Click to Kill

By John Carlo

1

Balorat had been waiting at the rendezvous for what seemed like an eternity. He nursed his coffee, taking tiny sips as he read the *British Medical Journal*, eyes skating over the articles, failing to stop on anything of interest. He'd chosen it as part of his cover, along with a leather valise, brown corduroy trousers, a blue button-down shirt, and a sleeveless navy jumper. The idea was to present himself as a classic British doctor: a man of means, comfortable in his own skin, and those of the crocodiles who'd given theirs to make his Gucci loafers. So far, it had worked. Staff at his Belgrade hotel all assumed he was in town for a conference. He'd be one of the last people anyone would suspect of being involved in a homicide.

A stream of people came in and out of the bar, mostly old codgers arriving for their afternoon *raki*. They played cards at plastic tables, counting out their coins, toasting good health, '*Zively, Zively*'. Almost an hour after the rendezvous time, the man he'd been waiting for, a marksman named Underson, finally arrived. Balorat's heart fell as soon as he saw him. Stumbling drunk, Underson managed only a few steps before he tripped and crashed into one of the old men's tables, knocking over their glasses. He slurred an apology, but it wasn't enough. They began demanding refills. Balorat looked away, hoping to disassociate himself. Unfortunately, the marksman had spotted him and staggered across.

'Professor Balorat, it's been a long time ...'

The barman came towards them. He was a small man, dressed in tight jeans and a black T-shirt, with his shiny hair scraped back in a ponytail. He pointed to the old men's table, and then at Balorat. 'You pay for drinks,' he said.

'Me? What does it have to do with me?'

'Your friend is drunk.'

'This idiot? Never seen him before.'

'Charmed, I'm sure,' Underson garbled, before spinning around unsteadily to face the barman. 'And you can fuck off too.'

The barman stuck a finger in Underson's face. 'No-one talks to me like that.'

'Okay, stop!' Balorat said, standing up and pushing himself between them. 'I'll cover it.' He pulled out a roll of notes from his pocket and peeled off a 1,000 dinar note. Less than ten quid. Painless.

The barman snatched it from him and stashed it beneath his apron. He retrieved a bottle of *raki* from the bar and made his way to the old men. That would have been the end of it if Underson, in his wasted glory, hadn't decided to take a swing at him as he came past. Being a foot taller, and seeing double, he missed completely, and the barman, instead of going down, wrapped his arms around Underson and shoved him against the wall. He collided with a sideboard, sending glasses crashing to the floor. The barman caught Underson's wrist, spun him, slapped him twice across the face, and then stuck a leg behind and shoved. He hit the floor with a thud. The barman grabbed one of his hands and pushed it towards a broken tumbler. Balorat gasped. A marksman with a sliced arm was as much use as a surgeon with crushed hands. He picked up another glass off the floor and stuck it near the barman's neck. 'Don't make me ...'

The barman glanced over his shoulder and growled. He let go of Underson's arm, but then spat on him and kicked him in the side. The men at the tables cheered. The barman spat again then continued to their table, a fist thrust high in the air.

Heaving a sigh, Balorat got up, dragged Underson off the floor, checked him over, and then shoved him hard towards a booth at the back.

A voice behind them yelled, 'No! You out!'

Balorat ignored him. Settling Underson in the booth, he went over to the barman and peeled off another thousand.

The barman shook his head. 'Out!'

'He'll behave, bring coffee.' He peeled off two more notes and pressed them into his palm.

The barman took them reluctantly, then wiped sweat from his beard. 'Don't fuck with me. I call my friends.'

Balorat's eyes narrowed. He hated it when plebs talked tough. He fixed him with a stare. 'Like I said, he'll behave.'

The barman seemed to understand, instinctively, that he was dealing with a character far more dangerous than a drunken ox like Underson. Walking back to the booth, Balorat realised that in his long career, with all of its early-hour call-outs and blundering detectives, he'd never felt as angry as he did right then. He wanted to crack Underson's head against a wall, but he *needed* this idiot. He remembered meeting the marksman over a decade ago, when they were both standing at the scene of a suspected bomb attack in the West End. Underson had been part of a Met Police armed response unit. Balorat remembered smelling drink on his breath, despite the marksman devouring an entire packet of Extra Strong Mints while they stood there. Now, pensioned off, he didn't bother hiding it. Today's episode confirmed everything Balorat had feared when K said she'd recruited him. They were expanding too quickly. First the tosher, and now this. If it continued, they'd all be nabbed. Balorat was damned if he was going to let that happen.

'Look up at the light,' he said.

Underson didn't move. Had he not heard, or was the processing of language now beyond him? Balorat grabbed his thinning hair and wrenched his head back. The light hit his eyes and he tried to pull away. Balorat held him tight. Underson's pupils constricted. Slo-o-owly.

'Did you drink your duty free for lunch?'

'Just a few beers.'

'Pisshead like you getting arseholed on beer? I don't think so.' He'd probably been relying on having the afternoon and evening to sober up, Balorat guessed, feeling mildly revolted by the webs of spider veins that had overrun Underson's cheeks. He checked his watch. 15:03. The girl had been instructed to get the target out of the restaurant by 20:00. Five hours. Heavy drinkers produced a greater quantity of the enzyme that broke down alcohol, so processing two units an hour might be feasible, but the amount ingested would be critical.

'Spirits? How much?'

'None.'

He rapped Underson on the nose with the *BMJ*. 'If we don't deliver, a clean-up team arrives. They don't leave loose ends.'

Underson managed a shrug.

Balorat rapped him again, harder this time. Underson tried to swat the magazine away, but Balorat grabbed his wrist. 'Getting this drunk takes effort. How much?'

Underson belched in his face. There was no point trying to be scientific. Even with twice the enzymes, he'd be far from sober at 20:00. He walked up to the bar.

'Where can we find a sauna?'

'Sauna?' the barman said, surprised. Then he slapped his bicep and laughed. 'You his bone?'

Balorat gripped a hypodermic filled with Midazolam, a fast-acting sedative, that he kept in his pocket. He resisted the temptation to stick it in the barman's arm, and instead peeled off another five thou. The barman sneered with contempt, then he took out his order pad and scribbled an address.

They caught a taxi. As soon as they walked in, Underson took one look at the red velvet wallpaper and bolted for the door. 'This is a bender place.'

Balorat grabbed his collar. 'Shut it. I'll get us a private room.'

He signed the bill without even looking, then took him to the changing room and told him to strip. A group of men sitting by the lockers stared curiously at the two Anglos, the big one undressing, and the little one still in street clothes, carrying a medical valise. What was this, some kind of domination game?

'Hurry up,' Balorat snapped. He threw Underson a towel and guided him toward their private room. Opening the door let out a blast of humidity. Whoever had been in before had poured far too much water on the coals. Normally he would have been irritated, but today it served his purpose. Shutting the door, he pulled down the roll-a-blind, then took out a rubber tourniquet, a sterile needle, and a bag of electrolyte solution. It was intended for treating serious injuries if a mission went wrong.

'Give me your arm.'

The marksman complied. Balorat tied-on. A network of blue rivers popped up. He stuck the needle into the widest, attached the tube to the bag, and released the tourniquet.

'Keep it high,' he said, placing the bag in Underson's hand and raising his arm. 'I'll be back in half an hour to change it.'

'Where are you going?'

'To recover my sanity.'

Thirty minutes later he returned to find Underson standing outside the sauna room, an empty IV bag resting on his head.

'How long have you been out?' Balorat said.

'Couple of minutes.'

Lying drunk. 'You have to stay in.'

'I'm roasting in there.'

'That's the idea. Look at the light.'

His pupils constricted more quickly than earlier, but still ridiculously slowly. Balorat hooked up a replacement bag.

'I'm not going back in,; Underson said.

'Yes you are. Or I'll call the clean-up crew myself.'

Two bag changes later, Underson began to sound sober. His pupils were almost as they should be. He dressed and they caught a taxi to a restaurant near the original rendezvous. It looked brand new, its white façade a stark contrast to the old town's dilapidation. Balorat pointed to a wooden fence at the side.

'Put two in there, no more. You're meant to be an amateur, but not a total muff. The others should connect. One through the heart.'

Underson said, 'If there are bodyguards it might take more.'

'He's on a date.'

'Hell of a time to go. The mark, what did he do anyway?'

Balorat felt his fists tighten. The mark's name was Tudor Clarke, and he was going to get exactly what he deserved. He forced himself to breathe. The last thing he needed was a loose canon like Underson – a small-time gunman who'd do anything for a few quid – realising that this one was *personal*. He gave an exaggerated shrug. 'Who cares. He's getting off lightly. Take it from a pathologist, there's a lot worse things than a nice clean death.'

A pair of tourists approached, checking the menu. Balorat turned his back and twirled his finger for Underson to do the same. The couple had no reason to remember, or even to notice, another pair of foreigners walking the bohemian quarter, but best not to take any chances.

Balorat said when they'd gone, 'Do what you have to, but aim towards the fence. Keep it an easy story: single shooter, opportunistic, revenge motive.'

Walking to the front of the restaurant, Underson traced a path with his finger, running from the front door to the bottom of the stairs. 'I'll take him here. What are you going to shout?'

'Dalje ruke ona je moja.'

'What's it mean?'

'Hands off, she's mine.'

'Corny.'

'Who are you, Ricky Gervais?'

Underson's expression darkened. 'What about the hired help?'

'She clears his pockets.'

'And?'

'Forget it, she's brainy.' He'd briefed her himself, and she got it like snap.

'Where's the van going to be?'

Balorat led him up a pedestrian street, past a dozen more restaurants, to where old Belgrade gave way to the modern world. Cars blew past on a four-lane boulevard lined with roll-front stores and graffiti. 'Green Renault. It'll be here in front.'

'And if it's not?'

'Make your own way home.' Balorat would have been tempted to ditch him for real if he could be trusted not to screw that up too. Most marksmen needed a handler. This one needed a nanny. In his prime, Underson's shooting had been Olympic quality. He would normally find the target without fail, even with the thirty-year old Makarov that Balorat had given him. He could only hope that Underson was now sufficiently sober, and the range so short, that he couldn't miss.

By 20:00, the cobbled street had filled with groups of people milling around the *kafanas*. Balorat had been told that Serbian women were among the most beautiful in Europe, and he'd noticed a few stunners earlier, but now he kept his eyes firmly fixed on the restaurant door.

First to exit was the hired help, all five feet ten of her, in four-inch stilettos, blonde hair spilling off her shoulders, slinky black dress painted on, and prancing behind her, in jeans and a white t-shirt – as if he were Brando in the fifties, as if she actually *liked* him – came Tudor Clarke. Balorat wished it was him holding the Makarov.

The girl turned to Clarke and kissed him full on the lips: that was the cue. Balorat cupped his hands to his mouth and hollered: '*Dalje ruke ona je moja!*'

The girl shoved Clarke away. Shots echoed in the tiny street. He fell. The girl let out an ear piercing scream, then slipped off her stilettos and ran into crowd.

Balorat resisted an instinct from somewhere deep in his training to go and check for signs of life. There was no need. He'd seen two bullets enter the middle of Clarke's chest. The traitor dropped instantly, like a toy with dead batteries. The medical examiner in him knew there was zero chance of survival.

Walking calmly up the boulevard, he began to wish that Clarke's death hadn't been so quick and clean. The little bastard deserved to suffer. Said he'd shop them if they didn't give him a bigger cut. He was only a tosher, for God's sake. A bit bunny. A cleaner. Expunging digital data, how difficult could that be? They'd made him rich beyond his dreams, and this was how he paid them back. Pathetic.

Balorat had cautioned K that Clarke had gone crazy down in Belgrade. It was containable, she said. Leave it to her. Then Clarke had gone and planted the screenshots for the National Crime Agency to find, just as a warning, but the repercussions were echoing louder than anyone had ever imagined, far louder than the gunshots which, in the end, had been the only way of settling the matter.

At 20:10, the Renault was parked exactly where Balorat had said it would be. They climbed in and headed for the airport.

'Four rounds,' Underson said. 'Two in the heart, two in the fence. As requested.'

Balorat felt relieved. The clean-up crew had never been more than a threat, but still failure was best left to fuckwits.

He held out a chamois for the Makarov.

Underson offered the gun, then just as Balorat was about to take it, he tossed it out of the window.

'Idiot!' Balorat shouted. 'I'm responsible for that.'

Underson laughed at him. 'Relax, bottom of the Danube now. You're scouse, aren't you? I can hear it. Are all scouse as uptight as you?'

'K won't be happy.'

'Sod K. What does she know.'

More than he realised, clearly, Balorat thought. That was him off the roster, for good.

They caught the late flight to Athens. By the following afternoon they were checked into a hotel on Santorini. Underson had insisted on a suntan as part of the deal. Balorat had protested. His pasty skin would turn bright pink in seconds. Unfortunately, K agreed it would make for good cover, so while the big man lay in the sun turning his hide to leather, Balorat hid under beach bar umbrellas, sipping Greek coffee, praying for rain. He needed to get back to London as soon as possible. Things were unravelling fast. Where the NCA were going with their investigation of Clarke's leak, he couldn't be sure. Only one thing was for certain: with Clarke gone, they were going to need a new tosher. Their NCA insider, Mark Putts, said he'd found the perfect replacement, but that provided zero reassurance. Putts was about as much use as a chocolate teapot.

2

Rigby clipped his shoes into his pedals and glowered at the rainclouds. The challenge he'd set himself earlier in the week was to try to achieve a new personal best every morning on the way to work, and again every night on the way home. It was Wednesday morning and so far, so good. Two days. Four records. But they'd been set in dry conditions, and he had no intention of trying to beat yesterday's time in the rain. He'd seen his fair share of wet-road accidents, like the loony – now ex-loony – who'd lost his rear trying to beat the lights at Shepherd's Bush roundabout, and slid into three lanes of oncoming traffic. He'd ride hard – of course he would – but a PB was out of the question.

A mile from his house, everything changed. The dedicated bike lane on the Goldhawk Road looked bone dry. He checked the skies over his shoulder. The rain had shied away. Traffic had been light so far, making a decent run possible. He rode flat-out around Shepherd's Bush, psyching himself for the sprint up Holland Park. Here, technique was everything. If he caught red at the first traffic light, there would be no way to recover – he'd get reds all the way up, and his time would be ruined. He counted seconds: thirteen, fourteen, fifteen ... Go! He sprinted hard, catching the light before it turned yellow. Green ahead: he sprinted again. Go! Three more like that, and he might be on for a PB.

He tore along the top of Hyde Park, and then along Oxford Street, hurling himself along the red corridor between lanes of double-decker buses. At Oxford Circus the traffic lights were kind to him again, and Regent Street opened wide.

Three minutes later he passed through the Oriental Arch on Gerrard Street and tore the phone from his armband: he'd made it by two seconds. Beaming, he typed in the passcode for the small garage they used for bikes, chained his Pinarello F10 to a rack, re-locked the garage, walked down the steps to the office, and buzzed in with a key card.

The lights were on and he could smell coffee, but couldn't see a soul. 'Anyone here?' he called. No reply came.

Content with some peace and quiet, he sat down to check his emails at one of the picnic tables they used for workstations. There were no offices at Pangolin. He would have loved for it to be more like one of the really funky places that tech companies in Brick Lane and Hackney went for – Airstream caravans, converted tube cars and the like – but he'd decided when he left the National Crime Agency four years ago to be as inconspicuous as possible. He'd settled for a basement in Chinatown, with a landlord who wasn't fussy about how they decorated. They'd taken the walls back to bare brick and ripped out the plasterboard to make a single, cavernous area.

He checked the main phone first, and, seeing nothing, pulled out his crypto phone. He required everyone at his company to carry two handsets: a regular one that used all the normal services and apps, and which could be tracked and intercepted, and was as susceptible to eavesdropping as anyone else's; they also had to carry a crypto, which used software modified by Rigby himself to defeat all known surveillance systems, including Stingray cell tower simulators, the telecom weapon of choice both for law enforcement agencies and for the dozens of foreign intelligence services who'd turned the capital into a world centre of eavesdropping.

There were a couple of emails from clients in Asia which had come in overnight. He needed to reply, but from across the room the espresso machine was beckoning to him. He found himself heading straight toward it, a prisoner to its charms. He filled one double filter handle and then another, slotting them into place, and stopped dead. The milk nozzle wore a two-inch long coating of white residue. Rigby wanted to scream. How many times did he have to tell them to wipe it? Every layer of gunk attracted another, and then another, until …

Counting to five, he wiped the nozzle and flicked open the pumps. Molasses-coloured loveliness flowed. He sipped. Magnificent. Bearing it before him like a sacrificial offering, he went to the men's room to change out of his cycling gear. He pulled on his jeans, then selected from his locker one of half a dozen identical charcoal-grey, long-sleeved T-shirts, all with the labels cut out. Why couldn't they make clothing without labels? They scratched. They irritated. No-one ever seemed to understand. One of his ex-girlfriends had even sniped, 'Try wearing a bra some time'. 'Ex' had become the operative word.

Over the T-shirt he slipped on his grey moleskin coat. He didn't need it in the office, but then Rigby didn't require any excuse to wear it. It had a loose, double-breasted cut, with the smoothest, silkiest feel he'd ever found in any garment.

He'd begun replying to one of the client emails when a toilet flushed. Steadman Jones, their head of profiling, came out of one of the stalls. Rigby quickly reached into his backpack. He pulled out a dispensing pack of hand sanitizer and held it out it for Steadman.

'Alcohol gel.'

Steadman did a double-take. 'Good morning to you too. How was your ride in? Weren't we lucky that the rain stayed away. *Yes we were, Steadman. And how was your ride?* Mine wasn't very enjoyable at all. *No?* No. A taxi cut me up on Theobalds Road and I almost ended up under a bus.'

'Sorry to hear that,' Rigby said. He offered the sanitizer again. 'Surgical grade.'

Steadman shook his head. 'I don't care if it spent a week on the space station. What are you doing here anyway?'

'I work here.'

'Didn't the woman call you?'

'What woman?' Rigby double-checked both phones. Nothing.

'Came by about ten minutes ago looking for you. Short. Asian. Nice looking. Sharp dresser. Not what you expect from an NCA officer.' He added, 'Flashed her card.'

'Did you get a name?'

'Kaur. K-A-U-R.'

'*Mesh* Kaur? That's a blast from the past.'

'She said to meet her at Sherry's,' Steadman said.

'Sherry's, why Sherry's?' Sherry's Diner was a burger and shake joint with a Rockabilly theme, a few streets away.

'How should I know?' He added with a grin, 'Want me to go instead?'

Had Steadman taken a shine to her, Rigby wondered? If so, he was barking up a very strange tree.

'Did she say what she wanted?'

'Nope.'

Rigby felt puzzled. He hadn't seen Mesh in four years. Why now? 'Better go see what she wants, I suppose.'

'Ops Meeting starts in twenty minutes, will you be back?'

'How should I know? Go ahead and start without me. Please.'

Steadman shook his head. 'I have a surprise for you.'

'Two in one morning. Isn't this just my lucky day.'

Sherry's was empty, except for a solitary head of black hair, scraped back tight, and rising barely high enough over the booth to be visible. Seeing her again felt strange. She was typing on her phone, and barely bothered to look up as he approached.

'Hi Mesh,' he ventured.

'Take a seat,' she said, continuing to type. 'I just need to finish this.'

He sat. After a minute, she looked up, 'Hi Rigby, nice to see you. It's been too long. How's business?'

Her abruptness took him by surprise. Empathy had never been one of her strong suits, but this was a studied coldness. Was she angry with him?

'It's going great, thanks. The world is full of rich scumbags wanting their online profiles sanitized, and we're only too happy to oblige. How's life at the Citadel?'

The National Crime Agency's headquarters on Citadel Place in Vauxhall, London, were known to staff simply as 'the Citadel'. Rigby had been employed there for four years, part of a team who specialized in tracking, and sometimes erasing, digital footprints. They were known as the 'toshers', after the Victorian sewer kids who dug around in humanity's effluent, hunting for coins and anything else of value.

She went back to typing. 'I'm running the Sweatbox,' she said.

A pang of jealousy shot through him. The Sweatbox was the investigative engine room where they all sat. Mesh was a detective, and Rigby a geek. They'd been paired up, and had worked cases together for over two years.

She spotted his reaction. 'It could have been yours, you know, if you'd stuck around.'

'I'm not a bureaucrat.'

'You're saying I am?' She dispatched her email with a little whooshing noise, and seemed about to launch into an explanation for her visit when a waitress arrived to take their order, wearing a Gingham swing dress, her hair in victory rolls.

'May I take your order?'

'I'm fine,' Mesh said, pointing to a half-finished cup.

Rigby was about to give his order, but the waitress beat him to it.

'I know, triple espresso,' she said, scribbling on her pad.

Rigby tried to say something in response but the words became garbled as they entered his mouth.

'It's what you always have,' she said, with a smile.

Rigby could feel himself blushing.

When she'd gone, Mesh said, 'An admirer. You should ask her out.'

'What? Come on, she's about twenty.'

'So what? Do you have a girlfriend at the moment?' She said it like she already knew the answer.

Rigby folded his arms. 'You didn't come here to discuss my love life.'

Before she could speak, his nose twitched, and not in a good way. He leaned in closer. 'What are you wearing?'

Mesh rolled her eyes. 'A suit.'

'No, I mean your perfume.' He waved away the scent.

'Wow. You haven't lost your charm.'

'Really gets me, remember?'

'Sorry,' She said. 'I'd forgot you're ... on the spectrum.'

'I'm not on any spectrum!'

'It's not an insult. It's a description.'

'I don't need describing. Why does everything have to have a label? There's just things that irritate me.'

Mesh took a deep breath. 'Sorry. I already said that. But I am sorry, okay. I don't how to refer to it. Your thing.' She added, 'I'm better at police work.'

'Then let's stick to that.'

She took a deep breath. 'Your name came up as part of an investigation, and I need to ask you some questions.'

'Better already,' Rigby said, but he was feeling a pinch of anxiety. That he might have stepped in something seemed entirely possible. He and Steadman, along with their head of tech, Gloria, spent much of their time patrolling the dark web. It was humanity's sewer, riddled with dealers, scammers, nonces and other scum. But it was also frequented by countless law enforcement agencies from all over the world, often posing as criminals. 'Did one of my people blow someone's cover?'

She shook her head. 'Nothing like that.' She glanced around, then lowered her voice. 'A few weeks back, my wireheads were clearing out some ancient laptops. They belonged to your team, back when you were with us. They said they'd checked all the drives and everything had been backed up. But they can be a little sloppy at times, so I thought I'd better take a look myself.'

Rigby groaned inwardly. He'd sat next to Mesh for the best part of two years. She was one of those people who waited silently in meetings until the very end, and then, when everyone thought something had been agreed, put her hand up and picked away at a tiny flaw in the previous discussion until the whole edifice came crashing down.

'So what did you find?' he said, dreading her answer.

'Screenshots.' She let the word hang in the air.

'Screenshots of what?'

'Website pages. Databases. Public records. I didn't think anything at first, just some old crap left by a careless tosher.'

'We were never careless,' Rigby said indignantly, but his heart had begun to race. 'We kept accurate records.'

'Like I said, I didn't think it was anything,' she countered. 'But then I noticed that one of the files was labelled "UKPPS". Personal Protection Service. *Witness* protection.'

A quiver went up Rigby's spine. 'I know what it stands for.'

'I had the screenshots analysed to get an accurate date for when they were taken, then I tracked down copies of official databases and witness protection records from the same period. We put them side-by-side – the original PPS documents and the toshed documents – and it was as plain as day: the PPS documents had been altered to remove all reference to the individuals in question.'

'Well no shit,' Rigby said, with a shrug. 'That's what toshing is.'

'I know. The problem is, the individuals in question weren't part of PPS.'

'What are you talking about?' Rigby said, genuinely confused. 'They had to be.'

'No. The master list containing the names of all the

people who were toshed for PPS did not contain the names of the individuals we found in the files.'

'But that's impossible, unless ...'

'Unless what?' she said.

'Unless the PPS records had been toshed too.'

Mesh nodded. 'Now you understand why I'm having to spend time with a man who says I stink.'

'And have you checked?'

'Of course. We cross-referenced the names against the national criminal database: nothing.'

'Since when do police databases match?'

'Which is why we cross-checked against everything else. HMRC. Customs & Excise. NHS. Nothing.'

'But it doesn't make any sense,' Rigby protested. 'We never toshed internal records, that would be ... illogical.'

'It would also be *illegal*. My theory, which I can't prove yet, is they were never part of witness protection. They were on the list for toshing, but they weren't supposed to be.'

'Why would anyone do that?'

'I can think of a lot of reasons. Maybe they wanted to disappear. Having the NCA erase their records for them would be a good way to start. Or maybe someone else wanted them to disappear.'

Rigby felt his stomach fall away. He rested his head on his thumbs, unsure how to respond. Eventually, he said, 'You tried to track them down, right? Some of them must have turned up.'

She shook her head.

'So maybe they were invented,' he said, hopefully.

'No such luck. We talked to some old snitches, just floated the names. They remembered them, but said they hadn't been seen in years. They were mainly low-level gangsters. We got the names of relatives. We're interviewing them now.'

'So what do you need from me?' Rigby asked. He knew she'd have her demands prepared in advance, and he braced himself.

'Three things,' she said, counting them off on her fingers. 'First, I want you to go back through your own records and see if it was you who toshed these guys.'

'I don't have any records.'

She pushed a piece of paper across the table. 'Here are their names. If you can corroborate that you toshed the public records, but not the internal ones, that would be helpful.'

'Mesh ...'

'Second, I want you to confirm to me the names of any of the toshers who were part of your team at that time.'

'Okay, that one's easy.'

'And third, and I want you to be honest with me, has anyone ever approached you to tosh privately, and if so, have you done it?'

'No! Come on, you know me better than that.'

'I used to.' She eyed him closely for a moment, then seemed to relax. 'Look, everyone at the Citadel says you're one of the good guys. You bring some great leads, scum we'd never catch by ourselves. All your charity stuff too, hell, it's wonderful. I'd hate for all that to get lost ... But sometimes even the best people make bad choices. If you made a mistake ...'

'I didn't make any mistakes!'

Rigby felt furious that she'd even suggest it, but he was also racking his brains trying to work out what might have gone wrong.

He said, 'Okay, I'll tell you where I might have screwed up, I never questioned the lists. They'd say, here are the people we want toshed, and I'd do it. I never double-checked anything.'

'That's what I guessed,' she said, with sympathy. 'It's possible you had a hand in this without realising.'

It was why she'd come to see him, he thought, and felt grateful. He was about to say, 'so can you help me', but then he remembered this was Mesh. She was too honest – and too ambitious – to bend the rules, even for an old friend. He said,

'What does Putts think about it?'

Mark Putts was their old boss at the Sweatbox, who'd now risen to be one of the most senior officers in cybercrime. Two decades earlier, cyber had been a career cul-de-sac. Now it was the new anti-terror.

'He broke Usain Bolt's sprint record trying to distance himself.'

'Did you even talk to him? Toshing was his baby.'

'You wouldn't know it now.' She shook her head and laughed. 'I book an appointment, he cancels at the last minute. Sees me in the corridor, walks the other way.'

'Do you want me to try?'

She looked surprised. 'How do you mean?'

Rigby twitched in his seat. He'd felt bad about not staying in touch with her, and in trying to be nice, he'd walked himself into a trap. She might not appreciate what he said next.

'If I ask to see him, he'll meet me. You might not know this, but all those great leads you were talking about, I spread them around. Some go to you, some might go to someone else ...'

'I know, I know, a lot of it goes to Mark. Who do think he dumps it on?' She laughed. 'Were you worried about what I'd say?'

Before he could back away, Mesh leaned forward and gave his shoulder a playful rub. Instinctively, he shoved his chair back to escape, banging his knees and sending his coffee flying across the table. Seeing it, Mesh sprang up, but she was a fraction of a second too late, most of it had already landed on her skirt.

'I'm so sorry,' he said. 'I'll buy you a new one.'

'It's fine,' she said, dabbing it with a napkin. 'It'll wash out.'

Rigby wasn't so sure. 'Get it cleaned, send me the bill.'

'It's okay, really. I should have remembered.'

Why couldn't he be normal, Rigby asked himself, not for

the first time in his life. Why did he have to have to cut labels out of clothes, and carry disinfectant, and have to be warned in advance when someone tried to touch him?

'I'll let you know what Mark says,' he said, by way of a peace offering.

'And don't forget the other things. You know the score: the faster you can get them to me, the quicker I can eliminate you from enquiries.'

3

As soon as Rigby arrived back at the office, Steadman stuck a hand up and waved at him. 'Ready for the Ops Meeting?'

Rigby grimaced. 'I said to start without me.'

Steadman laughed. 'What did she want?'

'I'll tell you later.'

Together they climbed the creaky staircase that led to their one and only meeting room. It was cantilevered precariously out from the side wall, propped up by two hollow metal poles which could be tapped with a pen and played like tubular bells.

Waiting for them were Gloria and Warren, the other two members of their board. Warren ran their identity consulting business, the public face of the company. Mostly, the job involved managing their clients' online profiles. Most of them were wealthy, and often dubious. Warren's team kept a close eye on social media, keeping track of what was being said about the clients, and countering negativity with more positive spin. Sometimes, when things got a little more fun, he called in the others for special services like deleting hacked photos from websites, and landing viruses on persistent trolls. With his narrow face, woolly hair and glasses, Warren reminded Rigby of a highly intelligent llama, and he couldn't help but feel fond of him, but he could also be hard to take. With most people, they were happy when they were happy, and sad when they were sad. For Warren, it didn't matter. If he was happy he was happy. If he was sad he was happy. And if he was pissed off to the point of wanting to kill someone, he could still put on a smile and no-one would know the difference.

Of the four of them, Gloria was the one who was most irritated by Warren's endless optimism. She'd grown up on a different side of London from Rigby and Steadman and Warren. Both Rigby's family and Steadman's came from the affluent suburbs to the west, Warren came from the stockbroker belt in Essex; she came from New Cross, a poor neighbourhood south of the river, home to many Afro-Caribbean families, like hers. With a first class honours degree from Imperial, she could have landed a job almost anywhere. Rigby felt lucky to have her on board, not just for her computer skills, but for her unwillingness to tolerate any form of bullshit. Rigby knew from experience that the Ops Meeting could be flashpoint for her and Warren, and he climbed the stairs slowly, preparing himself.

'All ready to go?' Rigby said, as he and Steadman arrived.

'Of course,' Warren replied immediately, flashing a smile. He launched straight into his presentation. His graphs and charts all went in one direction: up. Rigby found it difficult to concentrate; there was no tension, no drama. So much good news was hard to take.

'So, in summary,' Warren said, getting to his final slide, 'sales and profit are both increasing. Oh, and, I forgot to say, our fame is beginning to spread. We've had customer enquiries this week from Dubai and Monaco. My only problem is hiring enough freelancers to handle all the work.'

'It's like mugging cripples,' Steadman said.

'So there's the rent paid, anyway,' Warren said. He turned to Gloria. 'Now for the main event.'

Rigby caught a hint of jealousy in Warren's voice as he said it. He turned to him. 'You're doing a fantastic job. We all think that.'

'I saw a cartoon the other day,' Warren said, upbeat again. 'Kid says to his Dad, 'what are clouds made of?' Dad says, 'Linux servers, obviously.'

No-one laughed.

'I thought it was funny,' Warren said.

'It was,' said Gloria, 'first time I heard it.'

Warren said. 'Zella liked it. She works with cloud software.'

'Who's Zella?' Gloria said.

'The girl I'm taking out tomorrow night.'

'I thought you were dating a girl called Deirdre.'

'I am.'

'So who the hell's Zella?'

'Another one. Is there a problem with that?'

'If you're Deirdre,' Rigby said.

Steadman cut in, 'Says the man who's had five dates in two years.'

'So I'm picky. Shoot me.'

Gloria laughed. 'Picky? Poor girl wants a kiss and you hand her the cleansing wipes.'

Rigby didn't mind being ribbed by them, but it was truer than they realised. 'My sheer physical magnetism overcomes a great many barriers.'

She rolled her eyes and plugged her laptop into the projector, then began to enter the first in a series of passcodes. Her machine accessed different networks and servers from the other computers in the company. Its location was disguised with a VPN, a Tor browser, and a number of other secret tweaks she'd made to conceal its whereabouts.

As she went through her security protocols, Steadman seized the opportunity to take a chocolate muffin out of a bag. He split it in two, popped half in his mouth, and washed it down with a slug of coffee. He was about to pop in the second half when Gloria said, 'You going to chew that or swallow it whole?'

'I missed breakfast,' he said, with a shrug.

She rolled her eyes. 'Which one?'

'Just get on with it.'

She responded with a sigh. 'We're still tracking six stalkers from last time,' she said, turning to the screen. 'There are two females, both of whom we've checked and I can confirm that they are women, who advertise rape fantasies. Three groomers, but they're very, very careful. They seem to talk to each other off site because they say similar things.'

'Could they be the same person?' Rigby asked.

'I checked that,' Gloria said. 'They talk at the same time.'

'He could be double-geeking. Or using automatic text entry.'

'Pretty sophisticated.'

'Some of these arseholes are.'

'I'll double-check. Do you want to move on?'

Rigby nodded.

To keep the leads flowing they bought banner ads on porn sites, using code words like 'teenies' to mean underage, and 'punish' to mean sexual violence. Anyone who clicked could then be tracked, setting off red flags if they went to other sites known to contain harder material.

'The big news is we've made progress on the Bexley ring,' she said, clicking to the next chart. 'And I think Steady has a little surprise for you.'

She looked over at Steadman, who sat slumped in his chair with his hands pushed deep into the kangaroo pockets of his Chelsea FC sweatshirt.

'So he keeps telling me,' Rigby said.

Without saying a word, Steadman reached into his bag and retrieved another laptop, this one sealed in an evidence bag. He set it down on the table.

Rigby eyed it suspiciously. 'What's that?'

'Always wanted a MacBook Air,' he said, 'so I bought one on eBay.'

'I saw your expenses claim.'

'This isn't it.' Steadman smiled. 'You said to follow the video director.'

'And?'

'Well, we did, and we noticed that everywhere he went

he took one thing with him: his MacBook Air. And I mean everywhere. Home. Work. When he went for a crap.'

'Puh-lease,' Gloria said.

'But he flies a lot on business, so ...'

Rigby had guessed the answer. 'Security check?'

'We knew he was flying to Dusseldorf, so I bought a ticket, and then waited for him at the bag check. Got right behind in the line. Two MacBook Airs, side by side in the trays. I slipped a magnet into his pocket to set off the metal detector, and cut in front of him. I got to the trays while they gave him the full body scan. I slipped his laptop into my bag, then I went straight back out landside and met Warren in the car park.'

'So that's his Air?' Warren said, pointing to the one on the table.

'And he's got Mr eBay,' Steadman said.

The room erupted in applause.

It was a classic Steadman play, and Rigby felt once again vindicated for having placed his faith in him. On paper, starting a company with Steadman had been a terrible idea. He was one of those kids, Rigby always thought, who teachers say will come to no good. In his twenties he'd done a stretch in Belmarsh for hacking into the Land Registry database and changing the title deeds of abandoned properties to his own name, then selling them. 'An essential part of the male Afro-Caribbean experience,' Steadman joked about his time inside, trying to make light of it, but he hadn't fared well in prison. His parents were academics, and all through his adolescence Steadman had been torn between their world of classical music and documentaries on Radio 3 and Radio 4, and the hip-hop world of his friends. In Belmarsh, he didn't have the choice. Classical music and documentaries were a one-way ticket to getting the shit beaten out of you.

'How about a password for the laptop?' asked Warren.

'We already had that,' Gloria said. 'Followed him around coffee shops until he was sitting with his back to a window. Filmed him from outside as he logged on. Just had to go back and watch it a few times.'

'So what's on there?' Rigby said.

'Mostly his work stuff. Corporate videos. Scripts. But then we found a hidden folder. This was inside.'

A Word document flashed up on screen. It looked to Rigby like a film script.

Gloria said, 'There was a voice-over file, a read-through of the script, so I took a copy. Want to hear it?'

'Sure,' Rigby said, surprised.

From Gloria's computer came a strangely mechanical voice:

> 'Childhood as we know it today was a 19th century invention. Before that, they were little adults. They had the same rights and protections as anyone else. Now, we may think that in pre-Victorian times – prior to the adoption of an independent police service, or even any concept of national law – people enjoyed very little protection. But this was not the case. The citizens of the villages and hamlets – there were few real cities in those days – policed themselves. They were responsible for deciding what they did or did not find acceptable, and for punishing those who transgressed the accepted boundaries.'

'Sounds like a history lesson,' Warren said.

'Wait for it,' she said, scrolling to the top of the script.

'My God,' Rigby said.

The title read: *The Love of Children, A History.*

'A paedo documentary ... he was going to film this?'

'The whole production schedule is there, with budgets, and a list of all the backers and how much they put in. There's lots of other stuff he'd shot on there, too. All kids. Hardcore.

He's the ringleader, there's no doubt.'

'Warren said, 'I know that voice, too.'

'Course you do. It's Zira,' Steadman said.

'Who?'

'The Windows generic audio voice. He must have been worried about voice recognition, so he put the whole script into it and then played it back and recorded.'

Rigby stood up and paced, plunging his hands into his pockets. He was aware of the others watching him. They'd be wondering: why wasn't he excited? It was so easy to get carried away by a piece of evidence. 'What are you planning to do with this?'

'We're going to deliver it to the Child Exploitation and Online Protection Command,' Gloria said, swelling with pride. 'Taking it round there this afternoon.'

'That's what I was afraid of,' Rigby said.

'What?'

'Rigs, come on, man,' Steadman said. 'Don't piss on this.'

'I'm not pissing on anything. You've done a fantastic job, but this was illegally obtained. It's not admissible in court.'

'They don't know how we obtained it,' Gloria said. 'We can drop it off. Anonymous tip.'

Rigby shook his head. 'Let's say they arrest him. It goes to court. He tells how someone stole his laptop at the airport. That makes it illegally obtained. The case will be thrown out so fast you could dry your hair in the revolving doors.'

'So what do we do?' Warren said.

'We give it to someone who has the manpower to do it all over again, this time by the book, so it stands up.'

'You have someone in mind?' Steadman said.

'Maybe. What's next?'

'Nothing,' Warren said. 'We're finished.'

'Whoa, I'm not finished,' Gloria said. She pointed to the Air. 'What are we doing with this?'

Rigby shrugged. 'Lock it up until I figure out what to do with it.'

Gloria shook her head in frustration.

'Now, while we're still here, I have an important question,' Rigby said.

All eyes turned to him.

'Who used the espresso machine this morning?'

'Oh God, here we go,' Warren said, pushing his chair back. Gloria did the same.

'No, wait a minute,' Rigby said. 'I'm not asking you to give yourself up, but whoever it was, listen: clean the milk nozzle after you use it. Because, I've said this before, heat causes the proteins in the milk to stick to the metal. Proteins are like glue for other protein, so a layer of residue welds itself on, and then another, and another, until eventually your nozzle gets this ball on the end ...'

'And nobody likes a sticky nozzle,' Warren said.

'No sir,' Steadman said. 'Wouldn't taste too good in your coffee.'

Warren hooted. Steadman slapped his thigh, laughing.

Gloria pulled a face. 'It's all men ever think about.'

'No, it's not something I ever think about,' Steadman said.

'I'm not laughing,' Rigby said, trying hard not to join in. 'Really, I'm not laughing. Steadman, could you stay for a minute.'

'Wasn't me, boss. I swear.'

They waited for the others to leave. When they'd gone, Steadman said, 'Is it about this morning?'

Rigby nodded.

'What did she want?'

Shifting in his seat, Rigby took a deep breath. There was very little he kept from Steadman, but when it came to NCA activities his golden rule was not to tell him anything which would put him in danger. 'When I was part of Putts's team in the early days, one of the things we were working on was a technique called toshing.'

'I know,' Steadman said, 'you told me about that before.'

'And we invented toshing for the Protected Persons Service, like a single scoop of anonymity for those who didn't merit the full banana split.'

'You told me that too.'

Rigby hesitated. The golden rule was about to be broken. 'Some guys we toshed years ago, as part of PPS, have vanished.'

'Uh oh, public enemy numbers one to five on the run.'

'I'm not joking. These weren't wise guys, they were tumbleweed.'

Steadman looked puzzled, and Rigby wasn't surprised. It didn't make any sense to him either. 'Whoever toshed them went way overboard, took them out of the NCA database and everything. They're gone. I mean like totally gone.'

'You mean they're dead?'

'Most likely.'

'But if they were low life, and it's four or five years ago, then ...'

'Why does anyone give a damn? Because it stinks. To get the record this clean takes a lot of effort. You'd only do it if you ...' he tailed off.

'If what?'

'If there was more to it. If they weren't the only ones.'

Rigby watched as Steadman drew a deep breath. The implications of what he was saying were sinking in.

'And do you have any idea,' Steadman said, 'who might have done the toshing?'

He nodded. 'If you look at the dates, and who was in our department at that time ... quite possibly me. But even if I did the initial work, there was no way I erased internal records. No way. Someone else must have done that later.'

'Can you prove it?'

Rigby shook his head. 'I wish. And when anyone asks what the motive might have been, there's one obvious answer.'

Steadman rubbed his fingers together: money.

'Exactly.'

'You gotta talk to Putts,' Steadman said. 'Give him the Air. That's a good conversation starter.'

Rigby nodded. 'That's what I was thinking, but this could still go sour. I need you to do something for me.'

'Sure, anything.'

He reached into a pocket and pulled out a memory card. 'This is an insurance policy. It's a record of everyone I ever toshed. Needless to say, this information should never have left the Citadel.'

'You want me to stash it for you?'

Rigby nodded. 'The NCA are probably watching me.' He put the memory card on the table and slid it across to Steadman. 'Don't go anywhere out of the ordinary. Put it someplace that would be normal for you to go.'

'Okay. No problem.'

Rigby felt relieved. He said, 'Am I going to see you at the meeting tonight? Lana asked me to do the chair.'

'With all due respect, I've heard your chair before. More than once.'

'Oh,' Rigby said, surprised, and a little deflated.

Steadman laughed. 'Knobhead. Of course I'm going.'

Rigby called Putts's office and left a message. An assistant called back and instructed him to meet him at the Decades Club. She gave an address. Rigby had heard of it, a private members' club located on the Thames near Blackfriars Bridge. It was mainly a City dealers' haunt, but they were a crowd Putts enjoyed hanging with. He loved playing the markets in his spare time, and gleefully dished out stock tips and other investment advice. Rigby had followed his suggestions a few times and made money. When Rigby worked for him Putts had often talked about how he'd bought his house in Richmond entirely with dosh he'd made on the markets, and joining a club like the Decades was the kind of move he revelled in. He could invite the NCA top brass or other senior government officials, just to show off. Rigby liked him for it. He didn't share his avarice, but gaming the system always appealed.

He chained his bike to a railing then strode into the courtyard, past the Mercs and Teslas, and into the foyer. The receptionist did a double take at his urban camo cycling jacket, but when he said he was Putts's guest she directed him to the top floor. The lift whisked him up. At the end of a dark corridor he found a woman in a dark suit guarding a pair of black doors. A plaque read: Dining Suite.

'Could I take your name, sir?'

'Goode. Rigby Goode.'

She examined her list and frowned. 'And who are you here to meet?'

'Mark Putts.'

She straightened her back and flicked on a professional smile. 'Please go through.'

Rigby came into a moonlit room. Above him, a glass dome gave a panoramic view of the heavens. Stars gleamed in the night sky. A female jazz singer and her piano accompanist were purring their way through a Chet Baker number. The aroma of fresh seafood made him feel like he was on vacation, a summer evening somewhere in the Mediterranean. Twenty or so tables laid with white tablecloths were spaced far apart on a thick blue carpet. Were they expecting dancers, perhaps, or acrobats to perform between them?

He recognised some of the members seated at their tables, including Dr Liz Bracelyn, the paediatrician who hosted a morning show about child raising. As he passed her table she gave him the subtlest of knowing glances and a tiny smile played on her lips. She'd come to him the previous year when her estranged husband began writing a book about their marriage, claiming that she was a bad mother. A week before he was due to the deliver the manuscript, Rigby's techs had accessed his computer and deleted it. The publishers were furious and asked for the advance back. He'd started again, but they deleted that too and sent him a message from Dr Liz: *find a new meal ticket.*

He spotted Putts sitting at a table apart from the other guests. He seemed relaxed in his polo shirt and blazer, but seemingly alone. Rigby knew better. He did a quick check. Four beefcakes sat in a line on seats at the bar, their backs turned, scanning the room in the mirror behind the bottles. They sported identical haircuts – short back and sides, clipped extra close – with only their hair colour to identify them: two brunettes, one raven black, and a skullpube redhead. Putts stood up and stuck out a hand. Rigby shook it. He looked even taller and skinnier than Rigby remembered him; a stork in human clothes.

'Glass of wine?'

A half-consumed bottle rested in an ice bucket. Rigby read the label: Bâtard-Montrachet. He shook his head.

'Suit yourself. Have a seat.'

Rigby shrugged off his backpack and held it on his lap.

Putts eyed it. 'Is it my birthday?'

'It could be.'

He smiled. 'Speaking of birthdays, Lydia's taking GCSEs this year, can you believe that?'

'None of us is getting any younger.'

Putts gestured toward the jacket. 'Except you, maybe.'

He was verbal boxing. Rigby remembered the NCA patois all too well. Jab and retreat. Jab again, feint, then the sucker punch. Not that Putts didn't have a point. The jacket was *way* too young for him. He'd been wearing it for over a decade. The texture of every other cycling suit he'd ever tried made him feel physically ill, but this one was soft and comforting. He'd bought four of them; this was the fourth and last. The question of what he was going to do when it wore out had caused more than one sleepless night.

'Wait,' Putts said. 'What's that around your ears? Paint? Have you been decorating?'

Without meaning to, Rigby touched a hand to the grey flecks that had begun to sprout along the bottom of his hairline.

Putts chortled. Rigby waited while he swigged the wine and filled his glass.

'So what did you want to talk about?' Putts said.

'Mesh told me about the screenshots.'

Putts's lips tightened. 'Why do you think I ordered you guys to stop taking the bloody things?'

'It wouldn't have been a problem if everything was above board.'

'Everything *was*,' Putts growled. 'Or are you suggesting something else?'

'I'm not suggesting anything. Someone erased information.'

Putts shook his head. 'Don't even go there. It's a records anomaly. Happens all the time.' He added with a shrug, 'Maybe you were just too good at your job.'

'*Me*?'

'You!' Putts laughed and reached out to slap him on the shoulder. Rigby pulled away just in time. Putts pointed at the backpack. 'What you got there?'

Rigby cradled it. 'I want some assurances.'

'Give it a rest, mate. How long have we known each other? I'll help you however I can. What you got?'

Rigby sighed and took the Air out of the backpack. 'Nonce ring in Bexley. This belonged to the leader. He makes corporate videos by day and kiddie porn by night. He got all of his sick friends to put money into the productions. All of their names and investment details are on here.'

Putts whistled. 'I do wonder sometimes why you dig around in this scum. The Mariana's trench of the dark web is not exactly a fun place to go exploring. Presuming, of course, there's no money in it for you ...'

'So who's going to get it?' Rigby said, ignoring him. 'You or Mesh?'

'*Mesh?* Are you serious? This whole thing is her fault. As soon as she heard about this she started firing off emails about possible misuse by terrorists and threats to national security. They set up a task force with some whizz-kid from the Home Office. If this hits the media they will not hesitate to hang it on someone, and a former officer is always better than a current one …'

Rigby sat bolt upright. 'Is that a threat?'

'It's a stone fucking certainty. The only good news is, technically Mesh still reports to me, so I see everything. I'll try to keep your name out of it, but …'

Rigby's mouth had gone dry and he could feel a clamminess in his armpits. He tapped the Air. 'That's why I brought you this.'

Putts took a gulp of the wine. 'And I appreciate it, but helping you means putting my neck on the line. I'm going to need a little more.'

'It's a *big* lead,' Rigby insisted.

'Just fell from the sky, did it? You and I both know it won't stand up in court.'

Rigby tried to stare him down but Putts held his gaze, and soon Rigby could feel his own nerve starting to crumble. He thought he'd arrived holding a decent hand, now it turned out he had nothing. He was bluffing without even meaning to. He said, 'Okay, what do you want?'

'I need some toshing.'

'Jesus! That's what …' Rigby checked himself and lowered his voice. 'That's what got us into this mess.'

'I know, I know. It's nothing heavy, he's not in protection or anything.' Putts reached out and took his arm. Rigby recoiled, but Putts gripped firm. 'He needs to lay low for a while. Don't worry, I have a safe house organised. Tosh the records, give him a change of hair and clothes, be there if he needs anything.'

'Who is he?'

'Just some arsehole. Got himself in a bit of bother, needs to disappear for while.'

'How long do I have to babysit for?'

'Couple of weeks, max. And it goes without saying – not another word to anyone.'

'What about Mesh and her task force?'

Putts sat back and smiled. 'Sod Mesh. Leave her to me.'

4

Mesh was running late. She raced through the Citadel, not stopping to talk or even to acknowledge anyone, head down, lips tight, adopting a demeanour known to insiders as 'the Zombie'. It meant that a critical point in a case had been reached, or that a key argument needed to be rehearsed mentally without disturbance. Accepted practice when encountering a Zombie was to anticipate their expected path, and then to make way, allowing a two-foot gap. Under no circumstances should one be approached or interfered with.

Ever since she'd heard about the screenshots turning up out of the blue, Mesh had been a Zombie. The case made no sense. The people they found on the computer had been professionally toshed, but the toshers had gone far beyond their usual remit. Initially, she thought they might be officers in deep cover, but they made enquiries and it didn't check out. Then she thought maybe they weren't real people at all, just names invented for training purposes, but then they found the relatives. And if the toshers had been that thorough, why had they been sloppy enough to leave the names on an old hard drive? The thought had crossed her mind that there could be a conspiracy within the NCA.

The Sweatbox, she thought as she arrived, lived up to its name in every way. In other parts of the building sunlight streamed in through acres of tinted glass. Somehow, in the partitioning of rooms, they'd managed to create a particularly airless and dank space in which the temperature hovered around a point where even a small amount of physical exertion resulted in a film of perspiration appearing on the skin.

Then there was the male factor. Testosterone was the dominant hormone, even among the women. It was one way of getting on at the Citadel, but Mesh had never gone for that tactic.

One of the few other women who didn't dress in the uniform of cargo pants and a black polo shirt was Aisling Cockburn. She should park the silk bomber jackets for when she was on a date, but she gave as good as she got from the men, which earned her a few brownie points. Mesh had selected her to work on the case along with Brien O'Brien, an expert in Sybil attacks and other forms of social network deception. She'd picked the two of them out from the rest of the Boxers for their ability to think outside the screen, which was disappointingly rare in this crowd. Brien had joined the NCA after completing a PhD in information security at UCL. Like most PhDs that Mesh had met, he carried himself with an air of not really caring what anyone thought of him, guaranteed to poison his career chances at the Citadel. Aisling, by contrast, was clearly ambitious.

Mesh had told them that she knew one of the toshers who had been employed by the NCA around the time that the screenshots would have been taken, Rigby Goode, and that she would interview him herself. Their task had been to identify the others.

They were waiting for her in her office, coffee cups in hand. They said their greetings, and Aisling pointed to a spare cup on the desk. 'We got you one, too.'

'Brownnose,' Mesh said.

'Everything alright at nursery?' Aisling said, ignoring it.

Mesh smiled inwardly. She'd never discussed Satinder with Aisling. This was an unashamed attempt to demonstrate investigative skills. Brave too – being a personal subject it could backfire. These were traits she approved of.

'Fine, absolutely fine,' she said, without batting an eyelid. 'My mother takes care of him, actually. I drop him on the way here.'

'Sounds good to me,' Brien said, trying to join in. 'Gets to spend the day with Gran.'

Mesh's mind filled with an image of her mother shuttling obsessively between her kitchen and computer, emailing relatives around the world while cooking enough food to feed an army, and poor Satinder playing by himself on the floor. The sooner she got him into a proper nursery the better. 'Sure, what could be nicer? Should we get started?'

'The first thing was to divide up tasks,' Aisling said, eagerly. 'I asked Brien to try to find the names of the toshers, and I would take responsibility for tracking them down.'

'I feel like I'm on The Apprentice,' Mesh said. 'Okay, Brien, how did you get on?'

Brien smiled nervously. His eyes, enlarged and partly obscured by thick lenses, did not twinkle with confidence.

'Did you find any names?' Mesh said to him.

He said, 'It wasn't that easy, but in the end I was able to access the right area.'

'What do you mean, access? Did you hack our own systems?'

'Yes,' he said, unable to conceal his delight. Mesh scowled at him. He handed her a sheet. On it were three columns: names, dates of service, and last known whereabouts. She scanned it quickly. It contained four names, the same four that Rigby had sent to her in an email earlier. She felt relieved.

Brien said, 'The program was terminated three years ago. There was only a handful of officers who finished the training and became accredited. Of those, four were active during the time frame. Two of them, Michael Quick and John Vashon, have transferred to the Intelligence services.'

Mesh had guessed as much. 'And the other two?'

'The others have both left government employment. One of them, Tudor Clarke, is now believed to be living in Belgrade.'

'Belgrade?' Mesh said, surprised. 'What's he doing there?'

'Could be a few things. It's a drug route. There's no extradition treaty. I wondered if perhaps he was toshing people involved in genocide?'

'Possibly,' Mesh said. 'But that was almost twenty-five years ago. Has he had any further contact with the NCA?'

'Not that we know of. We're trying to find contact details.'

'Okay, good. Anything else?'

Aisling said, 'The fourth tosher, ma'am. We haven't discussed him yet.'

'The one I said I'd talk to,' Mesh said.

'And ... did you get a chance?'

Mesh hadn't decided how much she was willing to tell them. She was glad these two were both relatively new to the Sweatbox. Anyone who'd been around a while would be aware of how close she and Rigby had been. 'Goode and Should', they'd been known as. Mesh had hated the nickname. She knew why they called her 'Should'. She'd been called a bossy boots ever since she was a little girl. 'Tell me what you know,' she said.

Brien's face brightened. 'I did some background research. He runs a company called Pangolin. They describe themselves as identity consultants.'

'How interesting,' Mesh said, feigning surprise.

'I asked around and some of the CEOP team know him well. The whole Pangolin thing is a front. They're vigilantes. They run websites with names like Doggerland and Punishment Towers, and those are the clean ones. There are some with illegal content. They're bait. And it works. The NCA gets anonymous tip-offs, but everyone knows who they're from.'

'Fascinating,' Mesh said.

Aisling said, 'Leaving a steady job to go chasing nonces, it takes commitment. Is he some religious born again or something?'

Mesh felt a rush of old frustrations well-up inside her. She'd pleaded with Rigby not to leave, but he hadn't listened. She still didn't understand it. 'If chasing paedos is what you want to do, then the NCA is the best place in the world to do it.'

'Yeah, so why'd he leave?' Brien asked.

'You'd have to ask him,' she replied, but it was a question she wished she could answer. He'd never explained himself. One minute he was sitting beside her, the next he was gone.

Aisling said, 'I found a photo in his file.' She put it on the desk. 'He doesn't look like I thought he would.'

'In what way?' Mesh said.

'He's kinda handsome. That dark, Celtic look.'

Brien laughed. 'Not like a nerd, you mean?'

'Who says nerds can't be good-looking?' she said.

'He's a cycling nut,' Mesh said, well aware that Rigby's athleticism and relative good looks had made him the subject of office chatter. 'His perfect weekend away would be riding a section of the Tour de France.'

Aisling raised an eyebrow. 'He could be our man. I checked his home address. Chiswick. Costs a fortune to live there. Identity consultant could mean anything. What if he's still toshing, except he's doing it for money?'

'That's what I asked him,' Mesh said.

Aisling looked surprised. 'What did he say?'

'He denied it.'

'Of course he did. He could be working with organised crime, helping people disappear, or even helping to get rid of them. They'd pay big for that.'

Mesh wasn't so sure. 'Maybe. But think about this: data's like magnetized confetti, the toshers pick it off piece by piece. Driving licenses, self assessment, travel documents, etcetera. So it works best for people with tiny lives. Drifters. Small-time criminals. Some of the relatives have given us photos. I've sent them to people working as medical examiners at the time and asked them to review John Does for the past ten years. It'll take a while, but while we're waiting get on to Intelligence Liaison and see if we can interview Quick and Vashon.'

Aisling typed a note into her tablet.

'What about the one in Belgrade?' Brien said.

'That's your assignment,' Mesh said. 'For me, he's our prime suspect.'

An excited expression grew on Brien's face. 'Do you want me to go there?'

'Find him first, bucko, then we'll talk about who's on the plane.'

Balorat opened the email from Mesh Kaur NCA, and smacked his office table in frustration. Could nobody do what they were supposed to do? He called Putts. 'Have you seen this?'

'Seen what?'

'The email from your bloodhound. You're copied. "Reaching out to pathologists involved blah blah blah to reconsider every John Doe in the last ten years to see if it matches the description and photographs attached." Call her off.'

'She's not a dog, Vincent. I told you to expect something.'

'We're stretched already. I know exactly where those bodies are, and I can assure you none of them ever passed through a sodding path lab.'

He heard Putts heave a sigh. 'Please calm down, and go through the motions.'

Balorat felt anything but calm. 'Sod that, I'll get it rescinded.'

'She'll go to the Director-General.'

'Then I'll go over *her* head. What's happening with that new tosher?'

'It's good news. He's taken the bait.'

'Then reel him in. Do you now how much work K has lined up?'

'You keep thinking of that island,' Putts said in his nauseatingly optimistic voice. 'Little boat ride to the landing strip. Private jet waiting.'

'Don't patronise me.' But he had to admit, it was all Sylvie ever talked about. The archipelago. A string of islands off the coast of Turkey for sale. It had been a mistake to show her the map. When K had shown it to him, he'd known it was a ruse, the proverbial carrot dangled like a glittering bauble – reach for it, grasp, yearn, work harder, follow orders. What he hadn't counted on was his wife falling for it: 'Oh, Vincent, that's going to be our island! Oh my word.'

'So when are you going to turn him?' he said to Putts.

'Be patient. He's more than a tosher, he's a superstar. He writes the apps, does all the coding himself. NCA have been trying for four years to crack what he's written since he left. Once we get him, we can open up all kinds of new revenue streams.'

'Then get him, for fuck's sake.'

'I *am*. Don't you listen? He's not like Clarke, he doesn't have any bad habits, and he doesn't need the money because he's raking it in. He won't come willingly. The cage has to be carefully constructed, and then we shut the trapdoor at just the right moment.'

'Spare me the David Blaine crap. Just get him.'

5

Rigby made it from Chinatown to the church in Stoke Newington, where Lana ran various groups and meetings, in a time impressive enough for him to post it on Strava. In the churchyard, a group of people were sharing out cans of Diamond White cider. They weren't kids, they were in their twenties and maybe even thirties. It was hard to tell exactly, most of them had pulled their hoodies over their heads. They wore more layers than was necessary, a sure sign, Rigby knew, that they were homeless. The same church hosted a food bank and a drop-in centre where they provided basic services like haircuts and free clothes. The group had come to grab anything on offer, and then stayed for pre-dinner drinks.

The church, built in the Gothic style, seemed incongruous and antiquated next to the modern blocks that had sprung up round it. He was glad he'd arrived early, it would give him time to survey the room, get a feel for it, maybe even recite some of the speech he'd been preparing in his head. He'd done chairs before, but they never got any easier. Feeling nervous, he made his way up a path at the side and knocked on the door of a less ornate building that adjoined the main church.

'I'm not open yet,' called a voice from inside.

'It's me. Rigby.'

From inside came the tinkling of keys. Eventually the door opened and Lana peered out. In her mid-forties, with a liking for long skirts and floppy tops with loose sleeves, she reminded him of one of those actresses who'd tasted glamour at an early age and run for the hills – only to turn up many years later in clickbait: You'll Never Guess What These Once-Famous Celebs Look Like Today.

'Rigby! Thank you so much for coming.' She threw her arms around him.

Instantly, he coiled up and struggled out of her embrace.

'Oh, I'm sorry. I forgot,' she said. 'I know other people like that. Like Zelda, she's high-functioning, and ... how are you anyway?'

'I'm fine,' he said. He was glad to have got away, but her patchouli perfume was so strong he could feel it in his nostrils.

'Come in, come in.'

Lana led him into a room filled with racks of clothes. It had a lacquered wooden floor that made him think it might once have been a school gym.

'Now we have a clothes bank to go with our food bank,' she said, sliding hangars along the poles. 'A couple of the girls from a fashion college went around stores pestering them for donations. It's all designer gear. We'll have the best-dressed homeless in town.' She laughed. 'Actually, they'll probably refuse to wear most of it. They're surprisingly picky. You're picky too, aren't you ... You can have a look through if you want.'

Rigby flicked through the racks, dismayed by all the loose fibres.

'How's Steady?' she asked.

'Not going to fit into any of these, that's for sure.'

'Has he found a young lady friend? He deserves someone. He's such a sweet man.'

Rigby laughed. 'Last time he went on a date he took the girl to a fine dining restaurant and insisted on having the tasting menu. After the fifth course, she said she had to make a phone call, then never came back to the table.'

'That's awful!'

'He said he didn't mind – he didn't like her all that much, and had two desserts.'

'I'm glad you came early,' she said. 'There's something I wanted to talk to you about.'

'About the chair?'

'No. Something else. Come through here.'

She led him through a doorway into a kitchen area. A cauldron large enough to feed half the neighbourhood bubbled on the hob.

'Health and safety have condemned this whole section of the building. There's a rats' nest. Do you want to see?'

'Not really.'

But she'd already begun to move towards the back of the kitchen. She pulled a stainless steel table away from the wall and lifted a piece of plasterboard.

Rigby spluttered and covered his mouth.

'Sorry!' Lana said.

He held his nose. 'Is that what rats smell like?'

'Dead rats. I put poison down. I hate to kill anything. The rats did nothing wrong, they were just being rats. But with health and safety being so tough these days, I didn't have any choice.'

'Can you put the board back, please.'

'Of course, sorry.' She closed the up the hole. 'It's not just that, the whole kitchen is crumbling. The foundations are faulty, that's what Tom Talbot said, anyway. Tom worked in construction before he retired. We're in danger of being shut down.'

'So what do you need?'

Money, he guessed. That's why she was happy he'd arrived early, so she could pump him for a donation.

'We need to rebuild the kitchen.'

'Rebuild? The whole thing?'

She nodded.

He said, 'But that could cost, I don't know, tens of thousands.'

'More. One of Tom's partners came to take a look. He says we have foundation problems. His estimate is a hundred and thirty thousand.'

'*One-thirty?* I was thinking maybe like twenty.'

She shook her head despondently. 'There are all sorts of problems. Even the problems have problems. I wouldn't be asking if we weren't desperate.'

She wasn't the only one. 'Lana, I'll help any way I can, but I don't have that kind of money.'

'I wasn't asking for money,' she laughed nervously. 'I want your help.'

'Sure, but ...'

She couldn't resist reaching out and taking his arm. 'Couldn't one of your anonymous benefactors put something our way? We probably need new appliances too.'

'I'm sorry. Benefactors?'

Lana steadied herself. 'Maybe I shouldn't be saying this, but I was told in confidence, and I'm respecting that confidence because I'm only talking to you, that on occasion you had been able to persuade wealthy individuals to make charitable contributions. Instead of, well, things coming to light that perhaps those individuals would prefer stayed in the dark.'

Rigby didn't know whether to laugh or cry or shout out in anger. There was only one person she could have got this from. Did he know Lana was going to be making a plea? Was that why he was being coy about coming tonight?

He said sternly, 'What did Steadman tell you?'

She didn't reply immediately. The idea that she'd overstepped seemed to come as a surprise.

'It ... it wasn't Steady,' she said.

'Lana ...'

'No, really it was somebody else, um, one of the gals who brought the clothes.'

Rigby knew she was covering for him, but decided to let her off. If it had been anyone else, he would have told them to take a hike. 'Whoever you heard it from, it's not true. What you're describing is called coercion, and no matter how well-intentioned it might be – or how noble the cause – it's illegal. Now, I don't believe you'd request anyone to engage in illegal activities ...'

'No, of course not.'

'So could you please be a little more careful about what you're requesting.'

'Oh, no, Rigby, please, please, I'm not requesting anything. I'm not even describing. I'm just ... I was hoping you might know someone, that's all.'

He sighed. 'Let me think about it.'

She looked relieved. 'You'll still do my chair?'

'Of course. That's why I'm here.'

He sipped disgusting instant coffee, watching the minutes tick by on the wall clock, until the ninth – and presumably last – person came through the door to join their meeting. Rigby had attracted bigger audiences just by complaining in cafés. He took a minute to look over the audience. Most of them were regulars. There was Lilian, in her fifties, a nervous character, who probably always had been and probably always would be. Farouk, thirties, bearded, overweight, hardly said a word. Abney, a real upper-crust guy, who spoke through his nose and always wore a tweed suit, even in summer. Claris, tall, willowy, aquiline features, elegant movements. She could have been model, Rigby thought; perhaps she even had been. And, of course, Frank, who made it to every meeting. In his sixties, with grey hair down to his shoulders, he wore a pale-blue Adidas tracksuit cut in a style that would have been in vogue for the Montreal Olympics, and prided himself on existing quite happily with no apparent income. Frank knew all the soup kitchens and food banks in town, and they knew him. Rigby had long suspected there might be some alternative source of funds, such as shoplifting, which possibly explained why Frank was paranoid about the police, whom he referred to as filth. Whenever he said it, he spat the word, as if using the term was a badge of honour. Like himself and Steadman, all of them had been coming to Lana's group for a few years. There was also a pair who looked as if it was their first time. You could always tell newbies, they tried to put on a brave face like they really didn't belong here.

Rigby was about to turn to Lana and ask if she was ready to start, when he noticed Steadman slip in. A little voice inside said, 'Leave it until later,' but he'd gone deaf to little voices inside. Steadman had pulled a baseball cap low to cover his face, which for Rigby was the final straw. He sprang from his seat and grabbed his friend by the arm, steering him back outside.

'What did you tell Lana about anonymous benefactors?'

'I didn't say anything,' Steadman pleaded.

'Then where did she get the idea we could raise one-thirty large?'

Steadman shrugged. 'We could.'

'That's not the point.'

'Maybe we *should*.'

'So you're admitting it was you.'

'Why does it have to be anyone?' Steadman said, shaking himself free. 'Maybe Warren nailed it: we're getting famous.'

'Of course, why accept the simple when something preposterous is on offer? Was Brexit your idea too?'

Through the window he could see Lana craning her neck, trying to get his attention. They should be starting now.

Rigby said, 'Why are you here, anyway? I thought you'd heard my chair before, more than once.'

Steadman grinned. 'And each time it gives me a new and more profound sense of hope.'

'Get in there.'

Lana gave them each a stern look as they entered. As everyone settled themselves, she reminded them that they were in a safe and confidential space, and that nothing said inside the meeting should be repeated outside. She then introduced Rigby, saying that he'd been a member of her group for eight years.

'When I first met him,' Lana said, 'he was a young man of obvious talent and capability. He had landed himself an important job with the police. He was well paid. He lived in a nice flat. He rode his bicycle, a lot, which he still does, and it was a rather flashy number as I recall. But despite these outward signs of success, the truth was that he was – and I don't think he'll mind me saying this – broken inside. He had no friends. He rarely spoke to anyone. He told me that even at work he kept conversations to an absolute minimum. He was twenty-six years old, but had never had a long-term relationship with another person. He had not spoken to his parents or to other members of his family for five years.' She turned to him. 'I'm sorry, I'm stealing your story. Would you like to pick it up from there?'

For all his mental preparations, Rigby felt dazed staring out at the audience. He was relieved when he felt his main phone buzz in his pocket. Careful to cup it in his hand, he slid it out and stole a glance. It was from Putts. Rigby was to meet him outside the Pangolin office at 9pm sharp to collect his delivery.

Rigby did his chair and stayed around for the general sharing, but as soon as the clock hit 8:30, the scheduled finishing time, he made up an excuse about having a date, and bolted for the door.

Outside, as he unlocked his bike, he became aware of a presence of behind him. He turned. It was Steadman.

'Date?'

'Okay, it's a little errand,' Rigby said.

Steadman's eyes narrowed. 'I wouldn't send you for Smarties. Who's it for?'

Rigby sighed. 'Putts.'

'What's he want?'

'Nothing difficult. But I'll be out of the office for a few days.'

'Really? Where?'

'Nowhere special. I'll be at home. Working.'

'You hate working from home.'

'No, I don't.'

'Yes, you do.'

'Well, I'm going to do things a little differently this time, see if I like it any better.' He clipped in and pushed off before Steadman could ask any more questions.

When he arrived in Chinatown, two men were waiting for him. One was the unmistakable heron-like figure of Putts, dressed in his usual polo shirt and blazer, and the other a man whom he guessed to be in his mid-seventies, with a white beard, round spectacles, and what was left of his hair forming a ring halfway down his otherwise bald head. He was dressed in a green duffle coat, a pumpkin-coloured scarf, heavy yellow cords, and two-tone red and beige boat shoes. He could have been an average grandfather, had he not checked the time on his watch every thirty seconds – which, even at a distance, Rigby could tell was a TAG Monaco. Whoever this was standing with Putts, he was a wealthy man, and he wasn't used to being kept waiting. That was bad news. The chance of any toshing being completely successful declined in direct proportion to a person's means and social standing. It was a lot easier for a pauper to disappear than a prince. Fame equalled followers. Money equalled friends. Despite the great promise of the internet as a tool of democratisation, in Rigby's experience the class divide was alive and well in cyberspace.

Putts said, 'Rigby Goode meet Father Christmas. Real name, Frederick Ascott.'

Ascott kept his hands in his pockets and didn't smile. He acknowledged Rigby only with the tiniest dip of his head.

A set of keys dangled from Putts's finger. 'It's in Bethnal Green, close to the tube. The address is on the tag.'

'I'll take him there now,' Rigby said.

Putts said to the man, 'You're clear about staying in touch, yes?'

'Yes,' Ascott said, irritated.

'Rigby will be your contact. If there are any problems, he's your man.'

'Yes, I understand, fully.'

Rigby led Ascott into the tight maze of streets north of Shaftesbury Avenue, where he planned to pick up a Zipcar. The sooner he dropped off the old fart, the better. The sun had dipped down below the tight-packed buildings and what was left of it fought to peep around corners. When did Daylight Saving Time end, next weekend or the weekend after? It would be pitch black at this hour once that happened. If Ascott disappeared for good, Rigby wondered, how many people would give a damn?

He stopped dead in his tracks. Was that what he was walking into? Toshing would be the perfect precursor to dispatch.

'What?' Ascott grumbled, turning to see why he'd stopped.

'Nothing.'

'Forgotten the key?'

Rigby carried on walking straight past him. He'd dismissed his concern as quickly as it had arrived. Putts could be manipulative, that was par for the course for NCA officers. He was avaricious, but what government employee didn't need some extra cash. But a murderer? No way. He'd known the guy for almost a decade. It just wasn't in his make-up.

He cocked an ear to check if Ascott was still behind him. Boat shoes squeaked on the wet pavement. Unfortunately, he was still there.

6

Steadman was right as always, Rigby thought. He hated working from home. Houses, as everyone knew, were breeding grounds for bacteria and fungi. A thousand of the little buggers left on food residue could become thirty-two million within just five hours, and as few as ten, of certain strains, could cause serious illness. He'd find himself breaking off from his work to get a bottle of spray disinfectant, then go around the house on a search and destroy mission. Hours could be lost to what he knew was absurd behaviour. Fortunately, he only ever worked from home on the rare occasions when he needed to shield his colleagues from something dangerous. Unfortunately, this was one of those.

Ascott had him worried. There was too little data available on the man – far too little. On the face of it, Rigby should have been pleased: there was hardly anything to tosh. But that would be a rookie error. Frederick Ascott had once been an important individual, and there was no way anyone that important could be so clean. Even more worrying was the way he'd faded from sight. He hadn't vanished in a puff of smoke, he'd been toshed to the point where he existed at the fringes of society, with just enough public info to assuage any thoughts of a disappearance.

Rigby had sent out three waves of identity bots, part of the suite of toshing tools he'd conceived years ago when he'd worked with Putts. None of them had returned with anything useful. Inspired by Google bots, the identity bots crawled the web, hunting down any data they could find, and then delivered to Rigby a catalogue of appearances – everything from official records to informal entries, like Amazon reviews. Once he was in possession of the catalogue, toshing the information from the various sites was simply a matter of hacking in and deleting. With an average person, it would take the bots a few hours to compile the catalogue. As he waited, Rigby settled down with a triple espresso to catch up on reading and commenting on posts on *Cognoscenti*, a cycling website where fellow devotees of the two-wheeled arts discussed races, routes, legendary riders, and, of course, their equipment. He'd barely drunk half his coffee before an alert flashed up. The bots had completed their mission. It was too fast – *way* too fast – like completing the Tour de France in three hours instead of twenty-three days. It was just wrong.

Despite his misgivings, Rigby toshed what was left of Ascott's public persona. He began with school. Ascott had attended Abingdon, and from there he'd gone to Cambridge, to study Computer Science. Then straight into the civil service. Rigby couldn't find a record of his date of birth. His wife – or *a* wife – had died in 2004. He found the death certificate online, and the marriage, in 1984, also showed up on a register. Rigby hacked the relevant sites and deleted the originals.

Toshing Ascott from Abingdon was equally simple. Its alumni included a number of outstanding musicians, which earned it a slightly longer than average listing in Wikipedia. The bots had found a Facebook page, to which alums could submit news of themselves and classmates. Someone had posted a photo of Ascott on the Isle of Man attending the annual meeting of a Maserati owners' club. Using their time-tested Facebook hack – which the techs at Pangolin had to keep updating whenever Menlo Park spotted the intrusion – Rigby toshed Ascott from the page. Right before he made the final keystroke to delete, he took a screenshot, and made a mental note to add it to his archives. He then remembered that he'd given the archive – the SD card – to Steadman to keep safe for him. Hmmm. He'd have to store it on his laptop until he got the card back.

He then went to the actual site for the owners' club. The site was hosted at an engineering company in Swindon. Gaining entry was simple. He deleted all mentions of Ascott, again recording what he was about to delete, and added it to the same folder.

Erasing anything from Cambridge, he knew from experience, could be a tiresome affair. With all the different colleges keeping their own records, it took time to track things down. He skipped lunch and completed that part of the task by early afternoon. Travel came next, removing records of trains, flights or other means of transport. Pangolin had hacked every air, rail, and bus company at some point in the last few years. Ascott hadn't taken many flights, but he was a very heavy user of Le Shuttle. Rigby guessed this was to do with his Maserati. He toshed all record of Ascott having taken it. He followed that by deleting medical and dental records, and then finally bank accounts and credit cards.

Ascott had no LinkedIn entries, Twitter accounts, Instagram pages, or any other social media presence, according to the bots. There were, however, a large number of emails. The average person had two email accounts, but some had hundreds. Still, the only ones that mattered were those that other people remembered, and Rigby believed that the best way to deal with email was to find a person's one or two main accounts, break in, and delete them entirely.

Towards the end of the afternoon, he called Putts.

'Mark, it's Rigby. If Father Christmas ever existed, he doesn't anymore.'

'Thank you for letting me know. We'll talk soon.'

'Wait a minute,' Rigby said quickly, before Putts could hang up. 'You said he was a nobody.'

'Yeah, just an average guy with some personal issues.'

'He's anything but average.'

Putts hesitated for a moment before replying. 'What makes you say that?'

'For a start, his employment records don't stack up. He

took a government job in '72, moved up through the ranks, switched departments a couple of times, and then in the mid 1990s he disappears.'

'Retired.'

'Nah. He never draws the pension.'

'Maybe he doesn't need it.'

'With his classic car habit, I think he'd need it.'

'What are you suggesting?'

'I'm suggesting he's not who you say he is. He's been toshed before, professionally.'

'Is that a concern?'

'Damn right. We weren't the only people that did toshing. Some of the other government agencies use it ...'

'Yes ... and?'

'Is he a bloody spook?'

Putts laughed. 'Father Christmas? Pull the other one, it's got sleigh bells on.'

Rigby wanted to believe him. They'd been associates for over a decade. Bust-ups were common between officers, but never him and Mark. They were usually the ones at the back watching it go down, swapping little knowing looks – *we're above this crap.*

'Seen something he shouldn't at the North Pole?' Rigby said.

'Forget about it. Soon as he's out of your hands, whole thing never happened.'

Rigby felt his skin tightening. He'd guessed right. 'What whole thing? What is he involved in?'

There was silence on the other end. Eventually, Putts said, 'I can't tell you. DV and above only.'

Rigby knew very well what that meant: accessible only to people with Developed Vetting clearance – police in specific roles, NCA, and security services. 'I was DV,' he said, hopefully.

'*Was*.'

'Bastard!'

He rushed to shut down his computers, unplugged his router, and removed the SIM cards from his phone. Wondering what to do next, he took out a bottle of disinfectant and began patrolling the house for bacteria while he worked out his next move.

As he examined the body on the slab in front of him, Balorat could imagine all too easily the procedure by which it had ended up there. At a hotel in Paddington earlier that evening, a businessman sat in a bar nursing a cocktail. A woman slipped into the seat next to him. She was in her late twenties, perhaps early thirties, a few years younger than him, and attractive in her professional clothes. He noticed her and smiled. To his delight, she smiled back. From there, he offered her a drink. They flirted. They had more drinks. She made the first move; touched his hand. Two drinks later they went up to his room.

The kill was clean, but the tosher had left far too much information. All Balorat had to do was Google his name and whoosh – link after link came flying up, stuff that should have been toshed long before the hit. The victim was from Glasgow. He was married, with two teenage children. He worked in commercial property. He'd been in London for a trade fair. He drove a BMW. He had a bank account and a credit card. He paid his taxes. His house was worth £687,000 and he had £456,000 left on the mortgage. It was far more than was required for an ID. Fortunately they'd done their job properly in relation to his property holdings. He was no longer the owner of a warehouse space in Greenock, nor of a strangely dispersed chain of newsagents, with shops in Liverpool, Leeds, Newcastle, Glasgow, and Edinburgh. The properties – and all of their contents – were now registered as belonging to a company in the Channel Islands.

The cleaning staff had found the man on his bed at the hotel, cold. Cause of death wasn't obvious, so a post mortem examination had been requested. Balorat, who was in charge of scheduling, had sighed loudly enough for anyone interested to hear, and then offered to take on this boring, workaday case. Yet another middle-aged man had clearly had too much to drink, mixed it with prescription medication, and triggered a heart attack. Barely worth breaking out the toothed forceps. But hey-ho, needs must. Balorat would do his fair share of the mundane work. Lead by example and all that.

Later, on the slab, he rolled the body over to check for a puncture mark. There had to be one somewhere. He'd prepared the hypodermic himself, measured the dosage exactly, packed it in a sterile bag, put it in an old glasses case so the girl wouldn't prick her finger, and hidden it in a backpack. They'd done a bag-switch in a hideous Starbucks on the Edgware Road. The hypo contained Midazolam. As with most sedatives, a too-large dose would kill. It had been used in prisons for lethal injection, and had become a favourite in his work for K. He'd even begun carrying a hypo in his pocket when he was on field jobs in case of unexpected threats. Fortunately, he'd never had to use it, a fact he attributed to his unerring ability to spot trouble.

He wondered how the girl had done the actual injection. The police report said the victim had been found on the bed, on his back. Maybe she'd offered him a hand job, pinching him hard once or twice as she did it, asking him if a little pain turned him on. Was she naked? Had she mounted him to further distract his attention while she slipped in the needle? Death wouldn't have been instantaneous. Had she held him down, astride him, as he writhed in agony? Balorat would have given anything to see the look on the man's face when he realised this was the end.

He couldn't wait to get home and tell Sylvie about it. They'd go down to the playroom in their house and re-enact it. He'd stroke his wife to orgasm as he related the way that he found a tiny puncture mark in the fold where the top of the thigh met the gluteus, invisible to the naked eye. He chuckled to himself as he completed the autopsy report:

No external markings. Cause of death: heart attack

brought on by a combination of alcohol and medication. Pathologist-speak for: stupid fucker, should have known better.

Later on he called K. 'The girl did a beautiful job. But whoever Putts is using for toshing is a fucking amateur. Google the vic, there's still a ton of stuff.'

'I already did,' she said.

'Well, what are we going to do about it?'

He expected her to tear a strip off him, speaking to her like that. Instead, she said, 'My God, are you feeling remorse over Tudor Clarke?' Her voice made him go weak. Throaty and unashamedly superior, every word came with a sharp edge of disapproval. 'I forgot. He was your friend, wasn't he.'

'He was a greedy, coked-up, double-crossing little shitbag, as you very well know,' Balorat said quickly.

'He was still your friend.'

'A long time ago. A very fucking long time ago.'

'So what do you want me to do? I'm not closing while we get a replacement, we'll lose customers.'

Balorat chewed a hang-nail that had been bothering him for days. 'I'm not asking you to close, I'm asking you to get chocolate teapot to hurry up.'

'From what I understand, it's coming along well.'

'I'll believe it when I see it.'

'I have a new brief,' she said, changing the subject. 'Finland.'

That was different. 'What are they doing, fighting over an ice-fishing hole?'

'It's about a patent.'

'Where is it up to?'

'Toshed and ready for dispatch.'

'Toshed? You're sure about that?'

'It was one of Clarke's final jobs.'

Balorat had recently paid the boys' tuition at Charterhouse and it had cleaned out his current account. Thirty-eight grand a year. Each. He had four of the little shits.

'So long as it's not Underson.'

K snorted. 'You made your point about him. But the target and Underson have a problem in common. Might be an opportunity for us.'

'Which is?'

'The target's a known lush. Liver failure is a credible COD. Fairly easy to arrange.'

Balorat seethed. He hated it when people played doctor. 'It's not as simple as you think.'

'For a man of your ability? I'll give you a couple of days to consider.'

She knew he'd do it. *He* knew he'd do it. Finland. Wasn't it meant to be some sort of socialist paradise? Just went to show, people were the same everywhere. What would one less Finn mean to the world? Not much. Especially if he'd never existed in the first place. That was the one thing he liked most about K – apart from the way that men wilted in her presence – she understood efficiency. No loose ends. One thing Balorat knew for certain was that criminal cases were solved by tiny errors, they dangled like worms over the mouths of baby chicks. Take away the worms, and the chicks had nothing to feed on.

7

Nice neighbourhood, Rigby thought to himself with a deep sense of irony as he rode into the square in Bethnal Green where Frederick Ascott was staying. It had been night when he'd taken him to the safe house, and he hadn't gained much of a feel for the area. Now, in the daylight, its desolation became clear. Most of the windows and doors at street level were covered by metal grilles. Every spare wall had been scarred with graffiti. At the end of the street, a skinhead walked three pit bulls up a narrow strip of grass.

He locked his bike to a streetlight, taking care to wrap his cable through both wheels, then rang the doorbell. After a short wait, an inner door opened behind a grille. Ascott's face poked through the gap.

'Who is it?' he said, warily.

'It's me. Rigby.'

'Rigby?'

'I dropped you off the other day.'

'Oh, you.' He sounded surprised. 'I don't remember calling.'

'No, you didn't. I heard there was a disturbance in the area. Have you had any strangers knocking on the door?'

'No. No-one.'

'Good. Have you been outside at all?'

Ascott didn't respond for a second. 'Would you prefer to come in?'

'Sure.'

The inner door closed. He waited while Ascott unlocked the grille wearing pyjamas and a dressing gown, with his ugly boat shoes poking out from underneath. His hair was unkempt, and there was two or three days of grey stubble on his chin.

'I thought you said you'd come only if I called?' he said.

Rigby didn't answer him. 'Hot in here,' he said.

Ascott closed the grille, but left the inner door open. He mock-mopped his forehead with the sleeve of his robe. 'Thermostat's on the blink. At least it's not summer.'

A short hallway led to a kitchen and a small TV room.

Ascott said, 'I can offer coffee. We're out of firewater.'

'Nothing thanks.' Rigby helped himself to one of two identical Ikea recliners in the sitting room. Ascott took the other.

Rigby said, 'You must be bored here by yourself.'

'I get by. There's food, a music system, a few dreadful books.'

The first time Rigby had met Ascott, he'd found it difficult to get a fix on what kind of man he was, and he was finding it no easier now. Like most Englishmen, Rigby had developed from an early age a tendency to judge a person's wealth, upbringing and social status by listening to their accent. It was a trait he profoundly disliked in himself. He'd tried hard over the years to unlearn it, although, he had to admit, it sometimes came in useful. Ascott was proving baffling. He'd attended a private boys' school, which accounted for his pronunciations and priggishness, but all those years working with IT geeks and engineers should have softened it more. At the same time, he was slouching around in a dressing gown at lunchtime, unshaven, like some trailer-trash wino.

As if reading his mind, Ascott said, 'It can be difficult, having no routine.' He waited barely long enough for a reply before adding, 'Very important in prisons, I'm told, to keep a routine.'

'I've never spent much time in one,' Rigby said, 'except when visiting.'

'I visited an open prison once. It was rather like this.'

'Except that you're not locked in.'

'I think I am,' Ascott said, with a wry smile.

Rigby guessed from the prison reference that Ascott had him pegged as an ex-con who owed Putts a favour. His tone carried an implicit message: whatever predicament he was in, it was far above Rigby's pay grade.

'As you're here, perhaps you could run an errand for me, down to the store.'

Finding out what Ascott craved might be useful. 'What do you need?'

'Something to break up the monotony of tea.'

'Like a bottle of wine?'

'I was thinking Grey Goose, tomato juice, and Worcester sauce.'

'You're making Bloody Marys?'

'And a bottle of Fino sherry. My personal twist, the Fino. Do you know what that is? Possibly not. It's the dry sherry, not the sweet one. And if they don't have Grey Goose, get whatever vodka is the most expensive. I value my insides.'

Rigby forced himself not to react to the condescension. If Ascott wanted an ex-con, an ex-con he would get. 'I'm not sure Mr Putts would approve of that. Keep them on the straight and narrow, Rigby, he always says to me.'

'You're not going to go whining to Master, are you?'

'My friend who was in prison, he got to be friends with one of the screws. That happens a lot, apparently, one of the cons and one of the screws hitting it off – I don't mean that way – and they start to confide in each other. What would that be, Stockholm syndrome and Oslo syndrome at the same time?'

'I don't think it's either, actually.'

'Anyway, the screw told him that they had to be careful about not letting personal information become public, because when an inmate is released they don't want them coming around to the screw's house. So when you become a screw, all that information has to be deleted from public records. It's like one day you're there, and the next you're not.'

'I'd never heard that,' Ascott said, in such a way as to make clear that he thought Rigby was making it up.

'There are other jobs where you have to have your identity erased.'

Ascott eyed him warily. 'I'm a systems engineer. Not interesting enough to require anything like that.'

'The only people who think their jobs are interesting are record producers and film directors, and most of them are broke.'

Ascott's eyes narrowed. He was wondering where this was leading.

Rigby asked him, 'Did Putts tell you what I do for a living?'

'No,' he said, irritated.

'I manage people's online profiles.'

'How very modern.'

'He asked me to manage yours.'

For the first time since Rigby had entered the safe house, an expression crossed Ascott's face that was instinctive and unfiltered. It clearly rattled him that Rigby could be messing around with his personal information. 'I don't believe I authorised that.'

'But you're aware of it?'

'What?'

'Your public profile. You pay attention to it.'

'I don't bother with things like Facebook, if that's what you mean.'

Rigby wasn't buying it. 'There's a lot of information out there about you when you were younger, but not much recent stuff. And it's not only your public profile. Your presence on private networks – like government mailing lists – gets less and less with every passing year.'

'I'm an old man now. Thank you for reminding me.'

'I'm saying this out of professional respect. A sudden disappearance is noticed. What happened to so-and-so? Is he sick? Is he dead? But a slow fade, so that no-one notices, that takes skill.'

'I wouldn't know.'

Nice try, Rigby thought. He didn't buy the wide-eyed act. 'The funny thing is, toshing – that's what it's called – helps people disappear, but when you meet someone who's been toshed it makes them more interesting.'

Ascott's eyes went cold. 'Is that some sort of threat?'

'No, I've been asked to protect you. But that will be a lot easier if you tell me what I'm meant to be protecting you from.'

'What I do is confidential.'

'That's what I guessed,' Rigby said. 'I found a home address for you. I couldn't help noticing it's near Cheltenham.'

'I'm retired. The entire world moves west when they retire.'

'You moved there when you were still working.'

'I think you'd better leave,' Ascott said.

'What was your job at GCHQ? The codes expert? Were you in The Cage, or maybe on the Russian desk? Why do you need to disappear now?'

'Get out!' Ascott shouted, rising from his chair. He pushed past Rigby and unlocked the iron grille. 'And stay away from me!'

Rigby pushed past him again in the narrow corridor. 'Still want your Fino sherry?'

Ascott ignored him. 'I will be reporting this to your superior.'

'My superior?'

'Mark Putts.'

Rigby laughed. 'Not even when I worked for him.'

Mesh was lifting her laptop bag from the rear chute of the X-ray machine when the security guard reached out and placed a hand on the strap.

'Sorry, ma'am. Visual inspection.'

Not again. Could this really be happening, in a government building? They were so obvious about it. Did they think no-one noticed?

She said, 'Five people just went through. None of them required a visual inspection.'

The guard shook his head in apology. 'Standard procedure.'

Mesh reached into her coat pocket and pulled out her NCA card. 'Will this help?'

His eyes opened wide with surprise. 'I'll be as fast as I can.'

She released the bag, still furious. There was nothing in her attire to arouse suspicion. She wore heels higher than most, but then she was not tall; she had a liking for suits that gave a bit of width to her shoulders, but again, she was not the broadest; and yes, her skirts tended to fit well, but she visited the gym three times a week and what was the point of that if she was going to hide everything? When the guard had finished, she accepted the bag silently and walked at a dignified pace up the grand staircase. Focus, she said to herself, this is a big opportunity, a way to rise beyond being just the manager of the Sweatbox.

Dale's office stood at the far end of a corridor on the third floor. She gave a sharp knock.

'Come in,' he called.

His vast windows overlooked Westminster. A collection of old photographic equipment on the shelves made the room seem more like a museum than a part of the Home Office. Dale, bright-eyed and appearing even younger than his twenty-nine years, wore a dark grey suit with lapels so narrow they were almost stripes, a white shirt, and a thin blue tie. Mesh remembered thinking the first time they'd met that if his accent had been Boston Brahmin, instead of perfect BBC English, he could have been a Kennedy.

'Well, hello, Mesh,' he said, setting an antique Leica back down on the shelf. 'These belonged to my grandfather. He had them in his office in the Commons ...'

Mesh didn't know what to say. She knew nothing about cameras, and always felt daunted by people from upper-class families.

When she didn't reply, he said, 'You seem a little flustered. Has something upset you?'

It caught her by surprise. 'I didn't appreciate the way the security people treated me.'

'Gave you an ASBA did they?'

'ASBA?'

'Always search Blacks and Asians.'

What had she done to deserve this? Double-first in computer science and law. Trained at the Police Central e-Crime Unit. Talent-spotted and promoted when the unit had become part of the NCA. Now this teenager thought he could make casual racist comments and she'd have to grin and take it.

'You're lucky I'm not recording this,' she said.

'Don't worry,' Dale laughed, 'the whole place is bugged.'

She told herself to take it as some kind of weird compliment, as if he felt sufficiently comfortable around her to let his guard down.

'So, you requested this meeting,' he said. 'How can I help?'

She cleared her throat and tried to put the last ten minutes behind her. She'd been rehearsing for this moment since early morning. 'We've been working hard to corroborate what little information we have about the people in the screenshots. We've identified relatives and others who knew them, and we've taken statements.'

Dale frowned. 'The people you took statements from, how many of them have underworld connections?'

Mesh swallowed. 'Most of them.'

'Then none of it will stand up. Opposing counsel would rip it to shreds, if it even got that far.'

'It's only one part of the picture.'

'And what's the other part: asking all our pathologists to review John Does?'

'Yes it is,' she said, trying to sound confident.

'So now I have an inbox full of complaints. Professor Balorat, over at Guys Hospital, he's on the warpath. Says the whole thing's a records anomaly. Says he'd lay his reputation on it.'

She remembered Balorat from work he'd done on one of her cases. An obnoxious little man. 'Let him.'

'He plays golf with the Home Secretary. And whatever you think of our esteemed leader, he's the one with a seat at the Cabinet table. It's not a fight you can win.'

Mesh felt the floor falling away. She'd always known Dale might bail out, ever since she'd first been informed that the case had been assigned to him. He was too nakedly ambitious to take such a big risk.

'Now don't get me wrong,' he said, 'I'm not trying to wriggle out of this. But we have to remember who we're dealing with. These people would have been street thieves, fringe members of crime gangs, drug dealers. Who are we trying to achieve justice for? Their families? Because I don't hear any cries for help. Are we even sure they're missing? People like this, they go on the run, live on the streets, sometimes they're in the nick, or sleeping rough.'

'And sometimes they're dead,' Mesh said.

'And what if they are? Is anyone weeping? I'm not saying this in jest, these are the questions I'm asked every day.'

'I understand, but as I said from the start, the absence of any data about these individuals, in the context of them being part of witness protection, suggests that they were professionally toshed. Proof of life will be thin on the ground. And you agreed,' she said, pouncing on the opportunity to quote him, 'that we should treat them as possible homicides.'

Dale didn't appreciate his words being thrown back at him. 'Mesh, I am under extraordinary pressure to close this case. Bring me some hard facts. Do you have anything? Any suspects?'

'We've narrowed the field,' she said. 'There were only four toshers working for the NCA at the time. Two of them transferred to the security services, so we're focusing on the other two.'

'Anything useful?' Dale said, perking up.

'One is in Belgrade.'

'*Belgrade*? What the hell's he doing there?'

She cleared her throat nervously. 'We're not entirely sure.'

'You'll find out, presumably. What about the fourth suspect?'

Mesh tensed again. 'I wouldn't call him a suspect. His name is Rigby Goode. He's former NCA, and still works with us, albeit not in an official capacity.'

'How long ago did he leave?'

'Four years.'

'And what does he do now?'

'He's an identity consultant.' She explained how Pangolin worked.

'So he's a fixer and a vigilante,' Dale said. 'Sort of a shady character.'

'Not at all,' she said quickly. 'They're a successful company. He has a house in Chiswick.'

'Chiswick? Bloody hell, I'm in the wrong business.'

Mesh resisted the urge to laugh. Dale's family had been multi-millionaires for generations. Their estate in Sussex stretched to over a thousand acres.

She said, 'We learned that in the early days toshers used to keep screenshots of everything they deleted. Once the higher-ups found out about it they stopped them doing it. But Rigby Goode was one of the first, so it's possible he still holds a record of the people he toshed at that time.'

Dale's face lit up. 'Now that, *that*, would be the kind of evidence we need.'

'I'll talk to him,' she said. 'If he has the records we can

eliminate him from enquiries.'

'*Eliminate*?' Dale stared at her like she'd lost her mind. 'He's the prime suspect.'

'Sir, I worked with him for four years ...'

But Dale wasn't listening. 'People wonder how I got this post.'

She resisted the urge to urge to blurt out 'nepotism'. 'I think it's very impressive. Your hard work paid off.'

'Pish, posh. My grandfather and I crafted the strategy, and then we gathered the family: my father, my brothers, cousin Eugene from Investec, Aunt Helen from Oxfam. We got them on-message, and then sent them out to spread the word.'

'What was the message?'

'That's irrelevant. It was an ambush. We'll do the same with Mr Goode.'

'How?'

'Raid his offices. Confiscate their equipment. Take everything. Those records have got to be there somewhere.'

'Sir, it won't work.'

'Why not?'

'He's too clever, he'll have it hidden it.'

'Never underestimate human stupidity. Get the paperwork prepped and I'll sign it. We've got to show progress on this. If we don't, they'll close it down, and I am not in the business of having cases closed by my so-called superiors.'

8

The caller ID on Putts's phone came up as 'unknown number'. He was tempted not to take it. Only one person ever called him from a burner: K. No doubt Vincent Balorat had been bending her ear, telling her everything was going south; insisting it was all his fault. Like hell it was. He was the only sane one. With luck, K might have told Balorat to put up or shut up. She'd had an empathy bypass. Sometimes it worked in his favour. He took the call.

'Your ladyship.'

'I'm not in the mood.'

'What's little Vincent told you now?' He should never have got him involved. Short man syndrome had metastasised into borderline personality disorder.

'I haven't been speaking to Vincent. Ascott called me. He's a gibbering wreck.'

A siren sounded in Putts's head. 'Why? What happened?'

'Seems your friend Rigby Goode paid him a visit.'

'First I've heard.'

'Is this investigation going to cause us problems?'

'I'm containing it.'

'So why is Goode asking him about GCHQ?'

Alarms. Cold fingers. 'Bollocks, it's bollocks.'

'No, it's not. How did Goode find out about that?'

'I've told you, he's far more than just a tosher.'

'And I believe you, so when are you going to bring him over to our side?'

'He can't be bought. We have to make it impossible for him not to.'

He could hear her sigh of disapproval down the phone. What would she be thinking, that Balorat was right, that everything was going to hell, and that the blame lay at his door? She said, 'Everyone has a price.'

'No, they don't. Some people cannot be bought.'

'Stop arguing with me, I don't do arguing.'

'I'm not arguing, it's a discussion.'

That sigh again. 'I don't discuss.'

He said, 'Just give me a week. Things are moving.'

'Mark ...'

'Vincent's in Finland, yes?'

'So what?'

'Give me until he gets back.'

Silence.

He said, 'When's he getting back?'

'What does that have to do with it?'

Nothing. It had nothing to do with it. It was just time. 'Because if it went okay in Finland, maybe he'll stop whining about toshers.'

'Or at least complain about something else ...'

'So until then?'

'Fine.' She hung up.

There were times, he felt, that the best course of action would be to fire up an onion browser, head onto the dark web, go to K's site, and take out a contract on both her and Balorat. Right now would be highly appropriate. Unfortunately, there was also no point. The hit would be traced back to him, and one of the marksmen, annoyed at losing their paymaster, would come after him. Before even thinking about something like that, he needed to make sure that him and his family were toshed beyond any hint of traceability. For that, he needed Rigby.

It always came back to sodding Rigby.

Back in her office, Mesh landed with a thud. If she wasn't

careful, the whole thing could get pinned on her old friend. She also suspected she might need Rigby's help to solve the case; bursting into his offices would surely mean that he never trusted her again.

Then, out of the blue, she received an email from Aisling inviting her for a drink after work. Normally, she would have rejected it. Mesh took great care around socialising with colleagues. She didn't drink, so that negated the main pleasure of a visit to the pub – all the men in her family drank like fish, not every day but enough, and always the same stuff, Chivas Regal, the thought of its sweet and resinous odour made her shiver – but Aisling had done good work recently, and she was older than the rest of the Sweatboxers. Maybe they could relate more as people. Maybe she wouldn't screw up her face when Mesh ordered a Diet Coke. She replied 'yes'. Aisling came straight back, suggesting a sports bar in Pimlico. The suggestion surprised her, but she had that sporty vibe.

Mesh walked in to discover the bar to be much brighter and more civilized than she expected, with sane-looking men sharing reasonably appetising food. It still wasn't to her taste, and she braced herself for a wolf-whistle as she strode past half a dozen male-only tables. She found Aisling in a booth at the back.

'So what is this place? A favourite of yours?' Mesh said.

'I'm the only girl in a family with four boys. I'm surprised you don't know it. NCA lads come here a lot. Security Service too. And MI6. This bar is lasting proof that all terrorists are idiots.'

'As if we needed that.'

'At six o'clock on a Friday evening, a carefully placed explosive could take out a good swathe of Britain's anti-terrorism capability, but they're too stupid to realise it.'

'We're fortunate they're not as clever as you.'

A waitress came. Mesh ordered a Diet Coke.

'Going back to work?' Aisling said.

Mesh ignored the comment. 'So, what did you want to

talk about?'

'Nothing in particular. I thought it would be nice to get to know each other better.'

Mesh smiled. 'Save it. I need to get home for my kid.'

Aisling laughed. 'Okay, cut to the chase. I want to do more on this case.'

Just as Mesh had hoped. 'There might be an opportunity coming up.'

'Really?' Aisling said, visibly excited. 'Does it have anything to do with your meeting this morning with Mr Dale?'

'No,' she said quickly. The last thing she needed was Aisling thinking she was acting on a direct order from the Home Office.

'Oh. What did he want?'

'Nothing significant,' Mesh shrugged. 'Just a bunch of SFQs.'

'SFQs?'

'Stupid fucking questions.'

'Mesh, I'm sorry, tell me if I'm getting out of line. Sometimes my enthusiasm gets the better of me.'

'I will, don't worry.' She reached out and put a hand on Aisling's arm. 'Let me confide something to you: Rigby Goode and I have history.'

Aisling's eyes went wide with surprise.

'Not that kind,' Mesh said quickly. 'We were rivals in our first couple of years. Our bosses used to think it was funny, so they made us sit together and work cases as a pair.'

Aisling nodded in recognition. 'So that's why I've heard the term Goode and Should?'

'Yes, and you'd be wise to forget it.'

'Wiped from memory. But if you were working in the Sweatbox around that time, you must have known Tudor Clarke, too.'

Very good, Mesh thought. This girl was as bright as she'd hoped. 'Yes, but not as well. It was over fifty people, even then. Clarke was a quiet one. I didn't have much to do with him.

What I do know is that in the beginning the toshers used to keep screenshots of everything they deleted. Clarke and Rigby both would have done this. If those files still exist, if we could get our hands on them, we could prove their involvement.'

'Did you ask Rigby?'

Mesh smiled. 'Flat out denied it, which makes me think he's probably lying. We need to raid his offices, seize the equipment, go through all the hard drives.'

'Okay,' Aisling said, getting excited.

'But here's the thing, I can't lead that raid. I can't have colleagues thinking I'm settling old scores.'

Aisling took a second to comprehend what Mesh was hinting at. 'You want me to do it?' she said nervously. 'I wouldn't know where to start.'

Mesh glanced down the bar. She thought she'd recognised one or two faces as she came in. She checked again. Sure enough, sitting at a table near the front there was a group of NCA operations boys sharing a pizza. They were young and well-built, showing off their muscles in tight T-shirts. She was pretty sure she'd met them before.

'Well,' Mesh said, 'tonight's your lucky night, because I've spotted a couple of gentlemen who might be able to help you.' She pointed to the table with the pizza.

'The beefcake boys?' Aisling said. 'Who are they?'

'They're from Operations. Let's go talk to them.'

'You're serious?'

'Actually, no. I have to rescue my son from his grandmother. You talk to them. They'll take care of the whole thing for you.'

'Why would they do that?'

Mesh laughed. 'The way men look at you? Don't think I haven't noticed. It's not complicated. You brief Ops on what you want, then go with them, record everything, and be the one to write the report.'

'What if we don't find anything?'

'Then we'll have an angry ex-officer to deal with. But

don't worry about him, he's a pussycat.'

'Why do I think you're not telling me the whole truth?' Aisling said.

'That's the NCA for you,' Mesh said, standing up. 'If it were that simple, anyone could do it.'

Mesh strode down the Embankment towards her car feeling ten feet tall. Dale would get his raid. She wouldn't get the blame. And Aisling and a pair of a beefcakes had zero chance of finding anything that could damage Rigby. All in all, a very satisfactory evening's work. Now, if traffic wasn't too bad, she'd be able to pick up Satinder and get him home in time to put him to bed properly, rather than him conking out in the car as usual. But maybe that was asking too much.

9

Rigby was in a luxury flat on the forty-fourth floor of St George Wharf Tower at Nine Elms, trying hard to not to be distracted by the view down the Thames, when his crypto rang. He pitching to a new client, and didn't appreciate the interruption. Embarrassed, he switched it to silent, but not before noticing that the caller was Steadman. He placed it on the table in front of him. Two minutes later, he saw Steadman ringing again. Something was up. He made an excuse about needing the bathroom and phoned back.

'What's so urgent?' Rigby fumed, straining to shout and whisper at the same time.

'Where are you?' Steadman said. 'Sounds like you're in the khazi.'

'I'm in the middle of a sales pitch.'

'In the khazi?'

'No ... what the hell do you want?'

'You need to get back the office, now.'

'I can't, I told you.'

'They're raiding us.'

'Who is?'

'NCA.'

Rigby racked his brains to remember which of his clients might have done something that could have led to an NCA investigation. It didn't take long to come up with a lengthy list. 'Which client are they investigating?'

'It's not a client. It's us.'

'Us? What about?' A cold worm wrapped itself around his insides.

'I don't know. They say they'll only to talk to you.'

Feeling anxious, he went back to the living room and told the client that he'd been contacted by a hospital: his brother had been taken ill, and they couldn't get hold of his wife. He was extremely sorry, but he had to leave immediately.

Sticking his bike in top gear and standing on the pedals, he raced back to Chinatown, building up a heavy sweat under the moleskin coat. His route took him along the Embankment, not far from the Citadel. He tried not to look, but couldn't help remembering going into the building for the first time, and how for weeks beforehand he'd fixated on what it would look like inside. He'd been disappointed when he entered the main reception with its chairs and coffee tables straight out of an office supplies catalogue. It could have been anywhere, from a local council office to a biscuit company. There was nothing special at all.

Later on, working there, his feelings changed completely. He grew to think of their team of toshers as a little army of silent protectors. Every day, riding his bike to and from work, he felt different and separate from everyone else on the streets – not better, but special: one of a select few. And then inside the Sweatbox itself, he didn't just feel connected, he felt like he was in the beating heart of the country, the place through which every human corpuscle passed at some point in its life, even if represented by nothing more than tiny strings of data. Truth was, he missed it.

When he arrived at his office in Chinatown, streaming with sweat, he found his staff standing out on the street, bewildered. Tourists milled around, wondering what was going on. He spotted Gloria in the crowd.

'They showed up an hour ago,' she told him. 'They're taking our equipment.'

'Everything?' he said, beginning to panic. 'What about your laptop?'

Gloria smiled. 'I didn't grow up in New Cross for nothing. First sign of trouble you stash the merch.'

'Where is it?'

'Pat me on the back.'

She was wearing a light jacket over a T-shirt. Rigby patted. Her back was hard and flat.

Gloria laughed. 'Soon as I heard the word 'warrant', I grabbed the duct tape, and zzzzt-zzzzt-zzzzt.'

Rigby laughed with her, delighted at Gloria's quick thinking. Then he stopped abruptly.

'What is it?' she said, seeing his face fall.

Rigby tore the backpack from his back. He unzipped and rifled through the contents. 'No! Shit! Shit! Shit!'

'Did you forget something.'

'*My* laptop.'

'Did you leave it behind?'

'No. Yes. I mean earlier. I didn't take it with me, I was using the iPad.' He pointed to the office. 'Laptop's in there.'

'But there's nothing on it, everything's on this one.'

'Not everything.'

Rigby ran to the door. It was locked. He fished his keys out and let himself in. Half a dozen men in black NCA jackets were piling everything they could find into plastic sacks. One of them held up a hand. 'You can't come in here.'

'I'm the owner.'

'I don't care who you are, you need to leave.'

'Is Mesh here?'

'I told you to get out,' said the officer. He put down his sack.

A second one saw the first making a move towards Rigby and set his sack down. 'Need a hand there?'

'I'm just looking for one computer, alright?' Rigby said. 'It contains sensitive information. NCA material.'

'Can't you read?' the second officer said, pointing at the letter on his jacket.

'The information is ... look, just call Mark Putts. The information belongs to him.'

'So why do you have it?'

'Because I'm working for him.'

The officers exchanged a glance: *bullshitter*. The first man said, 'Our orders are to take everything. You need to leave.' He added, '*Now*.'

'Come on guys, I used to work for you,' Rigby said, and he started to walk toward the picnic table where he'd been sitting that day. As he passed between the officers a fist hit him in the gut.

Rigby wasn't expecting it. He doubled over, winded, unable even to call out.

The two men laughed. 'You're walking the wrong way, son.'

'Maybe he needs a little help turning around.'

Another fist caught him on the side of the head. True to the promise, it spun him a perfect one-eighty. He saw the door and was about to run for it when a woman's voice shouted, 'What the hell is going on here?'

He turned, blinking hard, still dazed. She had short blonde hair and an athletic build. Her face was striking, slightly narrow, with wide blue eyes.

'Are you alright?' she said to Rigby.

Her voice was deep for a woman, and he found himself checking her out. She was physically very fit, slim and toned. He wondered if maybe she was a cyclist? She'd look good riding in front of him... Wait a minute, get a grip! She wasn't here to be chatted up.

'It's a misunderstanding.'

'You're the owner, is that correct?'

As she said it, Steadman and Warren emerged from the conference room. They watched from the top of the stairs.

'Yes,' Rigby said. 'And you are?'

She flashed her wallet. 'Aisling Cockburn, NCA. We have a warrant to search your premises and confiscate equipment.'

Rigby held up a hand. 'As I was trying to explain to your colleagues, there's material here that's highly confidential.

NCA material.'

'That's okay, we're NCA.'

'No. It's higher than that. DV level.'

Her eyes narrowed. Rigby glanced up to the top of the stairs. Steadman and Gloria looked as puzzled as she was.

Rigby said, 'You need to call Mark Putts. He can clear this up.'

She thought for a moment. 'Where is this information?'

'On my laptop. You can take everything else. I just need that one machine.'

'Do you know where it is?'

Rigby had spotted it, on a picnic table, exactly where he'd thought it would be. He pointed. 'That one.'

Aisling went over and examined it. Satisfied that it looked normal, she brought it over to him. 'You're sure this is the one?'

'Absolutely,' he said gratefully, holding out his hand.

She passed it to one of the officers. 'Bag it.'

'No!' Rigby yelled, but before he could move, the other officer grabbed his arm.

'It's nothing personal,' she said. 'I'm just doing my job.' She turned to the officer holding the computer. 'Make sure it's sealed as evidence.'

'Putts isn't going to be happy,' Rigby said.

Aisling nodded. 'We'll seal it for his attention.' She nodded to the officer holding him. 'Take him outside,' then she looked to the top of the stairs. 'Them too. Get them all out of here. We have work to do.'

Rigby went outside and called Putts, who picked up on the first ring.

'Thought it might be you.'

'What the fuck is going on?'

'I've only just heard. I'm as angry as you are.'

'I kept my end of the deal. First, Father Christmas is a spy, and now the stormtroopers are in my office. What the hell is going on?'

'I told you. It's Mesh. Trying to make a name for herself. I wasn't even aware they'd applied for the warrant. Dale signed it without asking me.'

'Who's Dale?'

'Makepeace Dale. A kid over at the Home Office.'

'Well, I saved your bacon. There's information about Father Christmas on one of the laptops.'

'That was careless.'

'I got them to place it under seal, not to be opened without your authorisation.'

'A small mercy.'

'It's a damned big mercy, and I want it back.'

'What. The laptop?'

'Intact.'

'I can't do that. It's evidence.'

Shitbag. He knew the value of it. 'Who is he, Mark? Who the fuck is Father Christmas?'

Putts paused. 'He's who you think he is. Only worse.'

Putts phoned K.

'He's not back yet,' she said.

'Wouldn't matter if he was.'

'You have good news?'

'Oh *yeah*. I can feel it, baby.'

'You're making me puke.'

'The net is closing.'

'Call me when it does.'

Mesh saw the caller ID and rolled her eyes.

'Hello Mark.'

There was a pause at the other end. It was something all senior officers did when trying to convey that they were irritated. Mesh did it herself with her own subordinates.

'What the hell do you think you're doing?'

'Following orders.'

'From Dale?' Putts laughed. 'Does he shave yet?'

'I wasn't even there. Aisling Cockburn ran the show.'

'Let's not play games. You deliberately kept me in the dark.'

'Did I? And are you going to keep me in the dark about what's on that laptop?'

'I want it on my desk first thing in the morning. Seals intact.'

Putts hung up. Why was he always the first to hang up? Mesh wondered. She slammed the phone shut in its case. She'd hang up on him next time. There was something going on between him and Rigby, and she didn't like it one bit. Ideally, she'd like to sit on both of them, but trying to run surveillance on a fellow officer was always dangerous, and doubly so when it was your superior. She'd go the easy route. Besides, he went everywhere on a bicycle. Even a button masher like herself ought to be able to keep up with him.

10

Rigby had found an inn for himself and Steadman to stay on the outskirts of Little Greystock, the village where Ascott lived. He'd thought it would be a good idea to pretend to be bicycle tourists, so they'd put their bikes on the roof of Steadman's Subaru. The only problem was that the road leading from the inn to Little Greystock was, like most roads in the Cotswolds, one hill after another. It didn't bother Rigby, as he rode a couple of hundred miles a week, but Steadman – who only ever cycled in London, which was like a pancake by comparison – was puffing and wheezing behind him. As they crested a large hill, Rigby slowed and came to a stop. He dragged his bike onto the grass. Steadman pulled in behind, with sweat streaming down. Rigby handed him a Lucozade Sport.

Steadman grabbed the bottle and chugged it. 'Why are we doing this again?'

'It's the perfect cover. Cyclists are self-righteous jerks.'

'Like you, you mean.'

'Exactly. If you're wearing the Lycra, everyone leaves you alone.'

Steadman wasn't convinced. 'How much further?'

'Five miles, give or take.'

'I'm going back for the car.'

'But we're almost there.'

'White man lie. We halfway. I came uphill. I go back downhill.'

'It's downhill both ways.' He added, 'Check the map if you don't believe me.'

'If you're lying, I'm going to go get that chip you gave me and send it straight to the NCA.'

Rigby laughed. 'Yeah, that would do for me. Where did you hide it anyway?'

'At Lana's.'

'*Lana's*?'

'You said put it somewhere they'd never think of. That's what I was doing there. I don't need to hear your chair, I've heard it a hundred times.'

Rigby didn't have a reply, he was still processing. 'Where at Lana's did you put it?'

'I didn't, I gave it to her and asked her to put it somewhere.'

'*Why?* Why would you do that?'

'I was running late. What's the big deal?'

'It's my insurance policy.'

'Exactly. So I gave it the one person you might trust.'

Rigby pushed off, annoyed. Didn't Steadman realise he'd put Lana in danger? He rode harder the rest of the rest of the way to Little Greystock, hoping Steadman was feeling it.

The village consisted of no more than fifty workers' cottages, built in sandstone and in perfect rows like desert rats ready for inspection. Unusually for the area, Ascott's house stood by itself down a small lane. They made their way up the gravel drive and stashed their bikes around the back. There was no sign of life in or around the house. None of the doors or windows showed signs of forced entry.

Alongside the house was a garage. Rigby tried the garage door, but it was locked. Walking around, he found a door at the side. For a man who could break into almost anything online, gaining entry in the offline world remained something of a mystery. Steadman had given him a few lessons in lock picking a few years back when Pangolin had first opened and they'd spent long afternoons waiting for the phone to ring. He'd brought his lock picking set with him now, but having it in his possession and being able to do something useful with it were two very different things. Fetching Steadman was out of the question. He'd never live it down.

Opening the plastic wallet, he spread it out on the ground. The tools, shaped like screwdrivers with malformed heads, made as much sense to him as if someone had cut Chinese characters out of paper and tossed them in the air. He remembered something about holding the bottom pins down with a spatula-shaped wand, then scraping the top pins with one of the bent pokers. At first he couldn't even get them into the hole, and then, with a little wiggling, he eased one of them in. He pressed down and held it with one hand, then tickled the tumblers at the top. Had he done enough? He tried turning the barrel and, to his astonishment, the door opened.

Inside was a pair of classic sports cars: Maseratis, road-going darts with pointed snouts, and lines sharp enough to cut a finger.

'Hey Steady,' he called out of the door, 'even you could score with one of these.'

On the far side of the garage was another door with another single latch. He picked this too. It opened into the kitchen. He already knew that Ascott was uptight, but the house took him by surprise. The way everything was placed in meticulous order: the chopping boards in colour sequence, the knives in size order in the knife rack. But, despite his fastidiousness, Ascott didn't appear to be a cold-hearted man, quite the opposite. The walls and shelves were full of pictures of his family. Most of them featured a younger Ascott with his wife and a daughter. He loved his classic cars too: there were pictures of him at the wheel from his twenties all the way up to the present day. Ascott's wife had died a few years ago, Rigby recalled, and she was missing from the later shots.

He heard a noise behind him and turned. It was Steadman.

'I can score any time I want. Don't need no Khamsin.'

Rigby shook his head. 'Maserati.'

'Khamsin is the model name, pillock.'

They headed upstairs. The old boards creaked. On the landing they split up and went opposite ways down the corridor.

'This one's occupied,' Steadman called. 'Looks like our man sleeps alone.'

Halfway to the other end, Rigby had found a box room. The walls were covered with Maserati memorabilia. 'Here's the auto showroom.'

'Guest bedroom,' Steadman said.

There was one door left at the end. They opened it, expecting more storage. It was an office, with an old desktop computer and two ornamental frames perched either side. One was an old picture of Ascott, his wife, and his daughter as toddler. The other looked like a medal. It was star-shaped, with eight points, and hung from a crimson ribbon.

'It's a Victoria Cross, isn't it?' Steadman said.

'Can't be. I never saw any record of him being a soldier.'

'What is it then, OBE?'

Rigby took a closer look. 'Might be.' He took out his phone and snapped a picture. Steadman went back down the corridor. Rigby followed and found his friend in the hallway, pressed up against the wall, holding a finger to his lips. He motioned toward the window with his eyes. Rigby flattened himself and they shuffled along until they could see out. Two men were getting out of a black BMW 5-series.

Rigby held up his phone to show he was switching the volume off. He didn't want a random ring to give them away. Steadman nodded and did the same. He whispered, 'If they go around back, they'll see our bikes.'

'Shit!'

They tiptoed down the stairs. The men's voices echoed around the courtyard. Rigby went through the kitchen to the back door and opened it. Outside, the bikes were untouched. He walked lightly as he left the house, but the gravel made a crunch underfoot. There was no way they were going to get away unnoticed. Dancing on their toes, they made it to the bikes and clipped in.

'Where do we go?' Steadman whispered.

'Look for a trail.'

Rigby stood on the pedals. His tires skidded on the gravel as he set off, his rear almost giving out from under him, but he managed to control it, steering his bike around the side of the house and onto the drive. He couldn't see the men as he accelerated and he thought maybe they'd gone around the back, but his hopes were soon dashed.

'Hey! Come back here!' shouted a voice.

They made it out of the drive and onto the road. Without stopping to worry about directions, Rigby turned away from the village. The road dropped in a steep descent and soon they were going so quickly that he couldn't pedal. Normally this would have been fast, but with a car on their tail it meant nothing. Rigby glanced back. The BMW was already turning out of the driveway.

Up ahead he could see a gap in a fence leading into a cornfield, and a sign for a hiking path, the arrows pointing to a track running downhill. Certain that Steadman would follow, he squeezed the brakes and steered hard to his right. He shot through the gap in the fence, soaring into the air as he flew off the side of a ditch. He kept his balance as he came down, and once he'd regained control he looked back, expecting to see Steadman bouncing through the gap. Instead, all he saw was his friend's head going along the top of the corn.

'What the fuck?!' Steadman shouted, waving in desperation as he carried on along the road.

There was no way Rigby could go back. Ahead of him lay an open field with a dirt path leading down a slope. There were no roads, nowhere for the BMW to catch up with him. Besides, they'd soon be busy with poor Steadman. Rigby could only hope that Steady would find another gap in another fence, or some other way to get clear of them.

He needed to stop worrying and concentrate. His bike had skinny, slick tires, and he was riding on dirt. There was nothing he could do but keep pedalling, and hang on for dear life.

He got lost, he was rained on, he de-chained twice, he came close to being flattened by a school bus, but two hours after disappearing though the gap in the fence, Rigby made it back to the inn. The only question now was, what had happened to his friend? They'd come in Steadman's car. Rigby checked the car park, and the Subaru was exactly where they'd left it. He went inside and asked the landlord, a plump man in a cardigan who reeked of cigarettes, if he could store his bike in the room. The landlord said no, but gave him a key to a shed at the back.

'You might want to clean up too,' the landlord said. 'There's a tap and some washing up liquid.'

Rigby looked down at his hands. They were black with chain oil.

Once his hands were cleaned, he fished his phone from his shorts. There were half a dozen missed calls, all from Steadman. He called back.

'Rigby, where the bloody hell are you?'

'At the inn. Where are you?'

'About five minutes from death,' he said, struggling for breath.

'Still on the road? Did they catch you?'

'Yeah, right after you ditched me.'

'I thought you were behind me.'

'They wanted to know what we were doing at the house. I told them an old girlfriend lived there. We were in the area and we wanted to see if she was home.'

'And they bought it?'

'They let me go.'

'How long are you going to be?'

'No idea. And I'm not hurrying either.'

'Take your time. Call me when you're ready and I'll buy you dinner.'

'Damn right, you will.'

Rigby entered his room, desperate to get his clothes off and climb into the shower. Locking the door, he'd pulled his cycling suit down to his waist before noticing a figure sitting in the corner. Startled, he pulled it back up.

'Don't stop on my account.'

Rigby blinked. He couldn't believe his eyes. It was Mesh.

'What the ...? How did you ...?' the questions came faster than he could get them out of his mouth.

'What am I doing here?' she said. 'I want to ask you some questions.'

'Is this a matter of life and death? Because I was going to take a shower.'

'Don't let me stop you.'

He waited a second, wondering if she was going to get up. Instead, she stared at him, the way she always stared at everyone. When he'd first met her, he thought she did it on purpose to unnerve people. Then he realised she was just nervous, socially awkward.

He said, 'Why don't you go get a drink in the bar. I'll be down in a few minutes.'

'What are you doing out here, anyway?'

'You tell me. You have the whole Sweatbox at your disposal.'

She gave a tiny smile. 'I thought you'd be pleased for me.'

He was, but jealousy had got the better of him. 'Why are you stalking me?'

She scowled at the idea. 'Whose house were you at?'

He shrugged. 'Look it up.'

'I did. It's registered to a Ms Katisha Ascott, a student in Paris.'

'Steadman's old girlfriend,' he said, thinking fast. 'We were in the area. He's overweight. Needs exercise. These hilly roads are just the ticket.'

She looked disappointed. 'Why are you lying to me?' She said it as if she was hurt by it.

He took a deep breath. 'I need a shower. Can we talk in

the bar?'

'Do you take hot showers?'

How was that any of her business? 'Steaming.'

'It's bad for your skin. You should only use warm water, not hot.'

'I'll bear that in mind.'

When he came out of the bathroom, she'd gone. Downstairs, he found her sitting far apart from everyone else in the bar, sipping what he assumed was a Virgin Mary – she didn't drink, he remembered. She'd chosen to sit at exactly the table he would have selected, had he been in her shoes. They shared their training. He texted Steadman, but didn't get a reply.

'I'm surprised you came,' she said, as he sat down.

'I was going to jump out the window, but it was too high.'

She didn't smile. She didn't look at him either, her eyes were darting back and forth around the room. A waiter came to take their order.

Rigby said, 'Triple espresso.'

'You shouldn't drink so much caffeine, it's bad for you,' Mesh said.

When the waiter had gone, he said, 'Mesh, what are you doing here?'

'We need to talk.'

He took a deep breath. 'I'm listening.'

'What's going on between you and Mark Putts?'

'Nothing.'

'Bollocks. What's on the laptop that you don't want me to see?'

Rigby took a deep breath. 'I can't tell you. It's above your security clearance.'

'How do you know what my security clearance is?'

'I don't. But just in case, I'm not telling you.'

'The Official Secrets Act is not your biggest problem right now,' she said, sternly. 'We have six missing people. Tampering with official records. A potential homicide investigation…'

'Come on, you know I would never have done that.'

'… And people at the Home Office thinking you're the prime suspect. I can't protect you. And neither can Mark, whatever he says.'

Deep down, Rigby knew she was right. 'None of this makes any sense,' he said. 'These missing names, they can't have been in PPS, there'd be some record somewhere.'

'Exactly. That's what I keep saying. Not that anyone wants to listen.'

'Have you cross-referenced John Does?'

'You can imagine what the pathologists thought of that idea.'

He could imagine.

She said, 'Tell me about toshing. How did it begin?'

Surely she knew. 'You sat next to me.'

'I joined the Sweatbox a couple of years after you. It was already going on.'

He'd forgotten. He always thought of them as having been there at the same time, but early on it was only him and Putts, plus a few others, not the empire it was today.

'You want a history lesson? Fine. Cybercrime was booming, but policing it was a mess. There were five or six different agencies, who all thought they were in charge. So they brought in consultants, who recommended merging everyone in together. Were they still there when you arrived?'

'Hanging around like a bad smell. Do you remember the hours we used to work? Eighty, sometimes ninety a week. And then the consultants wanted extra reports on top.'

'And then all that crap about cross-functional teams. They sent us out into the field with Operations. We'd go for a beer and they'd start having a go at me. They said the internet had killed informing. I asked what they meant, and they said that PPS was next to useless because it was so easy to trace records online. Word had got out. Grasses had been tracked down and killed.'

'Was it true?'

'We were in the dark ages. One example: NHS. They always wanted to ensure the grass had medical care, so they made sure they were signed up with a surgery in the new location. All you had to do to find out the new identity was get into a computer at the old surgery. Right there would be the forwarding address for the new one, so they could send the medical records, complete with patient info, including the patient's new name and address.'

'So you came up with the idea to erase all of that?'

'Basically, yes.'

'And you wrote all the apps, did all the coding yourself?'

He nodded, but inside the alarm bells began to ring.

'Where did the name come from?' she asked.

'I don't know who came up with it, it's just what they called us. Toshers were people who lived in sewers in Victorian times, looking for coins that had washed down. We were the modern version, digging around in humanity's effluent.'

'Has anyone asked you to do any recently?' she said.

'No! I told you that before.' He added, changing the subject, 'Have you found Tudor Clarke yet?'

She looked at him quizzically. 'He's in Belgrade, apparently. Any idea what he might be doing there?'

Belgrade? What the hell was Clarke doing in Serbia? He said with a shrug, 'Heroin trafficking, people smuggling, no extradition treaty...'

'Sure, but what's any of that got to do with toshing?'

'Nothing. And everything.'

She said, 'I'm flying there tomorrow morning.'

'To Belgrade? For six old rats?'

'It's more than six old rats, Rigby,' she said, getting flustered. 'There's something else going on here and I'm going to find out what it is.'

He was about to say that he agreed with her when he saw Steadman out of the corner of his eye entering the bar.

'We'll have to continue this another time,' he said.

As Steadman gazed around, not seeing them yet, Mesh said, 'Why the hell did you have to leave?'

He turned, surprised. 'Leave what?'

'The NCA. I could really do with you being on this case with me right now.'

He knew how she felt. Alone. He wanted to confide in her, but until he found out the truth about Frederick Ascott and why he needed to disappear, he wasn't going to be confiding in anybody. 'I'm on it, Mesh. We're getting the band back together.' He reached into his pocket and took out his crypto. 'I'll prove it to you. Take this number, very few people in the world have this number. It's my crypto phone.'

Mesh grinned at the name. 'Your *crypto phone*,' she said, mockingly.

He rolled his eyes and gave her the number. 'The staff like it.'

'He's seen us,' she said, pointing at Steadman.

Steadman came towards their table. A few yards away, he stopped. His eyes ballooned.

Mesh said quickly, 'How much does he know?'

Rigby gave a small smile. 'Hardly anything.'

Her eyes narrowed. She knew he was lying. 'Why is he staring at me?'

Steadman came closer. 'H-Hi, Steadman Jones,' he said, extending a hand.

Mesh was sitting too far away to shake his hand, and she made no attempt to move closer. 'Mesh Kaur,' she said.

Unsure what to do next, Steadman took another step forward, his hand still extended. Mesh looked cornered. Her eyes darted to Rigby for help.

'She's 11th dan Taekwondo, my friend. I wouldn't get too close.'

'Oh for God's sake,' Mesh said. She shook Steadman's hand. 'Nice to meet you.'

'Enchanté,' Steadman said.

For a second, Rigby thought Steadman was going to kiss her hand, but she took it away, blushing.

He wanted to puke.

Flustered, Mesh said, 'I'd best be going. I'll leave you two to your evening.'

When she'd gone, he said to Steadman, *'Enchanté?'*

'I was trying to be friendly.'

'Friendly? You stuck your hand in her face.'

'It's gentlemanly. A lady shouldn't have to move. The gentleman should go to her.'

'Since when are you a gentleman?'

'Since you rejoined the NCA.'

'I'm not rejoining the NCA.'

'You gave her your crypto?'

Rigby was about to answer, but stopped himself. 'Look, I'm starving. Let's get something to eat. I'll explain over dinner.'

11

Steadman seemed genuinely annoyed by the inn's menu. 'You have to worry,' he said, 'when the most exciting thing is barbecue wings with sesame seeds. So come on, what was that all about?'

'She needs help with her case.'

'And you leapt straight in there.'

'You can't just rejoin the NCA. It's not like a band, you can't go, hey, I hear you lost your bass player.'

'Yeah? Well here's something you don't know. There's no 11th dan in Taekwondo. It goes up to 9.'

'11.'

'9.' He added, 'It's Korean.'

'So?'

'So who makes their own kimchi?'

'You.'

'Exactly. So it's 9.'

Rigby changed the subject. 'Back at the house, there was no sign of forced entry. The cars were still there. He'd even left his medal behind.'

'Left in a hurry.'

'More than a hurry. Like my old teacher used to say, he fled like a bird to the mountain. But here's the thing: who's he running from? The only people in his life are his daughter, and the spooks. Something tells me he did something very bad up at GCHQ.'

Steadman frowned. 'So what's your plan, hack a world-renowned eavesdropping service? If they can handle the FSB, the Chinese, Iran and North Korea, what chance do we have?'

'Every chance. All of them want to know what's happening today. We want to know what was happening three months ago. Or three years ago.'

'Well that's easy, we'll just Google "GCHQ backup drive, 2015."'

'No, you're not following me. For some reason, Ascott is running away from his employers at the GCHQ. He had to leave in a hurry. He called Putts, and asked for help. Putts called me, and asked me tosh him.'

'Yeah, we know that,' Steadman said, chewing a wing.

'So, if you're GCHQ, what do you do next?'

'Go looking for him.'

'But how? They're listeners. What if he never picks up a phone or goes online?'

'You need eyes on the ground.'

'Exactly. And they have their own police force. I remember, I had to deal with them once. Ministry of Defence Police – known as Modplod. They guard the nuclear bases and Aldermaston, plus GCHQ. People were shit-shared of them. They can invoke national security and slap D-Notices on you. He knew Modplod was after him, so he legged it.'

'Right, but how does that help us?'

'I came across Modplod because they needed help. Like I said, there aren't many of them. So if they're on a manhunt, they might well have asked for help.'

Half an hour later they'd found what they were looking for. Hacking into a couple of regional police forces, they found an alert that had been emailed from a generic MOD Police account to all local forces in the country. It gave no name, only a description of a missing man wanted for questioning. It made Ascott sound like a harmless old tramp, but the physical characteristics matched him perfectly.

'So they've sent it to every police force in the country,' Steadman said.

'Let's go pick him up before someone beats us to it. We'll hand him over to Modplod, then I'll call Putts and hand him his arse.'

By the time they arrived at the safe-house in Bethnal Green the innocent drizzle that had earlier settled over London had grown into a deluge. Rivers sluiced down the flat fronts of the pebble-dashed flats.

Rigby said, 'Go around again, make sure no-one's watching.'

Steadman drove a slow lap of the square.

'Looks dead to me,' Steadman said.

He pulled up at the end of the street. They got out and walked to the safe house. The curtains were closed but lights burned inside. Rigby cocked an ear. There were voices, more than one. He felt the hair on his skin rising. He rang the doorbell and a dog barked. That was a surprise, he didn't remember a dog before. Taking a step back, he checked the number on the house. It was correct, but he noticed a new sign in the window: 'No salesmen, No surveys, No canvassing, No leaflets, No cold calls.'

'Sure you've got the right place?' Steadman said.

Rigby nodded nervously. He rang the doorbell again.

They could hear footsteps, and an irritated male voice. A second later the inner door swung open; the metal grille stayed shut. A man in his twenties, with bleached-blonde stubble for hair, stared out at them. 'Yeah?'

'Hello,' Rigby said, thinking fast. 'My name's David Smith. I'm here on behalf of the Labour party. I was here a couple of days ago and the person I met, I think his name was Frederick, said he wanted to make a donation, but didn't have any money. He asked me to call back.'

The man's eyes narrowed, whether out of disbelief or general annoyance, Rigby couldn't tell. In the background was a television, and a child's voice.

'I don't know any Frederick. And if I did, I'd smack 'em.'

Rigby managed a nervous laugh. 'May I ask your name?'

'No.'

'Like I said, I'm from Labour party. Are you the owner of the property?'

'None of your fuckin' business.'

A woman's voice called from inside, 'Who is it, Blenny?'

'Fuckin' Labour.'

'Tell them to piss off.'

'You heard the lady,' Blenny said. He turned to Steadman and glared. 'What you lookin' at, bwa? Put de lime in de coconut and fuck off home.'

Steadman reached through the grille and grabbed the man's T-shirt, yanking hard and pulling his face tight against the metal. Blenny yelped.

'Who are you working for?' Steadman said.

'Let me go!'

'What is it?' called the woman.

'You heard me,' Steadman said. 'What's the name?'

'Nobody. I ... been on vacation.'

'How much they paid you?'

'Fuck off!'

Steadman pulled even harder. Blenny let out a yelp. 'Where's Frederick Ascott?'

'Shelby!' Blenny called, as best he could. 'Get the dog!'

A second later she appeared in a leopard-print leotard, with a bull terrier straining at its leash. The dog saw its master in trouble and began bouncing up and down, snarling.

'Carlton, shut up!' She smacked the dog on the mouth.

'What about you?' Steadman said to her. 'Ever heard of Frederick Ascott?'

'Fuck off, Windrush. I'm calling the police.'

'He was living here while you were gone. Just tell us where he is.'

'We've never heard of him,' Shelby said.

'They don't know anything,' Rigby said to Steadman. 'Let him go.'

With one last tug on his shirt, Steadman released Blenny. But instead of going back into the house, he grabbed the dog's collar and let it off the lead.

Rigby grabbed his sleeve. 'Run!'

They turned and sprinted for the car. Behind them, they heard the key in the lock, as the bull terrier howled. Stedman blipped open the doors, and they both jumped in, slamming shut as the snarling dog arrived, scratching at the windows and baring its teeth.

Steadman was about to pull away when Blenny ran in front, whipping Carlton's leash in the air like a lasso.

Steadman leaned out of the car window. 'Oy, Pale Rider, out the fucking way.' He put his foot down and the car lurched forward. Blenny jumped to the side, but gave a last swing of the lead. The metal clip smacked the roof.

Steadman stood on the brakes, ready to get out.

'No!' Rigby shouted, throwing an arm across Steadman's chest. 'Leave him.'

Steadman's eyes burned. 'He needs his arse kicked!'

'Do it later. Go!'

Steadman put the car in gear and floored it.

At night, the city shrank. Twenty minutes later they were passing Stamford Bridge. The Chelsea FC stadium was lit up. A late match. Steadman hadn't said a word the entire journey. Rigby felt concerned.

'About time we went to a match again,' he said.

'Yep.'

'Your uncle still involved on the youth setup?'

'Sure is.'

'So he could get us some tickets.'

'I suppose.'

Rigby turned away, wondering what he'd done wrong. He and Steadman had their moments, but he never usually blanked him. They cruised the last few miles in silence.

When they stopped, Steadman turned to him. 'What

the fuck was that all about? Who was that arsehole?'

'I don't know. Don't take it personally.'

'I don't care about that. I'm talking about who we're trying to take on. NCA. GCHQ. These are serious people. We're going to get rinsed.'

'You're right.'

'I know I'm right. So what are we going to do about it?'

'Only thing we can do. Find Ascott.'

He opened the car door.

'That wasn't the answer I was looking for,' Steadman said.

'I know. But it's the only one I have.'

The following morning, Rigby showered and put on his cycling suit as normal, but when he arrived downstairs he felt in no rush to get on his bike. He hadn't slept well. He'd been woken by a nightmare in which he was cycling through Piccadilly Circus when his chain snapped. His feet spun round and round on the pedals and he couldn't get out of the way of an oncoming bus. Hundreds of tourists were filming him on their camera phones and laughing as the bus flattened him. He'd hoped that by going through his morning routine he could forget about the dream and things would become clearer in his mind, but instead he'd become more frustrated and confused. The previous night's rain hadn't abated and he was seriously considering, horror of horrors, to drive into work, in his only vehicle, an orange VW Combi, that he'd bought to ferry himself and his gear to and from cycling events.

As he forced down a protein smoothie, his crypto rang. He didn't recognise the number, but answered anyway.

'Rigby, it's me, Mesh.'

A friendly voice, on a burner. He felt a pang of hope. 'Are you in Belgrade?'

'I'm at the airport. Where are you?'

'At home,' he said, surprised by the urgency in her voice.

'Listen, you need to get out of there. Now. A warrant's

been issued for your arrest.'

'For what? Is this your Task Force?'

'No. Nothing to do with us. The charge is abduction.'

'Abduction? Who am I supposed to have abducted?'

'I don't know. One of the Sweatboxers woke me to tell me that your name had flashed up on an alert. There's a team on its way to your house now. You probably have minutes. Get out now!'

He grabbed his crypto and ran for the door, leaving his regular phone in the house, double-checking to make sure it was switched on. He checked up and down the street for cops, then started to zigzag through the back alleys of Chiswick. As he doubled-back over Duke's Road, he saw a line of unmarked cars, plus a couple of Met police vehicles, crossing the intersection ahead. No prizes for guessing where they were going.

He made it to the Combi and climbed in. Praying for ignition, he turned the key. The engine coughed and spun but wouldn't catch. He told himself not to panic, it usually took a little coaxing. On the third try, it fired. He feathered the throttle. Wiping his sweaty palms on his cycling suit – he really needed to change – he stuck it in gear and pulled out. Even at 7am, Chiswick High Road was thick with traffic. He forced himself to stay calm, chugging along in the queue.

When he finally made it to the M4, traffic speeded up and he was able to relax. He pulled to the left, into the slow lane, avoiding attention. As he exited onto the M25, his crypto rang. Once again, he didn't recognise the number, except that this one was different to the previous, so it wasn't Mesh. He took the call and put it on speaker.

'Hello?'

'You sound like you're driving somewhere.'

He recognised the voice instantly. Putts. His instinct was to shout at him – to scream even – but he was surprised at how he found himself able to speak in measured tones. 'Just on my way to work, Mark.'

'Driving to work? That's unlike you.'

'It's raining. Wouldn't want to have any unexpected situations.'

'Yeah, they can be pretty bad. But I thought there might be more to it than that. More than the rain, I mean.'

'Oh really? Like what?'

'Do you remember that laptop of yours? Someone nicked it off my desk. I think they must have sent it to Mod-plod.'

Rigby's throat went dry. He felt his knuckles tightening on the steering wheel. 'What do you want, you fucking bastard?'

'Language, language,' Putts taunted.

'Just tell me what you want!' Rigby screamed, finally losing it. He slammed his hand into the steering wheel and the bus swerved. A passing car blared its horn.

'Rigby, Rigby, you still there?'

He took a moment to compose himself. 'Yes. Unfortunately.'

'Calm down, it's not as bad as you think. Trust me. Do what I say and I can protect you.'

The words were knives stabbing at his ears. But did he have any choice? 'You played me from the start,' he growled.

'Like I said, it's not that bad. All I need is a little more toshing.'

'No.'

Putts gave a small laugh. 'I'm not going to take that as your final answer.'

'You can take it however you want.'

'I don't think so, Rigby. You won't last out there, not by yourself. At some point you're going to come back to me.'

'I will never work for you again. Got it?'

Rigby hung up. He waited, his heart pounding, for the phone to ring again, but nothing came. He aimed a fist at the handset, perched on the dash, and sent it flying. 'Damn it! Damn it! Damn it!'

As soon as he could, he left the motorway and continued heading north on smaller roads. As towns and villages zipped by, he had a chance to think back on what had happened in the preceding two weeks. Putts had played him, that was certain. Getting him to take Ascott off his hands, drive him to Bethnal Green, and then to tosh him – it had been an illusion, staged to deceive an audience of one: himself. If it wasn't for Mesh, the trick would already have reached the next stage: Rigby in custody, Putts paying him a visit, offering to get him off the charge. Fortunately, that hadn't happened. Yet.

He made a call to Steadman. Once he'd explained what had happened, he said, 'We need to pay a little visit to Mr Makepeace Dale.'

'Who the hell's he?'

'Home Office.'

'Rigby, for God's sake, I've told you ...'

'We *have* to. He's the one person that can put an end to it, but we need some leverage. He lives in West Sussex. Meet me tonight in Petworth, and bring the others.'

12

Mesh's flight from London to Belgrade hit turbulence over Germany, bucking and writhing on the air pockets. A flight attendant spilled red wine over a young executive in business class who stood up and began shouting, and simply wouldn't stop, even after the first officer came down from the flight deck to try and reason with him. Some of the passengers in coach began yelling at him to sit down, but when others in business began taking his side, Mesh began to worry that a full-scale class war might break out. She stormed up the aisle brandishing her NCA badge.

'Who wants to spend the night in a Serbian prison? Didn't think so. So sit down. Shut up. And be polite to the cabin crew. And you,' she said, pointing at the original troublemaker, 'start apologising.'

It earned her a round of applause from the other passengers. Mesh laughed to herself; she had no jurisdiction over an Air Serbia aircraft, but none of them knew that. She returned to her paperwork. Her team had reviewed everything they could find about Tudor Clarke, which wasn't much, but included a home address in Dedinje, a suburb of Belgrade. It didn't surprise her: the most successful felons lived entirely on-grid. After landing, she caught a cab to her hotel, where she checked in and dumped her bag, before setting off to the house.

It was an impressive Italianate white stucco villa located on what was, according to the cab driver who spoke surprisingly good English, one of Belgrade's most desirable residential streets. High walls overflowed with fuchsias, and these, plus the pantile roofs, made it one of the more elegant fortresses she remembered seeing. She pressed the button on the entry phone at one side of the gate. A light above a lens lit up for a second or two, then dimmed. Nobody answered. She tried again with the same result. With a growing sense that she was being watched, she turned around and spotted a neighbour observing her from across the street, behind a metal fence. She walked across. The neighbour scurried away but Mesh called to her in English, 'Excuse me, have you seen the man who lives in that house?'

The neighbour, a young woman in her thirties, dressed head to toe in pale denim, stopped in her tracks, intrigued. Mesh asked again, 'Have you seen the man who lives in that house?'

The woman came to the fence. 'More than one month. Gone.'

She then began speaking in Serbian. Mesh couldn't understand, but the expressions on her face were clear enough. The woman clearly knew Clarke and was concerned about him, perhaps even angry with him. She seemed to be asking for help.

Mesh took a card out of her wallet, wrote the name of her hotel on the back, and pushed it through the fence. 'If you hear anything, please contact me.'

The neighbour nodded, then headed quickly for her front door. Where could Clarke have gone? Mesh wondered. A month was too long for a vacation. A business trip maybe? Or had he bolted?

It was early evening and Mesh was in her hotel room replying to emails when the room phone rang. It startled her. No-one used room phones any more. It was the front desk, saying she had a visitor downstairs. She asked for a description and was told the visitor was a 'Mrs Clarke'. Intrigued, she went straight down, only to find dozens of people milling around in the lobby. She asked at the front desk, and the receptionist pointed to a woman with three forlorn children blocking the entrance, as if they were unsure of where they were supposed to go, and had simply stopped once they'd passed through the revolving door.

'Mrs Clarke?' Mesh asked, approaching the woman. Up close, she could see the children were upset. They weren't making any noise, but the youngest had teary eyes and the other two stared into the mid-distance.

The woman, underneath her unkempt hair and angry expression, must have been in her late twenties and was very attractive. She turned to Mesh and eyed her up and down.

'Tijana,' she said brusquely. 'Where is my husband? What have you done with him?'

Mesh felt annoyed by her aggression, but not entirely surprised. 'I don't have your husband. I'm looking for him.'

Tijana looked unconvinced. 'Who are you?'

Mesh flashed her ID. 'Mesh Kaur, NCA.'

The woman's face softened. 'You don't know where he is?'

Mesh shook her head and ushered her towards some sofas. 'Could we sit down?'

Tijana took no persuading and scooped up the children. Mesh waived a waiter across, and before anyone said anything more, Tijana ordered hot chocolate for the kids, and for herself, 'Malt whisky. Glenlivet.'

'You know your scotch.'

'It's what my husband drinks.'

Mesh asked for a Diet Coke. 'Do your children speak English?'

'Of course. But you can say anything in front of them.'

Mesh nodded. She took a breath. 'When did you last see your husband?'

'In summer.'

It took Mesh by surprise. 'He's been missing for four months?'

She shook her head. 'No, no. For about one month. Last

summer he sent us away.'

'Sent you where?'

'He did not say where. He just said go. I choose. We go to my sister.'

'Why?'

She shrugged.

Mesh frowned at her, hard. Tijana Clarke didn't look to be an unintelligent person, quite the contrary. She was also attractive, with long, dark-brown hair, deep hazel eyes, a small mouth, and a nose so perfect Mesh felt tempted to punch it. Was it possible, she wondered, that Tudor Clarke hadn't settled in Belgrade for any criminal reason, but for a more positive one: love?

'Mrs Clarke, if you want me to help find your husband, you need to tell me the truth.'

'I don't want to find him. I don't give a fuck about him.'

'Then why are you here?'

'Because the selfish prick owes me money.' She pointed at the children. 'I have to buy food and clothes, and everything else.'

'I can help you,' Mesh said, 'but you have to tell me the truth. Why did he send you away?'

Tijana shook her head and turned, avoiding Mesh's eyes. 'I don't ask questions,' she said, sadly. 'There's no point. I give up long time ago. Me and the children, we live our life.'

'But you and Clarke lived together?'

'Together, together ... Maybe in the same house, but not together. We never see him. He spend all day and all night in his basement. He say, "I have to work," but he wants to be by himself. If the children knock on door, say "Papa, Papa," he shout at them, "Leave me alone!" So we don't care about him. But always he gives money. Every week. And now, no more.'

'He's dead,' said the oldest child, a girl. Mesh guessed her to be about seven or eight.

Her mother snapped at her in Serbian.

'What work did he do?' Mesh asked.

Tijana shrugged. 'You know,' she said, deadpan.

'Papa works on a computer,' said the middle child.

Mesh turned to him and smiled. 'Do you like computers?'

The child nodded and grinned. 'I play Minecraft.'

Mesh turned back to the mother. 'Do you have a picture of him by any chance?'

Tijana reached into a pocket and produced three different photos, one from a vacation on a lake, a second in what Mesh assumed was the garden of the house, and a third at a party in a restaurant. Clarke looked much older in the third. His curly hair, which had been almost down to his shoulders in one of the earlier photos, had begun to recede, and had been cut back above his ears. His large, dark eyes stood out prominently in a narrow face, like his children's.

'Did he say anything at all about why you needed to leave?' Mesh asked, scanning the photos.

'He said he was going to do something dangerous. But that was normal.'

'What, he always did dangerous things?'

'No, he always saying, "It's super dangerous," or "every government wants to kill me," or "only ten people in the whole world know who I am."'

'Self-aggrandising,' Mesh said, under her breath. 'Had he ever sent you away before?'

Tijana nodded.

'So what made this time special?'

The eldest child, who had seemed to be staring off into the distance ever since her mother had chided her, now piped up. 'He was going to ask the people he worked with for more money.'

'Esme!' the mother said, then launched into another tirade. This time, Esme barked back.

'Who did he work for?' Mesh asked, not waiting for them to finish. When they didn't answer, she grabbed Tijana by the arm, 'You must know.'

'For you!' Tijana snapped angrily, pulling her arm free. 'Stop being stupid.'

'For me?'

'Yes. For British government. For NCA.'

There was a desperation in Tijana's eyes that Mesh felt guilty for not really noticing before. It now seemed clear to her that Tijana had come to the hotel hoping that Mesh was there on her husband's behalf, to negotiate some kind of financial settlement.

'Of course he did,' Mesh said quickly. She didn't have the heart to say that Clarke hadn't worked for the NCA for many years.

A waiter arrived, carrying drinks. The children squealed with delight. Their hot chocolates were so thick and set they should have been called blancmange.

Tijana saw her looking. 'It's Serbian chocolate.'

Mesh watched for a moment, entranced as the children ate it with spoons. 'I bet my son would love that.'

Tijana laughed. 'How old?'

'Four.'

They watched for a few seconds, enjoying the moment. It struck Mesh that the paranoid, uncaring man Tijana Clarke was describing was a very different animal to the shy, diffident one she remembered. Something had taken hold of him to produce what sounded like a mild form of psychosis. He'd become lost in his own web of fantasy and lies. 'The NCA isn't the sort of place where asking for a pay rise puts your family in danger. Do you have any idea what else your husband might have been mixed up in?'

Tijana didn't like the question. 'My sister can't afford to pay for all of us. If we can't give her some rent, we will have to leave. Then where will we go? My husband never told me anything except that he work for NCA.'

'Do you have keys to the house?'

She shook her head. 'He took all of them.'

'Did you report him missing to the police?'

'What police?' she said, growing frustrated and annoyed. 'You are police. He is police. What else can I do?'

'And you have no idea where he might be? Anything you can give me?'

'I thought he was in England.' She added, 'Probably in jail. But you are here. So I am wrong.'

Mesh changed the subject, asking about how she and Tudor Clarke had met. Tijana was happier talking about the past. She said that she'd been working as a model in London while attending the LSE. She'd met her future husband when he came to give an informal lecture on cybercrime. She'd been impressed by his stories.

'I thought he was James Bond,' she said. 'I was young and stupid.'

As soon as her children had finished their chocolates, she whisked them off, with a final exhortation, 'Find him, please, or my children will starve.'

Thanks for that, Mesh thought. Overdramatic it might be, but the plea from one mother to another still struck a chord.

The next morning, working through Interpol, she was able to schedule an appointment for later that day with Janko Petrovic from the Serbian Police, who worked on the missing persons desk. The police offices were in a newly-modernised building in the heart of Belgrade. Petrovic was younger than she expected, clean-shaven, with dark, questioning eyes that reminded her of Al Pacino. He didn't seem impressed when she explained the details of the case.

'His wife didn't report him missing, but I thought I should check. Someone else might have reported it?'

He took the photo from her and said he'd look into it.

'How long will that take?' she said. 'I'm only meant to be here a couple of days at most.'

Petrovic raised an eyebrow. 'Normally, two or three days.' He smiled. 'But the British Embassy did me a favour earlier this year, so I guess I can repay it.'

The favour equated to him promising to complete the task in a couple of hours. She was getting a bite to eat when her phone went.

'I think I might have a match for you,' Petrovic said.

'Someone reported him?'

'Not exactly.'

When she arrived back at his office, he handed her an incident report, and a coroner's report. Both were dated from six weeks previously, the same time as when Tijana Clarke said her husband went missing.

'Four 9mm shell casings found at the scene,' Petrovic said. 'Two slugs in a wooden fence. The other two were in his chest.'

Mesh flicked through the first couple of pages. The mugshot taken by the coroner was a perfect match for the pictures the wife had given her. There was no mistaking the corpse: early forties, medium height, receding curly hair, poppy eyes. This was Tudor Clarke. He'd been shot outside a restaurant in Skardalija. No ID was found on the body. Police had interviewed the restaurant manager. The deceased had been dining with a woman. He paid in cash.

'They never found her?' Mesh said.

'Seems not. Almost certainly an escort. Probably a student, making money on the side. There was no wallet. She probably took it. Everything pointed to a jealous boyfriend. They ran the guy's prints, but nothing came up. With no ID on the body, there wasn't much they could do except wait for someone to report him missing. No-one did.'

'What about CCTV?'

'They have it by the government buildings, but not in the old town.'

She flicked through the reports. Petrovic gave her a summary, translating the pages.

'Can you get a warrant to search his house?'

It took him by surprise. 'He had a house here?'

‘And a wife and three kids.’

‘What? But he’s British?’

She nodded.

Petrovic looked baffled. ‘Who was he?’

‘He was one of ours,’ she said, ‘until a few years ago. Then he got mixed up in something. I’m pretty sure this wasn’t a jealous boyfriend.’

Petrovic scratched his chin. Mesh could guess what he was thinking: if this was big enough for an NCA officer to come for, then it might be a feather in his cap too. She wondered how much of a risk he might be willing to take. She had no way of proving anything yet, it was all speculation.

He said, ‘It will take a while to get a warrant. Unless maybe your embassy can pull some strings.’

She shook her head. ‘It’s not important enough yet.’

The detective thought for a moment. Eventually, he said, ‘Out in the rich suburbs, where he lived, people get broken into all the time. Neighbours don’t report it.’

‘Do you think that could happen at the Clarke residence?’ she said, arching an eyebrow.

He shrugged. ‘If there’s no-one living there, I would say it’s more than likely.’

‘See you there at eight?’ she said.

‘See you there.’

No bulbs burned inside the white stucco villa in Dedinje. Dusk’s final glimmers had long since vanished, and the house all but disappeared into the surrounding trees. Hip-hop music blasted out from a party in full swing further up the street. The blue glow of TV screens could be seen through the windows of some of the other residences. Petrovic tried the front gate. It didn’t budge.

‘Wait here,’ he said.

Hoisting himself onto the wall, he negotiated the wrought-iron spikes on top, and then dropped down into the courtyard. Mesh lost sight of him. A pair of partygoers walked up the street on the other side. She froze for a second. Had they seen him? They were too into each other to care about anything else. She pressed herself back into the shadows.

A few minutes later the gate swung open.

'Coming in?' Petrovic said.

He'd unlocked the front door of the house too. Inside was freezing cold; Clarke had left without turning off the air conditioning. Mesh remembered what Tijana Clarke had said about her husband spending day and night in the basement. She found a light switch and began searching for a way down. Underneath the main stairs was a padlocked door. It wasn't high security: the hinges were on the outside, held in by mismatched screws. She went to the kitchen to look for a screwdriver.

As she passed the living area she saw Petrovic poring over a shelf full of family pictures, trying to piece together a life for the former John Doe.

'Looks like he might have met her in the UK,' he said. 'And then they moved here to have a family.'

'That fits with what she told me. She was a student in London when they met.'

She found a Phillips screwdriver in a drawer beneath the cutlery. 'Follow me.'

Removing the screws, she opened the door to the basement. They followed the stairs down into darkness. Hoping there might be a light cord, she swung an arm in the air ahead of her. Halfway down she found it and pulled. Fluorescent lights blinked on, and both of them gasped. Ahead of them on every wall were pinned dozens of pictures of faces. Some were cut-outs from magazines. Others were mugshots. Many were low quality, taken with long-distance lenses and blown up on a photocopier. At the far end of the room, a bank of computers and screens hummed away, still switched on.

'Who are these people?' Petrovic said.

'My guess is it's more like who *were* they? I'm going to need to get a forensic team down here.'

'Hold on, hold on,' Petrovic said quickly. 'We're not even supposed to be here.'

'I can sort that out,' she said. 'I'll call the Home Office.'

She stopped. Petrovic had raised his hand. 'I did you a favour bringing you here.'

'You did.'

'And I got you into the house. We don't know where this is going to go.'

She knew what he wanted. He was a young cop trying to make his mark. And he was right, she owed him. 'If you can get one of your forensic teams down here then it's all yours, so long as one of my people can observe.'

'I can do that,' he said. 'And I have to call his wife and tell her. It's the one part of the job that I hate.'

'Not this time,' Mesh said. 'She'll be thrilled.'

Petrovic looked at her strangely.

'She couldn't stand him, and she's broke,' Mesh explained. She took out her phone and sent him the contact details. When they were back outside, she called Brien.

He sounded cheerful. 'Hey, boss. Find anything?'

'How are you fixed for coming to Belgrade?'

He made no attempt to hide his delight. 'For real? When?'

'Now. Get onto Travel Services and book a ticket.'

She called Dale and told him what they'd found. 'This is bigger than we think,' she said.

He didn't share Brien's immediate glee. 'Make sure it gets processed properly,' Dale said. 'Are you staying there to supervise it?'

'I'm bringing over one of my guys.'

'Does he know what he's doing?'

'Yes,' she said, more shakily than she would have wished.

'You sure?'

'Yes,' she said again, more firmly this time.

'Okay, come see me as soon as you land.'

13

Rigby found a café in Petworth which stayed open late. Warren was the first to arrive. He looked concerned.

'Should you be out in public?' he said quietly, sitting down at Rigby's table.

'Relax. I doubled back. Switched cars. No-one's looking for me in a twee little town like Petworth.'

'Okay, if you say so.'

He said it with an attempt at insouciance, but Rigby could tell he was worried. He tried to make light of it. 'You'd have been a terrific actor and a lousy poker player.'

Warren looked at him strangely. 'What are you talking about?'

'Your face. It's like a map of worry-land.'

Warren gave him a look of mock-defiance, 'I'm actually pretty good at cards. I can act, too.'

'Is that so? A regular Omar Sharif.'

'Who?'

'*Who*? One of the greatest actors of his generation. And a well-known card sharp.'

'Never heard of him.'

'Lawrence of Arabia? Dr Zhivago? Millennials. God help us ...'

Warren was typing something into his phone. 'He wasn't very good at cards.'

'He was a world champion,' Rigby protested.

'Says here he lost his house.'

'Omar Sharif? No way.'

'Five million dollar mansion,' Warren said, a smug grin

growing on his face. 'Lost it in a card game in 1973, right after he'd finished building it.'

'He got better.'

Warren began making a digging motion and mimed offering Rigby the shovel. 'How deep are you going to go?'

Rigby frowned. 'Why are you always so damn happy?'

'Ah-ha,' Warren said, 'now we see who's *really* worried.'

Gloria and Steadman joined them soon after. Hoping to head off any opposition to what he was about to suggest, Rigby took out his laptop as soon as they sat down. On the screen was a map of a mansion with tennis courts, a pool, and so many outbuildings it was almost a small village. 'Chamberlin House,' he said. 'Home of the Dale family for the last three generations. Current occupier Makepeace Dale, of the Home Office.'

He watched as the three exchanged nervous glances. 'I know it sounds dodgy,' Rigby said, 'but we badly need some leverage. He leads the Task Force that raided our offices and ordered my arrest. I want to get onto his system, find something, and then use it to get him off my back.' He turned to Gloria. 'Did you bring your gear?'

She nodded. 'But how do you know you'll get anything?'

'Everyone has dirt. It's only a matter of finding it'

Gloria took a deep breath. 'If it's standard Wi-Fi, it shouldn't be a problem.'

Warren said, 'What if there's nothing there? It's an incredible risk.'

'Steady,' Rigby said to Steadman, 'how many home networks have we accessed?'

Steadman shrugged. 'I don't know. A lot.'

'Fifty?' Rigby said.

'At least.'

'And have we ever failed to find something?'

Steadman shook his head.

'Exactly,' Rigby said. 'Everyone has dirt. We'll find some.' He pointed to the online map. 'Here's the front gate.

Stables on one side. Two smaller guest houses on the other. Little gatehouse out front, and what look to be older stables behind. And there's the driveway leading up to the big house. Easily within Wi-Fi range. Are you guys with me?'

They nodded.

'Then let's get to it.'

A few miles outside Petworth they turned up a narrow country lane. After another mile, a stone wall sprang up on one side of the road, marking the boundary of an estate. They followed it until they could see a pair of gates in the distance. They got out. For field operations, standard procedure was to set up a conference call which they could all dial into from their mobile phones, and then use Bluetooth headsets, so they could walk and talk naturally, as if they were in the same room. Gloria slipped hers on, then took her laptop from her backpack, and began searching for a signal.

'Can you see the router?' Rigby said.

She moved around, holding the machine in different positions.

'Not yet. That wall's fairly thick.'

Rigby looked around. 'Perhaps we can get some elevation.' There were no streetlamps, but in the moonlight he could see, straight ahead of them, a large oak spreading its branches up and over the wall. It looked climbable. 'Try from that tree.'

Gloria looked terrified. 'I'm not going up a tree.'

'Why not?'

'Because I'm not,' she insisted.

'Gloria's afraid of heights,' Warren said.

Rigby laughed. 'I had no idea. Let me have the laptop.'

'Why?' she said quickly.

'I'm going up.'

'No way.'

'Why not? I can climb a tree. You think I'm an old man?'

'It's not that. They're after you. If someone sees us and

calls the police, you need to make a run for it. You can't do that if you're up a tree.'

Steadman said, 'Let me do it.'

'Not you either,' Gloria said.

'Why not?'

'The tree doesn't look strong enough.'

'Hey, that's uncalled for.'

Gloria laughed. 'Couldn't resist, but no, you've got a record. Get arrested again and they'll throw the book at you.'

'Then what about me?' Warren said.

'That's just what I was thinking,' Gloria said. 'What about you?'

Rigby didn't like the idea. He said to Warren, 'This isn't your area. Do you know how to do it?'

'I can talk him through it,' she said.

'Are you sure about this?' Rigby said to him.

Warren nodded confidently, but Rigby still wasn't convinced.

'Don't be a stick in the mud,' Steadman said. 'Let the front man get his hands dirty.'

Against his better judgement, Rigby said to Gloria, 'You're the organ grinder, he's the monkey. Make sure he does it right.'

'Of course I will.' She handed Warren her backpack with the laptop and he climbed the oak in seconds, soon sitting astride a high branch.

'It looks just like the satellite shots,' he called to them, his enthusiasm as bubbly as ever, 'plus some statues and topiary.'

'What about the router?' Gloria called up to him.

'Oh.' A few seconds later, he said, 'I'm getting a signal. Network is called Dalehouse.'

'Good,' she said. 'Now, on my desktop you'll see a file called Daleinfo. I downloaded everything I could find out about him and put into password character format. Double click and it'll enter all of that until it gets a hit. Could take a while ...'

The temperature dropped as night settled in. The three waiting below pushed their hands deep into their pockets.

'Soft touch,' Steadman said to Rigby as they waited.

'What?'

'You. Soft touch.'

He meant Warren. 'But you took his side.'

Steadman shrugged. 'I need his help with my tax return.'

Rigby was about to say something in response when he saw headlights in the distance. 'Get down behind the car,' he said quickly. 'Warren,' he called up, 'make yourself into a ball.'

The three of them ducked behind Rigby's car. The passing vehicle didn't slow. Rigby took it as a good sign. If they'd spotted Warren in the tree, the driver might have braked.

'Warren, you okay?'

'Yeah. I'm trying something else I found on the desktop.'

'What is it?' Gloria said, concerned.

'Port injection,' he said.

'Oh, no.'

'Initiating port scanners,' Warren said. 'Port identified, now we're getting somewhere.'

'This could take forever,' she said to Rigby.

'Starting injection,' Warren called.

'If this doesn't work in five minutes we should ditch it,' she said.

A few minutes later, Warren shouted down, excited. 'Houston, we have ignition!'

'Keep it down!' Rigby said under his breath.

'And guess what the password is,' Warren continued, ignoring him, 'Zero-L-D-M-Zero-N-E-Y.'

Gloria rolled her eyes. 'Maybe we should blow the place up.'

Warren said, 'What do you want first? His iPad or his laptop?'

'I don't care. Copy what you can and let's get out of here.'

'Okay, sit tight.'

They waited in the cold, willing him to hurry. After no more than five minutes, a bright beam appeared from near the house, lighting up Warren like noonday sun.

'He's busted!' said Steadman.

Behind the wall a dog began to bark. A man shouted for it to be quiet.

'He's there,' said a different voice. 'Look, up in the tree.'

'You, what are you doing up there?' said the other.

Rigby wished he'd never allowed Warren to go up. He'd frozen in the glare.

'Warren, come down,' Rigby said.

Warren didn't move. He sat, spellbound.

'Warren!'

He was clearly terrified, and yet had the presence of mind to realise that he was still holding Gloria's laptop.

'Catch this!' he called, holding it out. Rigby ran to the tree, positioning himself underneath to receive it.

Warren let it drop. It would have been an easy catch had the computer not collided with a branch on the way down. It flipped over in mid-air and began to spin. Rigby moved to line himself up, and he got half a hand to it, but it landed on the ground with a loud smack.

Gloria ran to pick it up. 'Dumbass.'

'Gloria, get Steady out of here. Warren and I'll come later.'

'I don't want to leave you guys,' she said, starting to panic.

'You know how it works. I'll get a fine. He'll get ten years. Please, get him out of here.'

She didn't argue any further. Rigby felt relieved as he watched her and Steadman run to his Subaru and drive off. He looked up, expecting to see Warren making his way down. Seeing him still fixed to the branch, he yelled, 'What the fuck are you doing!?'

'They told me not to move,' Warren said.

'Come down!'

'There's a rifle pointing at me!'

Warren sounded terrified, and with good reason. 'Let yourself drop.'

The dog was now barking uncontrollably. In front of them, the lane filled with light as the gate began to swing open.

'Okay, I'm coming!' Warren shouted.

'Wait!' Rigby wasn't prepared.

Warren came off his perch as a gunshot rang out. Rigby braced himself, expecting to see him fall like game. Then came a sickening crack from a branch. As with the laptop, his leg had caught on a limb, and he flipped over in mid-air. He travelled the last few feet upside down, striking the ground head-first.

'Warren!' Rigby ran to him.

Warren lay motionless. Rigby tapped his face with his hand but there was no response. He felt for a pulse and checked the breathing, and to his relief both seemed steady.

He heard footsteps running in the distance. Figures were coming through the gate.

'What's going here?' shouted a man's voice. 'Who's that on the ground? Is he hit?'

There was no way out of this, Rigby knew. He wouldn't have time to load Warren into a car.

'He's alive,' Rigby said, turning in the direction of the approaching men. There were two of them: one younger, one older. 'But he needs an ambulance.'

'Sweet Jesus!' said the younger man. 'That's all I need.'

Still full of relief that Warren was alive, Rigby stood and looked at them closely for the first time. The younger man, he assumed, must be Makepeace Dale. Who the other was he had no idea.

'Don't move him,' the older man said. 'I'll get some blankets, then drive him to the hospital.'

He was a Scot, Rigby noted, and spoke with a stern, but

well-educated voice. Ex-army, he guessed. Officer class. He looked the part too: short and wide with close-cropped sandy hair, about Rigby's age or maybe a little older. He wore heavy brown trousers and what appeared almost like an ordinary wax jacket except it was unusually rigid around the chest. Kevlar? He wondered.

'What the hell were you playing at?' he barked at Rigby. He came over and examined Warren. Then he said to Dale, 'You need to get back inside. I'll stay with him.'

'I'll stay too,' Rigby said.

'No you won't,' the Scot said, firmly. 'I'm not having any tricks.'

'It's not a trick,' Rigby protested.

'Were you spying on my house?' Dale said.

'I can explain,' Rigby said.

'Oh, I'm sure you can,' Dale said.

As he said it, Rigby noticed Dale looking at him closely. He trained the light on him and came a few steps closer.

Lomax said to Rigby, 'What are you, climate protestors or some such?'

'Not exactly,' Rigby said. 'Let me explain ...'

Dale was standing over Rigby now, with a look of disbelief on his face. 'Lomax, we have a serious problem here.'

'I'm already aware of that sir. I wish you'd let me deal with it.'

'No, it's worse than that,' he said, pointing at Rigby. 'This is a wanted man. I know, because I signed his arrest warrant.'

On instinct, Lomax raised his rifle and trained it on Rigby.

'Put it down,' Dale said to him, placing his hand on the barrel. 'You, come with me,' he said to Rigby.

He turned and marched back toward the gates. Wasn't Dale just going to turn him in? Rigby felt confused. Lomax saw him standing and waved his gun at him to follow. He wasn't about to argue.

14

The house was an old manor, done up inside like a medieval castle with suits of armour in the cavernous entrance hall. Rigby wondered what kind of man would live in a place like that. Dale led them through a small door and into a kitchen. A brand-new Aga sat in a corner, heating the room like a sauna.

'Take your shoes off,' Dale said.

'What?' Rigby said.

'Shoes off.'

'You shoot my friend and now you're all house proud?'

Dale didn't reply. Rigby slipped off his Converse and flicked mud from his jeans.

'Follow me,' Dale said.

Rigby followed him down a stone hallway. The flags felt warm beneath his feet.

'Underfloor heating,' Dale said. 'Powered by solar panels.'

'Shucks, that's wonderful. Meanwhile there's a man dying outside.'

'It's a flesh wound,' Dale said with disdain. 'Lomax was a Colonel in the Paras. He knows what he's doing.'

Dale opened a door to a living room furnished with sofas and tables that looked as though they'd been handed down for generations. 'Sit,' he said. 'It's about the most comfortable you're going to be for a while.'

'Before they ship me off to the big house?'

Dale ignored him, settling himself in an armchair and tapping his forehead with his fist as he pondered what to do. For the first time, Rigby had an opportunity to study the man at close quarters. He wasn't handsome by any means, his face a sharp intersection of planes, none of which joined together well, but there was a fiery intelligence in his eyes that gave him an undeniable charisma.

'I'm trying to work out the charges,' Dale said. 'Intercepting signals from the home of the government official who'd just authorised your arrest. What would that be: trespass, high treason, or just felony fuckwit? Then there's your involvement with the missing informants case.'

'Mesh knows I had nothing to do with that.' Rigby said, hopefully.

'Mesh is a little cog in a machine where not every part gets to be connected.' Dale gave him a hard stare before adopting a more conciliatory tone. 'But she's loyal. You have more than a few admirers, it seems. They think you're doing society a favour.'

'What do you think?' Rigby said.

Again, Dale didn't reply. Outside, a car was pulling out of the gates.

'That's Lomax,' Dale said. 'Taking your friend to hospital. Your other two friends ran off, am I correct?' Rigby's surprise must have been obvious, because Dale added, 'Please, who do you think you're dealing with? We were watching the whole time.'

Rigby kicked himself. He'd underestimated not only the difficulty of the operation, but the sophistication of Dale himself, and he'd put his friends at risk.

Dale said, 'But there a might be a way out of this for you. How about we start with a few questions.'

'Fire away.'

'Do you have Frederick Ascott?'

So that's what this was about. 'No.'

'Do you know where he is?'

'No.'

'Did you abduct him?'

'No.'

'But you Toshed him. They found evidence on your laptop.'

'I was helping him disappear.'

Dale seemed slightly surprised. This was easier than he expected. 'And why did you do that?'

'Mr Dale, in my line of work, you learn not to ask too much, because clients never tell the truth. If someone wants to disappear, that's their problem.'

Dales eyes narrowed. 'So he was a client?'

Rigby nodded.

'He Googled "disappearance services" and your name came up?'

'We're getting more famous. We have customers in Dubai ... Monaco ...'

Dale frowned. 'Do you know what Frederick Ascott does for a living?'

'He worked for GCHQ,' Rigby said, feeling his arms tighten. 'I found that out after he disappeared. If I'd known at the beginning, I wouldn't have touched him.'

Dale wagged a finger. 'Do you know what he did for them?'

'No.'

'Does the name Genya Zaytsev mean anything to you?'

The tightness Rigby felt in his arms was now moving to his chest. He'd never heard the name, and that worried him even more.

Dale opened his phone. He held out an old black-and-white print of a young naval cadet wearing a white sailor's hat, and a dark shirt with stripes on its V-neck. He had thick, rounded eyebrows and he was smiling, revealing prominent buck teeth.

'People say is the last officially recognised photo of Zaytsev, and possibly his last-ever use of that name. He is, by our best estimates, eighty-one years of age today. That is, if he exists.'

'Why are you telling me this?'

'In intelligence circles, he's one of the last great mysteries. Some people deny his existence – they say he's a myth. We've never successfully identified him. It started when a jealous husband appeared out of nowhere about thirty years ago, saying that the man who stole his wife was a spy. They followed leads and found traces of him living in various places. Paris in the 1970s and 1980s. French surfing resorts in the 1980s and 90s. But from about 2000 onwards we are fairly certain he's been living in London. There's been a sighting or two in the South Kensington area. Makes sense, say the analysts. He's almost certainly a cultured man. But he could be anyone. You might be sitting next to him at the theatre and have no idea that it's him.'

'A master spy?'

'He's not spy, really. He's a thief. He obtains classified material and sells it to the highest bidder. Ascott was a source. We suspect this because we intercepted materials that could only have come from Ascott, on a fishing trawler in the South China Sea, heading for port in Hainan, China. Somehow Ascott found out we were onto him, because he disappeared three weeks ago.'

'That's a week before he came to me,' Rigby said, trying to sound like this was way over his head.

Dale eyed him cautiously. 'I'm going to ask you again, who hired you?'

'Frederick Ascott.'

'Okay, have it your way,' Dale said. 'But here's the bottom line: find him, and everything's forgotten. But until then, you're still a wanted man. So keep out of trouble, work from the shadows, and don't even think about using my name. This conversation never happened. Find Ascott, bring him to me, then you can go back to entrapping paedos.'

'I thought I was doing society a favour.'

'I never said you weren't.'

As soon as he was back on the road, Rigby called Steadman on the crypto.

'Need us to come bail you out?' Steadman said.

'I got lucky. We made a deal.'

'Oh you did, huh?' Steadman said. He was warming up to something. 'Well that's just great. What about Warren?'

'I feel terrible about that. How is he?'

'Bullet shattered his shoulder and he has a concussion from the fall, but he's alive, so he should be grateful, right?'

'Steady ...'

'He worships you, you know. Nothing would make that poor fool happier than to take a bullet for you.'

'You don't need to lay it on.'

'Don't I? What were we doing there anyway? What did you think you were going to get out of it? You're like one of your nerd heroes – like Steve Jobs or someone. You think you're a genius so you get to be an arsehole. Let me tell you, everybody wants to be an arsehole. Me, you, the waitress at Sherry's. All of us want to behave like selfish, lying sacks of shit. Except we don't.'

'Whatever you say.'

'I do say. And guess what, Steve Jobs wasn't a genius, either. He was just a good gizmo-maker, and a twenty-four carat arsehole.'

Rigby sighed. 'You need to be an arsehole to go one way when the whole world is going the other.'

'Bollocks! In a couple of million years no-one's going to remember us, but in the big book, where they write down the names of everyone who ever lived, with a little description, what's it going to say about you? Rigby Goode: arsehole.'

Rigby saw red. 'I'm paying the price. Unless I find Ascott, the next time you see me will be in the nick.'

'Hell of a deal you cut there.'

'I didn't have a whole lot of choice. I'm going to destroy this phone now.'

'No. Rigs, wait ...'

But it was too late. He hung up. He popped out the SIM

card, broke it in half with his teeth, then rolled down the window and threw it onto the highway. A few miles along, he did the same with the phone.

He suddenly felt alone and exposed. He needed to find somewhere to hide, and fast.

He woke up, startled. For a moment, he had no memory of where he was or how he'd got there. Sitting in his sleeping bag, he took in his surroundings. The interior of the camper was unfamiliar – it felt cold and smelled like a forest – and then it all came back in a flash. Warren being shot, the ultimatum from Dale, Steady giving him a dressing-down. He unzipped the bag and hopped out, surprised by the feel of a freezing floor beneath his feet.

A VW Combi was too conspicuous for someone on the run, he realised. But being equipped for cycling tours, it held some very useful stashes. Inside a small cupboard was a tiny refrigerator, and behind that was a money belt containing a hundred pounds in twenties, which he'd put there over a year ago in case the bus broke down in the middle of nowhere. He took forty out and zipped it into his shorts, then returned the pack to its hiding place. Going around back, he opened the hatch and pulled out a black refuse sack. Inside was a mountain bike frame and two wheels. He had it together in minutes.

The route into town wasn't as potholed as he remembered it from the day before. He'd set off north-west from London, heading for the most remote piece of wilderness he could find within a day's drive, and ended up parking for the night deep in the Shropshire Hills. He was heading now for Ludlow, a market town about ten miles away.

He'd been there once before, many years ago, and he'd chosen it as a place to hide partly because it was a tourist town, where people drifted constantly in and out, and it was a favourite area for outdoor sports. Nobody would pay any attention to yet another mountain biker tearing up the trails.

As he rode into town he was surprised to find the market square overtaken by tables draped in striped tablecloths. Shoppers with bulging bags squeezed fruit and eyed chops. Dogs hunted scraps. Cats watched from walls. It was the farmer's market day, and the crowds were so thick he had to dismount and push. Chaining up, he went inside the library and took a seat at a row of computer terminals. It took him only a few minutes to gain Admin rights on a PC and install a Tor browser to hide his IP address. Without hacking anything, only using the regular systems, he went into his online banking. He transferred all but a few hundred dollars of his money to a wealth management company in the Virgin Islands. He let the money land in the account, and then hacked the company. He transferred the money again to an account held for clients at the Japanese office of a global law firm. Using that account, he bought Bitcoin, and then used that to purchase two prepaid credit cards. He set up a PayPal account linked to one of the credit card numbers, and deposited five thousand dollars into it.

Using the PayPal, he went to Amazon and bought a satellite Wi-Fi hub – like a home router but connected via satellite – and asked for it to be delivered to a pickup location near Ludlow. It would arrive in forty-eight hours. Logging off, careful to erase his trails, he left the library and found a little stationery store. He bought some paper, a pen, and a hard-backed envelope. Stopping at a café for a much-needed triple espresso, he wrote a letter to Steadman:

> *PIN 5487. Use this card in Andover, PIN 5487, withdraw £500, avoid CCTV, then the next day in Salisbury, withdraw £500, avoid CCTV, and then the next day in Yeovil, and the next in Exeter, and then again as soon as possible afterwards in Plymouth. Use it finally to book onto the car ferry to France. At that point destroy the card.*

He then put his regular debit card and the letter in the envelope, wrote Steadman's home address on the front, and took it into the Post Office.

15

Mesh landed back in London and went straight to the Home Office. She'd asked Aisling to attend her meeting with Dale so she could debrief them together, and when she arrived they were both sitting in his office in silence, doing emails. They looked up with anticipation as she entered. She was about to say good morning when she spotted another person in the room, who turned to her and smiled. It was Putts.

'Hello, Mesh,' he said. 'Welcome back.'

She felt her skin turn to ice. She wanted to ask what he was doing there, but he was within his rights as the ranking officer on the case. The real question was how he'd found out the meeting was taking place. She'd follow that up later.

Seeing the surprise on her face, Dale said, 'I heard the good news. You have some new information regarding the witness protection records anomaly.'

Records anomaly? Talk about whitewashing. 'Our prime suspect checked out,' she said. 'We're processing the evidence but it looks like a conspiracy on a large scale.'

'And what about your other suspect?' Putts said. 'Rigby Goode.'

'The evidence is pointing very strongly at Tudor Clarke.'

'Let's not jump to any conclusions. Goode's wanted in connection with the disappearance of a GCHQ operative, which gives us every reason to suspect that he may be involved in other criminal activities. He and Clarke are old friends.'

'Friends is stretching it.'

'Colleagues, then. But they could be working together.'

Mesh felt her anger rising. She knew she shouldn't react but couldn't stop herself. 'There's nothing connecting Goode to Clarke.'

'Except everything,' he said sarcastically.

'You don't believe that. Why are you …?'

She didn't finish. Dale was holding up his hand.

'Don't raise your voice in my office,' he said firmly. 'I have some sympathy for your situation. He's an ex-colleague and that can be difficult. But up until about three weeks ago toshing was a footnote in history. Now, everywhere we turn there's another bloody tosher.'

Mesh took a breath and composed herself. 'Before we put everyone in the same bucket, can I show you some of what we found?'

Dale held up his hands. 'I'm all ears.'

She opened a folder and spread out on the table some photos she'd taken in the basement. Some showed the whole room, others focused on specific walls, the computer equipment, and three or four individual faces.

'What are we looking at here?' Putts said.

'This is the basement in Tudor Clarke's house in Belgrade.'

'So you located him?'

'He was shot.'

'So you said. Outside a restaurant, right?'

She nodded. 'He came in as a John Doe and the Serbs processed him six weeks ago. He had a family, but they never reported him missing. They thought he was away working … for us.'

'What?' Dale said.

'Oh yes,' she continued, 'Clarke had told his family he worked for the NCA. And they had no reason, it appears, to disbelieve him.'

'And he's not, I take it?' Dale said, aiming it at Putts. 'He's not part of some clandestine programme?'

Putts shook his head. 'Not that I know of.'

Mesh said, 'Clarke was toshing. I'm not sure who for. One of my team is down there now, checking every face, trying to get matches. So far, if you look at the pictures in front of you, we have tentatively identified three of the individuals.'

She held up the first picture: an African American man in his late twenties or early thirties, smiling, with diamond studs flashing in his front teeth. 'Anyone recognise him?'

The others shook their heads.

'Obviously we're going to double-check all of this, but this looks to me to be Shad Bendigo.'

'No way,' Aisling said, peering closer. 'Oh my God, you're right.'

Dale said, 'Who is Shad Bendigo, please?'

'He was a musician,' Aisling said. 'Rapper, producer. He was really big when I was in college.' She added, 'About ten years ago.'

'And he disappeared,' Mesh said. 'Famously.'

Aisling nodded. 'Yeah, I remember reading about it. They thought it was some kind of argument with his manager or his record company.'

'I remember the case,' Putts said. 'They found his Range Rover on the banks of the Thames at Purfleet. Glove box packed with crack. The fool went swimming at night and was caught by the tide.'

'The body was never recovered,' Mesh said. 'He was later declared dead in absentia.'

'Are you suggesting something different?' Putts said, icily.

'It's difficult to suggest anything with this case, because the records are gone, as is almost every trace of the man himself. You can play his music on Spotify, but there's no record of his birth, or where he went to school, if he had a driving license ...'

'Come on, he's well-known,' Putts said. 'Why would anyone bother to tosh him?'

'Out of sight, out of mind. Anyone following up the cold case, journalists, fans, they'll get nowhere. His mum probably has some paperwork. Friends might have photographs. But digitally? Nothing. It's like pouring acid on a corpse. Same with the six in the witness protection file.'

'Oh, Jesus,' Putts said. 'Nothing connects him with those cases.'

'Except everything,' she said, mimicking his sarcasm. 'Or are you going to suggest it's coincidence?'

'Not coincidence, incompetence,' he said, waving dismissively at the photos. 'Government records exist for one reason only, which is to make sure you pay your taxes. It's not a foolproof way to track anyone.'

Mesh wasn't going to argue the point. She held out another picture: a man in his late fifties or early sixties, with slicked-back silver hair. 'This is Adolfo Aguirregabiria, a Spanish politician. He ran off with another politician's wife and two million euros he embezzled from a school improvement fund. Spanish media reported sightings in Bolivia, but there was never any corroboration.'

'Oh sure,' Putts said, 'and who else was down there? Princess Anastasia, Lord Lucan ...?'

Dale joined in. 'How about Richie James?'

Putts laughed. Mesh scowled at him, furiously. Typical men, she thought, pretending to be joining in a cheap laugh, when all they are really doing is putting a woman in her place.

'You can make fun if you want,' she cut in, 'but there were dozens of them. And I guarantee you, all dead.'

'So he was some kind of necrophile,' Putts said. 'So what?'

'He was a tosher, and I'll bet you, when we finish processing this, that every single person in these photos is not just deceased but toshed clean. This was only one link in a complex chain of death.'

'Leave the headlines to the hacks,' Putts said. 'Who's processing it?'

'The Serbian Police.'

He looked at Dale and rolled his eyes. 'Well that's helpful. When it hits a British court, what's more likely to be believed, homicidal premeditation by British citizens, or incompetence on the part of a Third World police force?'

Mesh couldn't believe what she was hearing. 'Are you going to insult anyone else? Or is an entire continent's worth of law enforcement professionals enough for one morning?'

Dale sighed. 'So you found Clarke, that's progress. We'll see what the Serbs come back with. Now, what's happening with the other suspect, Goode?'

Aisling, who'd said little while the big fish fought, spotted her opportunity. 'I spoke with MOD Police.'

'You did?' Mesh said. She couldn't believe Aisling would do it without asking her permission. She was impressed.

'They've been trying to find Ascott for about a month,' Aisling said. 'Goode's laptop was the first lead they had. But they think Ascott must have been tipped off, because neighbours saw him leaving the house on foot only a few minutes before MOD police arrived to pick him up.'

'What'd I tell you,' Putts said to Dale. 'One of his old NCA chums.'

Mesh shrank inside.

Putts stood up, his six-foot-seven-inch frame towering above the table. 'We have to stop treating him as an ally and see him for what he really is: a criminal. Clarke and Goode trained together. They pioneered toshing, together. The logical conclusion is that they were working together.'

'You *know* that's bollocks,' Mesh said.

'How do I know anything? He was the genius. Maybe this whole thing is his idea. He could have ordered a hit on Clarke.'

Mesh did a quick check to see if Dale or Aisling were buying it. She was pretty sure they weren't. 'Why are you doing this?'

'It's my job!' he thundered. 'Why don't you try doing yours?'

An ear-splitting whistle stopped them.

Dale took his fingers from his mouth. 'Enough! You're acting like children.'

For a moment no-one said anything. Breaking the silence, Aisling said, 'The good news is that we have a lead on Goode's whereabouts.'

Dale said, 'Why the hell didn't you say so? Where is he?' He turned to Putts. 'Would you sit down, for Chrissakes. It's like having Peter bloody Crouch in the room.'

Putts fumed for a moment, and then sat.

Aisling continued. 'His debit card is being used to make cash withdrawals.'

'Oh, come on,' Putts' said, still angry. 'He's far too clever for that.'

'Where?' Dale said to Aisling, ignoring Putts.

'Various places, all in a pattern, heading west, towards Cornwall.'

Putts laughed, making no attempt to hide his scorn. 'A little trail of breadcrumbs, leading the wrong way.'

'So what do you suggest?' Mesh said to him. 'We head vaguely east, in the hope he's gone that way?'

'I don't have time for this,' Putts said. He stood up again, whipping the jacket from the back of his chair and pulling it on. 'I don't care what you do,' he said to Mesh. 'But I'll tell you this, as he's your friend. If Modplod find him first, they'll invoke a national security privilege, and you won't see him again for a very, very long time.'

Before any of them could reply, he left the room, closing the door loudly behind him.

Mesh said to Aisling, 'I need you to get in touch with Brien and set up a system to check in with him every hour. The key to this case is in Belgrade. Anything he comes up with, run it through our systems. Give the Serbian Police every possible assistance.' She turned to Dale. 'Would you mind helping with that? Expedite any international clearances we might need.'

Dale looked slightly taken aback that she was asking for

his help, but he nodded. 'And you two?'

'We're tracking down the withdrawals.'

Dale frowned. 'It's crap, you know that.'

'Of course. And Goode knows that we know it is. So what's he trying to tell us?'

When Mesh and Aisling returned to Sweatbox they found a group of eager officers waiting.

'We found him,' said one of them, a young woman.

'Goode?'

'No. The person making withdrawals. Looks like the card was stolen.'

They handed her a series of photos taken from surveillance cameras. Mesh looked them over. 'Afro-Caribbean male, early to mid 30s, heavy build. Have you been able to identify him?'

'Not yet.'

She frowned. 'Let me help you. His name is Steadman Jones. He's Goode's right hand man. He's an ex-convict, and in addition to being a university graduate he's also, according to Goode, something of a gourmand, and an amateur profiler.'

The young woman stared back, terrified. Mesh returned the pictures to her. 'Alert police forces in the area.'

Two hours later, Devon and Cornwall Police alerted the Sweatboxers that they'd picked up Steadman on the A30 outside Exeter, heading west. A small squadron of unmarked cars were tracking him.

Mesh caught a flight at London City airport to Exeter. On touchdown, she turned on her phone to find a message from a senior detective saying that they'd followed Steadman to a downtown restaurant. She called back.

'He's been there two hours,' the detective told her. 'Ate a plate of local scallops with bacon. Followed by a loin of West Country lamb. Then he had a sticky toffee pudding, and the cheeseboard.'

'Well, he won't be going anywhere in a hurry,' she said.

'He just asked for coffee and the bill.'

A car was waiting for her outside the airport. All the way into the city she had to answer questions from the young detective who was driving. What was it like to work in the Citadel? Had she ever met the Prime Minister? She toyed with telling him the unglamorous truth, but decided to do him a favour and keep up the mystique: the NCA was a constant buzz, you felt like you were at the epicentre of crime fighting, and her greatest fear was not being able to keep up with her colleagues, who really were geniuses. The Director-General and Command Team were paragons of fairness and sound judgement. As for her own superior, she'd never received anything from him other than unwavering support and sound advice.

A few silent miles later he turned to her. 'It's not really like that, is it,' he said quietly.

'No.' To cheer him up, she added, 'But if you want to send me your CV some time I'll pass it on.'

As they came into the central business district, the radio in the car crackled: 'He's walking up Southernhay.'

'Where's that?' Mesh said.

'I'm not sure. I'm from Plymouth.'

Mesh swore under breath, then got out her phone and brought up a map. She felt a small but agreeable rush of adrenalin. It was two streets away. At the next light, she opened the door.

'Where are you going?'

'Thanks for the lift,' she said, closing it behind.

A voice in her earpiece said, 'We've lost visual contact.'

Steadman had given them the slip. But he still needed to find a bank, she guessed. They were like petrol stations: they used to be everywhere, but no longer. She searched on her phone; the first one that came up was on Cathedral Green. It was only a minute or two away.

Once there, she walked the perimeter of the square, scanning faces, wishing someone would come on the radio saying they had visual contact. She was on her second pass when she spotted him in a gaggle of tourists. There was no mistaking Steadman; he was in the same black jeans and Chelsea sweatshirt that he'd been wearing when she'd met him previously. He was staring at his phone – following the map too, she guessed, probably trying to find the cashpoint. She took up a position behind a statue, holding her breath as he passed less than ten feet away, traversing the open space to get to the bank. Following behind, she almost laughed as he waved his arms in frustration when he arrived – the machine was out of order. Someone said something to him and pointed to another bank on the next corner.

'We have visual,' said the voice. 'Shall we take him?'

'Negative,' she said. She was curious what he might do next. After making his withdrawal he headed off down a side street, then ducked into a record store.

She said into her radio, 'Does anyone know Vinyl Demands on Fore St?'

After a few seconds, a voice said, 'I know it.'

'Is there a road at the back?'

'I'll cover it,' someone said.

'Let me know when you're in position.'

Thirty seconds later, the same voice said, 'I'm here. There's a back door. I'm going to try it.' Then, a few seconds later, 'It's open.'

Steadman's large frame was easy to see through the window. With the back entrance covered, a direct approach would be possible. She turned down her radio.

A bell on the door tinkled as she came in. Steadman seemed not to notice; he was engrossed in flicking through the stacks of old LPs.

She walked up next to him and picked up an old Donna Summer album, pretending to read the cover. She was about to turn and say something to him, but then waited. He hadn't noticed her at all.

She tapped him on the shoulder. 'Steadman?'

He turned, surprised, and then looked doubly surprised when he recognised her.

He stuttered his words, 'W-what are you ...?'

She put her finger to her lips. He nodded. Then a voice at the back of the store shouted, 'Don't move!'

They both turned. A young policeman was coming towards them.

'Wait, no!' Mesh shouted, jumping out, her hands in front of her. 'I told you to guard the back.'

The cop looked surprised. 'I said on the radio I was coming in.'

Behind her, Mesh heard the door chime peel. She turned to see Steadman hoisting himself through the doorframe and into the street.

'Idiot!' Mesh yelled at the cop, then ran after him. 'Steadman, wait!' she called.

He turned downhill, went towards the port. At the bottom of the street he took a sharp left down an old cobblestoned road, and she almost tripped over her own feet trying to keep up. For a large man who'd just eaten a huge meal he was surprisingly agile.

He turned to look back and as he did so a delivery van pulled out from a side street. There was a screech of brakes. The driver blared his horn. Mesh's heart almost leapt out of her chest, but Steadman cut sharply to the left and ran around the front. He looked back again, and seemed almost in two minds as to whether to give up, but then carried on, leaping over a row of bushes, down to a riverside path.

Mesh's lungs burned. How the could an overweight man like him run so quickly? She was going to lose him. She heard footsteps behind, and turned to see the policeman from the store and two other uniformed cops joining in the chase.

'We're losing him,' she said to them.

'Stubbs'll get him,' said one of the cops.

On cue, a tiny man burst past, his short legs pumping faster than she would have thought possible. Steadman seemed a long way in the distance, but within a minute Stubbs was closing on him, and Steadman, who never once looked back, didn't appear to be aware of him. The tiny officer launched himself into the air and landed on Steadman's back. Mesh winced as the pair of them tumbled over in a tangle of legs. Stubbs sprang up, pulled his handcuffs, and stood over Steadman like a pint-sized gladiator.

Mesh heaved a breath and forced herself to jog the rest of the way. When she arrived, the cops had already cuffed his wrists, and were about to do the same to his ankles.

'Hold off on that,' she said.

'We don't want him running,' said one of the cops.

'Let him run,' Stubbs said. 'Good rugby training.'

'I want to talk to him,' Mesh said. She pointed to a set of concrete steps at the side of the path and said to the cops, 'Put him over there.'

They pulled Steadman up, and as he turned to look at her he double blinked. 'It's really you?' he spluttered. 'Are you okay?'

What was he talking about? 'Am I *okay*? I'm arresting you.'

'For what?'

'Falsifying evidence,' she said quickly. She hadn't given it any thought: she'd been too focused on apprehending him. 'Where's Rigby?'

'I don't know.'

'Steadman, this is serious.'

Steadman nodded and wiped the sweat from his brow. He knew all about it, it seemed. He took an envelope out of his back pocket and handed it to her. He said, 'I had an option, depending on who tracked me down. If it was anyone else, I would play dumb, but if it was you then I could give you this.'

Mesh wasn't about to be taken in that easily. She examined the envelope. It had been opened. Shaking it upside down, she said, 'An empty envelope. Thanks.'

Steadman said, 'He sent me the bank card in that. Turn it

over.'

On the front was Steadman's home address and a Post Office frank.

'Ludlow,' she said, pointing at the frank. 'This is made by an old Post Office machine. To get this, he had to do it over the counter. He did it on purpose to let us know where he really is.'

Steadman double-blinked in amazement. Mesh felt pleased, her deduction had sounded impressive even to her.

'That's what I figured too,' he said.

She looked at him doubtfully.

He said, 'Now tell them to give me back my car keys.'

'What?'

'Car keys. You want my help, I need my car.'

Mesh thought about it. On balance, she needed him. It was worth the risk. She turned to the policemen. 'Keys.' When they didn't respond she said it louder, 'Keys!'

Reluctantly, Stubbs tossed them to her.

Steadman reached out for them, but she dangled them out of his reach.

'Where's Frederick Ascott? Rigby toshed him. Has he hidden him somewhere?'

Steadman shrugged. 'Frederick who?'

'Don't play dumb. Not if you want *my* help.'

He sighed. 'You're about a week late.'

'What are you talking about?'

'We had him. We went to pick him up, but he was gone.'

Mesh took a moment to process the information. 'You *had* him? Where?'

'Bethnal Green. This skinhead lived there, with some Eva Braun wannabe, and this loony dog.'

'Did Rigby tell you anything about him?'

'He was some kind of spy. We were going to hand him over.'

'To whom?'

'Modplod.'

Mesh took a deep breath. She didn't like the sound of that, not one bit. Why them and not her? It wasn't jealousy. It was concern. She offered the keys and Steadman took them, flashing her a broad smile.

'Want me to drive you to Ludlow?' he said.

'Who says I'm going to Ludlow?'

Steadman laughed. 'It'll be a lot better for you if I'm there.'

He had a point, she knew, but she wasn't ready to be all pally, and certainly not with uniformed cops around. 'I'll call you if I need you.'

A police van arrived. Cops spilled out wearing body armour, surprised to find the situation under control.

One of them said to the senior cop, 'Party's over, skip?'

'Never got started,' he replied, the disappointment evident in his voice.

'Can you give us a lift back?' Mesh said to them.

The senior cop looked at the others and shrugged. 'Suppose so.'

As they drove back into town, Mesh noticed Steadman's eyes settling on her as the officers joshed each other. What a curious fellow he was, she thought, and why did he keep staring at her like that?

17

Rigby had taken a large pack with him on the bike to collect the sat hub. He'd expected it to be heavy, but it turned out to be a couple of pounds at most. He rode back to the camp like a kid on Christmas morning, bouncing through the ruts, but as he rounded a corner and got his first glimpse of the campsite his heart missed a beat. A second vehicle was parked in the clearing. He sped up to get a closer look and felt relieved to find that it was only an old Ford Transit van. Just some deadbeat, he reasoned, driving a heap like that.

As he drew nearer he heard singing, and instruments playing. Sitting between the two vehicles in a pair of tattered deckchairs were a man – probably in his fifties, Rigby guessed – dressed entirely in denim, and a masculine-looking woman a few years younger in theatrical gypsy gear. The man strummed a red-sunburst acoustic guitar, the woman blew a penny-whistle. The scene should have been harmless, even joyful, but a shot of alarm coursed through him. Who were these people? Where had they come from?

He jumped off his bike and pushed it up where they could see him. 'Hi,' he said, trying to sound nonchalant.

The man sprang out of his deckchair and came over, carrying his guitar. 'Hey, camper, so glad you came back,' he said, with a heavy Birmingham accent. 'We were starting to worry that maybe the old VW had been abandoned. Such a beautiful vehicle.'

'Thank you.'

'Marco Monda, pleased to meet you,' he said, sticking out a hand. 'And this is Polly Amorous.'

'Pleased to meet you,' Rigby said, shaking his hand. 'And you too,' he said to Polly. They appeared too eccentric to pose any immediate threat.

'Come join us,' Marco said. 'We were playing a few old favourites. You got an instrument with you?'

'Sorry, I don't play anything.'

'That's okay, we'll do the work, we're used to it,' Marco laughed.

He man sat down again and the playing continued, although Rigby didn't recognise the tune. He wanted to get inside the bus and try out his new toy.

Marco spotted him walking away and said, 'We were surprised to find someone else parked here. This is our little spot, we've been coming here for years.'

'It's very peaceful,' Rigby said.

'Great place to get away from everyone,' Marco smiled. He plucked a sweet-sounding chord and let it ring.

Rigby smiled at him and walked on, towards the bus.

'How about we play something for you?' Marco said, stopping him again. 'We can do anything. What would you like to hear?'

Rigby had to think hard. He rarely listened to music at home, and never on his bike. 'I used to be kind of a Bowie nut.'

'Great choice, he's the man, or was the man,' Marco said. 'Hey, if you're going to be a nut about something, might as well be one of the greats, right? We can play David Bowie, can't we, Pol.' He hit two heavy chords and sang: *'I'm an alligator, I'm a mama-papa coming for you ...'*

He had an amazing voice, Rigby had to admit, deep and theatrical. Polly joined in on the whistle, adding a tremolo that made it sound professional, more like a synthesiser than a kid's toy. Rigby was impressed. As he watched her play, he looked at her closely for the first time and noticed something that he hadn't expected. Polly's eyes were etched with mascara. Her face was narrow and her lips a dark red. Below them, a small chin completed a pleasing face and below that, further down the neck, a prominent Adam's apple.

She caught him looking; Rigby smiled and turned away. He hoped he hadn't offended her. Marco caught his eye and grinned.

'Keep playing, I need to do something,' Rigby said.

'*Put your ray gun to my head*,' sang Marco.

Locking himself into the bus, Rigby took the hub out of the box, marvelling at its lightness. He switched on. Everything played nice. The device needed line-of-sight to a satellite, but it worked through glass. He put it on the front passenger seat and aimed through the windshield, keeping it low so his fellow campers wouldn't see.

He had a hunch that some tiny morsel of Ascott's existence might still be lurking in the user groups and bulletin boards of the classic car fraternity. Toshers tried their best, but if someone logged into different sites using different names and used different IP addresses – even inadvertently – there was bound to be something somewhere that didn't get erased. Big searches like the one he was imagining needed bandwidth, though, and he decided to try the sat hub for speed.

He called up a news site. The speed of the connection impressed him, but when he saw the headlines his blood turned cold. Under the UK News banner, the lead story said:

Disappearance of GCHQ Mastermind

Shit! They'd gone public. Embedded in the text was a video. The caption said: Last known whereabouts – house in Bethnal Green. He clicked on it. The video clearly showed Ascott walking alongside a man, who it said the police wanted to speak to urgently. He wasn't named, but the final shot contained an old photo of his face, and one of the Combi.

His brain went into overdrive. He needed to move. He needed to ditch the VW. He needed to change his appearance. He needed to do all of that without attracting attention.

He got out. Marco looked up from his guitar. 'How you doin', chief?'

'Wouldn't you know it,' Rigby said, trying to play it cool, 'just as I'm getting settled in, there's a message from the office. Need to head back to the city.'

Marco shook his head. 'Don't do it. Stay here. Make them dance to your tune.'

'I wish I had that choice. It was nice to meet you both. And great voice, by the way. I think even Mr Bowie would have enjoyed hearing you do his stuff with such, I don't know, gusto.'

Marco said to Polly, 'Hear that, he says I've got gusto.'

Rigby turned to get into the Combi.

'Uh, before you go...' Marco called.

'Yeah?'

'You might want to think about a trade.'

'What?'

'Vehicles.'

Rigby did a double-take. Was the man serious? He gave a polite chuckle. 'Mine's been restored. It's the 21 window version. I mean, I'm not trying to brag, but it's worth maybe fifty grand.'

'And old Betty here – I mean the Transit – she's probably worth less than five.' Marco added with a twinkle, 'But it's the price of freedom, right?'

Marco gave him a broad grin. Rigby felt his heart thumping in his chest. They must have seen the news.

'I've always fancied a Transit,' Rigby said.

'A wise decision, my friend. We've had a lot of adventures in her.'

Marco winked at Polly, who smiled at Rigby.

'You've played this game before.' He chucked them the VW key.

'That we have, sir,' Marco said, throwing the key for the Transit. 'That we have.'

'You need to change the registration and give it a coat of

paint.'

'I know just the man for the job, don't you worry.'

Rigby drove off, bouncing back up the dirt track he'd come down two days before, cursing Mark Putts as he went. Putts hadn't laid just one trap for him, but a whole series of them, each one intended to steer him towards a point where he would realise there was no hope of escape, and it was drawing closer. The time had come, he saw, to cash in his insurance policy.

The SD card contained screenshots of information relating to dozens of toshed people, and a lot of it would help in Mesh's investigation. If he could get it to her, she could have it analysed by the Sweatbox, and they could prove, conclusively, that he had nothing to do with the missing informants. It wouldn't clear him of everything, but it could buy time while he figured out what to do about Putts.

The fact that he was having to take action against a man who for years he'd thought of not as a friend exactly, but as a close collaborator, made him so angry that he found himself hitting the steering wheel over and over as he drove. Putts had been a boss not a buddy, but they had often been the ones who'd found each other standing at the back of a conference or in a lecture hall, looking at the rest with a degree of circumspection, exchanging a little knowing glance, a tiny roll of the eyes – *we're above this crap* – as the other officers riled each other and jockeyed for position.

Putts had defended him more than once. Rigby's annual assessments were always full of damning phrases like 'questions authority for the sake of it', 'combustible if things don't go his way', and 'takes everything *way* too personally'. Putts laughed it off. Then came the case with the Judge, where he really proved his loyalty. Rigby had been assigned to work alongside officers from CEOP, hunting for paedophiles grooming kids online. One of their tactics was for an officer to go into a chat room posing as a child, and to wait for pervs pretending to be children to come online. Over time, the officer would allow themselves to be befriended. On rare occasions, the new friend tried to arrange an offline meeting and, without trying to appear too eager, the officer would agree to meet. If they were lucky, the suspect would show, and if the 'friend' turned out to be someone different than they'd claimed to be, they would make an arrest.

But paedos were getting smarter. Like drug pushers using burner phones, paedos rarely used the same name twice, and they used multiple computers, all hidden behind VPNs, to go into different forums simultaneously. Rigby sensed they were the same people – little giveaways – but there was no evidence beyond gut feeling, and it was almost impossible for him to probe deeper to find out who they might be without unmasking himself in the process. He solved the problem by writing an application called ConvSim. It analysed chunks of text and looked for similarities in syntax, vocabulary and other key elements of discourse. The technology had been around for years, but Rigby's app enabled it to run in real time, cross-referencing hundreds of separate inputs simultaneously. After a few runs, CEOP were able to confirm that 90% of suspicious chats originated from a small handful of users, each of them working fast across multiple forums, and changing names with every visit. What it couldn't do was identify the individuals in question.

Rigby had a brainwave. Why not pre-screen? If they could obtain example text – such as emails – from previous offenders and other high-risk individuals, then the pre-screened text could be compared with the live text, and the perpetrators could be identified. He decided to test it to see if ConvSim could distinguish older, unrelated material from the live chat.

Putts encouraged him to go ahead, even though he was putting himself on the line assigning unauthorized man-hours to an untested app written by a junior operative. To test the system, they gathered a selection of random materials from

CEOP email accounts, and at the next ConvSim session included the some of it as one of the streams being analysed.

The random material should have been ignored by ConvSim, but instead they got a match. It upset Rigby at first. He thought it must be an error. ConvSim was meant to distinguish the unrelated older material from the live feed. He checked the system, but there seemed to be no problems. He tried it again and achieved the same result. ConvSim spotted strong similarities between the conversations of four supposed individuals in different chat rooms, who were now believed to be one person, with the text of the summing-up given by a judge at the County Court in Stafford in an abuse case. For Rigby, the implication was obvious: the judge was a groomer. His mistake was to state this, loudly and clearly, in the presence of half a dozen other NCA officers.

That an officer would make such an accusation against a sitting judge without double-checking the facts, without consulting his superior, and through the use of material that no-one could agree had been obtained legally, should have earned Rigby a suspension. But no. Putts stood up for him. He refused to punish him, and said if anyone was to blame, it was himself. Putts found out later that the judge had decided to retire – keeping his full retirement package – and that no other action had been taken against him. Incensed, he asked Rigby to keep running ConvSim every night using the same text sample. A few weeks later, they found a match. The judge had laid low for while, as Putts had suspected he would, then when he felt the heat was off, he'd returned to the chat rooms. They drove with a CEOP team to his house and busted him. It had been the happiest day of Rigby's NCA career.

Did it mean nothing to Putts? Had he just been grooming Rigby the whole time? And what about all those tips he'd given Putts since leaving – did they count for nothing? More than anything else, that wound him up the most. Those tips involved real victims and real criminals. Hadn't the fact that he'd entrusted Putts with such important material earned him even a modicum of respect? Apparently not, except in the most backhanded and hideous way – Putts recognised how good he was, and wanted him as part of whatever scheme he was mixed up in.

Until he could figure out how to fight it, Rigby knew his only option was to put as many miles as possible between himself and the Citadel. But time spent driving, he'd learned, meant time not looking for Ascott. The hub had proved to be useless on the move: it simply didn't work unless he was parked. So every time he wanted to search, he had to stop. He then had to aim the Hub at a satellite, do his search, and then download the results. He couldn't just stop at any old place, either. The hub was an unusual device, which was bound to attract attention. His best bet, he'd decided, would be to head to deep into Wales, and to find a secluded area where he wouldn't be observed either by people or security cameras, and which nevertheless had a good number of other vehicles in it, so his would go unnoticed.

Later that afternoon, after crossing into Wales, he saw a motorway service area that fit the bill. He turned off and drove to a far corner of the carpark, away from prying eyes. Putting the sat hub on the passenger seat, he fired it up and got a signal at the first attempt. Using an encrypted email service, he set up an anonymous account. Then he sent Mesh a one-line email: Ask Steady for the Insurance Policy.

He trusted Mesh. She'd do it by the book. This one was too important to get wrong. There could be no inadmissible evidence, or any other technicalities that would allow the worm to wriggle free. Steadman would thank him for it too, he thought, and he laughed out loud for the first time in many days.

Steadman would have doubted that a face could so perfectly express the feeling of suspicion until he watched Gloria tracking Mesh through Pangolin's reception. Her lips had drained of blood, her eyes narrowed to slits, and even though she sat at a desk, her weight had transferred to the balls of her feet and her thighs twitched, like a cat ready to strike. An Oscar-winner couldn't have done it better, except that Gloria wasn't acting: this was true, unadulterated mistrust.

He hurried past the desk and over to the coffee machine. Setting it up to brew, he dashed back to Gloria's workstation. 'Damn, girl, you look like you're about to kill someone.'

'What's she doing here?' Gloria demanded. 'Last time the NCA came, they tore the place apart.'

'No, that was someone else.'

'Don't give me that. It was NCA. Some kids learn how to tell Pikachu from Totoro. I learned how to tell Met from NCA from regular Old Bill.'

'Rubbish,' he said, dismissively.

'Fuck off. Old Bill, on the beat, they're just normal people doing a job. Detectives are different, they try to be all cool, think they're Idris Elba. They're like 'hey sister, what's going down?' And you're like, cut the act, clown. NCA are different. They're quiet, but they got this look on their face like they're king of the world.'

'Well, whatever. We have to talk to her. Meet us upstairs in a few minutes.'

He made coffee and carried the cups on a tray to reception where he collected Mesh, before taking her upstairs to the conference room. He managed the journey without spilling a drop, which he felt pleased about, because ever since he'd met her, a little voice inside his head had been telling him to ask her out. She was a cop, and much of what he did for Rigby strayed into areas that were only semi-legal, so that didn't bode well. Rigby himself had always said she was a nightmare to work with, which didn't sound encouraging. Then there was the investigation, in which he himself was undoubtedly implicated. These were the simple facts that made asking her out a very bad idea, but the little voice was like a politician: it didn't seem to be interested in inconvenient things like *facts*.

As they made their way up the staircase, he became

aware of heads turning. The male freelancers tried to get an eyeful of anyone of the opposite sex ascending the stairs. He hollered at them, 'Get back to your work!'

Warren had already arrived and was setting up. The bandage around his head had gone, but his arm was still in a sling. He had both his regular computer and the target laptop out on the table. Steadman introduced him to Mesh.

'So, you're the climate protestor?' she said to Warren.

He tried his best to look confused, but she wasn't fooled. 'Don't worry, you don't have to answer,' she said.

Gloria arrived, her face unchanged from earlier. Steadman caught a look of ice between the two. Was this going to be a huge mistake?

'Take a seat,' Mesh said to Gloria. 'And shut the door.'

Gloria glanced at Warren and rolled her eyes. He gave the tiniest of shrugs.

Gloria said to Mesh, 'Did you give the order to raid us?'

Mesh seemed surprised by the question. 'I didn't order it. But I approved it,' she said calmly.

'See,' Gloria said to Steadman.

'The raid didn't find anything, did it?' Warren said.

'We now know you a run parallel organisation,' Mesh said.

'And that's as far as you're ever going to get.'

Mesh gave a sigh. 'Look, guys, we all want to help Rigby, but if we're going to work together, then we're going to have to trust each other. And you,' she stared straight at Gloria, 'are going to have to change your attitude. Either that or take some acting lessons, because right now your face is like a teleprompter, and I don't like the script.'

'Hey, hey, c'mon, Mesh, Mesh,' Steadman said, hurriedly. He said to his own party, 'We need to put this hostility to one side. Can I see some cordiality, please?'

They took breaths and nodded.

'That's better,' he said. 'Now listen up. Mesh has had word from Rigby.'

The announcement took them by surprise.

'Is he okay?' Warren said.

'Where is he?' asked Gloria.

Mesh told them about the email, saying it was all she knew. 'So it doesn't sound to me like he's being held captive, or pinned down somewhere. He's still a free man.'

Gloria crossed her arms. 'There's no way anyone's going to catch him. He's too smart.'

'But he wants our help, which is why he sent Mesh the message,' Steadman said.

'What did it say, exactly?' Gloria said.

'It said "ask Steady for the insurance policy",' Mesh replied.

'And I know exactly what that is,' Steadman said.

'You do?' Mesh said, her turn to be surprised. 'Why didn't you say so before?'

Steadman felt himself blushing. He hoped no-one else noticed. 'I think he did this to bring us together, so I got us together.'

Gloria eyed him suspiciously. 'You want us to hold hands or something?'

'You wish.' He turned to Mesh. 'He came to me right after that first meeting with you. He knew it meant trouble.'

'So what is this policy?' Gloria said.

'It's an SD Card,' Steadman said. 'Contains a record of everyone he ever toshed. I think all the toshers did it.'

'They did,' Mesh said. 'It was in case anyone in witness protection was found and killed – the toshers could say "nope wasn't my fault".'

'That was back then,' Gloria said. 'How does that help him now?'

'It'll help me,' Mesh said, tentatively, 'with the original case.'

'And it'll help us find him too,' Steadman said.

'See, that's what I'm worried about,' Gloria said. 'He's laying a trail to bring us together so we can help him, I'll go along with that. But he didn't say anything about finding him. Maybe he doesn't want to be found.'

'I agree completely,' Mesh said.

'You do?'

'It's what they expect you to do. There's probably people watching you now, hoping you'll lead them right to him. So don't go anywhere. And if you do anything online, make sure to anonymise yourselves.'

'Oh, we're good at that,' Warren said.

'I'm sure you are. Steadman and I will go pick up the insurance policy and we'll meet you back here, agreed?'

They nodded.

Steadman smiled. 'Well praise the Lawd,' he said in a mock-Preacher voice. 'We have found agreement.'

Sunlight bathed the church in Stoke Newington in what Steadman wanted to describe as an angelic glow, but he refrained from saying it out loud as he wasn't sure how Mesh might react to religious references, even if they were tongue-in-cheek. He showed her the way through the churchyard toward the side entrance, which he knew all too well from attending meetings. He didn't tell her about those either.

They knocked on the door. When there was no answer, he tried the latch. It opened. He said to Mesh, 'She might be downstairs.' They stepped inside. 'Hello,' he called. 'Hello?'

A light flickered on in the basement, but still there was no reply.

'Shall we?'

'Lead the way.'

They came into a wide, low-ceilinged room with an array of mismatched chairs arranged around a ping-pong table. Scores were chalked up on a board. Steadman knew it well.

He said, 'They use it as a place where homeless people can come and get a cup of coffee. Guess they've been having a tournament.'

To his surprise, Mesh said, 'It reminds me of when I was growing up. My mum used to take me to the Sikh temple. The women would cook tons of food and take it to the all the homeless shelters. She used to drag me along. I don't remember much, but we might have come here.'

'It's been running a long time.'

'I never liked going inside. The people smelled bad and they had rotting teeth. I used to hide in the car.'

Steadman was enraptured, hearing her talk about herself, but a voice behind them broke the spell.

'Can I help you?'

Instinctively, Mesh spun around. He quickly put out an arm to reassure her or restrain her, he didn't know which.

'It's Steady,' he said, flinching when he realised his arm had ended up around Mesh's waist, closer than he would ever have believed possible. He removed it quickly.

A figure emerged from the darkness. 'Steady, what are you doing down here? And who's this?'

Mesh flashed her ID. 'Mesh Kaur, NCA.'

Lana came close and peered at the card, then wheeled around to Steadman. 'Why have you brought her here?' she said, angrily. 'You know this is a safe space.'

'No, it's okay, she's not looking for anyone.'

Lana's eyes flicked backward and forward between the two of them. 'People come here for food and a helping hand. We don't ask questions. All are welcome.'

'I appreciate that,' Mesh said. 'Really.'

Lana eyed the two of them suspiciously for a few more seconds, then she said, 'So what are you here for, then?'

'We need to talk to you about something. It's about Rigby.'

'Rigby? What about him?'

Steadman said, 'It's not about him exactly. It's about that thing I gave you.'

Lana's eyes narrowed. She checked Mesh again. Still uncertain about her, she said, 'You didn't give me anything.'

Where was this coming from, Steadman wondered? He hadn't considered that retrieving the SD card might be anything other than a straightforward exercise. He'd known Lana for years, but maybe not as well as he thought. Was she, like Gloria, instinctively mistrustful of the police? Or was her loyalty to Rigby so strong that she would doubt everyone else?

'Lana, please. She's a friend. Can we sit down at least?'

Lana was considering the request when a figure came down the stairs. A man's voice said, 'You alright, Lana?'

Steadman knew that voice, too. It was Frank, one of the regulars from their self-help group. Self-appointed guardian of Lana.

'I'll be a few minutes,' she called back.

As Frank came into the light, Steadman rolled his eyes. His Adidas sweats looked filthier than ever. Frank didn't have a malicious bone in his body, but he also had a one-track mind. He pointed a shaky finger at Mesh. 'She's the filth. What are you doing bringing the filth here, Steady?'

'She's a friend of mine.'

'Friend?' Frank said, as if the idea wounded him.

'I'll be with you soon,' Lana said to him. 'Please just wait outside.'

'Outside?' Frank said. 'More filth outside than in here.' He scratched his chin, waiting for her response.

Steadman said, 'That's why it's important you keep an eye on them for us.'

Frank blinked. He knew they were giving him the brush-off.

Lana said, 'We won't be long, Frank. I'll be up in a minute.'

He gave each of them a scathing look, saving the last and most disdainful for Steadman. 'If I was you, I'd be more careful about the company I keep.' He turned and proceeded to climb back up the stairs.

'Bless you, Frank,' Lana called after him.

When he'd finally gone, Mesh said to her, 'Everyone here

has immense loyalty to each other, I get that, and Rigby needs your help.'

Lana looked balefully at Steadman and he nodded in support. He said softly, 'When I was last here, I asked you to keep something for me. I said to put it in a safe place.'

She took a deep breath, then said, 'Okay, I have it. But it's not here.'

'Where is it?' Mesh said.

Steadman threw her a glance, but Lana seemed to have gone past the point of denial.

'At my daughter's school. It's safe, but it's being used.'

'Used?' Steadman said, concerned that the daughter might have erased data. 'What for?'

'You said to hide it. Well, they're for cameras so I put it in a camera.'

Mesh said, 'And your daughter took the camera to school?'

Lana nodded. Steadman felt his stomach fall away.

'She has a show coming up in her art class, and she came up with this idea – well it was wonderful but completely bizarre, but that's high school kids for you. It's a head. She wanted microphones for ears and cameras for eyes, and all the rest of it. So without asking, mind you, she comes up here to my office and starts hunting through all the donated items.'

'So the camera is now part of an art exhibit at a school?' Mesh said.

'And the judging is today, so we can't go and get it. Tiffy would kill me.'

Steadman and Mesh exchanged a glance.

'I suppose it's safe,' Mesh said to him.

'What?' he said.

'The *card*.'

'Yeah, of course.'

Mesh gave him a quizzical look, then turned back to Lana. 'Will the judging be completed today? Can we come and pick it up, tomorrow maybe?'

Lana smiled. 'That'll be fine. I'll make sure it comes back.'

Outside, the sun had burned away the clouds. Mesh stretched and yawned, triggering Steadman do the same.

She said, 'I'm glad to be out of there. It was more like a morgue than a church.'

He was about to reply when he saw that her attention had been diverted.

'Did you see that?' she said.

He followed her eye line to an empty parking space. A car was driving away at speed.

'Did someone take your car?' he said.

'No,' she said, pointing. 'My car's over there. But did you see the one that left?'

'It looked like yours.'

'Exactly. Identical. Mine's a pool car,' she said, explaining. 'That probably was too.'

Steadman felt the hairs on his neck start to rise. 'Was he following us?'

'Possibly. Maybe that's what your friend Frank was talking about: more filth outside than inside.'

As they drove back downtown, she said, 'We need to let Rigby know we're on the case.'

Steadman didn't know how to reply immediately. The obvious thing was to agree, but he felt that he couldn't. 'I'm not sure that's a good idea.'

'Why not?' she said, surprised. 'We need to let him know about Tudor Clarke, too. It changes everything.'

'I know but ...'

He was aware of her waiting for him to finish the sentence, and after a few seconds said, 'We told Gloria and Warren we wouldn't try to find him.'

'I don't want to find him. I want to contact him.'

Steadman felt pinched. He knew Mesh was right, but he

had to honour the agreement. 'Even that could give him away.'

Mesh was having none of it. 'I'm sure if you put your mind to it you can think of a some way to do it that wouldn't compromise him.'

Sounded like a test. 'Let me think about it.'

They arrived in Chinatown sooner than he expected. Mesh pulled over, expecting him to get out. 'Why don't you give me a call if you think of something,' she said.

'No, I got it, I got it,' he said. The idea was only half-baked but he couldn't let her drive away without him passing the test. 'Cognoscenti.'

She turned to him. 'What's that?'

'It's a website, kind of half-magazine and half-bulletin board, for cycling nuts. He reads it every day, and writes stuff, you know, gets involved in debates. It's all about the world's toughest rides and the rules you have to follow.'

'Racing rules.'

'No, really stupid stuff. Decorum and rituals, like you have to shave your legs, and have grip tape that matches the saddle. Wherever he is, if he has internet access, he will at some point drop in at Cognoscenti.'

Her hand hovered over the gear lever as she considered the suggestion.

'If we put something on there,' he added, trying to sell her on it, 'he'll see it, I guarantee you.'

She shook her head. 'I can't put my case notes on a public website.'

'I don't mean like that. I'm thinking we write a story as if it comes from a cyclist, but it's like in code, so only he understands it.'

He couldn't stop himself from smiling as she put the car in park and took her phone out.

'What's the URL?'

He gave it to her.

She navigated around the site. He watched enraptured as sunlight streamed in through the windshield giving her hair a lustrous sheen.

She laughed and said, 'This is the nerdiest site I have ever seen.'

'Exactly. That's why he loves it.'

'I'm going to sign up,' she said, tapping way. 'User name: Shouldbeme.' She looked up to see if he liked it, and he quickly averted his gaze.

'That's what they used to call us,' she said, 'Goode and Should.'

'I-I know,' he said, managing to get the words out. 'I remember him telling me.'

He was looking away, pretending to be interested in something happening on the sidewalk, so she tapped his shoulder for attention. Her touch felt electric.

'How long have you boys known each other, anyway?'

An easy question. He breathed again. 'Maybe seven or eight years. Why?'

'It's my job,' she smiled, but he could tell there was something else in her mind. 'Now ... to start a thread,' she said. 'How about "Cycling Trip to Belgrade"?'

It was a terrible title, Steadman thought. 'You have to get his attention first. Belgrade sounds too much like where someone might have been.'

Mesh seemed confused. 'That's the point. It's a cycling site.'

'That's why it won't work. You have to make it sound like something that a cyclist would never write about, but then write it like a cyclist.'

She laughed. 'You're making it *way* too complicated.'

Clearly, she didn't know Rigby as well as she thought. 'Nothing's ever too complicated. *Ever.*'

'So what would you write, smarty-pants?'

'I don't know. How much time do you have?'

'Why? What did you have in mind?'

The look on her face – she knew what this was. His heart felt like the drum of a marching band. 'How about we go get a bite and talk about it?'

'I'd like that,' she said with a smile, but then her expression changed – suddenly, she looked sorry. 'But I'll have to take a rain check. I have a meeting in half an hour.'

'Oh. One step at a time, I guess.'

She put a hand on his arm. 'They always say, never date a cop.'

'Do they?'

'Yeah.'

'Lucky for you I never do what anyone tells me.'

She laughed. 'That makes two of us. Write up your idea and send it to me.'

'I will.'

He backed away from the car and she drove off with a wave. He couldn't believe it. He'd asked her out and she'd said yes. All they had to do now was actually go on the date.

18

Balorat was in his office at Guys Hospital, admiring the set of skulls arranged on a shelf. Most people – well, everyone – would fail to understand both the significance of the arrangement, and its unlikeliness. That a private individual would not only possess such a collection, but display it in public, where anyone could handle the items, was patently ludicrous. The arrangement of the skulls never ceased to amuse him, and as his eyes drifted lovingly from one to the next, he wished he could talk about it more openly when people came to see him. But again, that would be ludicrous. How could he share with them the fact that the four full-size human skulls in his collection were in fact actual bone? It could lead to awkward questions about their provenance, and, more worryingly, to enquiries as to the nature of the fifth. A much smaller item, it was readily identifiable to anyone with half a brain and a working knowledge of human biology (which in Balorat's experience comprised a terrifyingly small pool and excluded the majority of the Guys staff) as a Neanderthal. Surely it belonged in a museum, they would opine, how had it come to be in his possession? The busybodies would no doubt ask questions about the second of the smaller skulls, and then the real problems would begin. It was a Denisovan, the Stradivarius of crania. It had cost him a fortune, and been smuggled out of China in pieces. Finally, but by no means last, not a skull at all, but a shrunken head, bought in Peru from an actual Achuar tribesman. Everyone assumed it was fake, but it was as real as the rest.

He'd arranged them oh-so-carefully, left to right. First,

the Indo-European, Asian and Asiatic skulls. Next, the Neanderthal, because, of course, ancient homo sapiens had mated with Neanderthal to produce the most recent, hybridised genetic line. Then the fourth human skull, an African, which unlike the others did not contain Neanderthal DNA. Then the Denisovan, which was a hybrid of the human, the Neanderthal, and a third yet-to-be-identified race. And finally the shrunken head, which was, he was assured by the tribe he'd bought it from at vast expense, not produced from the head of a member of another primitive clan, but was in fact the remains of an Indo-European – a Frenchman, no less – who had become lost in a mountain forest and was captured and killed, and his head shrunk. Balorat called his arrangement: The Descent of Man. Descent. *Descent!* With the hapless Frenchie last in line. What a tragedy that no-one else could share the joke.

A phone was ringing, the special phone, the one he kept only for K. He thought for a moment about not taking it – he was relishing the moment – but then, as always, the thought came to him that there was, in actual fact, no other person to whom he would rather speak – partly because he had little desire to speak to anyone, except, occasionally, his wife.

He pressed the green button. 'Good afternoon,' he said, suddenly aware that he was still laughing.

'Someone's in a good mood. Finland went well?'

Balorat took a moment to compose himself. 'That marksman, Hardy. He's incredible.'

'Former SAS.'

'Don't I know. Mentioned it every other sentence. You said the target was a lush, well, he was half-cut when we found him, slobbing out in front of the telly with a fresh bottle of vodka. Before I know it, Hardy has him tied to a chair with his mouth wedged open with a sunglasses case. "Get a tube in," he says to me. So I whip out the bag, stick a tube down his throat, put a funnel on the end, and start pouring in the hooch. Not too fast though, and I threw in half a bottle of antiemetic to help him keep it down.'

'Sounds gruesome,' K said.

'Not really, he never struggled. It was all over within an hour. He started having seizures, so we untied him and put him on the ground. I counted his breaths against my watch until they became irregular, and when hypothermia set in – it's obvious because the skin turns blue – I gave Hardy the nod to clean up. We got the suits on, and before I had time to lift a finger, the whole place was fresher than a nun's cunt on Sunday.'

K gave a snort. 'A good marksman is worth his weight in gold.'

'So,' Balorat said, noticing that he felt happier than he had in months, 'what's next? Is our new tosher in place yet?'

'Ah,' she said. 'That's where we have a little bit of a problem.'

The words hit him hard, and instantly.

'Chocolate teapot again?'

'The tosher's gone on the run.'

'Oh for ...' he began, but there were no words to express his rage. Why had she put someone in charge who clearly had no idea what he was doing? Putts was bearable so long as he was following orders. Ask him to do anything else and he was lost. It wasn't personal. Balorat had known him over twenty years, and on a day-to-day level they rubbed along fine, they'd even socialized once, with families. It hadn't been a roaring success. Balorat's boys had found the Putts children sickeningly dull, and the two wives hadn't ventured beyond schools. His wife had quipped afterwards that she found Mark Putts remarkably well-balanced, he had a chip on both shoulders. He talked non-stop about the car he'd just bought, their new house, the golf clubs they belonged to, and the amazing resort where they were planning to go on vacation. You couldn't trust a man whose only motivation was money, especially when it came to breaking the law. To be successful, a man – or any organization for that matter – needed a purpose. Without purpose, you were merely criminal.

He couldn't blame anyone else, of course. As soon as Putts had first approached him about the whole idea, he should have said no. He should have told himself, I've known this dunderhead for years, and he doesn't have the qualities to pull off what he's talking about. Ideas, fine, anyone could have ideas, but delivery was what separated winners from losers. He remembered the military adage: amateurs do strategy, professionals do logistics. Putts was all strategy. He was exactly the type of idiot who'd leave a squadron of the world's finest battle tanks stranded in the middle of an open plain, ready to be picked off from the sky, because he'd forgotten to book the fuel truck.

He said, 'Do you not realise that for a middle-age man with four teenage sons, simple happiness is very hard to come by.'

'I understand and share your frustration.'

'We need to take this into our own hands.'

'I've already spoken to him. He has one last chance.'

'Another one? I can't believe I'm hearing this.'

'There's a final lead he wants to follow.'

Balorat fumed. 'How long is it going to take?'

'It'll happen tonight. Could even be right now.'

It was K, he supposed, who'd won him over. It was clear as soon as he'd set eyes on her. It wasn't her looks, he was well past the age where he could be swayed by such things. But when she spoke it became obvious that everything Putts had told him earlier had come from her. She described how she'd met Putts at a conference on banking and identity fraud. She worked at a bank in the City, she said, in the compliance department, although the real value of the conferences were in all the ideas they gave her for her other businesses. Balorat didn't need it spelling out: she was running an identity theft and money-laundering operation on the side, using everything she learned at the bank to stay ahead of the NCA. He remembered the awe he felt the moment he worked out what she was up to. She'd planned her entire career as an exercise in getting someone to pay her to learn how to steal from them. Everything she gleaned along the way, every contact she made, was put to use. With a mind like that, she must have taken one look at Putts and known he was born to be used.

And Putts, the fool, tried to pretend he was the one in control. He charged around, volunteering for every task, no matter how menial. In the early days of any new venture, anyone willing to put their hand up was welcome. That was how Balorat had learned how incompetent the man could be. Everything he touched, *everything*, had some little fuck-up in it. Often it didn't matter, the chore was of little importance, and simply by getting things done he painted a sheen of dependability on himself. But when something required more than what an ape could accomplish, you were almost better off with the ape. Balorat had told K this more times than he cared to remember. She always agreed with him, but then reminded him how useful Putts could be, so long as they 'used him the right way'. Results didn't lie though, and they were now like the tanks on the plain, stranded.

He said, 'If he fails, he's out.'

'I agree.'

'And out means out.'

'I agree with that too.'

He gripped the bottle of Midazolam in his pocket. It contained an enhanced version of the drug, with an even faster onset, which he'd agreed to trial for a pharmaceutical company.

'And before you ask,' she said, 'the answer is yes. If it comes to that, you can be the one to do it. I know how much you'd enjoy it.'

Barely a minute went by, Lana mused, that someone wasn't phoning her, or emailing, or knocking on her door wanting something. Did they think she was a limitless resource? And couldn't they read the notice, which clearly stated the opening hours? She stopped and corrected herself. Such uncharitable thoughts! Many who came to her for assistance had problems which prevented them from reading. This one must need help badly, so loud and insistent was their banging.

'I'll just be a minute,' she called.

She'd been going though photos to put on their website. Ever since she'd begun using social media, both donations and offers of help from volunteers had increased. Some of it could be used for rebuilding, but they still had running costs.

Leaving the last picture to upload, she unbolted the door. She let out a gasp as a hand was thrust across her face. Two men lifted her and carried her back down the corridor. They stuffed a gag in her mouth. She bucked and writhed in their arms, but they held firm.

Someone kicked a chair out from beside the ping pong table. They sat her in it and tied her arms around her back. She heard the door being shut and the bolts slotted home. Her heart was beating so fast she worried it might explode. The gag made it impossible to catch her breath. Three men stood in front of her. Two beefy ones and a third, tall and skinny, like a beanpole. Beanpole took a chair, then sat down opposite her.

'Take out the gag,' he said.

One of the men untied the gag. 'No point in screaming,' he said to her.

As soon as the gag was released, Lana screamed for her life. She knew she was in a church basement with walls four feet thick, but that was no reason not to try. Then came the slap. She'd not felt anything like it in her life. Her head was suddenly resting on her shoulder, and her neck felt like it had been snapped in half. She could taste blood in her mouth.

Beanpole said, 'She does it again, don't hesitate.'

'I won't, boss.'

'Look at me,' Beanpole said to Lana.

She was too scared to move. Not even her eyes would budge.

'Look at me!'

Terrified, she turned her neck and tried to focus. The tall

man was holding up a wallet with a picture of himself in it.

'Do you know what that is?' he said.

'I haven't got my glasses.' It was true. She'd left them next to the computer.

'It's my ID from the National Crime Agency. We're the good guys.' He folded it away.

'Funny way of showing it,' she said.

One of the henchmen glanced at him, but Beanpole let it slide. 'One of my colleagues came to see you earlier.'

Lana stared at him blankly.

He said, 'You don't need to confirm it. We followed her here.'

Lana remembered the conversation all too well. She still hadn't fully forgiven Steadman for bringing her.

Lana said, 'She asked me about some money that had been donated to our charity.'

The tall man nodded. 'Oh yeah? What did she want to know?'

'Where the money had come from.'

Beanpole shook his head. 'Was it illegal?'

'Of course not.'

'Tell me what she wanted.'

'I told you.'

The man who'd slapped her before raised his hand long enough for her to see it. Lana flinched and screamed. Then he brought it crashing into her face. It felt even worse than the first. Her wrists burned as she struggled against her restraints.

Why was she doing this, anyway, she asked herself? Why didn't she just tell them? She was protecting Rigby, but what would he say if he knew? He'd say don't be brave, give them what they want. He'd survive. She needed to save herself and Tiffy, and carry on the work she did for others.

Beanpole said, 'We have reason to believe that someone associated with this establishment is involved with money laundering. The person who came to see you may be involved too. Answer my questions truthfully, and we may be able to prevent you becoming implicated.'

Lana didn't believe him, and it didn't matter anyway. She'd made up her mind. 'She wanted to know ...'

'Yes?'

'She wanted ... she wanted to know if I'd been asked keep something safe.'

'Safe? For who, Rigby Goode?'

Lana nodded. Her neck went into cramp and she had to hold her head sideways. Her whole body tensed in agony.

'Could you straighten my neck?' she said.

'What?'

'Straighten my neck!'

One of the men pushed her chin up and back.

'Hold it there,' she said.

After a few seconds, the cramp subsided.

Beanpole said, 'She asked if Rigby Goode had asked you to keep something safe for him, is that right?'

Lana nodded.

'And what did you tell her?'

'Nothing.'

Beanpole looked disappointed. He could tell she was lying. Her body language probably screamed it. She was blinking so quickly she might have been walking through a sandstorm.

'You told her nothing?'

Lana was about to reply when the slap landed. She wasn't expecting it, and his hand caught her on the cheekbone. It felt like an entire hive of bees attacking at once.

'You sure about that?'

Lana shook her head. 'No.'

'No, what? No there's nothing to tell, or no you're not sure? Why are you making this so bloody difficult? What did Rigby ask you to keep?'

Lana hesitated, she knew that if she told them about the camera, she'd have to tell them about Tiffy, and the one thing she wanted more than anything else was to protect her daughter.

'It wasn't Rigby, it was Steadman Jones.'

He rolled his eyes. 'Okay, so what did Steadman Jones ask you to keep? Tell us now or my men will rip this place apart, and we'll leave you here for the rats.'

'A memory card, like in a camera,' she said.

'SD card,' one of the men said to the beanpole. 'Christ knows what's on it.'

'I can guess what's on it,' Beanpole said. He said to Lana, 'Where is it?'

'My daughter has it. It's in the camera that's part of her sculpture. But keep her out of this. I'll go and get it.'

'No. We'll go. Where is she? Where's the camera?'

'At home.'

'What's your address?'

'I don't want you talking to Tiffy!' Lana shouted.

It earned her another slap.

Beanpole grabbed her chin and spoke in baby-words, 'The nice lady and her nice daughter are going to help the nice officer stop the bad guys. We'll be sweet to her, like apple pie with a scoop of fucking ice-cream.'

Lana was crying now. Beanpole tapped her lightly on the cheeks. 'There's a good girl. You do not mention this to anyone, do you understand me? If we hear different, if it gets reported, we will be back, for you and your daughter. And next time we won't be so fucking sweet.'

'But what do I tell Steadman?' she sobbed. 'He wanted the camera too.'

'Tell him it got stolen at school.'

Beanpole nodded to his men. It was time for them to go. Almost as an afterthought, he said to her, 'How do you know those two losers anyway, Rigby and Steadman?'

Lana wasn't sure if it was a rhetorical question, and didn't reply. It earned her another slap.

One of the men shouted at her, 'When you're asked a question, you answer.'

'They come to meetings.'

Beanpole looked surprised. 'What meetings?'

'Self-help.'

'What, like AA. Or NA?'

She shook her head.

'What meetings, then?' Beanpole said.

It was the one things she knew she should never reveal. They held both AA and NA meetings at the church, and people were asked to respect anonymity, but this was different.

Suddenly, she felt the legs of her chair disappear from under her. She was falling backwards and could do nothing about it. The chair hit the ground with a crash and the back of her head smacked into the floor.

She shut her eyes and screamed in terror. When she opened them again, Beanpole was standing above her. 'Stop making it difficult and tell me. What fucking meetings do they come to?'

Lana was shaking so hard it was hard to get the words out. 'For peo ... suffer ... buse ...'

'What?' he said. 'Say it again.'

She took a couple of deep breaths, and almost screamed it at him. 'For people who have suffered abuse.'

Beanpole's face took on an expression like someone walking into a surprise party. He spun around his men, excited. 'Get onto CEOP, see what they know about this group. Say it's laundering or whatever, get some names.' He turned back to Lana. 'We're going to station a man outside for a few days, just to keep an eye on the place. If you see him, you are to have no interaction with him, do you understand me? You do not point him out to anyone else.'

She wouldn't need to, Lana thought, as they left. Frank and the others could do that for themselves.

Lana called after them, 'Hey!! Hey!! Aren't you going to untie me?!'

They ignored her. The door clicked closed.

Lana panicked at first. She thought she might die, writhing on the floor like an insect on a pin. Only once she began to run out of energy and became thirsty, did a deeper, more primitive survival instinct kick in. She stayed quiet and still, concentrating on her breathing, and lost track of time. At some point, she guessed, she must have passed out. She regained consciousness to discover a youth worker named Timothy, who did the night shift, untying her.

'Lana, Lana, are you alright?'

When she tried to reply, her throat hurt too much to speak.

'I'll get you some water,' he said. He held a bottle to her lips and she drank. She coughed, and when she tried again, the words came out in a croak. 'Thank God you came. I'll be okay, I think.'

'What happened?'

She remembered exactly what had happened. She also remembered how much the slaps hurt. 'Burglars. They jumped me as I came in.'

'I'll call the police.'

'No,' she insisted. 'What time is it?'

'8pm.'

More than enough time for them to get to her flat and retrieve the memory card. 'Oh my God, Tiffy must be worried sick.'

'Who's that?'

'My daughter. Could you fetch my phone – I think I might have left it in the kitchen.'

'No problem.'

As soon as he was out of earshot, she retrieved her ancient Nokia from her trouser zip pocket and dialled Rigby. A message said his phone was no longer working. She brought up Steadman's number, and was about to press to dial it, but then decided against it. Steadman would feel duty-bound to do something, and it could get him in trouble. Beanpole was NCA. Steadman had been in prison before. He was black. He wouldn't stand a chance.

Lana heard footsteps. Timothy was returning. When he arrived, she gave a shaky smile and showed him the phone. 'Silly me, I had it all along.'

'I ought to take you to the hospital,' he said.

'Nothing's broken,' Lana said, waving away the idea. 'Let me call Tiffy, make sure she's alright.'

19

Balorat detested anyone impinging upon his carefully thought-through schedule. So a request to meet Putts at an ungodly hour in a ghastly location, on a morning when he should be enjoying a leisurely breakfast at home before delivering a long-scheduled lecture to a group of second-year medical students, who would treat him with the reverence a man of his standing in the profession deserved, was wholly unwelcome. He knew what Putts wanted: help clearing up his latest catastrophe, the tosher on the run.

For so much of his adult life, he'd felt at the mercy of others. In the middle of the night, if one human being decided to terminate the existence of another human being, then he'd be dragged from his bed to examine the body and crime scene. Or if a judge in a case where he was waiting to give evidence decided, as judges often did, that nothing further would be heard on a given day, then he would be required to travel back to the same court the following day, no matter how far away it might be, and regardless of what else he might have planned. As a younger man, he'd put up with being jerked around. Not now. He treated every claim on his time like an imposition, especially when made by an idiot.

Tracking devices were getting smaller, and he took no chances. He'd taken a shower as soon as he rose, washed what was left of his hair and run an extra-fine-toothed comb through it, and then dressed in clothes bought the previous day on his way home from work, and which hadn't left their wrapping until he put them on. The arrangement was for him to park on Snowsfield and then walk into the tunnel at the top of Bermondsey Street, where it ran under London Bridge Station. At that time of the morning, there should only be the two of them. Nobody was capable eavesdropping on a conversation between two individuals in a tunnel at 6am, that nobody else knew was taking place, not even GCHQ.

He parked as instructed and set off to walk. It wasn't raining, but a driving wind chilled him. He fastened the buttons on his overcoat and tightened his tie. The mouth of the tunnel became visible and he ducked inside, hoping for protection from the squall, but it blew even harder, straight into his face. Despite the conditions, there was no mistaking Putts, with that bony frame swaying like a reed. Balorat remembered meeting him for the first time when Putts was a much younger man. He'd been the pathologist on a case involving the homicide of a young mobster. Putts stood out a mile – the dumbest in a bright bunch. From there he'd taken a well-trodden course to get to the top of his profession, one that didn't involve talent, dedication, skill or even particularly hard work. It was called breaking the law.

'Beautiful morning,' Putts said. Despite the events of the previous day, he still expected it to be civil.

'Would be if I wasn't here,' Balorat said.

'Give it a rest, we'll find the tosher. Sticks a spanner in the works, but ...'

'I'll stick more than that in you if anything goes wrong.'

'Never took you for that type, Vincent.'

Pathetic. Not even worth a response. 'How are we going to find him?'

'We have two choices. Stay conventional, or go nuclear.'

'Stop trying to be clever.'

Putts stared at him in fury, then his right hand plunged into a pocket. Balorat braced himself, thinking he might bring out a weapon. When it emerged, he was holding something very small between his thumb and index finger. Putts said, 'Two days ago, I might have taken that from you. Not now.'

Balorat leaned in closer. 'What is that?'

He gave a smile that made Balorat shudder. 'It's a record of everyone he's ever toshed.'

Balorat felt a sudden pang of jealousy. For all his fuck-ups, Putts had gone and produced something genuinely valuable. 'K never mentioned that.'

'You think I asked you here for tiddlywinks?'

The precautions now made sense, Balorat had to admit. 'Where did you get it?'

'Little bird gave it to me.'

He sounded almost superior. Balorat didn't like it when people got uppity. 'Stop gloating. You're like Gollum with a fucking ring.'

Before he could step back, Putts grabbed him and stuck a finger in his chest. 'This is just the beginning. There's other information that'll make Rigby beg to work with us. So no more back-channel. You want anything from K, you go through me.'

Balorat had no intention of taking orders from this clown. He reached for the hypodermic in his pocket with the super-fast sedative and flicked off the protective cap. Switching his hand around so he could strike like a hammer, he drew it out. Putts's eyes widened in disbelief. He took a step back, but it wasn't quick enough. Balorat lunged forward and sunk the hypo into Putt's thigh, then drove home the plunger.

Putts yelped and leapt back, the needle still stuck in him. He pulled it out and threw it at Balorat. 'You're insane! What the hell was in that?'

'Something to calm you down.'

'You drugged me! K's going to kill you for this.'

'She's not going to hear about it.'

'Oh yes she is.'

'No she's not, because if she does, then I'll have to tell her about how you lost that memory card.'

'Lost the card? What are you ...'

Balorat laughed as the shock of realisation registered on Putts's face.

He turned and began to run. The sedative would normally require a few minutes to take effect, but running would speed it up. Balorat walked calmly after him, watching Putts struggle toward the tunnel entrance. His legs slowed, his knees stiffened, his feet dragged behind him. He fell more than once, only to haul himself back up and, through sheer willpower, soldiered on. Balorat was impressed. He'd be able to report back to the manufacturer that the new formulation was indeed an improvement.

By the time they reached the tunnel mouth, Putts could barely put one foot in front of the other. Still, Balorat couldn't risk him getting into the open air. He flicked Putts's heels with his shoe. Putts stumbled forward a few steps before collapsing. Balorat put a foot on his head. Putts yelped, but the words were lost in traffic noise. Balorat stood over him for another minute, waiting for the sedative to take full effect. When he felt the muscles go limp, he picked up an arm and let it drop. No reaction. He put a hand over Putts's mouth and nose. Still breathing. All was as it should be, but the SD card was still in his grasp. Balorat prized open his fingers, slipped the card into his own wallet, then found Putts's phone and dialled 999.

'I was walking into a tunnel near London Bridge,' he told the emergency operator, 'and there was a body. I think he's still alive, but I'm no doctor.' He gave a detailed description of the location. 'I'll wait with him until they get here.'

He hung up, then rolled Putts into the recovery position and walked back down the tunnel, stripping the SIM from the phone as he went. An hour later, he emerged from his office at Guys Hospital, ready to give his lecture to the medical students. The SD Card was now safely hidden in the skull collection. Many floors beneath him, he guessed, in the ER, another set of doctors would be trying to bring Putts back to consciousness. There was a chance they'd run a tox screen and come back with a positive on Midazolam, at which point they could administer Flumazenil to counteract it. He'd be right as rain in a couple of hours.

Steadman's ingenuity never ceased to impress Rigby. Thirty-six hours after leaving Ludlow, deep in the middle of nowhere, he'd pulled over for a well-deserved rest and fired up the hub, eager to relax by reading something familiar and comforting. He'd gone to his favourite website, Cognoscenti, and settled down in his bunk to catch up on the bitchy comments that flew back and forth between the riders. He only knew them via their postings, but no-one held back; everything became personal and people revealed far more than they ever intended, so they felt like old friends, even though they'd never met in person and half of them lived in the USA. Someone whose name he didn't recognise had started a new thread called *The Terrors of Cotswold Hills*. That had to be a joke. The Cotswolds were hilly, certainly, but they weren't terrifying. For most of the Cognoscenti, cycling was all about the hills. They bragged about the times they'd set on Alpe d'Huez and other Tour-level ascents. The Cotswolds would be a weekend training run. The only person he'd ever met who found it 'terrifying' was Steadman.

Then it hit him. He rushed to open the thread, which had so far received no comments from other Cognoscenti, and began to read:

The most interesting thing you'll find on a trip around the Cotswolds, as a rider, is what's inside the houses. Kind of like my recent trip to Belgrade, where I went inside the house of an old colleague. His basement had pictures covering the walls, of everyone he'd ever worked with. Many of them, perhaps all of them, were now deceased. He'd been very successful, it seemed. Built up a huge business with some partners in England. I think it was a cleaning and removal service.

His head swam. He almost dropped the computer. The

message wasn't from Steadman, it was from Mesh, and he thought he understood it pretty well. She'd gone to Belgrade to track down Tudor Clarke. She'd gone to his house, and into his basement. She'd found pictures all over the walls. The people in the pics were dead. Could that be what was going on here, that Tudor Clarke was part of an organised gang who toshed and murdered for money? How would you even go about something like that? Put up a site on the dark web called clicktokill.onion?

So much for a relaxing afternoon. He had to find Ascott, and fast. His search so far had proved fruitless mainly because all the toshers over the years, himself included, had succeeded in erasing any trace of the man. But there was one critical piece of information that Rigby knew about Ascott which the others weren't privy to, even despite the media attention. The safe house in Bethnal Green wasn't a government property, it was a ruse put together by Putts, somehow involving Blenny the lunatic. He'd viewed the news footage over and over, and it had been edited by Putts's gang so that the location of the house was never revealed. That gave him an advantage. Putts didn't want other law enforcement officials to know the address, or they'd begin to ask questions. He, on the other hand, knew it off by heart.

The listing for the property at the Land Registry showed that the safe house was owned by a company named Antrobus Holdings. A due diligence search on Antrobus revealed that it was a wholly owned subsidiary of another company, Karivolam, registered in Panama. Even if Karivolam turned out not to be the ultimate owner, the idea that a house in Bethnal Green would be controlled through such a convoluted arrangement struck Rigby as suspicious. He Googled the name, expecting to find nothing, or at best an email. Instead, after scrolling through pages of unrelated links, he found a website. It was barely anything, a single page with an amateurish logo. It had been put together using a web template package. There were no contact options, and nobody seemed to have bothered with SEO. He wondered what the point of it was. It didn't advertise anything. Nobody would ever find it, unless they searched and searched, like he had, or keyed the actual URL into a browser. If they did either of those things, then they already knew as much as the website told them, so why have a website at all? About the only useful thing was an IP address, which he used to identify a location in Panama.

He suddenly felt hungry. The place he'd chosen to park was a sea beach in North Wales with a boat launch and a campsite. It seemed the sort of place where someone might spend a couple of days without anyone turning a hair, but at this time of year there was hardly anyone around. The temperature was barely into the teens, and the clouds hung heavy with rain. Boats on their trailers looked like they hadn't been out of the water for months. He shut down his computer and the hub, and walked to a fishing tackle and general store a quarter mile back up the road. The man behind the counter eyed him strangely as he bought a disposable barbecue, a pack of sausages, and a loaf of bread. Had he been recognised, or was it just paranoia? As he walked back to the camper, he felt as though there were eyes watching him from multiple directions. At a house overlooking the road, he was sure he could see a figure at the window. A Land Rover passed him on the road and the driver took a long look at him, first through the rearview, then the wing mirror. Rigby decided it was all in his head. It had to be. No-one knew he was here. The picture in the media hadn't been high quality. The sat hub was next-to-untraceable.

He set off down to the beach. Despite the wind, which had picked up strongly after dusk, he managed to light the barbecue, and watched the wind etch patterns into the water's pelt, as the coals turned to grey. Half sausages disappeared in what seemed like seconds. He hadn't realised that he was so famished. The clouds had scattered, leaving a bright, starlit night. He walked back to the van feeling satisfied and ready for sleep. Climbing into a bunk at the back, he was soon dreaming deeply.

It was still pitch black when he woke with a start. He checked his phone: 4am. A car had pulled in next to him. The engine was running, but when he peered out the window he couldn't see anything. Headlights off? Why? As he waited, listening, his heart pounding, three more cars arrived.

A few seconds later a torch tracked around inside the Transit.

Probably the police, he guessed. They didn't like people sleeping in cars.

Then came was a sharp rap on one of the windows.

'Anyone in there?'

Rigby thought about replying, then held his breath. If they were cops, would they have switched their headlights off?

Another rap. 'Hello!'

Desperate to gain an advantage, he leapt out of bed and, in a single motion, grabbed the keys off the table and pitched himself over the front bench into the driver's seat. He turned the key. The engine coughed but didn't catch.

A side window shattered.

He cranked the key again, goosing the gas. Nothing.

'Get out of there!' someone yelled.

One last try. The engine caught. Rigby almost whooped for joy. He threw it in reverse and stood on the accelerator. Tyres squeaked. Men shouted. A gun fired.

Shoving it into first, he cranked the steering, heading for what he thought might be the other side of the parking area. Hearing shots behind him, he shoved it again into reverse and hit the accelerator, then forward again, spinning the wheel.

Thinking that he might be headed toward the exit, he switched on the headlights, but what he saw in front of him made his heart sink. Three cars had been parked alongside each other, blocking the way. Standing in front of the cars was half a dozen men, holding an assortment of weaponry. The headlights of the three cars came on, and the men began walking towards him.

He hit the pedal. The Transit leapt forward and as the men jumped out of the way he swerved hard to avoid going straight into the cars. Ahead, a dirt strip looked like it might offer a way to go around the back of them, and then out to the road. He headed for it, but as soon as the van left the asphalt it stopped with a jolt. The steering went dead. He tried to reverse out, but the wheels spun. The strip he'd driven onto wasn't dirt, he realised, but loose sand. He was beached.

Before he could open the door to run, torches surrounded him. More glass shattered. A voice yelled, 'Get out!'

Rigby glanced to his left. A gun was pointing at him through the broken window. Slowly, he opened the door and stepped down.

'Keep your hands where we can see them.'

Another set of torches arrived on the other side. He put his hands up. A second later, they cuffed him. He felt a shove in his back.

'Move.'

A stupider man, Balorat thought, would feel honoured to be invited to K's pad in Orme Square, a gated cul-de-sac of white stucco mansions on the Bayswater Road, opposite Kensington Gardens. That she would risk her own security by inviting them over could mean only one thing: trouble.

Her doorman was dressed in a black T-shirt, despite the freezing wind, his earpiece and gun holster clearly on show. Anyone passing by would have assumed the property belonged to an oligarch, or a deposed dictator. None would have suspected that, only a few years ago, its owner had been trudging to work through The City like millions of others, sitting in an office cubicle, attending dull meetings and lunching on overpriced sandwiches. The doorman asked him for ID. He examined it, then double-checked it with someone else over walkie-talkie. Satisfied, he opened the door.

Putts had already arrived. He was standing in the living

room with a pathetic grin on his face and what looked to Balorat like a glass of sherry in his hand.

'Christmas is it?' Balorat called from the hallway. 'Auntie Mabel coming?'

'Good evening, Vincent,' Putts said, still wearing his stupid smile.

'You told her?'

'Of course I told her.'

'Coward.'

A woman came behind him and pulled off his overcoat, hanging it in a closet in the hall. Balorat grunted his thanks. A butler stood in the corner, next to a Victorian drinks trolley. It matched other antiques in the room, all from the same period. Then, completely at odds with rest, what Balorat could only describe as a ghastly piece of modern art dominated the long wall. Next to the butler stood K, crunching a stick of celery. Her grey cashmere pantsuit hugged her figure, and as she turned to fetch something from the trolley, he couldn't help but admire her curves.

'Can we fix you a drink, Vincent?' K said.

'Scotch.'

'Any particular brand?'

'Decent malt. Or is it girls' drinks night?'

Putts laughed. 'Oh boy, are you in for some fun.'

K said, 'I have a twenty-five year old Dalmore.'

'Sounds perfect.' He caught Putts watching him. 'What?'

'Nothing,' he said, unable to conceal a smirk.

The butler handed him his drink. K raised her martini. 'Santé.'

She drank half then set it down. Balorat sipped his whisky. It was exquisite.

K said, 'I think we know why we're here, gentlemen. There's been some difficult behaviour of late.'

'Don't blame me,' Putts said.

'Why not?' Balorat growled.

'I discovered valuable information.'

'And I'm keeping it safe for you,' Balorat added. He tried to stifle a laugh but it came out anyway.

'This is what I mean,' K said, impatiently. 'Baiting and sniping. You're like a couple of bull elephants.'

'And an elephant never forgets,' Putts said to Balorat, icily.

'Who are you, the king of fucking cliché?'

'Enough!' She held her arms aloft. 'This is where it stops. Right here. Put your drinks down.'

Neither man moved.

'Down, I said!'

The two eyed each other, placing their drinks on side tables.

'You're going to kiss and make up.'

'Okay,' Balorat said, 'I'm *sor*-ry.'

'Thank you, Vincent. Mark?'

Putts laughed. 'Whatever. We're wasting time.'

'Say it!'

'I'm sorry.'

'Very good. Now kiss.'

The two men exchanged a nervous glance. 'Sod that,' Balorat said.

Her face hardened. 'Kiss!'

'I'm not doing it,' Balorat said.

'Yes you are.'

'Not for all the tea in China.'

'Now who's the king of fucking cliché, Vincent?' Putts said.

'You too!' she said to Putts. 'Pucker up!'

'No. Fucking. Way,' Balorat said. He picked up his Scotch and knocked it back, ready to march out.

K stepped forward to block his path, then reached out and swept the glass from his hand. It shattered against a coffee table. 'Think you're clever, do you? Putting your colleague in the hospital? Using prescription drugs that could be traced back to you?'

'Told you she wasn't happy,' Putts said.

'And you,' she said, swinging around to him, 'taking weeks to turn this tosher.'

'I've got him in the palm of my hand,' Putts said, calmly.

'Oh, please,' Balorat groaned.

'He's on his way to the farm right now.'

Balorat spun around. 'You *found* him?'

'So this where it stops, gentlemen,' K said. 'We're finally getting on top of this situation. The biggest risk factor now is your bickering.'

'We're going there,' Putts said, 'to seal the deal.'

His smile grew an inch wider as he said it. Balorat wanted to put his foot through the mouth.

'We need you to come with us,' K said to him.

He didn't like the sound of that. The farm had been Putts's idea. 'When?'

'Now.'

'*What?* I can't just leave.'

No wonder Putts had been wearing that smug grin all evening. He'd arrived early and spilled his news. They'd had time to cook this up together.

Balorat said, 'What am I going to tell Sylvie?'

'Got you on a tight leash, huh?' Putts laughed. 'But you like that, right?'

'Should have finished you off in the tunnel,' Balorat hissed.

'Can you call her?' K said. 'Make something up.'

Sure, *K*, anything you want, *K*. 'Of course, but she worries. Loves me too much, that girl. Always has.'

K shrugged, 'It's okay if you can't make it. Mark can do it just as well.' She gave a little smile. Just to rub it in, Balorat thought.

'Alright, I get it,' he snarled. 'What's the job?'

'We'll brief you in the car,' Putts said. 'But get this straight, the party's over. From now on we do it my way.'

Balorat looked to K for a correction. She gave a tiny nod.

Fuck!

20

Dawn broke over the rolling hills as a band of solid indigo, interrupted only by dust clouds from a convoy of cars travelling at speed along an unpaved road. The general stink of the men, and their overnight breath, already had Rigby in agony, and now the pollen and sprays from the fields began assaulting his eyes and nose. He sneezed uncontrollably. Snot flew down over his lips and onto his chin, but with hands in cuffs he couldn't wipe himself.

'Can I get a tissue or something?' he said.

Benjy, who was sitting next to him, curled a lip at the mucus pasted across his face. 'Lick it.'

Rigby tried his best, stretching his tongue as far as it would go, but it wouldn't reach.

'Come on, help me out here. Even a towel.'

'You're not my problem.'

Furious, Rigby pressed his face into Benjy's jacket and rubbed back and forth.

'Fucking pig!' Benjy shoved him hard into the door.

'Ouch!' Rigby said, as his head hit the window.

'Knock it off!' came a voice from the front. It was Maddox, who Rigby had learned was the boss of the operation. He was on the small side and lean, but with bulging muscles that suggested a lot of gym work, and curly red hair – the *skullpube redhead* he'd seen at the Decades Club. 'What's your problem?' he said to Benjy.

If this had been a gangster movie, Rigby thought, Benjy might have had the nickname 'Babyface'. He was chubbier and younger than the others, with close-set brown eyes, freckles and straw-coloured hair. He also had agonising – for Rigby – halitosis.

'Bitch wiped his nose on me.'

Rigby said, 'How about taking the cuffs off? I'm hardly going anywhere.'

Maddox thought for a moment, then nodded at Benjy. 'Do it.'

'Boss,' Benjy complained.

'Do it. We're almost there anyway.'

Ten miles later, his face cleaned, Rigby spotted a grain silo next to a breeze-block building with a corrugated roof, and a couple of minutes later they parked next to a row of tractors and threshers. His door was opened and Benjy shoved him out. He felt queasy and unsteady on his feet.

As Rigby waited with the rest of the men, Maddox went inside one of the barns. A freezing easterly wind whipped across the open plain and everyone gazed longingly toward the doorway, praying for Maddox to return and let them in. Eventually, a door slid; light flickered across the asphalt. Maddox came out again, flanked by a much taller man, draped in a long overcoat.

Rigby felt an immediate rush of fury. His fists balled and he began marching forward, but hands grabbed his arms and held him back.

As he came closer, Putts raised a palm in apology. 'I know you're angry, but hear me out.'

'Hear me, Putts. I know what you want, and you can fuck yourself.'

As angry as he was, Rigby also felt strangely relieved. When the men had apprehended him, he hadn't been sure who they worked for, Putts or Modplod. Right now, it was probably better to be in the hands of the bad guys. At least the bad guys wanted something he could give them. Modplod only wanted Ascott, and Rigby was no closer to knowing where he was.

With his long legs kicking out, Putts strode straight past the group towards a farmhouse on the other side of the parking area. 'Bring him,' he called to the men.

Maddox led Rigby across to the farmhouse and took him inside. The first thing he noticed was how cosy and quaint it felt – a world away from the armed goons who'd brought him here. With its flowery wallpaper and the smell of wood smoke, it reminded him of his grandmother's cottage. It even had the same layout, with a corridor leading from the front door down the middle of the house, and rooms on either side.

His head swam. He waited in the hall, as instructed, glad not to have to go any further. After a few minutes, Putts stuck his head out from a doorway and beckoned them through to a sitting room. Stuffed armchairs surrounded an iron hearth. A fire burned peacefully. Rigby felt like he was going to be sick.

Putts said, 'Have a seat. Relax.'

Maddox glared at him like sitting wasn't an option. Dreading having to roast in front of the fire, he settled into one of the chairs.

Putts said, 'I bet you could use a drink.'

'Triple espresso,' Rigby replied, automatically.

'I meant something convivial. Whisky? Cognac?'

Before he could reply, Putts walked behind him to a drinks cabinet. Two glasses were filled with ice. Liquid poured. Putts came around and put a glass into Rigby's hand. He clinked it with his own. 'Knock it back. You'll feel better.'

Rigby took a sip. It was sweet and cold. He took a larger gulp and almost coughed it back up.

Putts laughed. 'Always were a lightweight.'

Setting the glass on the table, with no intention of picking it up again, Rigby said, 'You can try anything you want, but it's not going to change my answer.'

Putts took a long swig then looked at him over the rim of the glass, his expression hardening. 'We're past the time of choices. So let's just have a drink. Two old friends.'

Rigby couldn't believe what he was hearing. 'You are completely deluded.'

Putts let out a laugh, but Rigby wasn't even sure if he

was paying attention. He stared into the fire, deep in his own thoughts.

At length, Putts said, 'One thing about you always puzzled me.'

'Only one?'

'I could never work out why you left the NCA. Techie like you, with all those toys to play with. A noble purpose. No family nagging you to spend time at home. Okay, the pay is rotten, but you never seemed that interested in money. So why?'

'I couldn't stand the people.'

'Feeling's mutual,' Maddox muttered from the corner. He was still standing guard, gun in hand.

Putts rounded on him. 'I'd like you to leave. This conversation is privileged.'

Maddox's eyes narrowed and flicked towards Rigby.

'He's not going to try anything,' Putts said.

Maddox departed, closing the door firmly behind him.

When he'd gone, Putts said, 'We don't need the world to know our little secrets, do we.'

'Your little secret?' Rigby said. 'You mean the click-to-kill service you've been running out of the NCA? Is that what happened to Ascott? Is he at the bottom of the Thames? If you think I'm going to be Clarke's replacement, think again.'

Putts's eyes narrowed momentarily. He seemed surprised that Rigby knew as much as he did. 'Clarke got greedy. Started trying to boss us around. Look, we need a tosher, you're the best candidate, simple as. We're not asking you to kill anyone. All you have to do is pretty much what you do now.'

Rigby didn't have to think about it. 'No,' he said firmly.

Putts shrugged. 'Okay, we'll do it the hard way.'

Why was he so damned sure of himself? 'For fuck's sake, Mark, there's got to be other people that can do this for you. I can help you find one.'

'I thought you were refusing to help me,' Putts said, dismissively.

'I'm not going to join your team. But it could be what was like before. I provided the leads but you did the arrests.'

'And we locked up some serious scum.'

'Exactly,' Rigby said. He seemed to be getting somewhere.

Putts set his glass down on the table then picked it up again, downed the drink in one, then put it down. 'Nice try.'

'Mark, be reasonable ...'

'No!' Putts said, standing up, towering over Rigby. 'Get it through your head. This is not a negotiation.'

He left the room.

As Rigby wondered where he was going, he felt a chill come over him. He slid closer to the fire and warmed his hands. Maybe Putts was going to fetch someone. During his tour of Wales he'd reached the conclusion that there had to be a mastermind, somewhere. A conspiracy of the scale he was imagining would take a greater intellect than Putts to conceive and organise. He'd always been one of those people about whom others asked, 'Putts, eh, how's he done so well?' And Rigby remembered trying to explain: 'He's great at letting other people think they're in charge. He does the whole loyal, dependable thing. It's why the brass like him. He lets them be master.' That had to be the case here, too. So who was master?

The door swung open. A woman entered, with Putts trailing behind. Rigby had his answer. She was in her mid-thirties, dressed in jeans and a cashmere roll-neck, with an athletic build, and a face that was impossible to forget: round with wide, bright grey eyes, and dark straight hair cut at an angle across her face. She carried a brown leather satchel. He didn't think they'd ever met before, but there was something very familiar in the way that Putts followed at a distance, just as he used to trail along behind the Director-General, or any of the various Deputy Directors, on the rare occasions that any of them deigned to come down to the Sweatbox.

She looked Rigby up and down, her face betraying no

particular opinion. 'So this is the tosher?'

'He does amazing things,' Putts said.

'I've heard a lot about you,' she said to Rigby. 'You can call me K.'

As she spoke, he listened hard to her accent, hoping to gain some sort of insight into her. To his frustration, it was completely neutral. She could have been from anywhere.

'Kay?'

'Like the letter.'

'How mysterious,' he said, unimpressed.

'There's no mystery about your situation,' she shot back. 'Here's the deal: work with us, or Mark goes back to London with these.' She took from her satchel an SD card and a laptop. 'Recognise them? The card shows clear as day what you knew from day one: that you were the one who toshed those six names that Mesh Kaur found. They were never part of witness protection. You knew that all along.'

'No I didn't, they were just on my list to process. I never questioned it.'

'Try getting a jury to believe it. And this,' she said, holding up the laptop, 'is the one taken from your office. And again, clear as day, it shows that you toshed Frederick Ascott, national security asset and fugitive.' She turned to Putts. 'How many years will he get for this, Mark, realistic guess?'

Putts shrugged. 'Multiple counts of conspiracy. Potentially, conspiracy to murder. The CPS would ask for life in prison as a start.'

Before Rigby could raise an objection, K said, 'Let me tell you what we really want.

We're upscaling. Clients love our process. They ask me all the time – how can we take it to the next level? I'll tell you how. We need more toshers. We asked Tudor Clarke to train some. At first he refused, then, with a little persuasion, he came around, but then he started demanding money. When we said no, he threatened us. We called his bluff. Next thing we knew half a dozen old names mysteriously turn up on an NCA computer. You know the rest.'

Could that be all they wanted, really? 'That's what this is about, *training*?'

'We need a dozen or so, who can do what you do. Once they're in place, you go back to your old life.'

'You're insane, both of you,' Rigby said. 'Completely fucking insane.'

K turned to Putts. 'I don't think I like his tone.'

Putts shook his head. 'Me neither.'

'So what are you going to do about it?'

Putts shrugged. 'As we discussed.'

His feigned nonchalance sickened Rigby. 'Oh, so cool, Mark,' he said. 'Do whatever you want. I'm never going to work for you.'

He barely had time to get the words out of his mouth before he became aware of movement behind him. Turning to look, he saw only Benjy's boyish face and the blur of an arm as it reached around to grab him. A hand covered his mouth, and then a forearm slipped under his chin and jerked him backwards. He tried to stay on his feet, but he couldn't keep up. He was dragged, gasping for breath, out of the farmhouse. Maddox led the way, barking orders. As they passed the cars, a gate opened and the hard surface gave way to mud. They pushed him down and he fell hard on his shoulder.

'Get in there!' Benjy shouted, pointing towards a tin tube, which he knew from the shape and the stench of animal urine was a pigsty. It was his worst nightmare, scratchy straw and an intense stench, but he was going in, one way or the other. He took the easy option, falling to his knees and crawling inside. They pushed a crate against the end of the sty, blocking the light. He knew better than to push it away and try to run. That would only give them an excuse to beat him.

21

Lying in the stinking straw, Rigby could hear screaming. It was faint and intermittent. At first, he thought – hoped – that it was a fox. They often made noises that were scarily human. But the more he listened to it, the more convinced he became that words were mixed with the wails. It wasn't a child, either; the voice was too deep. This was an adult, and probably male. The longer it went on, the more compelled he felt to go the person's assistance. He began kicking against the tube, feeling trapped and powerless, like an infant wrapped in too many clothes.

As his legs began to ache, his kicking slowed. He forced himself to take a few deep breaths. Once his rage had passed, he began to go over what he knew so far, trying to formulate some kind of plan for when they let him out. Putts, he guessed, had been running his service for years. He'd used Clarke to do the toshing, and they probably had other people on the payroll to take care of the physical evidence. It could make for one hell of a lucrative business. Putts had been at the NCA long enough to have built up organized crime connections, so there'd be no shortage of uses for the service – extortion, narcotics, blackmail, people trafficking, murder.

It also seemed obvious, now, how they'd tracked him to the lake: the website for Karivolam, the company which was the ultimate owner of the house in Bethnal Green, must have been bait. A spyware payload had been downloaded as soon as he'd landed on it, and they'd used that to track him. The website had appeared to have no real function – but maybe that *was* its function, to paint a digital target onto anyone who found their way to it, like the explosive dye they put in cash delivery boxes.

No matter how he looked at it, whatever K wanted, whatever 'training' meant, it would be a one-way ticket to hell. So long as he was useful they'd keep him alive, but once that usefulness had passed he'd be dispensable. Rigby had met people like K before. Some of his clients, he had to admit, had psychopathic tendencies, but she was the real deal. Letting him go back to his old life was a mirage.

The cool of the morning gave way to a warmer day, and as the temperature climbed, the sty became unbearably hot. He'd had nothing to drink since arriving except a glass of spirits, and now his throat felt like sandpaper. Some time later, the crate was pushed aside. It was almost dark when they hauled him out again. He clamoured for water. One of the guards threw a wet sponge at him.

'Clean yourself up.'

Instead of rubbing his face, Rigby sucked hard at it, wringing it in his mouth to get every last drop of moisture. Then three of them pulled him out and onto his feet, and marched him in the direction of the barn opposite the farmhouse. He walked slowly, dreading what he might face when he arrived. The guards kept shoving him in the back, trying to hurry him along. When they reached the barn, Putts slid open the door and they went in. It was freezing inside. Rigby shivered. They'd arrived in a small office area, with tables covered in computer equipment, all unused. Another room lay beyond, where K stood waiting with Putts.

As he entered, she said, 'Did you have a chance to think about our offer?'

'Yes. And I'm not the educator type.'

K's face fell. She turned to Putts, shaking her head. 'Maybe he's not as intelligent as you said he was. Time to show him.'

'Show me what?' Rigby said, his pulse picking up.

They led him through into the next room.

Putts called, 'Balorat … Where are you?'

Rigby remembered hearing that name before. Putts had mentioned him. A pathologist. That made sense, they needed someone to bury evidence.

A voice answered back, 'We're in the stable.'

Rigby felt a shove in his back. He followed the others through to an indoor paddock with rows of small stables. The walls were only about four feet high, with metal gates at the front to let the animals in and out. This was a pig farm, he realised. In the first stable, on his left, sat a man in a chair with a hood over his head and his trousers rolled up to his knees, exposing his calves. The hood was superfluous – Rigby took one look at his boat shoes and knew who he was.

'That's Ascott,' he said, surprised and strangely deflated. 'You had him all along.'

Putts laughed. 'Had him? It was his idea.'

Standing next to the chair was a short man in his late fifties, Rigby guessed, with thinning red hair, skin transparent as paper, and a face like an ugly rabbit. He knew this must be Balorat. He held in his hand a device like a giant hole punch, with a rubber brace on one side and a long needle on the other. Pulling on the handles, he opened the jaws of the contraption and placed it on Ascott's leg, just below his knee.

'This is just a demonstration,' Balorat said. 'But if I'm right, the intelligence community is going to thank me. They waterboarded Khalid Sheikh Mohammed one-hundred and eighty-three times at Guantanamo, and hardly got anything out of him. You can't tell me that's efficient. We need better ways to trick the brain. What I'm doing here is compressing the deep peroneal nerve. It causes the subject to lose control of their foot.' He let a hand flop in the air to mimic the effect. 'The mind panics. Why have I lost control? Am I *dying*? That's when they're vulnerable, when the only way out is to talk.'

Balorat pretended to squeeze the handles together and Ascott gave a fake howl of agony.

'What are you trying to prove?' Rigby said. 'Am I next?

Go ahead, do your worst. I told you already, I'm not going to work for you.'

'We don't need another test subject,' Balorat said. 'We already did one last night. Filmed it and everything. Worked perfectly.'

Rigby felt another shove. He almost lost his balance, and staggered a few feet to the right. When he'd got it back, he found himself standing in front of the next stable in the row. In a corner, lying in a heap, was a man. Just as he'd recognised Ascott by his boat shoes, this time he recognised Frank, from Lana's support group, by his blue Adidas tracksuit. Rigby's heart fell. The screams must have been his. He ran over and put a hand on him, to see if he was still alive.

'Frank? Are you okay?' Rigby said. 'What did they do to you?'

Frank flinched and grunted, trying to roll away, but he was pressed up against a brick wall.

'Go away!' Frank shouted. 'Fucking filth. This is what they do.'

Rigby turned, furious. 'What have you done to him? He's got nothing to do with this!'

'He's not hurt,' Balorat called from the next stable. 'He's just a bloody wimp.'

'Vincent …' Putts said to him in a warning tone.

'What?' Balorat jeered back. He snickered. 'I barely touched him, he pissed his knickers and spilled the beans.'

'*Vincent!*' K snapped.

This time, Rigby watched in amazement as the pathologist cowered.

'Told you what?' Rigby said to K. 'Told you *what?*'

'I never told them nothing!' Frank yelled.

Putts took a few steps forward towards the sty, leaning on the posts either side of the gate. His face wore a satisfied smile, as if this were a moment he'd been looking forward to for a long time. 'Like I said, Rigby. I always wondered why you left the Agency. Now I get it. It was poor bastards like him. You felt sorry for them. You used to go to those meetings, listen to their stories. You got angrier and angrier. And for all the good stuff you were doing with CEOP, it didn't come close to what you really wanted, which was to take revenge, for them, and for yourself.'

'Not revenge,' Rigby said, quickly.

'Of course it was. You can try to call it something else, but why not be honest. You couldn't just sit there, week after week, listening to them.'

There was truth in what he said. Sitting in meetings listening to other victims' stories had made him angry, but it was nothing compared to what happened outside. 'Over fifty thousand sexual offences against children under sixteen every year, about seven thousand of which are rapes of kids under thirteen,' he shot back at him. 'And one in three gets reported.'

Putts nodded. He knew the figures. 'That's it, boy. You let it out. It made you sick to your guts. Frank told us all about it. How once you and Steadman had the idea, you went around the meetings recruiting. You found Gloria and Warren, and convinced them to come in with you. You even left the filth. Frank liked you after that.'

So that was why Frank kept a lookout, Rigby realised. He thought they were a righteous band of outlaws. How could he have known that the strongest evidence they uncovered went straight to CEOP?

'Scared of his own shadow, that one,' Balorat said.

'You work with this subhuman?' Rigby said to Putts and K, pointing at Balorat. He turned to the pathologist. 'I bet you loved it. Did you get him to tell you exactly what happened to him? Did it get you off?'

Balorat shook his head. 'I don't like rape. They have to want it. But by nine or ten, they know what they're doing.'

Rigby tried to use the stable wall as a pivot and launch himself toward Balorat, but before he could make it out of the door, Maddox's fist collided with his face. He crumpled, holding his nose, and sank to his knees.

'Get him up,' K barked. Rigby felt a pair of hands under each arm.

'We'll bring them in here, one by one,' K said to Rigby. 'All of your little group. Steadman. Gloria. Warren. Interrogate them. Humiliate them. You idiots tell each other everything.' She pointed to Frank. 'He used to record you.'

'What?' Rigby said.

K held up a phone. 'This is his.' She put it on speaker. Rigby heard his own voice. He remembered saying the words. It was from his chair at Lana's.

'...it never really occurred to me that this was something that could happen, or that it was something I needed to be careful of. I just did what everyone else did. I went to school, I played football and made dens and threw rocks at wasps. And I was a boy scout.'

Rigby felt himself tightening. His throat went dry. 'Shut it off,' he croaked.

'Why?' she said. 'We all felt so sorry for you.' She pressed play.

'...We used to go camping. The father of one of the other lads organised it. We were in this campsite, and there must be about fifteen families. There were no women allowed, it was just for the fathers and sons. We were doing all the usual stuff, and the dads drank beer, and we made barbecues, and smores. I knew what was going to happen with my dad, because it didn't matter what the occasion was ...'

'Shut it off!' Rigby shouted. 'Shut it off!' He fought to get to K, grab the phone, smash it to pieces, but Maddox and Benjy still had hold of his arms.

'Most people went to their tents with their fathers. I went by myself 'cos my dad was gonna stay up and get blind drunk. I didn't care, I was used to it. I got into my sleeping bag and went to sleep. In

the morning I woke up, and there in the tent with me, looking at me, was one of the other dads, this little arsehole called Royston Tring. He was the one who organised the camping. Strange-looking man with a shiny bald head and this constant fucking grin, and he looked at me through his little glasses. He says, "We had a lot of fun last night." And it all came back to me. I thought I'd had a nightmare about someone pissing in my mouth ...

'How dare you,' Rigby said. 'How fucking dare you...'

'Tring says to me, 'This has to be our secret. If the other boys find out, they'll call you a poof. Just trust me. Do what I say, and I can protect you.'

K fast-forwarded.

'I found my Dad snoring, his head against a log, with an empty bottle of Jack Daniels nearby.'

'There's plenty more,' K said. 'We listened to the whole thing. And who can blame you, after hearing that, for being such a weirdo.'

Rigby flinched. She really didn't comprehend. She'd listened to it, probably more than once, extracting whatever she needed, but not understanding any of it. 'What happened to me is terrifyingly fucking normal,' he said quietly, forcing himself to stay in control. 'It's as common as cancer.'

K seemed not to have heard him. She was smiling now, convinced that she was taunting him. 'Can't stand to be touched. Get the disinfectant out the minute you see a speck of dirt. That's pretty weird stuff.'

His head dropped into this hands. Was it even worth responding? He looked up and said, 'It's unrelated. I'm mild Asperger's. What, you think everyone who's been abused turns out to be some King Jeremy the Wicked? We all shoot up schools or become serial killers?'

K nodded. 'Or internet vigilantes. Just like your friends. We know all about Gloria and her uncles, how they used to share her around. And Warren, wow, that foster home he grew up in.'

'Enough!' Rigby shouted, before he could stop himself.

'And what about Steadman? What about that. How bizarre. Doing it with his sister and filming it, that's some kinky shit.'

'It's not kinky, their mother was schizophrenic,' Rigby said, shaking with anger. 'Leave them out. They don't deserve any of this.'

'That's up to you. We can haul them all in here, make them relive it. We can film them, stick their videos on YouTube. They'd be overnight sensations – True Confessions of the Abused – it would get millions of hits. People are such sick fucks. But none of that has to happen.'

'Like to see you try that with Gloria,' Rigby said.

'Livewire is she?' Balorat said. 'Sounds like fun.'

'Shut up, Vincent,' Putts snapped.

K said, 'Rigby, listen to me. The abused become abusers, you and I know that. CEOP know that. It won't be hard to establish with a jury. How hard do you think it's going to be for us to dummy up evidence? Mark's men can insert fingerprints into files, Vincent can sign off DNA analyses. This isn't a threat or a bluff, it's a reality. Steadman, Warren, Gloria ... we'll make sure CEOP prosecutes *them* for paedophilia, unless you cooperate.'

Rigby blinked. Hard. He knew she meant it. With anyone else, even with Putts, it might be a bluff, but not with her. He took a deep breath and let it out very, very slowly. 'Let Frank go,' he said. 'Then we'll talk.'

There would be thousands of people, millions, including probably every member of every jury he might ever stand in front of, who would not understand what he was doing. But it was clear as day to Rigby. He had to stop them, and to do so meant becoming one of them, so that he could find a way, somehow, to put an end to it.

Despite a policy of hot-desking at Pangolin, individuals tended to sit at the same picnic table, and often in the same groups. Warren and Gloria had few friends in common, and usually parked themselves on opposite sides of the office. That they'd been sitting together for the past two hours, and had claimed a table entirely for themselves – telling anyone who tried to join them to piss off – caused more than a few tongues to wag. Not that they were paying much attention. The trail to Bethnal Green was far more interesting.

'Let's go through it again,' Warren said, 'from the top.'

Gloria sighed. 'We've done "from the top" twice already.'

'Okay. Just one more time. Land Registry shows that the property is owned by Antrobus Holdings.'

Gloria nodded, and went to her own notes. 'And Antrobus is a wholly owned subsidiary of a Panamanian company called Karivolam.' Odd name, she thought. What language would that be from? It didn't immediately conjure up any association.

Warren said. 'You checked all of this. What else does Antrobus own?'

She *had* checked it. Thoroughly. Being asked about it again made it seem almost like he didn't trust her, and that would be an *issue*. She might be the newest person on the team, but he worked client side, so who was he to start questioning her? 'A few other properties in England.'

'He could be at one of those.'

She shrugged. 'Why?'

'They could have captured him.'

There was no way Gloria would believe that. If there was one thing certain in her mind, it was that Rigby was many times cleverer than any of them. 'That's conjecture.'

'He sent Mesh that email, but he didn't respond to her reply.'

'He'll reply when he feels like it,' she insisted, but Warren had a point. It troubled all of them that Rigby seemed to have initiated contact, and then immediately disappeared.

Warren said, 'There's another thing that bothers me.'

Gloria took a deep breath, making no attempt to hide her frustration. 'What's that, Sherlock?'

'Karivolam. It's an amateur site, made using a template. You know, the kind you get free when you register a domain name.'

'And?'

'And it's easy to hack them.'

He waved her over to take a look at another PC he had running. On the screen were bar graphs and lists of IP addresses. 'I got inside and looked at the analytics for site visitors. All they ever get is bounce traffic – people who go there by mistake and they stay about a second or two, and then leave.'

Gloria scanned the data. It corroborated what he was saying. 'So?'

'So why have a site at all? I mean, what's the point?'

She shrugged. 'Everyone has a site. It's just something companies do.'

'Unless it's there for another reason. In this case, to attract one special visitor.' He pointed to a line graph near the bottom of the screen. The line was consistently flat, hovering just above zero, except for two tall, sharp spikes, one halfway along the graph and one at the end. He pointed to the one in the middle. 'That, right there, is a single visitor, staying on the site for half an hour. And it took place right around the time that Mesh posted that letter on the cycling website.'

Gloria felt goosebumps rising on her arms. She was surprised, it didn't happen often. 'Think that was him?'

Warren nodded. He pointed to the spike at the end. 'That's us, right now. And he would have followed the same leads we did.'

Gloria pulled up the Karivolam site on her own laptop.

She let it sit for a minute, then opened a command window. Code began appearing in it; the same string, over and over.

'What's that?' Warren said.

'The site's trying to cookie me. I use a cookie blocker, but it keeps sending it.'

'So what? Most sites try to load cookies.'

'Not like this one.' She opened another command window and typed something in.

A warning flashed up on Warren's screen, asking if he would accept a cookie.

'Hah!' Gloria said. 'Thought so.'

'What?'

'I sent it to you. It's a location identifier. The Karivolam site hits you with it the moment you land.'

The two of them looked at each other. She grabbed his computer and opened another command window. This time, she copied and pasted a long strong of code. 'Now, let's see if we can return the favour.'

They waited a few minutes while nothing happened. Warren was about to offer to get coffee when his computer bleeped.

'Hello world,' she said.

She typed into the command window and his screen changed to a map. A red dot appeared in the middle of Buckinghamshire.

'What is that?' he said. They zoomed in. 'Nearest town is Quainton. Must be a farm or something.'

She said, 'Where's that list of what they own?'

He pulled it up. They both scanned it.

'There!' he said. 'Bresnock Farm, Quainton. Let's call Steady.'

Gloria was already out of her seat. 'Call him from the car.'

'What car?'

'I don't know.' She called out to the staff. 'Hey! Anyone got a car?! We might have found Rigby!'

22

Rigby spent a couple of hours with Frank, calming him, then put him in a car back to London. He'd wanted to go with him, but K wouldn't allow it; there was something else they needed to discuss, she said. Once Frank had left, Maddox took him back to the farmhouse. K and Putts were waiting in the front room.

K wasted no time coming to the point. 'You're still a wanted man. The minute you surface, you'll be arrested.'

She reached into the waistband of her jeans and pulled out a Sig Sauer automatic. She offered it to him.

'What do I need that for?' Rigby said, feeling suddenly frightened.

'You're going to become a hero. Go rescue the old man. Make it look good.'

'*What*?'

Putts said, 'Go rescue Ascott, take him back to London, and hand him over. It's the only way we're going to get you clean. Otherwise you're no use to us.'

Rigby stared at the gun as if he were holding an extra-terrestrial.

'What's the problem?' K said, 'You're a trained NCA officer. You know how to use it.'

'Yeah, but I haven't, not for ...'

'You don't have to do too much,' Putts said. 'The boys are expecting you. Run in and fire a few rounds at the ceiling. They'll do the same. Then hit the deck. You'll get residue on your hands. Later they can match ballistics. Balorat's been taking blood samples and he's an expert at spatter. He'll make it look like someone got hit, but not too bad. No bodies. Once you've fired a few rounds, untie Ascott, put your prints on absolutely everything. Then drive back. I'll phone ahead and tip them off.'

'Simple as that?'

'Simple as that.'

'Should I go now?'

K nodded. 'Go get 'em, tiger.' Her eyes sparkled with flirtation, and it was almost hard when faced with such effortless charisma to remember just who she was. But her next words reminded him with a sickening thud that she was a psychopath through and through. 'But remember, any deviation from the plan and we'll start planting evidence against your friends.'

'What about Ascott? What's in it for him?'

'He's out cold,' Putts said. 'He won't give you any trouble.'

'But when he wakes up?'

K said, 'He's got something to trade too. Information about Genya Zaytsev.'

Rigby did a double-take. 'He's real?'

K shrugged. 'Lots of people think so.'

'Plenty at the NCA, Home Office, Modplod,' Putts added. 'It's suited them very well over the years to keep that myth alive.'

K threw her head back and laughed with derision. 'You can't protect the children from the bogeyman if they don't believe in him.'

One of the freelancers loaned Gloria and Warren his old Mini. Gloria drove, keeping her foot down, slaloming around the slower-moving cars as if they were road cones. Warren gripped tight to the dashboard, unable to speak, until the traffic thinned out north of High Wycombe and she was able to stick to a single lane for more than half a mile.

Relaxing a little, he said to her, 'Did you ever consider

the NCA yourself?'

'Consider in what way?'

'To work there.'

'*Me*?'

'Why not? You're clever enough. And you seem the type.'

'I seem the *what*?'

'You're perceptive, great with IT, don't take any shit.'

Gloria rubbed her head in disbelief. 'Wow. NCA. Is that what you think of me?'

Warren looked taken aback by her response. 'I meant it as a compliment.'

She thought about it for a moment. Maybe it *was* a compliment. 'Why not? My detective skills got us this far.'

'*Your* detective skills? I saw the connection.'

Gloria couldn't believe he was trying to claim it. 'Where are we going right now? Quainton. And who found that? *Me*.'

'But only because *I* looked at the site traffic.'

'You got lucky, okay. You're the front-of-house guy. Stick to the day job.'

His mouth, she noticed, was hanging open in dismay.

'Trying to catch flies?' she said.

'I ... I ...' he began.

'I ... I ...' she mocked. 'You sound like a bloody seal. Argh-argh-argh.'

He fixed her with a furious stare. She started laughing. 'I'm taking the piss.'

He did a double-take. 'I'd hate to see you serious.'

'That you would, boy, that you would.'

Two and a half hours later, they found themselves driving up a long gravel road, heading towards a grain silo on the horizon. Eventually, they found a turning and followed it. The path took them to a farm. A farmhouse and a breeze-block barn faced each other across an asphalt parking area. A couple of farm machines stood in a corner.

'Looks deserted,' Warren said.

They hopped out. It was a sunny afternoon with a cold wind from the north. As they walked towards the farm buildings, Gloria stopped. 'Someone left in a hurry.'

'What makes you say that?'

She pointed to the asphalt. 'Tyre marks. Little burnouts.'

'Are they fresh?'

'I'm not really a detective, you know. I'm just saying what I see.'

They walked to the buildings. All the doors had been padlocked shut. Around the side, a window looked in on a small office. It was filled with trestle tables.

'Look at those,' she said.

'What about them?'

'What's a farm needing tables like that for?'

Warren shrugged. 'Could be for anything. Classes. Crafts fairs.'

'Out here? Who's going to come? Badgers?'

She tried sliding the window. To her surprise, it budged. She slid it open all the way.

'No way,' Warren said. 'No way.'

'What? There's no-one around.'

'If the farmer comes back, we're toast. If you want to go in, I'll keep watch.'

'Suit yourself.'

Gloria climbed in. It took less than a minute before she let out a scream.

'Gloria! What is it?' Warren yelled. He was halfway through the window when she came running back.

'What was it? What's in there?'

She had her hand over her mouth like she was going to be sick. Once she recovered, she said, 'I'm sorry. I never realised ... but I can't stand the sight of blood.'

Warren suddenly felt the same way he had up the tree, when they'd turned the light on him. All along the drive, he'd been filled with visions of them discovering Rigby tied up in a small room, like a hostage. He'd imagined opening the door and pulling tape off his mouth, and driving him home to safety. Now all he could imagine was finding a body.

'Call Steady,' Gloria said.

Steadman answered on the first ring. Before he could say anything, Warren said, 'I don't know how to tell you this. We might have some pretty bad news. It's about Rigby. We found the place where we thought he'd be and ...'

'And what?'

'And there's blood on the walls. Looks like a fight, or maybe someone got shot.'

'Well, whatever you found, it's not him.'

Warren's heart leaped. 'It's not?'

'I spoke to him, two minutes ago.'

'You did? Is he okay?'

'He's fine.'

Warren heard an edge in Steadman's voice. Not everything was fine. 'What is it, Steady? What's the problem?'

'It's not a problem. It's sort of the opposite. He's found Ascott. They're travelling back to London together.'

'That's great news.'

'Yeah, sure. It's great news.'

'What's wrong?'

Steadman hesitated.

'What is it, Steady?'

'Mesh.'

'What about her.'

'She went all funny as soon as she heard.'

'Funny how? She wanted to be the one who found him?'

'No,' he said, dismissively, 'it's like she doesn't believe it.'

'But you talked to him.'

'Oh yeah, it's him alright. She doesn't doubt that. It's ...'

'It's what?'

'Hell, I don't know. I'm just glad he's safe. I'll see you

back in town.'

Gloria had climbed out of the window and came over to join him. 'What's all that about?'

'Rigby's fine. He's driving back now.'

'Thank God for that,' shaking her head in relief. 'So what's the problem?'

'Mesh isn't happy for some reason.'

'Mrs NCA thinks she's hot shit. She's just jealous 'cos we solved the case.'

23

The view from Dale's office windows across Westminster really were spectacular, Rigby thought. He knew he shouldn't be staring outside during an important meeting, but he was trying everything to avoid looking Mesh in the eye. He knew what she was thinking: were Dale and Putts seriously buying this rubbish? He was almost as surprised as she was. They were sitting at Dale's desk, and the two of them were grinning away like children in front of a roaring fire on Christmas morning while Ascott told them the story of his disappearance, from the beginning. Every word was a lie, Rigby guessed, and they were buying it.

There was a knock at the door.

'Enter,' Dale called.

His receptionist poked her head around the door to make an introduction, but before she could say anything it opened wider and was filled by a man in late middle age with receding hair and a portly frame ill-concealed inside an old brown suit.

'Detective Inspector,' Dale said. 'Very kind of you to join us.' He said to the others, 'Let me introduce you. This is Creighton Lasca of the Ministry of Defence Police. I asked him to join us. I hope you don't mind.'

From the frozen expression on Mesh's face, Rigby could tell that she most certainly *did* mind. She hadn't been expecting him.

Dale said to Ascott, 'Perhaps you could start over, from the beginning, for the Detective Inspector's benefit.'

'No need, I read the report,' Lasca said in his heavy Yorkshire accent.

'What report?' Mesh said. Aisling looked similarly confused.

'A high-level briefing I sent yesterday,' Putts said.

The female officers scowled. They'd been deliberately kept out of the loop.

Lasca sat down. 'Don't stop on my account,' he said to Ascott.

'Thank you, sir,' Ascott said. 'A pleasure to see you again.'

Lasca frowned in reply.

Ascott said, 'As I was telling the troops, I was at my favourite watering hole in the Cotswolds, reading the *Economist* – I manage my own portfolio – and enjoying a leisurely lunch. Now, in an urban bar no-one would have noticed the chap. He came in by himself and sat down at the table next to me. He had a shaved head and a biker jacket with jeans. Stood out a mile. I didn't bother with him – best to leave people like that alone – but after a few minutes he leaned over. "Frederick Ascott?" he says to me. I was shocked, naturally, but before I could respond he reached into his jacket and pulled out a wallet. I've seen enough in my time, both real and fake. This one was real. Ronald Bertray. Security Service.

"It's a courtesy call," he said. "Something has arisen that my superiors believe should be brought to your attention."

'So I looked around, and we were far from alone. I said to him, 'Are you sure this is the right place to be discussing it?

'And he's all nonchalant, "Oh yes, this is perfect, because you're going to tell everyone that I'm a solicitor. I travelled up from London to inform you that you've been named as executor of your cousin's will. This will require you to go away for a couple of weeks. I'll fill you in on the rest back at your house.

'He leaves and I finish my lunch. Driving home, I see an Audi S4 parked in my driveway. This tells me everything I need to know. I go in and he's sitting in the kitchen. I'd locked up, of course. I always do. This was him showing off. Just like the car.'

Lasca said, 'How old?'

'2014. Maybe 2015. I'm not an Audi fan.'

Lasca gave him a withering look. 'I meant the *man*. Bertray.'

'Oh, um, in his thirties, I'd say. He wore a tight black T-shirt. And he'd laid a black briefcase on the table. He starts taking out pictures, and begins to tell me about Genya Zaytsev, how they've been trying to track him for years. They have a lead, he says. He's been selling material to the Chinese. He wants bait. Something different from the usual intel chicken feed. Something that's going to get them slavering at the chops. Now, forgive me, but I've been in intelligence long enough to know when I'm being fed a line.'

Lasca fixed him with stare. 'Why didn't you come to us? Or someone in counterintelligence, or someone you could trust in the government?'

'I did,' Ascott said, staring straight back. He pointed at Putts. 'Him.'

'He's a bit-bunny,' Lasca objected.

'Well, forgive me for living in the twenty-first century. I knew I'd been part-toshed. I thought the best plan was to give this security johnnie a little bit of what he wanted, and then vanish completely.'

He'd rehearsed his lines well, Rigby had to admit. It sounded almost plausible, and his delivery was foolproof.

'But you thought he was fake,' Lasca said.

'No. I suspected he wasn't telling me the whole truth, but that's not uncommon.'

Lasca shifted uncomfortably in his seat. He and Dale exchanged a glance.

Ascott picked up the thread. 'Rightly or wrongly ...'

'Wrongly,' Lasca interrupted.

'Rightly or wrongly,' Ascott said again, refusing to be put off, 'I called an old friend. I said, "Mark, I need to be toshed, disguised, and hidden somewhere they'd never think to look for me." Mark called Mr Goode, and he did a good job. Too good, as it turned out.'

Dale jabbed a pen in Rigby's direction. 'I asked you to find him for me, and you had him all along.'

'I didn't have him,' Rigby said, shaking his head. 'I toshed him, and I took him to the safe house. You said everything would go away if I could find him. Seemed like the simplest deal ever. I thought all I had to do was pick him up.'

'Me and Mesh off your back for good,' Aisling said.

Rigby nodded. 'It was too easy. I should have known.'

Ascott said, 'The problem was that this fellow is too intelligent for his own good. He'd worked out my background. Came to ask about it.'

'I had to cover myself,' Rigby said. 'I thought, if I'm caught toshing a spy, I'll be rinsed. Spies are...'

'We're trouble, we're always trouble,' Ascott said, throwing in a chuckle.

It worked – Lasca gave a the tiniest of smiles.

Ascott continued, 'I didn't know if he was one of the good guys, or the bad guys. So I absconded, and that was my real mistake. That's when Zaytsev's boys nabbed me.'

Mesh could take no more. She threw down the notebook she was holding. 'Oh for God's sake, you expect us to believe this crap?' She spun around to face Rigby. 'I can't believe *you're* going along with this. What does he have on you?'

'Nothing,' Rigby said quickly, trying hard not to blink or raise his hands to cover the back of his head, his NCA training coming back to him. 'I told you everything I could at the time. Don't forget the pressure I was under. You'd raided my company.'

'Oh, *please*,' she said. 'There's no Bertray, or Zaytsev. When's Keyser Söze showing up?'

'Tell that to him,' Rigby said, pointing at Lasca.

Her eyes narrowed. He was daring her to come out and say that she'd tipped him off. Modplod would be very interested to hear about that.

Rigby said, 'I only had one play, which was to find him and bring him in. And I did it.'

'And you should have seen him,' Ascott said, waving his fingers like pistols in the air. 'He ran into the barn where they'd been keeping me. It stank of faeces and urine. I was tied to a bed, bruises and puncture marks all over my body. He didn't flinch, took out three of Zaytsev's hoods, bam-bam-bam.'

Putts applauded. No-one else joined in. Putts said, 'I just want to say this. For the record, I was personally very disappointed when Rigby left the NCA. I felt like we'd invested a lot of time and resources in him, and that he was leaving just as he was about to mature as an officer. It always bothered me that we never got the payback on our investment. Well today that account has been settled. Rigby Goode, you have repaid us handsomely.'

He clapped again. This time, Ascott joined in. Rigby thought about joining too. He raised his hands ready, but couldn't quite bring them together.

'You make me sick,' Mesh said to them.

Lasca turned to Rigby, who felt a shiver go up his spine as the brown reptilian eyes sunk into him. He said, 'I don't know how many sides of this you're playing, or how stupid you think we are.'

'None of that, Sir,' Rigby said.

Lasca ignored him. 'You've returned the asset, so we'll honour whatever agreement Dale thinks he made with you. Beyond that, so far as MOD Police are concerned, you remain a person of interest with respect to a number of other situations that are the subject of ongoing investigations.'

'Do you mean Belgrade?' Rigby said.

'I mean a number of other situations.' He turned to Ascott. 'Mark said you have information about Zaytsev.'

Mesh began to interject, but Lasca held up a hand. 'I've been hearing both sides of this for twenty years. If he's a myth, these people didn't invent it.'

'He's not a myth,' Ascott said. 'I did the simplest of

things. While Bertray was at my house, I planted a miniature tracking device on him.'

'You just happened to have one hanging around,' Mesh said, cynically.

'Officer Kaur,' Dale snapped.

Mesh shrank.

'It's actually a reasonable question,' Ascott said. 'I'm going to sound like something out of *Meet The Parents* here, but as you may be aware, I lost my wife a few years ago, and my daughter is the only thing I have left.'

'You were tracking her,' Putts said, with a rueful smile. 'Wouldn't be the first time a government employee did that to a family member.'

Dale wasn't seeing the funny side. 'I hope they realise that if the individual found out they could press charges.'

'My daughter did find out,' Ascott said, quick as a flash. 'That's why I had it spare.'

Rigby had to suppress a laugh. For someone who was making it all up, he was doing a masterful job.

'After Bertray left,' Ascott continued, 'he went to a hotel in Bayswater. I followed later, took a room across the road, and waited until he returned. He did, later, and when he left the hotel the second time, he was in the company of an elderly gentleman. I have seen many alleged photos of Genya Zaytsev, and I can tell you that in my judgment the person Bertray was meeting was one and the same.' He took out a piece of paper from his jacket and set it down on the table in front of Lasca. 'Here's the address.'

Lasca took it and thrust it in front of Dale. 'Copy this down.'

When Dale had finished scribbling, Lasca said, 'I'll raise the troops.' He took his jacket from the chair and headed for the door.

As he passed, Rigby caught his eye. 'Sir, whatever you think, please trust me, we're on the same side.'

Lasca scowled. 'Then you should have stayed with the

NCA, instead of strutting around like some kind of gigabit Batman.'

'I had my reasons.'

'So does everyone. But we put them to one side. It's called having character.'

Rigby glanced at Mesh. She turned away.

24

Four weeks later, with Christmas come and gone, Warren, Gloria, and Steadman inched their way through a blizzard from their office to the Chinatown Starbucks. It was only one street away, but scarves, gloves and hats were all required for a journey of less than a hundred metres.

'Why did she want to meet us at Skagbucks?' Gloria said. 'It's about the worst place there is.'

'Maybe that's why she chose it,' Warren said. 'No one there but pimps, whores, and junkies.'

'And drug squad,' Gloria said.

'There's no drug squad.'

'They sell them the dope. Pays for their vacation.'

Steadman said, 'You're cynical, you know that?'

He opened the door and rolled his eyes as they walked inside. 'Why don't you go find a table. Away from other people.'

'What does Mrs NCA want with us anyway?'

He shrugged. 'You'll find out. What do you want to drink?'

'My usual,' she said, turning to go upstairs.

'Same for me,' Warren said, following her up.

Steadman glanced around. They were right; it was the worst Starby's he'd ever been in. The drinks arrived and Steadman carried them upstairs. They'd found a table between a white man in a pork pie hat reading a newspaper – no other part of him was visible above the paper – and another man with a long white beard, wrapped in a down coat with the hood pulled over his head, asleep.

Steadman set the drinks down. Making conversation, he said, 'Anyone have any plans for the weekend?'

Gloria shook her head. She looked glum.

'Problems?' Steadman said.

'My Mum's planning a birthday party for me.'

'That's a good thing, isn't it?'

She sighed. 'Except we have to keep it a secret from my Dad. If he hears about it he'll show up, and then they argue, and then it's no fun.'

'So who's going to tell him?' Warren said.

'Maybe my sister, or one of my brothers. Reginald, especially. He always takes Dad's side.'

'He's his role model,' Steadman said.

'Exactly, they're both dipshits.'

Soon after, a manager came upstairs to check the tables. Eastern European, in his mid-twenties, he carried a rolled-up magazine in his hands. When he saw the bearded man sleeping, he whacked him on the feet with it. The eyes opened slowly.

'No sleeping here,' the manager said. He gave another tap with the mag. 'I told you already, no sleep.'

'I'm not sleeping,' said the Beard.

'And you,' the staffer said, wheeling around to face the man in the pork pie hat. He lanced the paper with the mag, knocking it flat and revealing the person behind. Like the Beard, the Hat was snoozing away. 'No sleep here.'

'I was reading,' said the Hat.

'Like hell.'

He made no further attempt to move them on, instead putting the magazine in a rack, and went back downstairs. As he descended, he turned sideways to let a woman past.

Steadman took one look as she came up and spilled his coffee.

'Damn it,' he said, wiping his fingers. He glanced quickly at Gloria and Warren to see if they'd noticed. Fortunately, they were watching Mesh.

As she approached their table he stood up. 'Let me get you something.'

'I'm fine, thank you,' she said, smiling.

His eyes melted as she took off one item after another – gloves, her bobble hat, a long woollen scarf, a parka, and then a body warmer – slowly revealing a trim figure underneath. His heart began beating so hard he could hear the blood in his ears.

Sitting down, Mesh said, 'It's nice to see you all again. How are things going?'

'Great,' Warren said.

'Couldn't be better,' said Gloria. 'How about you?'

'Same. Couldn't be better.'

None of them meant it.

Steadman said to her, 'How are things at the Citadel?'

He detected the hint of a smile as she turned to him. 'Crime never sleeps.'

'Thanks for coming,' he said.

'What do you mean?' Gloria said, quickly. 'I thought this was her idea.'

'No, it was my idea,' Steadman said. 'Because there's something I need to tell you.'

'Oh shit,' Warren said, his ever-present happy expression disappearing from his face. 'What is it? Are you sick?'

'No, it's not about me. It's about Rigby.'

'Rigby?' Gloria said, suspiciously. She looked over at Mesh. 'You aren't investigating him again, are you?'

Mesh put her hands up. 'I don't know anything about this.'

Gloria said, 'Rigby's been minding his own business. Ever since he came back, he's been working three days a week. Taking some time for himself, and after what he went through, I think he deserves it.'

'Well that's kind of what I wanted to talk about,' Steadman said

'Why, what's the issue?' Gloria said. 'He told me that being on the run had made him think about things differently. He'd reflected on his life and decided he needed more time to himself. Wanted to spend time on his other interests. What the hell's wrong with that?'

'He's doing a lot of long-distance cycling,' Warren added. 'Hill climbs in Snowdonia, that sort of thing. He's been developing new apps, too. Some of ours are getting out of date.'

'Seen any yet?' Steadman said.

'No, but his stuff is ground-breaking. It takes time.'

'And how about those long rides? Looked at his Strava account? Any videos posted on Instagram?'

'How about Cognoscenti?' Mesh said.

'Nice one,' Steadman said to her. 'I checked all of them. And you know what, the man who never fails to document a ride hasn't logged anything since October last year. Does that surprise you?'

'Maybe he's using a different site,' Gloria said.

'What are you wanting to tell us, Steadman?' Mesh said. 'Maybe you should just come out and say it.'

Steadman felt himself going to putty as she said it. They'd never gone on their date, and she simply hadn't been around for the past month, and he'd missed her. 'I'll tell you in a second, but first I need to ask you a question.'

'Okay,' she said.

Steadman swallowed hard. He'd never been disloyal to Rigby before. Sure they'd had disagreements, but he'd never accused him – or even suspected him – of anything serious, like lying to the team. 'I never bought that story about him rescuing the spy. Did you?'

Mesh looked cornered. Steadman worried that maybe he'd pushed her too hard. She probably wasn't supposed to comment on cases.

She said, 'How about you tell us why you didn't buy it?'

Sneaky woman, turned it back on him. 'They said he shot three of them. That's just not possible. Give him a gun and he'd most likely blow his own foot off.'

Mesh laughed. Gloria gave her an icy stare. Mesh covered her mouth and tried to stop. 'Sorry,' she said. 'I'm laughing because ... because that's exactly what I thought too.'

Warren let out a sigh. 'Oh, God ...'

Steadman said, 'So I started to wonder what he was really doing on those days off. I started following him ...'

'Following him?' Gloria butted in.

'I've been getting up twice a week, at 5am ...'

'... You never got up at 5am in your life ...'

'... driving to Chiswick before dawn,' Steadman continued, ignoring her, 'in a rental car so I couldn't be recognised. And at 6am every Thursday, Friday, Saturday and Sunday Rigby comes out and takes his car – that's right, not his bike – and he drives to an office park about a mile from Stansted Airport. He goes in. He stays there for the whole day. And then he comes out and drives home.'

The three of them stared at him, astonished. 'I have the pictures if you don't believe me,' he said.

'So he has another job?' Warren said. 'Do you know what it is?'

Steadman shook his head.

'Have you asked him?'

'Of course not. If I do that, he'll know I've been following him, and then he'll never speak to me again.'

Mesh said, 'I can run a check on the name of the company that leases the building.'

'I already did that,' Steadman said. 'It's a shell company, and the landlord says it's unoccupied.'

'Is he meeting someone there?'

'That's the interesting part. On the days he's not there, the building's unoccupied. But on the days he's there, fifteen people, mostly early twenties, get bussed in and out. They spend two hours there. I tailed the buses. Their pick-up and drop-off points are Stansted, Kings Cross, and Victoria.'

'This is fucked up,' Gloria said. 'I mean, what are you saying?'

'I'm not saying anything,' Steadman said. 'Except what it is.'

The four of them looked at each other, full of questions, but not knowing who to ask.

Eventually, Warren said, 'Whatever happened to that insurance policy you guys were supposed to be picking up? I mean, it sounds he could be in deep shit. Maybe it's time to cash it in.'

Steadman took a deep breath. 'Yeah, that,' he said, feeling embarrassed. 'It's a long story but ... I stashed it with Lana. Her daughter used a camera it was hidden in as part of a school project. A few weeks back I asked Lana about it and she told me ... well, it's not the best school ... the camera got nicked.'

'Oh, no,' Mesh said.

Steadman turned to her. 'Yeah. Typical.'

Off to their left, the Beard began snoring. Gloria was nearest. Steadman said to her, 'Nudge him.'

Gloria kicked him hard in the shin with the toe of her Dr Marten's.

The Beard let out a muffled yelp. 'What the fuck?'

'Shuddup,' Gloria said to him.

Steadman put a hand on her arm. 'I said nudge him, not break his leg.'

'Worked,' she said, pulling away. She turned to Mesh. 'So

what do you think of this?'

'I don't know what to think,' Mesh said.

'Well take a guess,' Gloria replied tersely.

Mesh shot her a look. 'I can understand why you find this disturbing,' she said evenly, 'but I was ordered to drop this case. I can't go near it. They'd crucify me.'

Steadman said, 'I'll tell you what I think. It looks to me like kids going to college.' He said to Mesh, 'Did he cut a deal with your lot?'

'*Deal*?' she said, surprised. 'What are you talking about?'

'I'm talking about him training toshers. Think about it, what's the one thing he's the world expert in? So is that the deal? You keep him out of the nick in return for training toshers?'

'Why would anyone want to train a busload of toshers?' Warren said.

'I can think of a busload of reasons, and every single one is evil. That's why I'm hoping he's working for the good guys.'

His agitation must have been clear – he'd been worrying about this for weeks, unable to tell anyone – because Gloria reached out and put a hand on his shoulder.

'It's alright, Steady,' she said. 'We're going to sort this.'

Mesh said, 'Unfortunately, I have more bad news for you. If Rigby was doing this for us, it wouldn't be in an office park. It'd be at a police college, like Bramshill.'

Steadman thought for a minute. 'Could you double-check for me?'

Once again, her hesitation made Steadman worry that he'd overstepped the mark.

She said, 'If I'm going to get involved, I'm going to need more than this.'

'I took photos of the people getting on and off the bus,' he said. 'Maybe we can find out who owns the bus, or who books it. Warren, can you get on that?'

'No problem.'

'What do you want me to do?' Gloria said.

'Make friends with the students,' he said. 'Find out what they're doing there.'

'I can hardly sign up for the class.'

He could feel Mesh's eyes on him. He'd been preparing his plan for a while, hoping she'd get a chance to hear it.

'You don't need to. Meet them after they get off the bus at Stansted. We'll get you plane tickets. Go through security like any other passenger. Some of the younger men might go for a pint, and there are only a couple of bars there. When they come in, try to get them talking.'

Gloria knew what that meant. 'Act like I'm available, you mean.'

'Send out the right signals and nature will do the rest.'

'I'm not doing any *nature*.'

'I'm not asking you to. Just get them talking, and listen. Can you do that?'

She nodded.

Mesh said, 'Guys, please understand, if I could help out with this I would.' She turned to Steadman. 'You'd make a pretty good officer.'

He felt himself blushing. 'It's going to take some time to do all this. Can we meet up here again, same time next week?'

She took a deep breath. Steadman watched in awe. He imagined her waking up next to him, stretching, and taking the first deep breath of morning.

'Fine,' she said. 'But don't tell anyone or I'll be the next one in deep shit.'

On the way back to the office, Gloria said to Steadman, 'You got some nerve asking me to be the honey trap.'

He stuck his thumbs in his lapels and gave a little strut. 'I would do it myself, except it might be too effective. You know, too many ladies giving me the eye.'

Warren said, 'Only one lady you have eyes for, Steady.'

'No doubt about that,' Gloria said.

Steadman's strut slowed. They couldn't possibly suspect, could they? His neck tightened with embarrassment. 'What you talking 'bout?' he said, barely able to squeak the words out.

'What you talking 'bout?' Gloria said, imitating him. 'Mrs NCA, that's what.'

'Her? No way. I hate cops.'

'She's not a cop.'

'I hate NCA too.'

All the way back to the office he had to endure their taunts.

'You hate NCA, Warren?' Gloria said.

'I hate NCA, especially ones with dreamy brown eyes.'

'Yeah, and them tight little skirts,' she said, running her hands down her hips. 'I hate NCA because they tease me.'

'I hate 'em 'cos they please me.'

'I hate 'em too, they make me spy.'

'I hate 'em all. Wait! That's a lie.'

Let them have their fun, Steadman thought. But deep down, it was maddening. They'd caught him out, and he hadn't even been on a proper date yet.

25

Mesh was in her office when the phone rang. It was Brien's number.

'Hi,' she said brightly, 'how are you doing? The Serbs behaving themselves?'

'Yeah, sort of. I can watch, but I can't touch.'

'So what have you seen?'

'That's why I'm calling. I'm not sure that this is what we thought it was.'

Mesh stood up. In some ways this was the phone call she'd been hoping for, and also the one she'd feared. 'Tell me.'

'He kept screenshots of all the toshing he'd done, and it tallies in ninety-five percent of cases to the photographs on the walls.'

'Wow.'

'Yeah. It's making it pretty easy to put together. But there's more. A lot more.'

'More victims?'

'Not exactly. More toshing, and not everyone's dead. The Serbian Police identified older guys who'd been in the army. They're pretty sure they were involved in war crimes.'

'Can they be tracked?'

'They're on it, but the new IDs are from every country you can imagine. It's not like everyone gets a Serbian passport. Some get Turkey. Some Egypt. Plus lots of EU countries, including the UK.'

'UK?'

'And Mesh,' he hesitated for a moment, 'there were kids too.'

'Kids to shed?'

'Yeah. From babies up to about four or five. Young enough not to really know what was going on.'

'And what were they doing with them?'

'Shipping them out. Again, everywhere.'

'But how? I mean, were they being shipped overseas? Were adults coming to pick them up?'

'I don't think we know yet. They're still working through the files.'

'Okay, let me know as soon as you have more.'

'Boss,' he said, tentatively. She could hear the concern in his voice. 'There's been a new development.'

Mesh felt butterflies in her stomach. She'd only initiated the original investigation to prove a point to her colleagues about how sloppy they were with data. For political reasons it had mushroomed into a Task Force. And now, with the discovery of Tudor Clarke's basement, that was metastasising into a major international case.

'There's email traffic between himself and a number of individuals, discussing what they were doing. They used encrypted accounts, and the IP addresses are mostly dead ends, except one. We traced it to Guys Hospital.'

'Really? Guys? Can you get a person?'

'Not from that. But I did some checking. During the time that Tudor Clarke was working in the Sweatbox, there was a forensic pathologist who worked a lot with that team. He's now a professor at Guys.'

'Got a name for me?'

'Professor Vincent Balorat.'

The butterflies stopped fluttering and turned to acid. She remembered Balorat. He was a ghoulish man who she'd always avoided when he was attached to the NCA, and his name came up again when he complained to Dale about her request to check John Does. This was way too big for the Sweatbox, that was for sure. It would be a feather in her cap, but only if she did it by the book. Everything had to be documented and reported up the line. As much as she hated the idea – and as much as she disliked her Putts – that meant involving her boss every step of the way. She thanked Brien and immediately made another call.

Putts answered, sounding somewhat surprised. 'Do you have news for me?'

'Yes. Very good news.'

'What's that?'

'O'Brien just called me from Belgrade. There have been some new findings. We can connect Clarke to a pathologist in London named Vincent Balorat. It looks like they were colluding. Without trying to sound overdramatic, we may have uncovered a major organised crime ring.'

For a moment there was silence on the line. Then Putts said, 'That's fantastic, if it stands up. Great work. Perhaps you could brief me in detail ...'

'That's why I was calling. I'd like to do so as soon as possible.'

Another pause.

'I'm free in about twenty minutes. How does that suit?'

'Perfect. Thank you.'

It was a Saturday afternoon, and, having completed his training session for the day, Rigby went shopping downtown. It wasn't something he normally enjoyed, but he needed a change of routine. The students were driving him insane. They all seemed to have been trained in different coding languages. Whoever had done the recruiting didn't seem to have taken it into account, but that, he guessed, maybe hadn't been their primary criteria. From what he'd observed so far, they'd looked for younger people (all of them were under twenty-five) who were smart but naïve, with a high level of computer skill, and who had been out of work for a while. Happy to be receiving both pay and training, they weren't asking questions, especially as they were mainly quiet types, and from places with high unemployment rates. He guessed that ex-cons and ex-military would have been filtered out too, along with anyone who'd previously been in government employment.

He was gazing at a model railroad in the window of a toy store, remembering building something similar as a boy, when he heard a voice behind him.

'It was my favourite toy when I was a kid.'

He looked up and saw a Putts's face reflected in the window. 'Mark?'

'Do you have time for a walk?' Putts said.

He seemed less confident than usual, glancing round, making sure that no-one was observing them.

'If you insist,' Rigby said. He felt certain that the day was about to get much worse.

'I hear the training sessions are going well,' Putts said cautiously as they walked.

Rigby glanced up at him. It was almost like small-talk, but Rigby knew that couldn't be what it was. This wasn't a social call. 'Some of them get it. Others are a little slower.'

'You want them to go as slowly as possible, of course.'

It took Rigby a second to work out what he meant. 'To drag out my usefulness? I worried about that too, but then I worked out that you guys wouldn't have gone to all this trouble just to get some toshers trained. Next up it's data harvesting, election rigging, altering newsfeeds ...'

Putts laughed. 'Sure, that and all the rest.' A few paces later, he said, 'But it could be irrelevant. Have you heard from Mesh?'

Strange question. 'No. Should I?'

'News from Belgrade. Tudor Clarke was sloppy. So was Balorat. They can connect them. It won't be too long before she has enough to put us all away. You included.'

'Me?' Rigby said, indignantly.

Putts grabbed his arm and pulled him to the side. 'Yes, you. But there's a way out, if you trust me.'

They were outside a restaurant with twenty-foot windows. Rigby suddenly felt exposed. This was a trap. It had to be. He shook himself free, and his arm connected accidentally with a shopper walking past. She shouted at him in a foreign language.

'Nice try,' Rigby said. 'Think I'm stupid enough to walk into that.'

'I'm in deeper than you are,' Putts said. 'Even having this conversation, I'm a dead man.'

Putts walked ahead and turned into an alley, waving at Rigby to follow.

He knew he should turn around and walk the other way. Listening to Putts the first time was what had landed him in this nightmare. But if Mesh was closing in, he had no choice but to listen.

They found a quiet bar and sat in a corner. Putts stared wide-eyed into the middle distance, reminding Rigby of a startled bird. He said, 'This whole thing has got way out of control. Ten years ago I was at a conference on money laundering. K worked for one of the banks, in the fraud department, looking out for people on watch lists trying to do money transfers. We were sitting next to each other. Then later, I ran into her at the hotel bar. She told me she was only there to be up on the latest techniques, and I knew from the way she said it that she wasn't doing it for the bank. I was intrigued, and you've seen her, Jesus. We started an affair. I told her about toshing, I don't know why, maybe I was trying to impress her. She said she knew people who would pay for a service like that. Before I knew it, there was one-fifty large on the table. Crazy money. Two years' salary for toshing. But it wasn't. The customer wanted a hit. K had found an ex-para to do the deed. I was petrified, said I wanted out. Next day, my wife got an email from a 'friend' suggesting that I was seeing another woman. I confronted K who showed me the dossier she'd put together – not only the affair, but the whole thing. The hit, everything. All the evidence pointing at me.'

'She had you from "hello".'

'She quit her job. Told me her plan to make a fortune. I had no choice, except make sure we didn't get caught. First thing was to tosh her. Then we recruited Vincent, and a team of marksmen.'

'And your customers?'

'Not everyone wants a hit. Sometimes it's only toshing. People on sex offenders lists. Rich and powerful bastards who need to cover their arses. Sports agents. But there's also governments, private security.'

'Where do you sell it, the dark web?'

'Forget Silk Road, meet Snuff Road.' He forced a laugh. 'Sure, there's a site, but most of it's personal connections. One of the growth areas is intelligence. They need to anonymise agents. It's getting almost impossible to go undercover these days because people can check your past data.'

'Sounds one hell of an operation.'

'And the money, Jesus.' For a moment Putts's eyes lost their hunted expression and gleamed. 'We've bought a whole chain of islands. We're putting in a landing strip. Mansions. Docks for our yachts.'

'You make me puke.'

'It's irrelevant now, except K refuses to see it. She's in this fantasy-land where she's untouchable. But we can get her. You and me. Set her up. Turn her in. Cut a deal. Maybe even get them to believe you never left. It was deep cover. Just you and me. All to bring down K.'

Putts was closer to the truth than he realised, Rigby thought. 'Now who's living in fantasy-land?'

'They've bought worse, believe me.'

He had to play along, see where this went. He had no intention of doing exactly what Putts wanted, but it was the first whiff of a break he'd had since the farm. 'How about if I tosh us – you, me, your family, Balorat, K. Really deep and thorough. No trace left. We get Balorat to dummy up the forensic evidence. We all die in the same plane crash or something.'

'And then what? I'm a little conspicuous. K can have more facial surgery, but what are they going to do with me? Saw my legs off? Anyway the others wouldn't go for it. No way.'

They sat in silence for a moment, until Putts's face suddenly brightened. 'Hang on a minute, hang on, you've given me an idea. This might just work.'

'What might?'

'Toshing K.'

'What, and get rid of her? How does that help?'

'No. You don't realise, but you already toshed her. Probably one of the last jobs you ever did. I put her in the pile for witness protection. It was part of our plan. She could become a ghost, like Genya Zaytsev.'

'So what?'

'For everyone we've taken care of over the years, there's someone else out there who wants revenge. Anonymity is K's only protection, and she knows that better than anyone. We can expose her. She's on that SD card.'

'You mean leak her identity?'

'Exactly. She'll have to run. It'll take her out of the game. Then we just need to figure out what to do with Vincent.'

Rigby held his hands up. 'Whoa, whoa, I am not going to be party to anything like that.'

'I'm not talking about anything too drastic, he's an old friend. You don't have to do anything, except get that card back.'

'But you have it.'

'No, that's the point. Vincent stole it.'

'Stole it? How?'

'Never mind that. But I know where it is. In his office at Guys.'

'How do you know?'

'I've worked with him for twenty years. He trusts nobody. Everything important is within arm's reach.'

'So, go get it.'

'Come on, if he finds it gone, we're finished. You put anti-copy protections on it, right?'

Rigby nodded.

'See,' Putts said, 'I know how you operate. You need to go in, make a copy, then put it back.'

'And then?'

'Send it to the NCA. But before we do that, there's one other thing I need you to do.'

Rigby took a deep breath. 'I'm not your damned lackey.'

'Tosh my family. Just in case. I can get them out of the country. Anything that happens to me, I've got it coming. But they don't deserve it. They're innocent.'

Just in case, just in case. It rang hollow. This was Plan A, dressed up to look like a contingency.

'Sixth floor,' Putts said.

'What?'

'His office at Guys. Sixth floor. Nearest tube is London Bridge.'

'I know where it is,' Rigby said tersely.

Putts smiled, though the hunted expression had returned. 'Good. Then there won't be any problems.'

Gloria passed through security at Stansted without a hitch. She bought a magazine, then did a quick tour of the bars and coffee shops in the departure lounge. She chose one that looked the sort of place where younger guys might have a couple of beers before getting on their plane. She sat down, spread her bag and coat onto other chairs, flicked the mag and sipped a cranberry juice, looking up every so often to see if anyone had arrived.

Sitting at the bar, she felt more relaxed than she had in many days. Being in the office was stressful. The approach they'd agreed at Starbucks would have been simple if Rigby had left the company. But he hadn't; he was still there, three days a week. She'd found herself watching him as he went through his usual routines, making too many espressos, berating people on weird aspects of cleanliness, wearing that dumb coat everywhere, his hands red and cracked from being sanitised every ten minutes. It put her on edge. Spying on enemies, fine. The, NCA, Met, Old Bill, no problem. But not someone she liked and, dare she say it, admired.

Her phone bleeped. An incoming message from Steadman: *Geese have flown.*

She sighed in exasperation. If his idiotic code wasn't bad enough – what was this, a Jackie Chan movie? – it also meant that the bus was only now leaving the office park. They wouldn't get to the airport, and through security, for at least half an hour.

She ordered another juice.

She swapped the mag she'd bought at the newsstand for one she'd brought in her handbag. In this magazine, she'd pasted photographs of the young men who Steadman had snapped going in and out of the office building. She'd cut them to size so that they fitted into the page layouts, making them less noticeable if anyone happened to be looking over her shoulder. After what seemed an excruciatingly long wait, she spotted one of them coming into the bar.

He was of medium height, in his early to mid twenties, although he could have passed for younger, with red hair, blue eyes and freckles. He wasn't her type, but he was far from ugly, with a friendly demeanour and a ready smile. Standing at the bar, he ordered a beer, and said something to the bartender that made her laugh. Sipping it, he noticed Gloria clocking him and offered her a grin. She flipped the magazine up to cover her face.

A few seconds later she looked again, and almost died. He was standing in front of her.

'Anyone sitting here?'

Gloria knew that she should feel pleased that one of her marks had come over to talk without her having to do a thing.

Instead, she was in knots.

'Help yourself,' she said, trying to sound uninterested. It was like being in a bar in the West End, and some creep trying to hit on her.

After a few minutes, still hiding behind the magazine, she heard him say, 'What are you drinking?'

She glanced over the page. 'Were you talking to me?'

He'd drained his beer. It had turned his face slightly red, making him appear as if he were embarrassed. Judging by the smile on his face, he was anything but.

'I'm going to the bar anyway. Can I get you something? What's that?'

'Cranberry.'

He nodded approvingly. 'That's smart, avoiding alcohol before a flight. I would normally, but it's been kind of a strange day.' He laughed.

Gloria knew she needed to open up. He'd dangled the conversation bait; it was time to take a bite. 'Oh? How come?'

His face lit up. She felt almost like giggling – he was so expressive. He was lucky that she wasn't in this to score, because she wouldn't have been able to take him seriously.

'Let me get that drink,' he said, all in a rush, 'and I'll tell you about it. Cranberry?'

She nodded.

'Sure you don't want a tiny little vodka in it?'

'I'm sure. Thank you.'

From the bar, he kept looking over and grinning at her.

Such a goofy kid, she thought. It was almost a shame she was going to have to milk him for information.

'So, a strange day,' she said when he returned. 'Bet it can't be any stranger than mine.'

'Really? What happened to you?'

'Nope. You first.'

He took a deep breath and launched in, barely stopping as he told her about how, two months ago, he'd been contacted on social media by a recruitment consultant. A company was looking to recruit and train IT contractors. He'd been between jobs, so he replied. As soon as they sent him the details, he told Gloria, it became obvious that the employer was a private security company, working very closely with the government.

'What makes you say that?' she said.

He head-checked, then said quietly, 'They made me sign the Official Secrets Act.'

'Wow. Should you be telling me this?'

'It's fine. They haven't told us any secret stuff yet.'

Gloria wondered how he could know the difference, but she didn't want to discourage him.

He said, 'I've been flying up from Newquay once a week. I meet up with a bunch of other people and we go to this place. There's a teacher, who's ...' he trailed off and began to laugh.

'What?' she said. 'What's so funny?'

'He's a great teacher, I love listening to him. He makes everything sound so easy. I sit there in class, and I'm like, yeah, I get it, I can do this. But then I go home and I try to do the exercises that he's given us, and it's like whoa, how did he do that?'

Steadman was right, she realised. Rigby was teaching them. But what, exactly? She forced a smile. 'So is that what happened to you today? Did you get in trouble for not being able to complete your homework?'

'No!' he laughed.

He was drinking his beer quickly, she noticed. Was he maybe more nervous than he appeared?

'Are you in a hurry?' she said.

'Yeah. My flight leaves in about twenty minutes.'

'Oh,' she said, disappointed.

'Where are you flying to?' he asked.

'Dublin. Sorry.'

'What a shame. We'll never see each other again.'

She was about to agree, when she realised there was no need to. 'Not necessarily.'

He laughed. 'What? You want to come to Newquay?'

'No, well, maybe one day. But I'm here with my company, and I have to come to London once a week too.'

'Really?' he said, all wide-eyed. 'That's amazing.'

'You could give me your email address. I'll let you know when I'm going to be here.'

He wasted no time, reaching into his backpack, tearing off a strip of paper, and writing it down.

'I should get my flight,' he said as he scribbled.

'You still haven't told me what happened.'

'Oh that. Nothing.'

'What do you mean?'

He laughed and turned bright red again, this time through genuine embarrassment. 'I wanted to talk to you but I couldn't think of anything else to say.'

'Oh, now that's naughty,' she said. 'Stringing a girl along like that.'

He got up. 'Will you forgive me?'

'I'll think about it.'

'It was nice to meet you,' he said, slinging the pack on his back.

'You too.'

'Email me?'

'I'll think about it.'

And then he was gone. Gloria felt elated. She'd pulled it off. She'd made contact, learned crucial information, and created a way to get more. She waited until he was out of sight, then stood up from the table. Steadman had told her to look for the exit being used by arriving passengers, and then to join the crowds. It would be easy, he said. So long as you weren't boarding a plane, nobody at an airport paid any attention.

She found the exit for arriving passengers. There was no-one else around, so she pushed open the double doors and walked straight through. At first, all she saw was a sign for transfers. Thinking she might have gone the wrong way, she turned around, but it was too late. The door had closed and there was no handle on her side. Rounding a bend, she ran straight into a T-junction. Frustrated with herself, she took a deep breath and chose left. It led her down an escalator and through another set of doors. She expected to come into the main arrivals area, but instead she found herself approaching a desk where a uniformed airport security guard and another man with short-cropped grey hair, jeans and a black windcheater were going through paperwork. As she approached, they both glanced up, surprised. Gloria forced herself to stay calm. The best thing would be to walk straight past them; there was space on the far side of the desk. Maybe if she just strode on by, like she owned the place, they'd leave her alone.

Fat chance. The security guard stepped out from behind the desk and held up a hand. He was a white male in his fifties, balding, with glasses. 'Excuse me, miss. The gates aren't this way.'

Gloria's heart was already pumping, and now it went into overdrive. 'I'm looking for the exit.'

'If you turn around, Miss, the gates are back that way.'

'I'm not going to the gate, I'm going out.'

He seemed puzzled. 'If you're coming from up there, then you've passed security.'

'Yeah, I came through.'

'So this is the wrong way.'

'I've come off a plane.'

As soon as she said it, Gloria realised she'd made a mistake. *Damn it, Steady, you said this was going to be easy.* The man in plain clothes, who she assumed to be a detective, looked up from the paperwork. 'Could we see some identification, please. Your passport.'

'Why?'

'Just show us your passport, please.'

Gloria took it out and handed it to him. He studied it for a moment and handed it back.

'What flight did you disembark from?' he said.

'Dublin,' she said.

He looked surprised. 'Dublin? Okay, let's see.'

Her heart sank as he typed something into the computer on the desk. He scrolled the screen. 'How long ago did it land?'

'About fifteen minutes.'

He scrolled some more, then shook his head. 'I can't see a flight from Dublin landing fifteen minutes ago.'

Play dumb, Gloria thought. They probably expected her to be some stupid girl, so that's what she'd give them. 'Okay, I lied,' she said. 'I'm not arriving. I was going to Dublin, but now I don't want to. I want to go home.'

The two men turned to each other.

'Can I see your boarding card?' said the guard.

She handed it to him.

He said, 'You still have thirty minutes to make this flight. If you go back down that corridor, you'll find your gate.'

'I'm not getting on the plane,' she said, trying to sound agitated.

'Miss, you can't book yourself onto a plane, come through airport security, and then not get on.'

'Why not?'

'Did you check baggage for the flight?'

'No.'

'You're going to Dublin with no bags?'

'Yeah.'

'If you're not going to get on, you need to tell the airline.'

'I'll call them,' she said, and began to walk.

She expected them not to bother with her, that they had better things to do. She couldn't have been more wrong. The guard moved to block her path and she bumped into him. When she tried to push past he grabbed one arm, and the detective grabbed the other.

'Let me go!' Gloria said. 'What have I done?'

'Stop struggling,' the guard said.

She wasn't struggling, her arms hung limp. The best she

could do now, she decided, was to keep up the stupid act and hope they lost interest.

'We need to go straighten this out,' the detective said.

'Straighten what?' she said. 'I've done nothing.'

'We need to contact the airline.'

'What about?'

They'd ceased listening. The guard said, 'Please just come this way.'

'Fine!' she said, shaking her arms to get free. 'Get your hands off me.'

They led her down a service corridor to a small room. It had a round table, four chairs, and felt uncomfortably warm. She sat.

The detective picked up her handbag from the table. 'We need to run this again through the scanner.'

Her hand shot out and grabbed the handle. 'That's personal property!'

'Miss, please calm down,' the guard said, levelly. 'We'll return with the bag in a few minutes.'

The detective nodded. 'We'd appreciate it if you'd cooperate.'

She let go of the bag and folded her arms. 'Not like I have a choice, is it?'

They left her to stew in her juice. She kept thinking about Warren, and how he'd ended up in surgery. How far was she willing to go? Ever since Rigby had recruited her, she'd loved every moment of working at Pangolin, and she believed one-hundred percent in what they were doing, but was she ready to go to jail for it? She'd broken the law many times online, she was more than aware of that, but it was always so well hidden that she never gave much thought to getting caught. This was different. This was real. The most important thing, she told herself, was to stay calm, and to use the time she had now to work on her cover story.

After leaving her alone for almost half an hour, the detective returned. He carried Gloria's bag in one hand and her passport and boarding card in the other. He handed her the paperwork, but kept the bag. Shit, she thought, had they gone through it?

'Miss Damson, you're probably wondering why we asked you to step aside?'

'I'm not wondering anything. You get paid to harass people.'

'Miss, we're not trying to harass anyone. It causes problems for the airlines when people don't board flights.'

The dumb girl she was pretending to be would change tack about now, Gloria thought. She'd turn on the charm. 'I can explain,' she said, batting her eyelids.

'Please do,' the detective said. 'But try telling the truth. We knew you were lying because disembarking passengers aren't routed down that corridor.'

She smiled as sweetly as she could. 'That was really stupid, I'm sorry.'

'Are you a former airline employee, Ms. Damson?'

'Me? No.'

'Because this is the kind of stunt that a disgruntled employee would pull. You know, delaying flights, causing emergency scares.'

Her act was working, Gloria thought. Now she could go for the cover story. She reached into her pocket for a Kleenex and began dabbing her eyes.

'I had a fight with my boyfriend,' she said. 'He moved to Dublin a month ago. I was going to go see him, but I just got a call from my cousin who lives there, and she's saying she's seen him carrying on with some woman. So now I don't want to go to Dublin.' She dabbed her eyes harder and let her voice break. 'I just want to go home.'

The detective frowned at her. 'Whatever the reason, this is a serious matter.'

'Why is it anyone's business?' she exclaimed, letting the emotion out. 'Why is it your business?'

He opened her bag and pulled out the magazine she'd

brought with her. Fanning the pages, he stopped on one with a pasted-in photo. It was of the student she'd been talking to earlier. 'Maybe you'd like to explain this?'

Thinking fast, Gloria shrugged. 'That's not mine.'

'It was in your handbag.'

'I found it. When I sat down in the bar, it was on the table. I thought, free magazine ...'

He raised a disbelieving eyebrow.

'Can I go now, please. I'm sorry for the inconvenience, but I've done nothing wrong and all I want to do is go home and have a good cry. Then I'm going to call that ratfink and dump him.'

He got up. She stood too.

'Sit down, Miss.'

'Sorry, I thought ...'

'You're going to have to wait a while longer. Some other people want to talk to you.'

Gloria's heart started pounding again. 'Who? What could they want with me?'

'Just some other officials.'

'You got no right to hold me. What law have I broken?'

But the detective wasn't listening. He reached for the door. 'Take a seat please. They'll be with you shortly.'

Before Gloria could say anything else, he shut the door with a firm click. Whoever these 'other officials' might be, she wasn't going to stick around to find out. The door would be locked, she knew, so she knelt down to examine the latch. A simple slide. Remembering a trick Steadman had showed her once, she reached for her bag and pulled out her purse. She rifled through her cards, trying to find one that was both flexible and springy, and when she'd found the best one, bent it into a U-shape. She then hooked it round the back of the latch and pulled. The door popped. Gloria stuck her head out. At the far end of the corridor, three figures were approaching, deep in conversation, led by a very tall man. There was no time to waste. She slipped through the door and walked back up the service corridor until she found the exit to the main terminal. The crowds of people and flight announcements felt like a breath of freedom. It was short-lived: a pair of airport cops walked past. Fixing her gaze straight ahead, she strode past, not slowing until she was outside the terminal.

She ran across the bus and taxi lanes and into the car park. To her relief, they hadn't taken the car park ticket from her purse, but there was a family ahead of her trying to pay their parking fee. First they argued about which way the slip went in. Then they started arguing which credit card to use. Gloria felt like smacking their heads together. A second machine came free. People were waiting, but she barged the line. Someone shouted a complaint. She ignored them. Her car was at the back of the lot. Picking her way through the parked cars, she kept her eyes peeled in case anyone had followed her.

Halfway to her car, she saw a man standing in the middle of the lot, his head whipping around, clearly looking for someone. She ducked into a crouch. Had he seen her? Squeezing between two cars, she peered through the windows. Two more cops were running out from the terminal. How the hell had let herself get talked into this?

They shouted to the man in the middle of the lot.

'Seen anything?'

'Not yet.'

The two cops prowled the bays. Gloria slipped from her hiding place, then dashed for cover in the next row. As they continued searching, she inched back towards the terminal, hoping to get to the train entrance. She'd barely set foot inside before she saw the tall man again, with his flunkies. Turning quickly, she walked the other way, keeping going until she spotted a group of backpackers asleep on chairs. One of them had rested a baseball cap on top of his backpack. Gloria reached out and grabbed it as she passed by, and put it on her head. Then she ditched her jacket in the ladies, made her way downstairs, and joined a crowd of passengers hauling luggage towards the train. She followed the throng up the escalators, and then waited on the platform. Airport cops milled. Gloria pulled the cap down, her heart still pounding.

She caught the train into Liverpool Street, then the tube, and surfaced at Leicester Square. She walked as fast as she could to the office. Only once the door had closed behind her did she feel safe again. A few people looked up and gave friendly smiles as she entered, unaware of what she'd just been through. She smiled back and waved, feeling strangely calm. It wasn't until Steadman saw her and came running over that her fury came flooding back.

'You lied to me Steady,' she said.

'Hey whoa, whoa, calm down.'

'You can't just walk out of an airport.'

'What happened, did someone stop you?' He added, 'Let's go upstairs.'

Once they were in the conference room, Gloria told him what had happened. When she'd finished, she said, 'Never ask me to do something like that again.'

'Come on, what are you talking about? You were brilliant.'

'I almost got arrested.'

'But you didn't. And you got the info.'

'I could have gone to prison.'

'You got away with it.'

'I'm not cut out for this kind of work.' After a second, she added, 'There's something else.'

'What's that?'

'They found the magazine in my bag. The one with the pictures glued into it.'

'So ...?'

'That was when they decided to hold me. I'm pretty sure they knew something was going on. The guys who were coming to question me, they weren't airport cops, they were NCA.'

Steadman said nothing for a few minutes. Eventually he

said, 'Are you sure?'

'Like I told you before, where I grew up you learn to recognise them.'

From the look on his face, she could tell that it troubled him.

'What does it mean?' she said.

He took out his phone.

'Who're you calling?'

'NCA, of course. Mesh.'

Mesh was busy trying to convince her son that it wasn't unreasonable to ask him to brush his teeth after eating an entire pack of Skittles when she heard the phone ringing. That his grandmother would have given him that much sugar was maddening! She was tempted to ignore the call, but when she saw the caller ID, she picked up.

'Hi Steadman.'

'I'm sorry to bother you, but this might be important.'

'What is it?'

Satinder saw her on the phone and took the opportunity to throw his toothbrush into the basin. He ran off down the hallway, laughing.

'Satinder, get back here!'

'Sorry, is this a bad time?' Steadman said.

'No, it's fine. It's just my son.'

'It's my fault,' Steadman said, his words tumbling out like water in rapids. 'I made Gloria the honey-trap. She's got no experience. They asked for ID, so she gave it to them.'

'I'm sorry what are you talking about?'

'She went to the airport and made contact with one of Rigby's students.'

'I see. Was there a problem?'

'She got busted.'

'Oh shit.'

'No, she got away. But they were trying to hold her there, and right before she got away she said the NCA were coming. They were going to interrogate her.'

That sounded unlikely to Mesh. 'They must have been Essex Police.'

'No, they weren't. Gloria knows the difference, and she's freaked out.'

'Did they show her ID?'

'No, but I trust her.'

Mesh sighed. Satinder had gone quiet at the other end of the hall. Too quiet. She dreaded to think what he might be getting up to.

'Is Gloria with you? Can you put her on?'

'Hold on.'

Mesh held the phone away from her head. She called, 'Satinder, what are you up to?'

'Hello?' Gloria said. 'Hello?'

'I'm here,' Mesh said. 'How can I help?'

'Steady asked me to go the airport to see what I could find out about the ...'

'Sorry, can I just stop you,' Mesh said. 'The people you were talking to would have been Essex Police. No crime was committed so it's unlikely they're going to follow up. I just wanted to reassure you.'

'I don't need reassurance,' Gloria shot back. 'Your people are in on this. They saw the magazine and whoosh, the NCA arrives.'

'What makes you so sure they were NCA?'

'Because they got that look, like they had part of their brain removed.'

Mesh wasn't taking that. 'If you're going to be rude, then ...'

'Wait no, I'm sorry, that sounded terrible. I don't mean it like that. I mean, like you guys are all really confident, like you have no self-doubt.'

Mesh took a breath and calmed herself. *What the hell was Satinder up to?* 'How many of them were there?'

'Maybe three or four. Couple of beefcake guys, and this

beanpole.'

An alarm rang in Mesh's head. 'What do you mean, beanpole?'

'Tall guy, really tall.'

'How tall?'

'Like a basketball player. But thin. And white.'

'How old?'

'Forty-five, maybe.'

'Did he identify himself?'

'I didn't stick around to get his name. He was the boss, though. The others were walking a couple of paces behind. Soon as I saw them I ran for it. Hold on, Steady wants to say something.'

Steadman came on. 'Mesh, are you double-sure the NCA didn't do a deal with Rigby?'

Until the phone call, Mesh would have sworn that they didn't have anything to do with it. But Gloria's description sounded unmistakably like Mark Putts. What would he be doing there, unless ...?

She said, 'I know you don't want to confront Rigby about this ...'

'But it's high time I did,' Steadman said, finishing the sentence for her.

A crash came from the front room.

'Satinder!' Mesh called, breaking into a run. 'Are you alright ...?'

26

Putts was the last person anyone should trust, Rigby knew, but getting the memory card back could benefit him in many different ways. Posing as a student eager to interview Balorat for his PhD thesis, he made contact with Guys. He asked them to provide some times when Balorat might be able to spare an hour, and from that information, plus a little extra conversation with the admin assistant, was able to work out when Balorat was certain to be away from his office.

The hallway on the sixth floor of Guys Hospital was dark, with offices both sides, and a grey linoleum floor. It was like stepping back in time to the 1970s, he thought. The offices had name plaques on the doors and at the far end, he found the one he was looking for: Prof. V. Balorat. He'd brought his lock-picking set just in case, but fortunately the old locks had been replaced by keycards. Rigby's crypto contained a keycard emulator app he'd written himself. All he had to do was hold it to the reader for about thirty seconds and ... *Click.*

He turned the handle and eased the door open. A cold draught, carrying a vague whiff of formaldehyde, flowed into the corridor. A voice within him said, don't go in. There was still the option, even now, of turning around and going home. Nothing had been taken; no damage done. The SD card was the size of a cornflake, how likely was he to find it anyway? He would have turned back, were it not for the fact that there was so little in the office: a desk, a solitary chair, a filing cabinet – how quaint – and a single shelf with a row of skulls. It wouldn't take very long to search. He could be in and out in minutes. In addition to the furniture, a pinboard with scraps of paper and business cards was fixed to the wall behind the desk. There were no family photos, he noticed, either on the board or on the desk, but next to the usual medical certificates hung a single picture. Rigby went closer to inspect it. The photo was of two men, at some kind of conference. He recognised one as Balorat, and the other – yes, he was sure – was Richard Dawkins, the geneticist. They were shaking hands. Balorat's head was dipped deferentially.

He slid open the desk drawer and rifled through it. There was nothing except pens, pencils, paper clips, and a box of latex gloves. Pulling a pair on, he rubbed his prints from the handle of the drawer, just in case, then went over to the filing cabinet. Its contents surprised him. It contained the deeds to Balorat's house, copies of his Self Assessment forms, plus payslips, some dating back more than fifteen years. Putts had been right, Balorat kept everything important within arm's reach. He pushed the file holders to the back and rummaged underneath. Nothing. He examined the desk, the cabinet, the photo frames, and the pinboard. Still nothing. Putts had insisted that the SD card would be there somewhere.

He turned to the shelf of skulls. They were of different shapes and sizes, and he wasn't sure if all of them were human. He picked up the first. The material surprised him. He'd assumed it would be plastic, but it had little crevices and discolorations like an original. More importantly, there was no SD card, not inside or underneath, or glued to it anywhere. Hoping for a better result, he picked up the next. No card there either. Or the next.

As he raised the fourth skull, he heard a 'ting' from the lift. Was someone coming? He hurried to check inside the skull, and the jawbone fell into his hand. He was lucky to catch it before it smashed on the floor. Willing himself to slow down and be more careful, he put the skull back together and arranged it carefully on the shelf. As he lifted the fifth skull, his heart gave a leap. A black object was visible through a gap in the teeth. That had to be it. All he had to do was fish it out and dash to the lift.

As he poked his fingers into the mouth, he heard a voice.

'Fascinating, isn't it.'

He spun. Standing in the doorway was Balorat. He wore a green operating gown; a surgical mask dangled from his chin.

'Put it down. It's a Denisovan, one of the rarest skulls on earth.'

Rigby swallowed hard. Slowly, he replaced the skull. 'I wanted to speak to you,' he said. 'It's about Mark Putts.'

'Save it,' Balorat hissed. 'I know why you're here.'

There was little point carrying on his charade. Rigby held up the chip. 'You mean this.'

'Don't swallow it, son. I'll slit you open.'

'You'll have to catch me first.'

Balorat wasn't expecting an attack, and he barely had time to get his hands up as Rigby grabbed a skull off the shelf and threw it at him. It hit him on the forehead, and he staggered into the filing cabinet. Rigby threw another, and then another. Balorat retreated towards his desk, allowing Rigby to inch closer to the door. He could make it out, but that wasn't going to be enough. With so many hospital staff and security around, he wouldn't stay free for long. Grabbing another skull, he launched himself at Balorat and brought it down on his head. The pathologist collapsed in a heap. Rigby saw an outstretched leg and jumped on the knee with his full weight. Balorat screamed, and Rigby felt sure he must have broken it. That was more like it; there was no way he'd come after him now. To make sure, he trod on the knee again. As he did, he felt a sharp, stinging pain in his left leg. He glanced down in shock. Balorat held a syringe. The pathologist snarled something Rigby couldn't catch, but he was too busy making his escape to care.

He ran first towards the lift, and then, remembering how long it had taken to arrive, turned back and headed for the emergency stairs at the other end of the hall. Before he'd made it even half way, he felt a leg give way underneath him and he tumbled to the floor. For a second he thought he'd tripped, but then felt the leg and realised it had gone numb. Using his arms and his other leg, he heaved himself up and started hopping.

Behind him, a door slammed. He turned. Balorat had made it out of the office. It was okay, Rigby told himself, he was almost there. A few hops later, he pushed open the emergency door, and then fell through it as his other leg gave way. Lying on the ground, winded, he felt the numbness spreading upwards through his torso. *Is this it?* Rigby said to himself, panicked. *Is this how I'm going to die?* Balorat's dead leg scraped along the floor, growing closer. How Rigby had the presence of mind to slip off one of the latex gloves and put the card inside, tying the end before he lost use of his hands, he would never know. As the numbness came into his shoulders and neck, he became aware, terrifyingly aware, of his senses going dead, one after the other.

His body was dead to him but his mind was still in overdrive. He put the glove in his mouth and choked it down, then tipped himself down the first flight of stairs. He felt nothing. When he arrived at the bottom, he almost laughed. Inching forward to the next flight, he tipped himself again. Once again, a tumble that would normally have left him wracked with pain had no effect at all. When he'd come to a stop, he waited and listened. The door to the stairway hadn't opened. It was possible, just possible, that Balorat had taken the lift. He rolled again. Just a couple more. He was losing consciousness now. Over and down he went, one last time.

Putts was in his office when the phone rang. Balorat. Right on schedule.

'Vincent,' he said breezily, 'how can I help?'

'That little twat was in my office.'

'Which little twat would that be?'

'You sent him, didn't you? The tosher.'

'Give me a break. What the did he want?'

'The chip, of course.'

'Jesus,' Putts said still playing innocent, and enjoying it. 'But you stopped him, right?'

Balorat hesitated. Putts bit his knuckle. 'Damn near broke my leg.'

He got it! If Balorat had fought him off he'd be crowing about it. 'Where are you now? We'd better find him.'

'I'm in the foyer. I went after him but I couldn't see him. I called hospital security. They're looking for him now.'

'That's good.'

'I stuck him with the hypo. He can't have got far.'

'Excellent. Good work.' Praising him came to Putts more easily than he thought it would, but now came the difficult part. 'You and I need to get together, talk about next steps.'

As he suspected, Balorat didn't reply at first. After a few seconds, he said, cagily, 'Why?'

'Because when hospital security find him they'll put him under watch. We need to get at him ... and get the card back.' He bit his tongue, waiting for the reply.

Balorat grunted.

'Did he swallow it?' Putts said.

'I don't know.'

'Well, if he did, you can have the pleasure of cutting him open.'

After a few seconds, Balorat said, 'Where are you now?'

Punching the air, Putts said, 'I can be there in a few minutes. Wait out front and I'll pick you up.'

He threw on his jacket and headed out to the lift. He walked slowly and smiled at the guards as he passed security.

Balorat stood outside the hospital, wondering where the hell Putts was. He'd said he'd be there in a few minutes, but it had been over a quarter of an hour. He was pulling out his phone, about to call the fool, when a motorbike blasted its horn. Balorat's head whipped around. The rider leaned over and swerved in his direction. There was a figure behind him riding pillion. Balorat realised in that instant what was about to happen. As they passed, the rider slowed for the passenger to raise an automatic and squeeze off three shots.

He fell hard. His neck and chest roared with pain. As he lay, unable to move, he was aware of still being alive. The physician in him reacted by trying to work out which blood vessels might have been hit, calculating how long he could hold himself together until help arrived. He had to live, there was no option. How else could he warn Sylvie? How else could he get a message to K? How else would he be able to go after Putts and Rigby and rip their fucking balls off?

He felt his body going cold. A blur of faces appeared before his eyes. He tried to reach out and grab them. He tried to shout, to name his murderer. There was no way Putts could get away with this. He'd got it all wrong. He was the biggest fucking idiot. How could he make such a stupid mistake? He reached for the hypo. It was empty. He wanted a refill. He wanted a gun. He wanted K. He felt colder. He wanted Sylvie. He wanted a blanket. He wanted it to stop.

The room smelled strongly of plastic. Rigby felt like he was going to be sick. He retched but nothing came up. His stomach sucked itself inwards half a dozen times as it tried to expel its phantom contents. When he eventually caught his breath, he held on, not wanting to let it out in case he never got it back again. After a while he had no choice but to exhale, and he counted the seconds, waiting for a convulsion. A few moments later, feeling calmer, he blinked his eyes open. A fluorescent strip flickered above, the brightness stinging his eyes. This wasn't the stairway, he surmised; the walls were white and he was lying on a bed. Somebody had found him and brought him here. Feeling panicked again, he tried to sit up. It didn't hurt, but there was no strength in his body. Hoisting himself an inch off the mattress, he saw an IV line in his arm.

The effort exhausted him and he lay down again. He

tried to keep his lids open, but eventually gave in to sleep. When he woke, the room was exactly the same, including the stench, but fortunately he was spared the dry heaves. Sitting up this time, he felt stronger and more alert. The drug that Balorat had shot him with was wearing off, he guessed. A blind had been drawn over the window, but it had a degree of opacity. Forcing himself to focus, he could make out a bright triangular sliver. The Shard, he guessed. He was still at Guys Hospital then. He felt relieved, but the feeling lasted no more than a few seconds before he remembered how he'd got here, and by whose hand. He could still be in danger. Ripping the IV from his arm, he threw the sheet off, then twisted around on the bed and launched himself forward.

It was a huge mistake. His legs didn't respond. He barely had time to put his arms up before crashing to the floor. Without thinking, he shouted for help, which brought a nurse. She called for assistance, and before he knew what was going on, he felt himself being lifted back onto the bed.

'Junkies, you're all damn fools,' a nurse said to him firmly. 'If it was up to me, we wouldn't treat you.'

What was she talking about? 'I'm no junkie.' He was aware of his words coming out slurred. He doubted if the nurse could understand.

'There was enough Midazolam in you to stone half the hospital.'

'Someone shot me up with it.'

'You're not the first, not by a long way. You were lucky someone found you,' she said, reattaching the IV. 'Don't take this out again.'

'Who found me?'

'Security, of course. They have to search every floor and stairway after a lockdown.'

Lockdown? What was that about? He felt his lids go heavy. Had they sedated him? He doubted it, not with all that other drug going around. But it made no difference, he couldn't stay awake.

When he came round, a blurred face floated over him. It wasn't the nurse; this was a white male. He tried to focus, then he heard a voice he recognised.

'Where is it?' the voice said.

Rigby blinked hard, wanting to double-check that he wasn't mistaken. His whole body stiffened. It was Putts. On instinct, he flattened himself into the bed.

Putts leaned in closer. 'I said, where is it?'

'Where's what?'

Putts's face was now right up against his, almost nose to nose. Rigby braced himself. 'Where's what?' Putts hissed, mocking him. 'Where's what?'

There was no point trying to pretend. 'Balorat took it.'

'Bollocks. We searched his body.'

Rigby felt himself go cold. 'Body?'

'That's right,' Putts said, icily. 'Happened right outside here. Shooter on a motorbike.'

That explained the lockdown.

Putts pressed his face up close to Rigby's ear. 'I'll ask you one more time. Where is it?'

Rigby swallowed hard – the stench of Putts's breath made him want to gag. He croaked the words out. 'It was in his office, just like you said. I was about to leave when he came in. Shot me up with drugs and took it.'

'You really are a weed,' Putts said sitting up. 'No wonder out of all the kids in the camp the poofter chose you.'

Rigby swung at him but his arms were putty. Putts caught his fist in mid-air as if it had been moving in slow-motion. He twisted hard. Rigby yelped.

'Where's the card, Rigby?'

'I don't know,' he squeaked. 'He took it.'

Putts twisted harder. 'Okay, have it your way. But if you're lying, you're a dead man. And don't try going to Mesh, either. You have nothing on me. *Nothing.* I am the only chance you have. Do things my way and I can still get us both out of it.

Do you understand?'

Rigby tried to nod.

'Do you understand?' he said again, twisting the arm harder.

'I get it. Fucking let go.'

Putts let go.

Rigby shut his eyes. When he opened them again, he had gone.

He counted to one hundred, then rang for the nurse. It took her an age to show up, and when she did, she didn't look pleased.

'What the problem now?' she said.

'When you're unconscious, what happens with your bowel movements?'

She blinked. 'I beg your pardon?'

'When you're unconscious, do you still, like, go?'

The question clearly irritated her. 'Why?' she said stiffly. 'Are you having problems in that area?'

He shook his head. 'I just want to know.'

'Why?'

'I just *do*.'

She shook her head. 'I have patients to attend to. I don't have time to play Wikipedia.'

He rubbed his stomach. This was the dangerous part. If he overplayed it, she might actually want to treat it. 'It hurts a little.'

Her face softened. 'When you're unconscious, peristalsis ceases. After you wake, everything starts up again, but if it doesn't, we can administer a laxative.'

'Thank you,' he said. As he spoke she came over and checked his lines, then turned to go. He said, 'I'm sorry to disturb your rounds.'

'It's not a problem,' she said, making clear that it was.

As soon as she'd gone, he twisted himself around and poked his legs out of the bed. He slid forward gently, careful not to go too far this time. Stretching out one leg, then the other, he gradually put weight on them. To his relief, he was able to stand. He shuffled forward, letting go of the bed, beyond the point of no return ... One foot, then the other ... His clothes were in the closet on the opposite side of the room. Could he make it? Sticking his arms out like Frankenstein's monster, he launched himself forward. His legs felt like they had gym weights stuck to them, but he made it to the door handle and grabbed hold, just in time before he fell. He dragged himself to his feet and checked the cupboard. As fast as he could, he pulled on his clothes. Happily, his debit card was still in the inside trouser pocket.

Would there be a guard outside the door? He cracked it open. Clear. Maybe Putts didn't want to draw attention, maybe the cop was in the gents, he didn't care. Tucking himself into doorways, he inched his way to the lift and pressed the down button. Outside, he hailed a cab.

'Where to?' said the cabbie.

'Chiswick.'

He fell asleep in the cab, and when he woke again they were in Hammersmith. He asked the cabbie to wait outside a chemist, and ran straight to the pharmacy desk. There were two people already waiting in line. He battled to contain himself as the pharmacist, a young man with bow tie, took his sweet time.

When he finally reached the front of the queue, he said, 'What's your fastest-acting laxative?'

The pharmacist looked surprised. 'Well, you don't necessarily want it to be too fast acting.'

'It's an emergency,' Rigby said, aware other customers were now waiting behind him.

'What kind of emergency?'

'The kind that needs a fast-acting laxative.'

Shaking his head, the pharmacist said, 'If you can't tell me your symptoms, then I can't recommend the correct remedy.' He glanced over Rigby's shoulder, ready to serve the person behind.

'I have something stuck in there, okay?' Rigby said. He held up his finger. 'Stuck right up there.'

The pharmacist's lips twisted in disapproval, then reached for a bottle of pills. 'This should sort you out,' he said. As an afterthought he reached for a tube of lubricant. 'You might need this too,' he said.

Rigby took two of the pills and ran out to the taxi. As soon as he arrived home, he grabbed a sieve from the kitchen and retired to the toilet, taking the lubricant with him, just in case, plus his crypto to contact Steadman. It wouldn't be long before Putts discovered him missing from the hospital.

27

The glove came out intact. It had to be about the most disgusting and one of the most painful activities he'd undertaken in a while, but now that it was over he felt jubilant. It could bring him real bargaining power. For the first time since he'd met Mesh at Sherry's, he knew who he was up against, and had the means to fight them.

Coming back out to the kitchen, he tossed the glove into a metal colander, drenched it in disinfectant, rinsed and dried it thoroughly, then took a sharp knife and slit it open. He was lifting the card out with a pair of tweezers when he noticed the low rumble of an engine outside. It couldn't be Steadman, not that quickly. He went to the living room and peeped out the window. His blood ran cold. A motorcyclist had dismounted outside his house. This wasn't Deliveroo.

Rigby had chosen his house partly because the previous owner had altered it substantially from the original layout. The master bedroom occupied most of the first floor. It had a walk-in wardrobe in a wing off to one side, and in the other wing a bathroom and shower with a steam room. On the floor above was an office, and a guest bedroom. A rear staircase, concealed behind a door in the guest bedroom, led down to the kitchen.

Sprinting upstairs, he took a place on the landing, listening for noise and hoping that whoever it was might come to the door, think no-one was home, and ride away again. No such luck. Glass shattered. A door opened and closed. He had to think fast. What would be the safest room? None of them. He needed a diversion.

Running to his office, he prized a bookcase away from the wall and pushed it over. It crashed to the floor, the books spilling everywhere. Then another. And another. Climbing over the bookcases, he ran to the guest bedroom, overturned a chest of drawers, and waited again.

His heart pounded as the rider came up the main stairs. As quietly as he could, Rigby opened the hidden door and closed it behind him. Walking on tiptoes, he descended the hidden stairs to the kitchen and pulled the door at the bottom behind him. He could hear the tread of feet, but couldn't tell over the rush and thump of the pulse in his ears whether the sound came from above him or on the stairs. There might be time, if he ran, to get outside.

Just then, the door he'd closed burst open. Rigby jumped back. The motorcyclist raised his gun. 'Don't move,' said a male voice.

On instinct, Rigby kicked out and knocked his attacker backwards into the kitchen table. The gun fired. Rigby sprinted from the kitchen, grabbed the banister of the main staircase and hurled himself back up towards the bedrooms.

Entering the master suite, he saw his iPad on the nightstand and picked it up. He still had his phone in his pocket. Taking it out, he tossed it onto the floor of the walk-in closet on his side of the room, then ran across to the bathroom on the other side. He opened the iPad and entered the passcode. It would only be a couple of seconds before the rider came in. *One chance.* Watching through a crack in the door, he saw him raise his visor.

It was Maddox. He said, 'Rigby, my orders are to bring you in alive. Don't make me do it the hard way.'

Bullshit. He was here for the card, that was all.

Locating himself in Contacts, Rigby messaged himself.

The phone chirruped.

Maddox wheeled around towards the noise.

'I could have taken you down any time,' Maddox said. 'Think about it. You're valuable to them.'

He sent another message, triggering a second bleep.

Doesn't want to go in, in case I jump him.

'The easy way is to come out. Hands in the air. Last chance.'

Like a stalking cat, Maddox took a step forward, then another. Rigby waited until he disappeared into the closet, then ran from the bathroom and slammed the door behind him. Grabbing a chair, he slid it under the handle, wedging it closed. *Won't hold for long.*

Splinters exploded from the door panels as Maddox began firing, but Rigby was already hurling himself down the stairs.

Cracking the back door, he stuck his head out. Clear. He came out and tiptoed down the side passage. Ahead of him, a shadow disappeared around the front of the house. All along the passage, bricks had been used to mark out a flower bed. He spotted one that looked slightly out of place, and kicked hard to loosen it. Then he bent down and dug at the earth with his fingers, wrenching the brick loose. He crept forward to where he'd seen the shadow.

As he poked his head around the corner of the house, he could see a figure in the bushes, but couldn't identify it. He raised the brick over his head, took a step forward, and a hand grabbed him around the neck. He swung with the brick. It connected with something hard, then he felt a hand grab his arm.

'Rigby, stop, it's me!'

He spun around.

Steadman! 'What are you doing here?'

'I got your message, dickhead. Now move.'

Steadman grabbed his arm and they ran together up the side of the house.

Behind them, a gun started firing. Bullets bounced off the path.

'Go! Go!' Steadman yelled, covering his head.

They leapt into the car. Steadman fumbled to insert the key while Rigby, craned round to watch the driveway, saw a figure in a visor emerge onto the pavement. The man raised his gun. Rigby pulled Steadman's head down as he ducked. There was a rapid volley of shots and a bullet bounced off the wing mirror shattering the glass. A second later the engine fired, and Steadman, ducked down behind the wheel, burned rubber.

As they tore through Chiswick, Rigby kept listening for sirens, but what concerned him more was the cut on Steadman's head where he'd hit him with the brick. It had come up like an egg and was bleeding down his face and shirt.

'Steady, you cannot believe how happy I am to see you.'

'Is that so.'

'You saved my arse back there.'

'Then how about you do me a favour and quit lying to me.'

Rigby did a double-take. He tried to laugh it off. 'Come on, what are you talking about?'

'About what you're really doing on your days off ...'

Alarm bells. *Days off? What did he know about that?*

'We know about Mark Putts,' Steadman added.

Jesus!

'Stop the car. Pull over,' Rigby said.

'Stop? Why?'

'Damn it, pull over!' Rigby grabbed the wheel. Steadman fought him off and pulled into a lay-by. Rigby reached for the door handle. 'Follow me.'

Steadman looked surprised, but Rigby waved at him to get out.

They were on Chiswick Lane, across the Hogarth Roundabout from Fuller's Brewery. 'If I leave it there, it's a ticket,' Steadman said.

Rigby ignored him, heading off into the underpass.

'Fuck it!' Steadman said, slamming the door.

'Hurry up,' Rigby called.

'Who saved who, eh, who saved who?' Steadman

shouted after him.

Rigby carried on, not looking back until he was at the riverside, then he did a head-check. Steadman was about twenty metres behind him. In front and to the sides, no-one. Above, drone free. Good. They could talk.

'What do you know about Putts?' Rigby said to Steadman, once he'd caught up.

'Gloria got pinched at Stansted. She was tracking some of your students,' Steadman wheezed, trying to catch his breath. 'She saw him there. He was coming to question her.'

That was already too much, *way* too much. 'Who else knows?'

'Just us and Warren. And Mesh Kaur.'

'You have to stay out of this. Never speak of it. They could have bugged your car, or the office, or anywhere. It's not safe.'

Steadman seemed angrier than Rigby had ever seen him. He shoved Rigby in the chest. 'Of course it's not safe.' He shoved again. 'Warren got shot.' And again. 'Gloria damned near got busted.' And another time. 'I had bullets flying past my ear.'

Rigby shoved him back. 'Exactly. So get out of here. Leave me alone.'

'I want some answers. You told us you were out riding, and writing apps, and the whole time you were colluding with Mark fucking Putts.'

'I'm not colluding!'

'Then what are you doing?' He shoved Rigby again, harder this time. 'You had the chance to stand up, and you went and joined those bastards.'

'I was trying to protect you!'

'How? How are you protecting me?'

'They know. About us. About how we all came together. About why I left the NCA.'

Steadman stared at him in disbelief. 'So fucking what?'

'So fucking everything. They kidnapped Frank and

interrogated him. Stuck probes in him. He told them everything. They know about your sister, your mum ...'

'You know what? I don't care. I never have. I got abused as a kid. But it wasn't my fault. I don't have to make reparations for it. That's not why I chase paedos, I do it to prevent it from happening to someone else.'

'But they said they'll falsify evidence, make it look like we're a ring, that we're preying on all these kids we're trying to help.'

Steadman's eyes burned red, but Rigby could see that despite in his anger, an understanding was beginning to form. 'That's what they threatened you with?'

'Yes! And they've people in the NCA, and a forensics guy. They can plant whatever they want, even DNA. The only way I can stop them is to get in with them.'

'Bollocks. You're a weak bastard.'

'No! We can stop them. And I need your help.'

Blood continued to race down Steadman's forehead. He pushed on the wound, trying to stop it. 'How?'

Rigby reached into his jeans pocket and pulled out the memory card.

'Is that the one I gave Lana?'

'Putts stole it from her. And then Balorat nicked it from him. I stole it back and almost got killed for it. That's what the guy was doing at my house. I didn't realise, but it has details of Putts's partner. I toshed her years ago. We need to get this to Makepeace Dale.'

'Shouldn't we give it to Mesh?'

'No, whatever you do, don't give it to her.'

Steadman frowned. 'Why not?'

'Too many people around her work for Putts.'

Steadman nodded. He dabbed at his forehead with his sleeve and grimaced when he saw the results.

'You want to get that looked at,' Rigby said.

'I'll be fine.'

'There's one other thing. Mark Putts is planning something. I haven't figured it out yet, but it's something that will earn him a shitload of money.'

'Is it part of this?'

'I don't know. He might be trying to buy his way out. He plays the stock market. See if he's made any big investments recently.'

'I'll get the team on it.'

The two men looked at each other for a few seconds without speaking. Rigby suddenly felt his guts turn to water.

'Oh no.'

'What?'

'The laxative.'

'You need the khazi?'

He held up a hand. 'Don't worry about me. We need to figure out a way to get that card to Dale without anyone else knowing about it. Assume there's 24-hour surveillance on him.'

Rigby felt his stomach about to explode. 'Go!'

Steadman called Mesh. They met at Skagbucks. He had the place to himself – no-one on the nod today – with a headache like fourteen rock drills digging into his cranium. He'd washed the cut, put a huge plaster on it, and taken four ibuprofen. None of it made any difference. Mesh was late, as usual. He wasn't offended. She did it to everyone. Despite his head, when she finally came up the stairs, his heart gave a little flutter.

She took one look at the injury and rushed to the table. 'What happened?'

Before he could tell her, she took his chin, pushed his head sideways, and lifted the bandage. 'You poor thing. You should get this looked at.'

'I'll be okay.'

'You might need stitches. I'll take you.'

'It's fine, really.'

'How did it happen?'

'Rigby hit me with a brick.'

'Rigby? Why?'

'I was saving his life.'

'*What*?'

He told her what happened. At the end, he said, 'You're sure no-one followed you?'

She nodded. 'I was careful. New clothes, fine comb, the works. You?'

'Same. I dress a lot better, normally.' He tried a smile, but she was too caught up in his injury. Giving the room one last check, he said quietly, 'It was Putts's guys. They were after this.' He held out the card. 'Rigby says the identity of Putts's accomplice is on here. The mastermind behind the whole thing.'

She stuck out her hand. 'Better let me have that.'

'No. Putts's guys are everywhere. We can't risk it being intercepted.'

'You can trust the Sweatbox, and we can get the information off it faster ...'

'No! It's got to go to Dale.' He put a hand on hers. 'I can't put you in danger. I just can't.'

She didn't argue, and instead looked again at his wound, probing with a finger. When he winced, she pulled away, and instead stroked his head. Suddenly aware of herself, she drew back.

Steadman said, 'Thank you.'

'What for?' She turned away, suddenly shy.

He couldn't take his eyes off her. She noticed him looking. 'What?'

Damn! Busted. 'There was something I want to ask you, and I keep thinking this isn't the right time.'

'In my experience, there's never a right time.'

He took a deep breath. Why had he found it so hard the last few years to tell anyone how he felt? When he was younger he used knock the girls over like bowling pins. 'When this is over, do you want to get a drink?'

She looked worried by the question. 'I don't drink.'

'Okay then, how about some food?'

'Like, lunch?'

'Sure. Or dinner. Hell, any of the meals.'

'Just the two of us?'

Why did women always have to ask that question? It was the I'm-going-to-double-double-check-that-this-really-is-a-date question. It sucked. 'Yes.'

'You need your head examined.'

'What?'

She pointed to his head. 'Don't look so shocked, it was a joke.'

'Sorry,' he said, trying to laugh it off. 'I ...'

She put a finger to his lips, then took it away and kissed him quickly. 'Yes. I'd like that. Now, what's your plan for getting that to Dale?'

He shrugged, feeling tired and not thinking as clearly as he would have wanted. 'Got any ideas?'

She nodded. 'He drives in every day. Never takes a meeting after 4pm because he likes to leave the office by five at the latest to beat the traffic – but he gets in early. Sometimes at six.'

'Where does he park?'

'He works in the Home Office Annex. There's a parking garage under a residential building at the back. Drives a Discovery. Silver. Brand new.'

'What time is it now?'

She checked her phone. 'One thirty.'

He watched intently as she chewed her lip. 'What is it?'

She said, 'I don't think this will nail Putts all by itself.'

Steadman heaved a sigh. It felt as though Putts had been more than a step ahead of them the whole way, and Rigby said that even now he thought there was something else up the guy's sleeve.

She patted his hand. 'You deliver that. I have another idea that I think might help.'

On his way out, he called Rigby.

'How are you feeling?' Steadman asked him.

'Like the world fell out of my arse. You?'

'Like it landed on my head.' He wasn't kidding. 'I talked to Mesh.'

'I said don't give it to her.'

'I didn't,' Steadman said, annoyed. 'But I found out where Dale parks, what he drives, and what time he leaves the office. Am I excused?'

There was a pause on the other end. 'Sorry.'

'So go get your bike. Meet me at Lambeth Bridge in ninety minutes.'

'I hope you've thought this through,' Rigby said. 'Last time we tried something with Dale, we underestimated him.'

'That was you,' Steadman said. 'This is me.'

Gloria felt herself shaking as she tried to blend into the tourist group making their way down Whitehall. The task Steadman had given her was to be the initiation programme, the boot file for the whole operation. Should she fail, nothing else would follow. Her job was to spot Dale coming out of the car park and alert the others. That gave her a problem, because the exit was on a road teeming with government buildings. There were dozens of security cameras, and anyone hanging around with no obvious purpose was going to catch the attention of the authorities. Fortunately, she'd thought of a workaround. It was one of those funny things that no-one else would ever know about – like writing a great a piece of code – but made her feel proud of herself.

Just after 3pm she'd arrived on foot, wearing a Gore-Tex jacket, hiking boots, a bush hat and backpack. She was carrying a large map. She walked the roads of Westminster, stopping outside the government buildings, snapping pictures of each and marking them off on her map. For anyone watching, she was nothing more than a nerdy tourist with a penchant for landmarks.

Heading up Monck Street, behind the Home Office, Gloria consulted her map, turning it this way and that, as if she were lost. What was really bothering her was that there were two parking garages. Fortunately, she'd brought more than one camera. She paused opposite the first garage, and leant up against a lamppost. Behind the map, she took from her pocket a tiny webcam. On the back she'd fixed a double-sided adhesive sticker. She peeled off the covering, reached behind, and stuck it to the post. Walking another twenty metres up the road, she checked the app on her phone. Sure enough, the camera was broadcasting perfectly, giving her a clear sight of the garage entrance. Pleased with her work, she repeated the procedure with the second. Keeping an eye on the phone to make sure she stayed within range, Gloria found a café and ordered a well-earned cappuccino. MI5's offices were only a stone's throw away, and she smiled to herself. The café she'd chosen was probably well-frequented by spooks. But even if it was crawling with them, they'd see her as nothing more than a tourist, watching videos on Instagram.

At four fifty-two, a silver Discovery came up the ramp to the gate. The driver waved to the gate guard. Zooming in, Gloria recognised Dale behind the wheel. *Bingo*. She called Steadman and Rigby. 'Our friend is leaving work now, heading south towards Horseferry Road.'

Rigby was waiting on his bike further down, at the Lambeth Bridge roundabout. While Gloria had been watching the screen, he'd been doing slow laps of the area, trying not to look conspicuous by staying in one place for too long. As Dale pulled up at the junction, Rigby pedalled hard and caught up, then slipped in behind. They expected him to come around the roundabout and head west on the Embankment, following it up through Chelsea to the A4. The plan was for Rigby to follow until the inevitable snarl-up around Earls Court, and then make an approach.

Everything went as planned until they hit Vauxhall

Bridge, then he called Steadman in a panic. 'I thought it was meant to be rush hour. There's no traffic. I can't keep up.'

He felt terribly out of condition. If they'd been doing this six months ago it would have been a walk in the park. He'd managed to stay behind Dale for the first mile, but his thighs burned and the car had begun to vanish into the distance.

Steadman said, 'Keep on him, you'll get him.'

His lungs felt like they would explode, but he pressed on, and soon Steadman was proved right. The traffic was growing heavier. Dale became struck behind a long line of cars at the Chelsea Bridge junction. Normally, Rigby would have slipped down the inside, but a bus had stopped to pick up passengers. He held his breath and swung out into the oncoming lane. It was empty, thank God, and he flew past the row of queuing cars. But ahead of him the traffic lights were already turning amber. Dale's Disco was one of the last to make it through. *Damn!* Rigby dug in, but the light went red before he arrived.

Holding his breath, he stood on the pedals, and sailed through the red into no-man's land. A car came at him from the side. He heaved on his brakes, almost sending himself over the handlebars. The driver swerved to avoid him, blaring his horn and swearing at the top of his voice. Other cars stopped to let Rigby through. There were more horns, more shouts. He rocketed away, but there was no sign of the Disco.

He hit his fist on the handlebars. 'I've lost him!'

'Where are you now?' Steadman said.

'Still on the Embankment.'

'Just keep going straight.'

Another vital few seconds passed. Rigby rode hard, feeling the sweat pour from his head, the icy air sweeping through the slats in his helmet.

'Hold on,' Rigby said. 'I think I've got him. No. Wait. Yep. No, definitely.'

'Make your mind up,' Steadman said.

'It's him, definitely.'

‘Still on the Embankment?’

‘No, we’re up on Warwick Road, stuck in a jam.’

They had one shot. He had to get to Dale before he turned onto the A4. It was too fast a road for a bike to possibly keep up, even in rush hour. He could see the Discovery up ahead. He slowed as he came nearer, then rode up next to it and rapped on the window.

Dale was talking on the phone. Concentrating on the conversation, he waved Rigby away without even looking at him. Rigby rapped again, but still Dale didn’t turn. The road ahead cleared and the Disco accelerated away. Rigby sprinted as fast as he could and caught him, but the lights at the A4 turning had gone green. If Dale made it through, the chase would be over. He sprinted again, and was able to inch his way past the Disco. As soon as he’d drawn ahead, he cut in front, slowed to walking pace, unclipped his shoes, and then hit the brakes.

There were moments cycling when all you could do was hope. This was one of them.

He felt his back collide with the bonnet of the Discovery, and the bike disappeared underneath with a sickening scrape. Dale came to a stop and gave a long blast on the horn. Rigby slid off the front of the car, and when he stood up, Dale was shouting at him through the windscreen, waving his fist.

Drivers in the outside lane, who’d continued to stream past, now stopped to have a look. One of them wound down the window to ask if Rigby wanted help, but he shook his head and gave a thumbs-up.

Dale stuck his head out of the window. ‘What the fuck were you doing?!’

‘Me? You drove into me!’

‘You didn’t even look where you were going!’

Nothing could be further from the truth, Rigby wanted to tell him. The manoeuvre had required pinpoint accuracy. ‘Says you in your Chelsea tractor. My bike is ruined.’

He bent down to pull it out from under the car. It came

out in one piece, twisted and battered. The front wheel was bent in half.

'That's a three thousand pound bike,' Rigby shouted.

Dale got out to assess the damage. Behind them, horns started blaring. Before he could say anything, Rigby tore off his helmet and sunglasses.

Dale did a double-take. 'What the fuck?'

Rigby whipped out of his backpack a folder containing the memory card, plus written instructions on what to do with it and what it meant, including everything Putts had told him about K. He thrust it into Dale's chest. 'Read this. All of it. Check the memory card. There's a woman on there who used to work for a bank. She's now the mastermind behind an organised criminal gang. Mark Putts is in it with her. Tudor Clarke was working for them. They're behind everything Mesh found in Belgrade. Earlier today they killed Vincent Balorat, a third partner. They tried to kill me too.' He added, 'Our only advantage is they don't know you have this.'

'I don't want it,' Dale said, wide-eyed. 'Give it to the NCA.'

'It's not safe. Anyone who works with Putts is compromised. Mesh Kaur is the one person there you can trust, but she needs your help. You have to read this.'

Dale's face drained of blood as he realised what it meant. He held up his hands. 'Sorry, I can't take this. It's not my fight.'

Rigby thrust it at him again, rocking him back on his heels. 'A secret NCA programme to tosh digital records. Abuse of the witness protection programme. A missing GCHQ agent. A murder-for-hire ring operating on the dark web. And to top it off, a rich brat at the Home Office who won't investigate because it's bad for his career. That's one hell of a story. It's either going to you or *The Guardian*. You have three seconds to decide. One. Two ...'

Dale blinked again, his face twitching as he processed the information. Behind them, more cars had joined in the honking.

'This will not play well!' Dale said, and snatched the folder from Rigby's hands. 'If it doesn't stack up, I'm shredding it.'

A string of cars was diverting around them. As they passed, each of the drivers made their anger clear, shaking a fist or tapping the horn. Terrified of being recognised, Dale covered his face with the folder and hurried back to his car. Rigby held out a hand to stop the line, then dragged his mangled bike to the side of the road and called Steadman to come and collect him.

28

Mesh was furious with herself. Aisling sat across from her in Mesh's office, both of them waiting for news from Rigby or Steadman, and powerless to do anything for the moment.

'How could I not have seen it?' she said to Aisling. 'He was my own boss. I dealt with him every day.'

'That's why you didn't,' Aisling said. 'But neither did anyone else.'

Mesh wasn't listening, lost in stream of self-criticism, 'I only discovered the names by accident. I go around in a state of constant irritation with other people's sloppiness.'

'You're pernickety. That's a good thing.'

'Is it?' They sat for a moment. At length, Mesh said, 'I can't believe I let it get this far. There were warning signs.'

Aisling looked up, curious. 'Like what?'

'He's obsessed by wealth. All that talk about the clubs he belongs to, the boarding schools his kids attend. He claims he makes all this money with investments, but if he's so good at it, why's he working here?'

'Perfect cover,' Aisling said. 'Access to resources. Access to personnel.'

Mesh nodded. 'I remember Tudor Clarke. He was immature, impressionable. Easy prey. And Vincent Balorat always gave me the creeps.'

'Do you think we'll ever be able to identify all the officers who colluded with him?'

Mesh allowed herself a small smile. 'Watch out watch for anyone requesting early retirement in the next few weeks. We'll nick them on the spot.'

Her phone rang. 'It's Dale,' she said. She put it on speaker. 'Have you read the file?' she said to him.

'This woman is an abomination,' Dale said. 'She was a cyber-security officer. Real high flyer.'

'Any link to Mark Putts?'

'Not yet.' He paused. 'Do we really think it's there?'

'She couldn't have done it without inside help. You know that.'

'But how can we prove it was him?'

'It was in his department. It's obvious.'

'This will not play well. We're going to need more. Lots more ...'

'We'll get what we need,' she said. 'It'll be good. For both of us.'

'I'm counting on you Mesh. This is not going to be easy.'

'But you're with us?'

He hesitated. 'I'm with you so far.'

The line went dead. Aisling hit the desk with her hand. 'What more does he want?!'

'He wants his arse covered.' Mesh stood up. 'Let's go.'

'Where are we going?'

'To get him something he can stick down his trousers.'

It had come to her in a flash while Dale was talking, and it was an unusual feeling for her. She knew she wasn't a Rigby type, who surfed through life on waves of intuition. She plodded. She sifted. She ground her way through data. But not this time. The answer had simply popped into her head: the car that she and Steadman had seen outside Lana's had been one of Putts's men. They'd been tailing them. Then they'd gone back later to question her, and taken the camera.

She and Aisling went around to the side entrance. A homeless man with greasy grey hair was sitting in the courtyard. He saw them and sniffed the air. 'I smell bacon.' They ignored him and rapped on the door.

Lana answered, and immediately tried to slam it shut.

Aisling stuck her foot in to jam it open, but the old wooden door weighed a ton, and she cried out in agony.

Frank cackled.

Mesh shoved the door ajar and followed Lana down the stairs. 'You lied about the camera,' she called after Lana. 'It wasn't stolen from the school, was it?'

There was no reply.

'Some other officers came here after we'd left, didn't they?'

A voice from nowhere shouted, 'No!'

They arrived at the bottom of the stairs. The room looked the same as the first time Mesh had visited. 'Come back. We don't mean you any harm. Did they hurt you?'

Someone was crying. The sound seemed to be coming from the kitchen on the far side of the room. They found Lana cowering beside a stainless steel table.

'I'm sorry I lied,' she wept. 'I had to protect my daughter.'

Mesh put a hand on her. 'Of course you did. No one's judging you.'

'I let everyone down.'

'No. You did what you had to do.'

'Is Rigby dead?' Lana said.

That took Mesh by surprise. 'No? Did you think he was in danger?'

'Steadman said to keep it safe. He said we had to help Rigby because he was in trouble,' she sobbed.

Mesh waited a few seconds for her to calm. Then she said, 'Can you identify the officers who came to get it from you?'

'No.'

'Did you see them?'

'No.'

'Lana, come on. Don't try to cover up one lie with an even bigger one.'

She stood up, and for the first time Mesh could see the

terror in her eyes. She really didn't know who to trust. 'I've let everyone down. Frank's so scared he won't set foot outside his room, Rigby's in trouble ...'

'Rigby's alive, but he needs your help. Tell me about the men who came to get the camera. What did they look like?'

Lana glanced away. Mesh touched her chin. 'Look at me, Lana. Look at me and give me a description.'

Turning to face her, Lana took a deep breath. 'There were four of them. The leader was like a giant.'

'Super-tall?'

She nodded.

'Skinny?'

'Yes.'

She took out her phone, pulled up a picture of Putts, and stuck it under Lana's nose. 'Is this him?'

'Yes.'

'He set Rigby up,' Aisling said. 'The whole way.'

Mesh nodded. 'Stay here and take a statement from Lana. Don't breathe a word of this to anyone, and don't file the statement until I tell you.'

'Where are you going?' Aisling said.

'There's someone else been telling lies.'

Mesh headed straight out to the Cotswolds. She'd never believed a word of Ascott's story, but hadn't been allowed to question him. Many times she'd thought about going ahead anyway, but contravening a direct order was career suicide so she'd talked herself out if it. She'd also lacked anything to pressure him with. Thanks to Lana that had changed. Ascott had given false evidence. The only question was how deeply he was involved. Had Putts simply paid him to do it, or pressurised him in some way? If so, she might be able to turn him, get him to testify against Putts. If not, if he was embroiled more deeply, she'd find out soon enough.

She arrived at his house and went straight to the door. No answer. A neighbour raking leaves in his garden – who looked 75 if he was a day – called to her from next door.

'He went cruising in the car.'

'What does he drive?' she called back.

The neighbour looked at her strangely. Had she said the wrong thing?

Mesh flashed her card.

'Well why didn't you say so,' the neighbour said with a broad grin. 'I was a Deputy Chief Constable once upon a time.'

That figured, Mesh thought, best neighbour for a crook to have.

'Mid-seventies Maserati,' the man said. 'Got a pair of 'em. Except one doesn't work. He says it does, but I've never seen it out of the garage.'

'What colour's the one that works?'

'Brown. Sort of dog-poo brown. You can tell him I said that. Ha-ha!'

She set off to look for a dog-poo brown Maserati. He couldn't have gone too far. Her satnav only showed a half-dozen roads in the whole area. The narrow country lanes felt more like playing a video game than actual driving. And she hated video games. How could anyone go out 'cruising' on roads like these for pleasure? Surely the point of transportation was to get from point A to point B. Forget what the stupid songs said, it wasn't about the journey, or the climb, or how you played the game, it was about getting there, preferably with some decent music along the way. Driving around in circles purely for entertainment was ... she could think of a dozen words, all of them impolite. Double that for ancient vehicles like the one Ascott drove.

She saw him up ahead, having hunted for him for over an hour, asking at petrol stations and cafés. Oh yes, they said, beautiful car – the throbbing dart, my wife calls it – makes a hell of a racket though. Whooshed past, ooh, half an hour ago, heading north, south, er ... that way.

She suddenly laughed out loud as she remembered the

moment between Steadman and herself in Starbucks. What would her mother say? The look on her face would be priceless: a *habshi* – and a tubby one at that. She didn't know how serious it was, but it was wonderful to feel desired again. But why had it come as such a surprise? Was it her fault? Had she made herself unlikeable, or was she just surrounded by objectionable people? And if that was the case, was it her fault too?

She saw the Maserati ahead and picked up the pace, closing the gap to his rear bumper. She could see him checking her out in the rearview. He accelerated, but she matched his speed. What would he be thinking – that some crazy woman wanted to race him? He couldn't possibly have 'made' her. This was about wanting his space, being king of the road. Did he think the countryside existed purely for his automotive amusement? The road dipped and swerved, then entered a forest. She stayed on his tail, even when he came up behind a slower car and flew past. Surely now he would know something was up.

As she suspected, within a mile he'd turned off the main road down a single-lane track, so tiny it didn't even show up on her sat-nav. It must be a farm path, she thought; not the sort of route a classic car enthusiast would normally choose for his prized possession. He was testing her, seeing if she'd follow. Well, now he had his answer. He'd stop soon to confront her, no doubt.

She had her angles ready. Was he going to come clean and help them make the case, or stick to his story and be charged as an accomplice? She'd put the choice to him as starkly as that. It was no bluff. She'd happily hand him back to Modplod in handcuffs.

She spotted something blue in her mirror. Concentrating on the narrow road, she waited for it to go straight before leaning forward to take a better look. Sure enough, a lorry was closing on her. Who would drive a vehicle like that, down a road like this, at that sort of speed? Farm hands, she said to herself, answering her own question. They knew these tracks.

They didn't expect anyone to be on them.

Her eyes returned to the road just in time. Ascott had stopped, dead ahead.

'Wanker!' she shouted, and stood on the brakes. She kept her foot planted as the car fought for traction on the mud and cow pat, coming to a halt inches from his bumper. Had the truck seen they'd stopped? Alarmed, she checked the rear-view. As she did, she felt a massive shunt from behind and her neck snapped back as the lorry collided with her back end.

The doors opened and two men climbed down. Her body went cold as she saw automatic rifles dangling from their necks. She reached instinctively for her own weapon, but it was already too late: starting a gun battle now, there wouldn't even be time for a suicide note. Ahead of her, a man she didn't recognise stepped from the Maserati.

He was at least forty years younger than Ascott, and was shaking his head – scolding her, it seemed – as if being in this predicament was her fault. Maybe he was right. Maybe it was her fault. She'd been stupid. She should have predicted this. She should have sensed the danger. If only there was someone left she could trust.

With her hand trembling, she reached for the door handle, then changed her mind. There was one person she still trusted. She took out her phone and sent a message. Then she stepped from the car, hands in the air, to face whatever fate she was due.

29

Rigby and Steadman holed up at a new café on Rupert Street, waiting for the phone call that Rigby was certain would arrive soon.

As they waited, he pointed to a stainless steel espresso machine behind the bar. 'That's a Synesso Cyncra,' he said to Steadman.

'Am I supposed to give a shit?'

'It's made in Seattle. Founded by a guy who used to work for LaMarzocca.'

'Kindly refer to my previous statement.'

'The key to great coffee is consistent water temperature. These guys can get less than half a degree of variability over the duration of the shot.'

Steadman took a quick sip. 'Sure, tastes great. Now shut up.'

They waited two hours. Even by his standards, Rigby thought he might have ingested a little too much caffeine. He was on his fourth triple when the call arrived. No number. No name.

A man's voice came on the phone. 'Italian Gardens. Half an hour.'

They walked to Piccadilly Circus tube station, then split up, travelling two different ways to Lancaster Gate. Riding on the tube, Rigby passed the nervous minutes by studying the London Underground map, remembering how, as a young boy, he'd been troubled by the pattern made by the lines. He'd checked other subway maps for comparison. NY was a multitentacled monster probing with its suckers toward the East. Moscow was a spider. Mexico City was confused and random – like a plan gone wrong. Washington DC was a multi-coloured swastika. London had a bottle in the middle, and all tracks led to it. He'd fantasized that an evil group were plotting to control the water supply; they owned the trains and the utilities – like his sister always did when they played Monopoly – and were biding their time to seize control of the capital. The Tube map was a symbol for others hidden all over the world. He'd even told his father about it, who'd laughed and suggested he turn it into a novel. Rigby got two pages in, before losing interest. He was twelve, and it was football season.

The Italian Gardens were four algae-filled ponds with fountains and Romanesque decoration at the head of the Serpentine in Kensington Gardens. Rigby assumed he'd be the first to arrive – he'd given himself the simplest route – but Steadman was waiting for him. It was clear to him why Dale would choose this as a meeting-place: it was completely open, you could see anyone coming or going within a hundred metres, it was filled with visitors, and yet there was no CCTV.

'It's an impressive set-up that Putts created, you have to admit,' Steadman said.

Rigby shook his head. 'Murder is still murder. You could say the same thing about the dark web – how impressive. But child abuse is still child abuse. The technology changes, but we don't. We think we're so clever, so advanced, but nothing ever really gets better.'

'So why do we bother fighting it?'

He knew Steadman knew the answer, but sometimes they had to remind each other. 'Because if we let up, for even an instant, they win.'

Steadman stretched out an arm and pointed. 'There he is.'

When they reached Dale, Rigby noticed that he looked troubled, he kept touching his face with his hands. Steadman was about to say something but Rigby put up an arm to stop him.

Dale turned to Rigby, annoyed. 'You have no idea how much danger you've put us all in. This woman still exists.'

'She's alive, sure,' Rigby said.

'No, I mean her identity. I ran it. She pops.' He held out his phone. On it was a photo of a woman in her thirties whose jaw and eyes bore a strong resemblance to K, but with a larger nose and heavier eyebrows. 'Katisha Ascott ... ten years ago, before she was toshed.'

'*Ascott*?' Rigby said. 'She's his daughter? Where did she turn up?'

'Exactly where you wouldn't want. In places an NCA tosher wouldn't have had access to. I had to pull in favours, go outside my own security clearances. She's still active. The intelligence agencies use her to do things to people they're not allowed to touch themselves.'

'Kind of like the dark web,' Steadman said.

'Exactly. The point is, she would have been shut down by now if they *wanted* her shut down.'

Rigby said, 'Who's *they*?'

'Come on. You know who I mean. MI5. MI6. Private security companies. Whole bloody viper's nest. We can't take this on.'

Rigby and Steadman exchanged a glance.

'So you're saying we should leave it?' Steadman said.

Dale looked at them both in turn. 'If you want to stay alive. And I know I do.'

Rigby felt furious. 'We put our arses on the line, and at the first whiff of danger you wimp out?'

'There's a difference between bravery and suicide,' Dale shot back. 'And this will not play well.'

As the two of them faced each other down, Steadman's phone cheeped.

Dale turned to him, horrified. 'What the fuck? Turn it off!'

'It's a crypto.'

'These guys can crack anything!'

'Well, technically, no, they can't ...' Rigby said.

'Both of you, shut up,' Steadman said, waving at them. 'It's from Mesh.'

'What does *she* want?' Dale said, dismissively.

Steadman held his phone out for them to read.

Both of their jaws dropped. The phone said: ABDUCTED ASCOTT.

'What the hell does that mean?' Rigby said. 'Has she taken him, or has he taken her?'

Steadman called her number. 'It's ringing.' Then, after a minute, 'No answer. Voicemail.'

'Try again,' Dale said.

He tried again. 'Same.'

A few seconds later, he received another message: EXCHANGE.

'What do you think they want?' Steadman said.

'The card,' Rigby said. 'K wants it, I'm sure.' He turned to Dale. 'Are you coming?'

Dale took a breath, his eyes darting between the two of them. 'Do I have a choice?'

30

Steadman's car was closest. They grabbed a cab to it, then set out west.

'Take the A40,' Rigby said to Steadman.

'Doesn't this car have satnav?' said Dale from the back seat.

'Too old,' Steadman said.

'Well, then take the M4, then turn off at Swindon.'

Rigby shook his head. 'No, A40 then M40, and then A40 again. It's straight to the Cotswolds.'

'But you'll be half an hour just getting out of London,' Dale said. 'I drive this way almost every week.'

Steadman shrugged. 'I'd go out on the A4, but then take the M25 to the M40.'

'*M25?*' the other two said in unison.

'Okay, maybe not.'

They were still in the West End.

Dale said, 'So are we taking the A4, or what?'

'We grew up in London,' Rigby said. 'Trust us.'

'I grew up here too,' Dale protested.

'No you didn't,' Steadman said. 'You grew up in a mansion in Sussex.'

'That was the summer house.'

Steadman glanced at Rigby and rolled his eyes.

Dale said, 'I'll look ahead on my phone, see if there are any hold-ups.'

'You do that,' Steadman said.

Ahead, Steadman saw a light change to yellow and he put his foot down.

'What are you doing?' Rigby said. 'That was a red light.'

'It was yellow. There's a woman's life at stake. I'm not slowing down for bloody yellow lights.'

'If we die on the way, we're not going to be much help to her, are we? What's going on between you and her anyway?'

'What are you talking about?'

'You never even met her two months ago.'

Steadman said nothing for a minute. 'I like her, she likes me. That's all there is.'

'That's *all*?'

Dale said from the back, 'You have to admit, she's attractive.'

Steadman wheeled around. 'Who asked you?'

'So are you like, going out?' Rigby said.

'No …' Steadman seemed embarrassed, tripping over his words. 'We haven't technically been out.'

'Have you asked her?' Rigby laughed.

'What's so damned funny?'

'You barely know her, you haven't even asked her out, and you're like Sir Galahad or something.'

Steadman looked wounded. 'I asked her.'

'She said no?'

Dale cackled.

Steadman wheeled around again. 'One more noise and you're out the door.' He turned back to Rigby. 'She said yes. But with all your shit going down, we haven't had a chance.'

'So it's my fault.'

'Of course it's your fault.'

'But I brought you together. So now you have to save her, or you're not going to get your date.'

'Shut the fuck up, Rigby.'

Steadman's car phone rang. It was Warren. He spoke quickly. 'One of the freelancers found this. Karivolam, the company in Panama, has taken huge positions in oil and gas options.'

'Long or short?' Dale called from the back.

'Long,' Warren said.

'In English please,' Steadman said.

Dale said, 'It means they've made a huge bet on oil and gas prices increasing. If they're right, they'll make a killing.'

The three men in the car exchanged glances. None of them knew what it meant, if anything.

'Thanks Warren. Call us if you find out more.' Steadman hung up.

Neither man spoke again, each lost in their own thoughts, until they were on the M40, heading toward Oxford.

Dale said to Rigby, 'By the way, how much were you paid to tosh Frederick Ascott?'

Rigby hesitated. 'I wasn't paid.'

'You did it out of the goodness of your heart?'

'I was paid in kind. Putts said your Task Force might try to blame everything on me, and he could … help …'

'So he blackmailed the blackmailer.'

Rigby coloured. Was he no better or different to Putts? That was the implication. 'He'd been toshed before, professionally,' Rigby said. 'They'd left just enough to substantiate his existence. I knew it was a risk.'

'A risk? It was a national security breach. What did they want from you, anyway?'

'They told me they were expanding. They wanted me to train dozens of toshers.'

'So what's that got to do with oil futures?' Dale said.

'I don't know.'

With a sigh, Dale said, 'You don't know. You've given them this power and you have no idea what they're going to do with it.'

'Hey!' Steadman said, growing irritated. 'Bust his balls later. Let's focus on getting Mesh out alive.'

'You really think it's that simple?' Dale said.

Wheeling around, Steadman tried to grab him by the shirt, but Dale slapped his arm away. 'Just listen to me for a second,' Dale said. 'What if it's not the card they want?'

'What else could it be?' Rigby asked.

'A person. They might want to trade her for safe passage for themselves plus someone else.'

'What do you know that you haven't told us?' Rigby said.

'Just that there's a limit. Everyone has a value, and we may not like it, but some people are worth more than others.'

'Where's this coming from?' Steadman said.

Dale hesitated. 'MOD Police.'

'*What*?' Rigby said. 'You spoke to Modplod?'

'Not me, my superiors. You should be thanking me, anyway. You can't deal with this by yourselves. Intelligence have been protecting K for years. The Home Office put up with it because we get intel on organised crime. But now Lasca's going ballistic. He's had it from Downing Street that under no circumstances can Frederick Ascott leave the country. He'll bring half the Army.'

'So where are they?' Steadman said, looking up into the sky.

'On their way.'

They came into Little Greystock. As they passed Ascott's house, Steadman tapped Rigby on the shoulder, pointing to a car in the driveway. 'That's hers,' he said.

Rigby felt a chill go up his spine. He'd never doubted that Mesh was their prisoner, but seeing the car somehow made it more real.

'Pull over,' Dale said, once they were out of sight of the house. 'We'll wait here until they arrive.'

Steadman frowned. 'How long's that going to take?'

'I don't know, but we sit tight. Agreed?'

Steadman glanced at Rigby, uncomfortable at having to fall in line.

'We're good,' Rigby said.

Half an hour later, the rolling thuds of a helicopter looking for a place to land filled the air behind them, and not long after that, a team of eight men came towards the house, weapons drawn. Dale, Rigby and Steadman joined them. Introductions were unnecessary. Lasca greeted them with a grunt. 'Gentlemen.'

The troop surrounded Ascott's house, spreading out along the fence. Two of them went around the back.

'Hold here,' Lasca said, holding out an arm. He signalled for Rigby and Steadman to back away. Four of the men, including himself, went into a huddle by the gate.

Not long afterwards, Lasca took out his phone and made a call. Rigby was too far away to hear what he was saying, but he guessed that he must be speaking to someone inside. A few seconds later, one of the officers brought out a pop-up screen and plugged it into Lasca's phone. Rigby and Steadman crept closer. An image of K appeared.

She peered out, her eyes flashing as she took in the faces staring back at her.

'Which one of you is Elvis?' she said.

'I am,' Lasca replied.

'And you've come here to make a trade?'

'Or you can hand him over.'

She looked at him as if he were an idiot. 'What's your plan for getting us out? You going to lend us your bird?'

'We'll stick you on EasyJet and wave good riddance. The deal is we don't stop you at the gate.'

'And my father.'

Lasca shook his head. 'He stays.'

K laughed. 'Oh really?'

She turned the camera: all they could see now was the side of Mesh's head, with a gun pointed at it.

The camera swung back to K. 'That goes online in thirty seconds. NCA officer killed live on air. Entirely preventable. It's your choice, Elvis.'

Lasca said, 'We have something that might change your mind.'

'What's that?' she said, offhand.

Rigby pushed forward so that his face was in shot. He held up the SD card. 'Your true identity.'

It only took K a split second to process what he was saying, then she threw her head back and laughed. 'That's all you've got?'

Rigby swallowed hard. He'd been expecting surprise, at least.

'Not only your name,' Rigby said. 'All my screenshots from when I toshed you, the moment when Katisha Ascott became the invisible woman. They're the last surviving record of the person you were.'

K gave him a knowing look. What did she want? 'Why are you standing at the back?' she said to Rigby. 'Push those gorillas out of the way so we can talk.'

Rigby said, 'Hand your father over, with Mesh, and this card is yours.'

K laughed again. 'The card? That piece of plastic isn't worth shit to me. There's only one thing I'm willing to trade for.'

'What's that?' Rigby said.

She shook her head as if it were obvious. 'You.'

31

What was she talking about? 'I already gave what you wanted.'

Rigby became aware of movement to his rear. He turned. Lasca had pulled back, along with two of his officers. They were making sure that Rigby didn't run.

Steadman, on instinct, went to grab one of them, but the other spun and cracked him in the chops with the butt of his gun. As Steadman held his mouth, the officer put him in a headlock.

'No-one do anything stupid,' Lasca barked.

'What is this?' Rigby said.

'She wants to make a trade.'

'I'm not yours to trade!'

K said, 'Rigby! Listen to me. Nobody wants bloodshed. It's beautiful where we have our development centre. It's warm, there are beaches, tennis courts.'

'I hate the tropics.'

'You're a single man. There are the most gorgeous girls you've ever seen. And so obedient. They'll do anything you ask.'

Rigby swallowed hard.

'Or maybe you want to do this the hard way?'

She swung her phone around again, but this time it was Mesh's terrified face that they saw. If she'd put up a fight earlier, her spirit was now exhausted. Looking at her now, it became clear to him that parallel universes were more than a theory, they existed here on earth, and that he and Mesh – and the rest of his friends, for that matter – were from a very different realm than the one in which they now walked. In Lasca's universe, the physics were familiar, but individual lives meant nothing compared to the needs of the nation. It was the same with the paedos he spent his life hunting – they had their own kingdom of the damned, with its own warped morality, and it was all they cared about.

Behind him Lasca said, 'Go with her.'

'No!'

Dale said, 'Rigby, believe what he's saying. We'll get you out. Go with her now, so we can shut this down. Do it for your country and we'll look after you. I'll get you out myself if I have to. You have my word.'

Rigby didn't believe him. Just as Putts had warned, all those weeks ago, a government agency would be all too willing to hang him out to dry. Whatever he chose to do now, he would do it for Steadman, and Gloria, and Lana, and Warren, and for Frank and all the rest who came from a universe he understood and believed in. Nothing any government could say would make a difference.

'Let her go first,' Rigby said, nodding toward Mesh. 'Then bring your father out.'

K said to someone else inside. 'Go get my father.'

'What now?' Rigby said.

Lasca said, 'We wait.'

Rigby turned. 'You can't expect me to shoulder all of this.'

K said, 'Life doesn't play fair. You have to make the best of what you get. You of all people should know that.'

'Fuck off.'

'No, come on, you're my hero. You took what happened to you in that boy scout tent and used it to your advantage. Vengeance is mine sayeth the Lord.'

'I'm not interested in vengeance.'

'Course you are. You wouldn't be human if you weren't.'

The front door swung open. Mesh came out first, followed by K holding a gun to the small of Mesh's back. Ascott came next, followed by Putts, who held two automatics, one pointing at Ascott, the other in the general direction of the officers.

'It's a simple exchange,' K called to them. 'One person for another. I want Rigby, and you get to choose which of these you get in return.'

'You already know the answer to that,' Lasca said.

'Why the hell do you want me anyway?' Rigby shouted to her. 'I already gave you what you wanted.'

She said, 'We have a big order to fulfil,' she said. 'Biggest one ever.'

'I already trained a battalion of toshers.'

'We need you to supervise them. Can't screw this one up, it's too important.'

'Got something to do with oil futures?' Rigby said. 'Who's the customer, Assad, IS, or maybe just some nice Saudi billionaires?'

Putts cut in, 'Rigby, shut up and walk. You're coming with us, you always were. So stop making this difficult, or more people will get killed.'

But Rigby had already made up his mind. He walked through the gate and into the garden.

K spun around to face her father. 'Dad ... walk.' She waved the gun at him.

Ascott looked devastated. His mouth had the deep, turned-down corners of a man confronted by a reality that was too much to bear. Whatever fate Lasca had in mind for him – a treason charge was entirely possible – was nothing compared to being betrayed and sacrificed by his own flesh and blood.

Rigby and Ascott walked slowly towards each other, matching their footsteps pace for pace. Then Rigby stopped suddenly. 'Let her go, too,' he said, pointing at Mesh.

K sneered at him.

'I'm serious. Let her go, or I turn around, and you can all kill each other.'

Ascott had continued walking, and he was about to pass

Rigby. K realised that she was in danger of losing them both.

'Walk!' she shouted at Rigby.

K released Mesh from her grasp, expecting her to run. But instead of sprinting for the fence, Mesh spun around and kicked K's legs from under her, then aimed another kick at her hand and sent the gun sliding across the lawn. Mesh ran after it, but she'd taken barely a few steps before Putts fired. Mesh screamed and fell forward.

Rigby ran towards the house for cover. Out of the corner of his eye, he saw Steadman hurdling the fence and running towards Mesh. He turned to join him, but an arm in his throat stopped him dead. He fell backwards, and looked up to see Putts standing over him, ready to fire. He curled up, instinctively, and a shot rang out. He expected a bolt of pain to rip into him but there was nothing. He looked up to see Putts's expression change to one of shock as a neat red hole appeared in his forehead. Time seemed frozen, then he fell like a collapsing tower. Rigby was so stunned he didn't even think about rolling out of the way. Putts fell on top of him and he felt a rush of revulsion, as if a billion bacteria had landed on him. He flailed his arms and kicked out wildly, until he heard a voice shouting, 'Enough, enough!'

It was Lasca. Rigby pushed off the corpse and sat up. In front of him, Lasca's men were dragging Ascott through the fence. Mesh was still lying on the ground, with Steadman leaning over her. He had his hand up in the air. Did that mean she was still alive? All around, Rigby could see men rushing forward, but he didn't dare to stand. Something hot had been pressed against his head, and he knew it was K's gun.

Lasca had seen it too. He dropped his weapon to his side in appeasement. 'Nice and easy now.'

Rigby stood. He was contemplating making a run for it, forcing Lasca to take down K whether he wanted to or not, when an ear-splitting wail came from the garage, along with a cloud of blue smoke. The garage door lifted. A black Maserati Khamsin rolled out into the driveway. In the driver's seat was

Maddox. Rigby felt a tug under his chin. 'Easy now. Get up.' Keeping the gun to his head, K began to lead him towards the car.

'He's all yours,' she called to Lasca. She meant Ascott.

'Kati, don't leave me!!' he shrieked.

She must have had some other plan, Rigby guessed, another elaborate deception that now could never be enacted. Ascott had never intended to sacrifice himself.

She dragged Rigby over to the car and opened the passenger door. 'Get in the back.'

He squeezed himself in. K sat in the front, keeping the gun trained on his head.

'What about your father?' Maddox said. 'We can't leave him.'

'He's had his time,' K said. 'This is ours.'

Maddox looked surprised.

'Drive!' she shouted, slamming the door.

Maddox put the car in gear. The tyres smoked as they accelerated away.

32

Warren was the first to notice the alert from one of the backup file storage systems to say it was full. His first instinct was to assume some kind of error. Its storage capacity was so vast that, in theory, it should have been more than adequate to handle all of Pangolin's requirements for the next decade. In years gone by, he would have passed the problem straight to Gloria – she was head of systems after all – but in the past three months, with Rigby gone, everything had changed, and they'd all been mucking-in wherever they could. Steadman had told them how K had threatened to frame them, and that Rigby had gone with her only to keep them safe. Warren, for one, wished he hadn't, but there was nothing he could about it now. All they could do was work hard, keep the ship afloat, and hope that he came back, some time.

The backup storage units were simple hard drives in metal cases which they kept on the floor in the air-conditioned server room at the back of the office. Warren opened the door, bracing himself for a chilly blast. He checked the connections and everything seemed in order. Its green LED shone as brightly as the others in the row. A single ethernet cable was connected. Nobody had attached a phone or a USB stick or dongle that could somehow be pumping data into the device. So where had all the memory gone?

Gloria rolled her eyes when he explained the problem to her.

'It's not stopping anyone doing anything is it?' she said.

'No.'

'Well then don't worry about it. I'll check it later when I

get a chance.'

He waited a day before nagging her again.

She said, 'I'll take a look, but whatever I find, you're going to have to fix it.'

Half an hour later, the pair of them sat stunned.

'We need to get Steady,' Warren said.

'Steady!' Gloria called out.

A little over two hours later, they were in Skagbucks, waiting for Mesh. Again.

'Tell me this, Steady,' Gloria said. 'Now that's she's your fancy lady, is she like a little bit earlier than before, or is she even later?'

'I bet she's even later, right?' Warren said.

Steadman gave a sigh. He'd had this every day for the past six months. If it wasn't timekeeping, it was conflicts of interest. If it wasn't conflicts of interest, it was his weight versus hers. If it wasn't his weight versus hers, it was had he met her son yet, or her mother. There seemed to be no end to the enjoyment they derived from teasing him.

'Try as ye may, I am Steadman the untormentable, the happiest man alive. And there is nothing you can do to take that away from me.'

Twenty minutes later, Mesh came up the stairs.

'Señorita,' Steadman said. 'You're late.'

Mesh walked straight up to him and kissed him on the lips.

'Hi guys,' she said to Warren and Gloria, slipping in next to Steadman on the worn leather sofa. 'What's up?'

Gloria lifted her laptop out of her bag and placed it on the table. 'We found a huge data dump on one of our storage units. It wasn't in any regular file form, so we had to do some conversions. Turned out it was screenshots.'

Steadman was watching for Mesh's reaction. As he expected, her eyes went wide. She turned to him. 'Is this ... is this what we were hoping for ...?'

'Damn right it is,' Gloria said.

Steadman put a hand on Mesh's arm. 'See what you think.'

Gloria handed the computer to Mesh. She clicked on the first image. Steadman watched her expression carefully, scrutinising every twitch of an eyebrow, every movement of her lips. She spent a few seconds scanning each one, then flicked to the next. After she'd viewed about twenty, she said, 'I need to get these analysed.'

'There's no time!' Gloria said.

Mesh looked taken aback. 'What makes you say that?'

'They're still alive,' Gloria said.

Warren added, 'Some of their phone numbers are in there.'

'You *called* them?' Mesh said, incredulous.

His mouth dropped open. He hadn't realised it might create problems. 'We didn't say anything. As soon as we found out they were alive, we hung up.'

Steadman said, 'We think Rigby's sent this now because they're about to be taken out. This is the moment.'

Mesh continued to flick through the pictures of email accounts, employment records, tax filings, phone bills, property deeds, air tickets, social media pages, bank statements, birth certificates and all the rest of the digitised paperwork that constituted a life. Or in this case, many lives.

'Look at the names,' Warren said. 'And the places.'

Mesh shook her head. 'I can't read most of it. It's in Arabic.'

'Exactly.' He leaned over and tapped faster on the arrow key. The photos flew past. 'Look at the stamps on the official documents. These people are Iranian, Qatari, Syrian, Emirati, Saudi, Palestinian ... Israeli.'

Warren added, 'Remember the oil and gas futures we found? ... Taking out all of these people would start a war. Prices would go sky high.'

'The toshing isn't to hide anyone,' Steadman said.

'These folks are way too high-profile. It's to make it look clandestine, like a hit ordered by an enemy state.'

Mesh's mouth hung open in shock. 'Multiple murders, and all the countries blame each other ... What do you need me to do?'

'To pay for the goddamned plane. What do you think?' Gloria snapped.

Mesh kept her cool. 'To do what?'

'We'll get Rigby, while you stop World War Three.'

Gloria opened her bag and took out a detachable hard drive. 'This is your copy,' she said to Mesh. 'Call us when you got a plan.'

Mesh nodded. 'Thank you,' she said. 'All of you. Rigby's a lucky guy to have friends like you.'

Mesh strong-armed Dale's assistant to free up a slot in his diary.

'He can give you five minutes later today,' she said.

Mesh emailed him a selection of screenshots with a short explanatory note. When she arrived at his office, he had printouts of them spread across his desk.

'You're saying they're all still alive?' he said.

'Some are, certainly. My people are checking on the rest.'

Dale nodded. 'Do we have any idea who's ordered this?'

'There's no indication about who's placing the orders, or when they're being delivered.'

Dale sighed. 'You make it sound like online shopping.'

'That's exactly what it is, sir.'

He gathered the pages together, stacking them roughly, and handed them back. 'Okay.'

'Okay what?'

'Go ahead and warn them. Tell them we believe they may be in danger and ... they need to get out of town for a while.'

Mesh couldn't believe what she was hearing. Surely Dale

understood the implications of what he was saying.

'Sir, Rigby planned this, from the moment he agreed to work with K and Mark Putts. He was looking for a way to put a bomb under their operation. He must have installed code into the apps used by every tosher he trained. This is all being sent automatically. If we warn these people, they'll be gone when the teams go to make the hits. It's going to be clear to K what's happened.'

'So you're saying they have to die so he can stay in place?'

'No!'

'Because you do realise that we are monitoring that archipelago day and night. The traffic we've intercepted has led to some of the best intelligence we've had in years on particular crime organisations.'

'I'll get you out myself if I have to.' That's what you promised him! Now you're saying he has to die down there?'

'No!'

'Then what's *your* plan?'

'We'll warn everyone. But we'll do it piecemeal.'

'It won't work, you know that. She'll put two and two together.'

Dale chewed his thumb, hard.

'I don't even understand why this difficult for you?' Mesh said. 'Or maybe you think Genya Zaytsev is behind it.'

'Alright, that's enough.'

'Sore point, huh? Took all those officers and it was the address of a bagel shop.'

'Kaur, you are insubordinate!' He paused for a few seconds, calming down. 'It's unlike you. This has become personal.'

'It always was, sir.'

He sighed again in dismay. 'Okay. Tell me what you want.'

Mesh didn't need to be asked twice. 'A Coastguard ship waiting just north of the archipelago – and don't tell me we only have two and they're being deployed elsewhere. A couple of inflatables for landing, with Ops teams. And I want all of Rigby's crew on the boat too, so they can greet him.'

'No way.'

She stood stock-still, her hands at her sides. 'Thank you, Sir.'

'I said no,' he said, surprised.

'To all of it?'

'The last part. Having civilians aboard is just too much.'

'I'm sure you can convince them, sir.'

He stared at her for a few seconds. 'Which part of "no" don't you understand?'

'The part where you're forgetting this is Rigby.'

Dale frowned. 'I don't want to hear about him again, for an awfully long time.'

'You won't, sir.'

He raised an eyebrow. 'Can you guarantee that?'

'No, sir.'

Shaking his head to make it clear that what he was about to say was against his better judgement, Dale said, 'Alright. Bring him home.'

33

A tap-tap-tap came on the window. And then another. Rigby waited a moment to see if it would come back. Tap-tap-tap. What could it be, he wondered? It wasn't unusual for there to be noises at this time, an hour or so before dawn, but usually it was birdsong, and not the tweety-tweety kind he was used to at home; these were tropical birds that made screeches like power tools working concrete. This was too rhythmic for them, too *considered*. Whatever it was, it had been enough to wake him from sleep. Could that have been the intention?

He stroked his beard, wondering for a moment if he should open the curtain. He didn't want to turn on the light. There were cameras and microphones everywhere. Slipping out of the single sheet, he pulled on a pair of shorts and a T-shirt, then slowly, slowly, so as not to make any noise, he went to the window and pulled aside the curtain.

A face stared back at him, illuminated only by moonlight; delighted and terrified. Gloria. She pressed a finger to her lips, then motioned towards the front door. His heart began pounding so hard it felt like it might run off without him.

Outside, he found her standing with Warren. 'I can't believe it. How did you get here?'

She whispered, 'No time to explain. The boat is at the river mouth. Follow me.' She started to run towards the edge of the forest.

'You next, I'll follow,' Warren said.

The three of them darted through the undergrowth, trying to stay as silent as possible, keeping alert to anyone coming at them from any direction. Rigby knew the river mouth was no more than a quarter-mile away. Barring any mishaps, they'd arrive in a couple of minutes.

When the jungle gave way to the beach, he could see an inflatable waiting for them. As they approached, another figure sprang up from behind the craft and began pushing out. Once everyone was on board, the engine fired.

As they sped out into the bay, a flash came from the pitch-black sea ahead. A larger vessel, Rigby assumed, signalling them. He looked back to the beach. A light had come on up the hill, where K had her compound. Had she heard them? It wouldn't matter now.

Steadman stood at the console, in the middle of the boat. Safely away from shore, and skimming along the waves, he took a moment to turn and check on everyone.

'All good?' he called.

Everyone shouted back positively, except Rigby. All the time he'd been at the compound there was one thing that had bothered him, above everything else.

'Hey Steady.'

'What?'

There was no other way than to ask the question: 'Did she make it?'

Steadman spun around. 'What are you talking about?'

'Mesh. Is she alive?'

Steadman looked surprised. 'Who do you think put this together?' He pointed to the boat ahead. 'You can't just order one from Uber.'

Gloria said, 'They'll do anything she wants right now, thanks to all that data that keeps getting sent to us.'

'You mean it worked?' Rigby said, feeling elated.

Warren said, 'Too right. We didn't realise what it was at first. Then Steady saw the screenshots, and he showed them to Mesh.'

'And Mrs NCA was like "give me that, now!"' Gloria added. 'They checked it all out and figured you'd snuck some code into everything so it sent us a copy.'

Rigby laughed. 'Twice I said to K – once at the farm, and then again out here – there are two ways of doing what you want: either we hire some people who know what they're doing and I show them how to write the apps they're going to need; or I write the apps, and you hire some less-goods who just have to operate them. Both times she wanted me to write the apps. All those kids you saw on the buses, they were clueless. People don't realise it's like speaking a different language, and if you can't speak it, you don't understand the person who does. They could be saying anything.'

Steadman cut the throttle and brought the inflatable alongside the large vessel. Up close, Rigby could see she wore Greek Navy markings. A ladder was thrown down and one by one they climbed on board.

The crew of the vessel seemed as delighted as the rest of them that the operation had gone smoothly. Rigby found himself being directed into a sparse and grey but perfectly comfortable seating area. A woman was talking on a phone with her back to him.

She became aware of movement behind her and turned. It was Mesh. She beamed at him and finished her call. Then came running over, throwing her arms around him.

'Rigby, it's you! It's really you!'

He recoiled immediately and flapped his arms to break loose.

'I'm sorry, I forgot,' she said. 'I'm just so happy to see you.'

'I'm happy to see you, too.' He braced himself. 'Try it again,' he said to her.

'What?'

'Just try it.'

She stepped forward and placed her hands on his shoulders. 'How's that?'

'It's okay,' he said, uneasily.

'Do you want me to go further?'

'No.'

Instead, he looked around at the others, who'd been watching. He waved them over. Gloria came first. Then Warren. Finally Steadman. It'd been four years since he'd brought them together, hand-picking them from the various groups.

'Do we have to go back?' Steadman said. 'I'm getting to like this Greek food.'

Mesh said to him, frowning, 'This poor man hasn't been home in six months, and all you can think about is your stomach.'

'And what's your rush?' Steadman shot back. 'You want to parade him around the NCA saying I'm the one who saved him.'

Rigby laughed. He turned to Warren. 'Are they always like this?'

Warren nodded. 'Always.'

'*Al*ways,' Gloria added.

Steadman said. 'Now we have to find *you* someone, Rigs.'

'Good luck with that.'

Mesh gave a tiny smile and nodded at someone behind him.

Rigby turned, and did a double-take. Standing there was Aisling, who he knew only as the officer who'd raided Pangolin. His immediate response was to feel angry with her, but it vanished as soon as she smiled.

'Hi Rigby,' she said. 'You look different.'

His hand went to his beard. 'I need a shave.'

'Oh?' she said. 'I kind of like it.'

Behind him, Mesh cleared her throat. 'We need to get you back home.'

'Sure,' he said, over his shoulder.

'But our route back to the mainland takes us past a couple of nice islands. We might need to stop for, um ... petrol.'

Rigby looked at Aisling, who was nodding. 'I've heard that too,' she said. 'These Greek Navy boats ... very small tanks.'

He laughed. And then Aisling reached out and touched

his upper arm.

'It's good to have you back,' she said, but he barely heard the words. All of his attention had been drawn by the hand that was now patting him. She hadn't given him any warning, and normally he would have recoiled as the hand landed. They'd never touched before that he could recall, and it felt exquisite. Why didn't it feel excruciating? What did it mean? Glancing around he saw everyone watching. Were they expecting him to jump back? He didn't feel like jumping back. He didn't want to pull away at all, he wanted to pull her closer.

He put his hand on top of hers. It felt fine. She didn't pull away.

'I'm starving,' he said. 'Can we go for breakfast?'

'Of course,' she said. 'Can I have my hand?'

'Of course,' he laughed. He saw Mesh watching and they exchanged a glance.

Aisling saw them looking. 'What?'

'Nothing,' he said, realising he still hadn't let go. 'It's... it's just amazing, that's all.'

18560774R00180

Printed in Great Britain
by Amazon